The Moon Temple

Eric Mayo

authors
On Line

Visit us online at www.authorsonline.co.uk

An Authors OnLine Book

Copyright © Authors OnLine Ltd 2006

Text Copyright © Eric Mayo 2006

Cover design by Siobhan Smith ©

All rights reserved. No part of this publication may be reproduced, stored in a retrieval system, or transmitted in any form or by any means, electronic, mechanical, photocopy, recording or otherwise, without prior written permission of the copyright owner. Nor can it be circulated in any form of binding or cover other than that in which it is published and without similar condition including this condition being imposed on a subsequent purchaser.

ISBN 0 7552 0249 X

Authors OnLine Ltd
19 The Cinques
Gamlingay, Sandy
Bedfordshire SG19 3NU
England

This book is also available in e-book format, details of which are available at www.authorsonline.co.uk

Dedicated to the Memory of

My Son
Stephen Mayo

And to

Nigel Madden
My stepson

1964 – 2006

ACKNOWLEDGEMENTS

There would be no book if it was not for the patience and hard work of my wife, Andrea. I am no good with computers but Andrea is – so, no contest. I'm sure I must have driven her absolutely mad with my re-writes, alterations and additions to the various drafts. It was Andrea who inspired me to write and I am deeply grateful to her for her encouragement and good advice. If she was not an occultist of great power and a thorough going pagan, I would have to approach the Roman Catholic Church and put her name forward for eventual canonisation. Of course, they would disapprove of her but that would be their great loss.

I also owe a debt of gratitude to my close friend, Anita Martin, an experienced occultist and shamanic practitioner. Anita took the time and patience to read several drafts and I was able to draw upon her considerable knowledge of the ancient, ancestral past. She gave me the name, Sela, the imagery of Pegasus, Tanith the cat and she inspired the 'Exmoor pony incident'. I think I tested her patience as well but she helped me a lot – that's what good friends do.

Thanks must also go to several other friends who assisted me by reading the drafts and who offered constructive criticism and, in some cases, ideas. I hope I have addressed these within the pages of this book. I am grateful to:– Kay Prideaux – artist, who gave me the 'jackdaw incident', Eileen Real – writer and poet, Janet and Bill McIntyre, Lindy and Mike Elliott, Sue England, Nigel Madden, Steven Prideaux, Clive Madden, Brian Adams – writer, and Beryl Adams.

The visit to Glastonbury comes from a time, in the early 1980s, when Andrea and I visited Chalice Well with the occultist Marian Green. There, within those peaceful gardens, the three of us drank from the eternal waters of Avalon, a memory that has always stayed with me.

Eric Mayo 2006

A NOTE TO THE READER

The magical techniques, described and discussed in this novel, are all real. Such techniques can be used for beneficial ends but, in the wrong hands, they can also be harmful to others as well as to the practitioner. The acquisition of occult skills requires dedication and hard work – there are no short cuts. Most people who set out to acquire such skills develop a sense of balance within their psychic beings. However, there are always the very few who act with malevolent intent. It is wise to avoid them.

If some of the events in this novel appear to be far-fetched, then I can only suggest that the sceptical person should take time-out to read widely, particularly in the areas of anthropology and the practices of witchcraft in the modern world. Thus, the opening sequence is based upon a malevolent practice which has been used throughout Europe and which is still in use in parts of the Americas and in Africa today.

In this novel all of the ceremonies, invocations and poetry are my own work. The only things I have left out are certain esoteric words of my own devising. My work has been influenced, in part, by a family tradition which has its origins in the Mediterranean region – my mother was born in Venice and my father's family came from Piemonte – and by an examination and practice of esoteric techniques.

Some neo-pagan practitioners will see a few similarities between the form of the major ceremony, described within these pages, and their own rites. This is inevitable. Almost all modern day practitioners of witchcraft and ceremonial magic in the West, owe a debt to the magical lodges of the 18th and 19th centuries who, in turn, claimed knowledge from previous centuries. Practitioners of modern day witchcraft owe a great debt to the work of one man who, in the 1950s, claimed initiation into a pre-Christian, pan-European tradition dating back into the very ancient past. This is not the place to go into a discussion of the origins of modern day occult groups; there are shelves of learned books which can deal with the subject far better than I ever could. However, I do touch upon some of this within the storyline. It is sufficient to say that the knowledge available to occult practitioners today is vast.

This has led me to consider whether or not to put a bibliography at the end of the book. I have decided not to do this as any such list would be entirely subjective, incomplete and unfair. However, there are some key pointers in the storyline, which may awaken the reader's interest and I suggest that those who are interested should browse the many bookshops and the internet and use their own intuitive powers. It has been said that when the time is right for you, then someone will come along who will guide you into the Mysteries. This is entirely true – after all, you have picked up this book.

Within this novel, two types of magical practice are depicted: the active and powerful path of Solar Magic and the equally powerful, mysterious and intuitive path of Lunar Magic. To those of you who are drawn towards the Solar path I say this. Remember Icarus! He tried to soar to the very heights but look what happened to him. The Lunar path is seductive and enticing but remember that, as you set out along your moonlit way, you must always be alert to what might be hiding in the shadows or to what might be stealthily creeping along the trail behind you.

Darkness Descending

PROLOGUE

The woman stood in the dark corner of the room and seemed to be contemplating the wooden box that lay on the floor before her. Bending down, she lifted the box, without effort, and carried it to the centre of the room, her bare feet padding softly across the chequered black and white stone floor. She lowered the box to the floor, placed it alongside an oddly shaped, earthenware bottle and knelt down in front of them.

   A single candle flame, flickering and dancing, cast an uneven light, which hardly reached beyond its immediate vicinity. The woman's face and naked body were pale and shadowed contrasts of shape and form, without any real definition, making her appear unearthly – spirit-like. From somewhere in the room, the recorded sound of drums thrummed on the still air, filling the room with an insistent rhythm, which grew in its intensity, until it settled into a powerful, throbbing, hypnotic beat.

   She undid the stopper of the bottle and a dreadful stench rose upon the air to mingle with the aromatic smell of burning incense. Laying the bottle on its side, the woman opened the lid of the wooden box and, reaching in, she lifted out the living, squirming body of a young rat.

   The candle's glow glittered in the creatures beady little eyes which were darting around seeking the origin of the smell, now permeating the room and which tempted its sensitive, twitching, inquisitive nose. The woman placed the rat close to the bottle's dark and open mouth and the animal poked its questing head inside. With a quick, firm movement she pushed the warm and vibrant body into the darkness, lifted the bottle and replaced the stopper. She stood the container upright on the floor and knelt before it, watching it intently. There was a pregnant pause and the bottle rocked slightly. The rat, caught within the stench-filled darkness, was trying to climb out but could gain no foothold on the curved interior.

   The kneeling woman continued to stare at the bottle but now she began to create a series of vivid mind pictures which were violent and terrifying. Her lips were moving, as though in soundless prayer and each successive visualisation became more real, more concrete as she focused the powerful and malevolent intentions of her Will. Slowly she rose until her body was in an upright kneeling posture and then she began to sway, moving her body in sinuous, serpentine, movements. As she swayed in time with the throbbing beat of the drums, she began moving her hands in a flowing motion as though weaving a net, or web, around the earthenware bottle.

   The bottle rocked again but the animal's soft, light body could not topple the heavy container. Not once did the woman remove her eyes from the bottle as she continued her strange dance. She was breathing hard now as though her body was undergoing great exertion and it seemed as though each breath was in time with the throbbing, driving beat of the drums. The candlelight glistened on the rivulets of sweat running down her face and body as her movements became more and more sensuous and extreme.

Then there was a scratching and scrabbling of claws as the doomed rat fought for a way to the light, to the air and freedom. The sounds became more urgent, frantic, the bottle rocking with the creature's futile hopeless efforts.

The mind pictures coalesced to form one dreadful and horrifying outcome. Then and only then did she let the pent-up power within her focus into a stream of incomprehensible words, culminating with a high, barbaric cry of hate directed at the bottle standing on the floor before her. As she reached this climax, she flung her arms outwards as, gradually, the sounds of scratching became fainter, more feeble and the rocking ceased.

The woman remained in her upright position, her arms spread out wide in a cruciform gesture. As the drum beats slowly faded away into silence she settled back on her heels and allowed her breathing to return to normal. She picked up the bottle and held it to her ear, listening, waiting. Satisfied, she stood up and, smiling to herself, carried the bottle from the room, closing the door behind her.

Of night fears and dead thoughts

CHAPTER 1

The strange and sudden death of his elderly aunt, Rita Palmer, had left Steven Downs with feelings of deep sadness mixed with a rather guilty sense of elation.

Rita had died in mysterious circumstances. Her body had been found on the open moor which formed part of her estate. She was clad only in her nightdress, with no slippers on her feet. Her legs, feet, arms and hands were torn and bloody; torn, it would seem, by the gorse and thorn bushes into which she had stumbled on that dark and freezing night. A coroner's report revealed she had died of a heart attack and subsequent investigations by the police uncovered no signs of an intruder inside the house. It was surmised that she had become confused and had, for some obscure reason, wandered out into the night and had died of cold and heart failure.

During her life, Rita had gained a modicum of fame as a singer and dancer during the 1930s and, in her later years, she had become very successful as a writer of rather mushy novels. With no other relatives save Steven, the elderly woman had lavished much affection upon her nephew who, together with his now deceased wife Ginny, would visit her from time to time. They spent many happy weekends at Rita's sprawling mansion, Hawkwood House, which nestled at the foot of the moorland hills of Porlock Vale in Exmoor. Steven had lost his parents in a car crash some fifteen years ago and Rita had become something of a surrogate mother to him. He greatly valued his visits to her, often taking the opportunity to carry out domestic repairs to the rambling Victorian building or to bring some form of order to the extensive grounds and gardens surrounding the property. The news and manner of her death had stunned and distressed him but he was astounded to learn that she had left not only Hawkwood to him but also had bequeathed a sizeable fortune, the proceeds of her novel writing, together with royalties. Hence his sense of elation and the mixture of emotions.

He drove his car into Porlock and was soon climbing up an impossible track, the entrance to Hawkwood House. Porlock was situated in a beautiful and stunning location set between the rising moorland and the Bristol Channel and, unlike other villages, it had a wide range of shops, restaurants and pubs enabling the community to be entirely self sufficient. Steven and Ginny had loved visiting Rita and they would often take her out into the surrounding countryside for long drives. As she had aged and Steven had become more conscious of her loneliness, he had bought her a dog for companionship, a Rottweiler puppy which they named, Perry. Rita had welcomed the dog with pleasure but her increasing age made it impossible for her to manage the now very large animal, so Perry was given the freedom of the grounds. Despite his huge size and ferocious appearance, Perry was extremely gentle when with Rita as though he could perceive her growing frailty and dependence upon him. Certainly he engendered an aura of security and he would growl and bark threateningly at any strangers who might approach the house. He did, though, have one peculiar mannerism; he would never go into the garden via the back of the house so Rita always let him out of the front door from where he would patrol the front of the property and, eventually, would then make his way to the extensive gardens at the rear.

Steven made a mental note to arrange to pick up the dog from the kennels at the earliest opportunity and as he parked the car outside the front door he pondered upon the death of Rita and felt certain Perry would have dealt with any threat to his owner. He took out his keys and opened the door which led into a large and lofty hallway. Hawkwood House was one of those sprawling Victorian mansions dating from the late 1800s, examples of which could be seen dotted around the countryside, displaying the wealth of the farmer-landowners who were not of the aristocratic class but who possessed an ancestry stretching back into the distant past. The Palmer family had lived in the region for centuries initially eking out a difficult existence through farming but, later, used good business acumen to increase the family coffers through some dabbling in the Bristol slave trade and then by some skilful investment in the expanding rail network and mining industries in the Mendips.

The upshot was that Rita's grandfather had demolished the old farmhouse and had built Hawkwood House. Some of the surrounding land had been sold off and Hawkwood was now surrounded by some eight acres of land affording it a considerable degree of privacy. Rita had never married and, as the inheritor of the property she had shown no interest in farming or sheep rearing and had quickly ditched that side of the business preferring, instead, to make her way on the stage where she met with some considerable success. Her later venture into writing brought in a substantial living and so she remained happily ensconced in the family home with only her one nephew, Steven, to visit her.

He stood in the hall remembering all the happy visits and his blissful weekends with Ginny. She had loved Hawkwood and got along wonderfully well with Rita so Steven was often given the opportunity to take Perry out for walks in the surrounding woods, something that was of great benefit to them both. He put his luggage down and walked into the large kitchen where Rita had spent most of her time. It was as though she had just gone out for a moment. Her coat was slung over a chair and there was a cup and plate in the sink where she must have put them before she went to bed.

Walking back into the hall he paused again, surveying his property. From the hall an intricately carved staircase led to an upper gallery giving access to the bedrooms. Four doors led off into various rooms; a large sitting-room, a dining-room, a library and to the small corridor leading to the kitchen. The former servants' quarters were in the attic but this was now stocked with the tangible mementoes of the Palmer family's past with a great deal of it a legacy of Rita's former show business life. He walked into the sitting-room and through the large glass doors which opened onto a conservatory, or was it an orangery? Steven was never sure.

He looked, with pleasure, out of the glass windows across the extensive garden area laid to lawn in part and with patio, a fountain and many shrubs. Beyond was a wonderful panorama of fields sweeping towards moorland hills. He turned back and noticed a glove, Rita's gardening glove. For some eccentric reason, she had only used one and he had seen her wearing it many times. He picked it up and felt tears welling up in his eyes as he sat, for a time, holding the glove and thinking of his aunt. Steven realised how much he would miss her intelligent, lively conversation and the many pleasant evenings they had spent together. He would miss her terribly and felt a great sense of guilt that he had not been present at the time of her death nor had he been able to attend the funeral. In fact it had been some weeks before he had heard of her death and cremation having been up in Scotland in the throes of dealing with his collapsing business. So involved had he been in the whole process affecting him that he had neglected to phone her – and now she was gone.

Steven sighed and went upstairs to the bedrooms. Rita's bed was unmade and in an extremely dishevelled state as though she had pulled back the clothes in a frenzy or panic. He noticed that her slippers were at the side of her bed and that her dressing gown was hanging behind the door. Clearly, the Coroner's report had been right. She had leapt out of bed and, barefoot, wearing only a nightdress, she had rushed out of the house and into the dark, to die a lonely and eerie death. He looked around. No signs of disturbance could be seen and the police had checked everything carefully. So, what had impelled her to go? If only a room could talk. As he studied the room, the light dimmed as a cloud passed across the face of the sun. The shadows, cast by the sun, merged, throwing the white sheets of the bed into sudden, high relief. For a brief moment he sensed a deadness within the room as though the fabric and structure were being sucked into a dark and endless void. He shivered and shook his head; the feeling was gone although there seemed to be a lingering memory, like an echo. The sun reappeared, lighting the room and he came out of his reverie, dismissing the feeling as fatigue from the journey. He shrugged and left her room and went into his usual bedroom which gave him a wonderful view of Porlock Bay. It was a beautiful day and the late spring sunlight was flashing and sparkling off the sea and lighting up the great hills so that the various shades of green, offered to the scene by moorland grass and forest trees, were thrown into bold colours almost crying out for a painter to commit their beauty to canvas; a skill Steven, unfortunately, lacked.

He unpacked his bags and started to do a bit of tidying up as it was still quite early in the day. Rita's bed was soon stripped but he decided to leave the rest of her things for now. He picked up the phone and got through to the kennels and arranged to pick up Perry after lunch.

There was nothing to eat in the house so he strolled down to Porlock, did some shopping and went back home where he made himself a sandwich and coffee. Then, taking the car he drove into Minehead to collect Perry from the kennels.

"He's been fine," said the woman in charge. "He's eating OK and isn't fretting. Of course, he's been here before so probably remembers us."

She took him through to the kennels where a cacophony of barking broke out as soon as they appeared. Dogs of all sizes stood yapping, barking and, in some cases, snarling as the woman led him to the very last enclosure where Perry lay nonchalantly looking out. He was a magnificent 'Rotty' with a huge head and powerful shoulders. On seeing Steven's familiar form, Perry's small stubby tail began wagging and he rose to greet them. "Hallo boy," said Steven and the dog gave a soft 'woof'. "Come on then, let's go home, eh! Yes, eh! Good boy." He took hold of Perry fondling and rubbing the big trusting head.

Perry leapt onto the front passenger seat and took up his usual position. Anyone looking at the car from the front, would see the dog's large and now happy face peering through as though he was the driver. They drove back to the house and, again, Steven pondered upon Rita's strange death. If she had been frightened or if there *had* been an intruder would not Perry have acted in her defence? He had seen Perry face unwelcome people and a terrifying sight that was. If there had been an intruder the dog would certainly have protected Rita. It was all so strange and he vowed to talk to Rita's doctor tomorrow. Remembering that Perry required dog food, he stopped off at the supermarket to pick up some tins and dog biscuits.

"Hallo, I didn't know you were down." The speaker was a small burly man whose name he remembered was John Simmonds, a friend of Rita's. Although in his 80s the man looked the very picture of health and had been out for a walk as he was wearing walking boots and carried a stick. "Sorry to hear about Rita – a great shock I must say. My condolences and all that. Are you down to clear up things? You didn't come to the funeral. Thought you must have kicked the bucket. Away were you?" He spoke in short clipped sentences almost in a military manner and then, of course, Steven recalled that he was known as 'The Colonel' and he was, indeed, an ex-military man; almost a caricature English colonel.

"Yes. Good to see you again Colonel. Yes, I was away settling up business matters. Thanks for your good wishes. Unfortunately, I didn't hear anything about her death until a while after the funeral. Do you know anything of the circumstances? I mean, she was found lying outside and in that cold – it doesn't make any sense."

He watched the colonel as the man shook his head, looked down at the ground and then up towards the hills where Rita had died. "No I don't know anything. I do know it was a strange end for her. Do you think she was losing it a bit, you know?" He tapped a finger against his temple. "We all seem to lose it as we get older. I seem to be having a lot of senior moments, myself, so Rita may have been becoming confused."

Steven considered this. "You mean senile or something? I don't think so. She was fine when I saw her a couple of months ago; always very lucid – enjoying discussions, so that doesn't sound like someone who was going gaga does it?" The thought had, indeed, occurred to him but he had dismissed it as being highly unlikely.

"I suppose not, still, very strange, very strange..." the colonel paused and then went on, "still, a bit of a surprise you turning up. I must say even *I* forgot you were her relative. I don't think many people have met you have they?" He looked at Steven, "You didn't mix much when you visited?"

"No, I didn't. We used to visit over weekends. Didn't mix much in the village." And this was so. He and Ginny usually remained at Hawkwood whenever they visited, only using the village facilities sporadically.

"So, you're down here to settle up her affairs, eh? I suppose you'll be putting the house on the market – you'd get a good price nowadays. Let me know. I've a friend who would be interested."

Steven looked at him blankly for a moment. "Sell? Oh no, I'm staying. I've no need to work now and I'll settle down at Hawkwood. Take some time to think things through. Might even try a bit of writing myself."

"Really?" The colonel gave him an odd look. "Well, well – staying on, eh? Ah well, I've got to get along – see you around I suppose." He moved off.

Once back at Hawkwood, Steven decided to take a stroll around the garden to see if anything needed doing. He let Perry out of the front door and then went into the garden via the orangery. This led directly onto a large patio surrounded by potted shrubs some of which looked to be in need of attention. He stepped out onto the lawn noting that a great many leaves needed to be tidied up and that the whole garden was in need of a considerable amount of tender loving care.

Perhaps it might be sensible to get someone in to give the garden a good going over he mused. He was not particularly fond of gardening but vowed that, once it was put in some sort of order, he would try to develop an interest. It was a lovely garden, or could be, and it had been laid out with an eye to low maintenance with plenty of shrubs. There was a rather fine fountain in the centre of the lawn and to the side an impressive stand of laurel bushes and a variety of trees.

Steven walked along the path that took him through the bushes and into the trees. Here, the ground was much more wild and it began to rise taking the garden towards a high hedge which formed a boundary between the formal garden and the high ground beyond. As he walked through the shaded area he heard the tinkle and babble of water and soon came upon the small brook which had been making its busy way down the rising ground to splash through a series of deep cut falls until it disappeared into the fields beyond and so on towards the Channel. The stream had deep banks indicating it had been cutting its way to the sea for many centuries. It appeared to emanate from the higher moors and was fed by two other, smaller, streams. Steven walked over to where it disappeared into a large jumble of rocks. It re-emerged and continued across part of the garden only to disappear again into a hedgerow forming the boundary of the garden and the fields beyond. From there the stream continued towards, and through, the shingle ridge bordering the Channel.

He re-traced his steps and made his way to the gate that gave access to the rest of his land, a series of fields separated by hedgerows. He stepped through the gate and Perry, who had been exploring the bushes in the main garden, bounded through after him. He went through a coppice of trees and stood on a knoll looking out across his new domain. To his left the grassland, bisected by the stream, entered another tree-line which began to ascend the moorland hills. To his right there was open land for a quarter of a mile to a long hedgerow which bordered another field owned by a neighbour. Beyond was the sea. Steven surveyed his land with a sense of pleasure at his good fortune and then, to his surprise, he saw two men emerging from behind the hedgerow. As he walked towards them, he noticed some newly dug holes and that the men were carrying objects. Steven felt a sense of unease and looked around for Perry but the dog was out of sight. The men looked up as he approached them and as he got closer, Steven saw that one of them held a spade and the other a metal detector.

"Afternoon," he said. "What are you doing?"

A tall young man with long blonde hair and a wispy beard looked at him and said, "What's it to do with you?" His tone was belligerent.

Taken aback by this surly response, Steven paused and eyed the other man who was now resting on his spade. He was a stocky, older man, very thick set. He was staring aggressively at Steven.

"It was a civil question," said Steven. "You're on my land and by the looks of things, searching for something; you're causing damage."

The men exchanged glances and the blonde said, "Your land – it belongs to Rita Palmer and she doesn't mind if we do a bit of digging so you can shove off." Despite his rather rough appearance, his voice indicated that he had been well educated, adding a sense of unreality to the unfolding confrontation.

Steven felt anger beginning to stir in him but he remained calm and said quietly, "There's one thing that really annoys me and that's people who can't be even a little bit polite. Rita is dead. The land is mine and *I* haven't given you any such permission. I might have but now you can whistle for it and I suggest *you* shove off and do it now." As he said this, he looked directly at the older man perceiving that if any confrontation did begin, the stocky man would pose the greatest threat.

"Come on Dan," said the older man, "let's go." But Dan was spoiling for trouble and put down the detector.

"No one tells me what to do." He began to move towards Steven and the other man, hefting his spade, joined him. Suddenly they stopped and began to retreat, moving slowly backwards, staring at a spot behind Steven. He glanced around and saw Perry. The dog was standing there like a statue, alert, menacing and beginning to growl.

Steven turned back to the men. "I suggest that you stand perfectly still." The men froze. "Here boy," he called and Perry loped towards him never taking his eyes off the men.

"Sit," he said and the dog obeyed. "You were saying?" he queried. "Now clear off. I don't want to see either of you again." The young man gave him a ferocious stare but took the advice and the two of them disappeared through the neighbour's fence. Steven watched them until they disappeared from sight.

"Good old Perry." He patted the now wagging dog. "Nasty customers," he mused aloud. But Perry's action had certainly confirmed one important point. The dog would have stood for no nonsense if someone had broken in on Rita thus confirming the police view that there had been no intrusion into the house. It made the circumstances of Rita's death even more puzzling.

CHAPTER 2

He awoke with sunlight streaming into the room and to the sounds of bird song. He went over to the window and looked out at the magnificent view which stretched, in a vast panorama, before him. Set up quite high on the side of the rising moorland, Hawkwood House enjoyed picture-book views in every direction. From the bay window situated on the side and rear of the house, Steven could see the hills above Selworthy round to Hurlestone Point and on round to a stretch of the Bristol Channel, as well as the low lying Vale of Porlock with its shingle ridge. The morning sunlight was bathing the hills but had not yet risen high enough to strike down into the sea which was masked by a soft mist. Other wisps of cloud and mist hung over the hills and would gradually burn off as the sun rose higher.

There was a clattering, thumping noise coming up the stairs and he opened the door to Perry who fawned into the room wagging his stubby tail. The dog had looked around for Rita and had sniffed outside her bedroom but seemed not to be fretting at her absence. This was probably because he had been left very much to his own devices over the previous years as Rita had aged. She had never taken him out, preferring instead to let him patrol the grounds. It was only when Steven and Ginny visited that Perry enjoyed a car ride and an outing on the moors or in the surrounding woods. Since Ginny's death, Steven had visited less frequently but, when he did visit, he always ensured that Perry was given a good outing, hence the dog's happiness at the prospect of more delightful rambles in the wild world beyond the confines of the grounds.

Steven showered, dressed and went downstairs to the kitchen where he and the dog each devoured substantial breakfasts. Later in the day Steven had arranged to meet Rita's doctor to clear up the mystery of her death and he would then drive to Taunton Crematorium to pay his respects to her memory in the rose garden where her ashes had been scattered. Before that, though, he decided to renew his acquaintance with the moors and woods and soon he and Perry were setting out along a stony track deep into a nearby coomb.

Exmoor was a strange and romantic place partly enclosed by farming needs but with huge wild areas, a mixture of deep wooded coombs or valleys, leading up to high, wild, bracken, heather and gorse covered uplands. In the hidden valleys or out on the high moors, the feeling of freedom and of being alone was something that Steven valued highly. He loved climbing the steep paths often bordering a tumbling brook, bubbling and splashing its strong and ancient way towards the sea. He loved that moment when the tough and sometimes difficult climb led him out from the strange, twisted, tree forms and onto the open moorland, where he could stand alone, miles from anywhere, beneath an overhanging canopy of sky and with the great open moorland stretching, it seemed, into infinity. Steven watched as Perry bounded and trotted here and there, sniffing and snuffling into dark and hidden corners alive with smells that were beyond Steven's own limited senses.

Steven was a spiritual man, not in the religious sense but more in terms of how he related to a sense of oneness with the Earth and with Nature. He was an environmentalist, a supporter of various causes which sought to redress the ravages and scourges of modern materialistic mankind. Like many people, though, this had not always been so.

As a youth and as a young man he had teetered on the brink of falling foul of the law. He had a strong propensity for violence and this had led him into the world of teenage gangs and the inevitable physical confrontations with others, fuelled by the dangerous mixture of testosterone and alcohol. He had been born into the Roman Catholic faith but had abandoned it as soon as he had left school where he had been seen as disruptive and difficult. He had never felt a need to return to the faith or, indeed, any of the Christian sects. Neither had he found Judaism or Islam of any interest but he had flirted, for a time, with Eastern Mysticism, a natural thing for someone who had played in a rock band throughout the 1970s. This had enabled him to open his mind, to be less judgemental and dismissive of the beliefs and ideas of others. Yet, still, he had felt no particular draw from any religious doctrine, whilst flirtations with philosophy had not borne fruit. A strange passion and fascination with Chinese Kung Fu movies had led him into the study of martial arts and the mental and spiritual disciplines that went with such practices. In effect, this had saved him from a downward spiral into violence and drink dependency. Gradually his skills in martial arts grew, so that the mindless violence and his growing drink problems were brought under control and channelled into a high degree of skill which he used, to advantage, in national and international competitions.

Now, standing on a high moorland summit and looking out over the forest spread below him he allowed his mind to relax as he began a Chi Kung exercise. As Steven breathed in deeply, drawing in the energy and power of the earth beneath him, he felt the warmth of the sun upon his face and a gentle breeze wrapped itself around his slowly moving body. As he drew in each deep breath he could feel the Chi, the life force, surging through him and, for a time, the earth upon which he stood, the air surrounding him and the light and warmth of the sun, merged together so that there was no man, no earth, no air, no sun, just one combined network of energies merged into a giant sea of everlasting and eternal power.

He brought the exercise to an end and looked again at the carpet of trees beneath him. The wind came up suddenly and eddied around and down into the valley causing some of the slender trunks to sway together as if dancing to the tune of a secret piper that they and they alone could hear. He called Perry to him and the two of them descended the steep hill and back down to the house. Before going in he thought he ought to look at the area where the men had been yesterday and in a short while, he and Perry were back at the scene where he had encountered trouble. He remembered that the men had emerged from behind a hedgerow so he strolled over there and found that there were several holes dug around the area close to where the stream ran down to the sea. He looked at the holes which were quite shallow; some were old but a few were fresh, obviously the product of recent digging.

It seemed that the two men were certainly intent upon finding something. Steven knew that this part of Exmoor had revealed the existence of early human habitation but had been disappointing in any artefacts from the Bronze and Iron Ages. The use of a metal detector indicated that they were looking for objects from those times or from later historical periods, perhaps even from World War II; there had been, after all, a few downed planes in the area. Steven knew that people who used metal detectors could be seeking coins or hoards or absolutely anything. Usually such people made only small openings into the earth to pick up a coin or buckle or other metal object. It was unusual for them to excavate so frequently and in such an uncaring manner. He looked over the hedge into the neighbouring field and was amazed to see a veritable procession of holes, always close to the stream. It was as though they had assumed every beep to be worth investigating. They were either stupid, highly inexperienced, or overly enthusiastic. He took Perry back to the house and then strolled down into Porlock for his meeting with Rita's doctor, at the Royal Oak.

Paul Hammond had been Rita's private physician for some ten years. He and Steven had met once or twice so after some preliminary small talk Steven asked him about Rita's death.

"It was a heart attack," said the doctor. "She was found outside the boundary of her land, quite high up on the moorland trail in the woods. She was only in her nightie and wasn't wearing any slippers. She must have died quite suddenly brought on by exhaustion and cold I should think. But certainly, the actual cause of her death was a heart attack. The only question that puzzles me is what she was doing out there – so high up. Her legs, arms and feet were badly torn as though she had stumbled about and got torn by thorns and brambles – terrible state and no shoes, no coat, very strange I must say." He took a deep gulp from his glass.

Steven stared into his own glass and then asked, "Could she have had some sort of nightmare or something? I mean, was she going a bit, you know, absent minded?"

The doctor answered immediately. "Senile, you mean? Oh no, no way, certainly not. Rita was far too lucid and anyway was still writing books. Look, I don't want to distress you but there was something about her death that certainly puzzles me although, of course, the police have found no evidence of foul play, hence the cremation. Coroners report indicated natural causes."

"So, what puzzles you?" asked Steven.

Paul Hammond finished his pint. "Well, so high up and so scantily dressed – bloody cold it was that night as well. No, the state of her, all torn up like that. It looked as though she was, well, trying to get away from something. I know it sounds odd but well, there you are. Almost as if she had run in panic so maybe a nightmare, I don't know." He tailed off.

Steven stared at him, "Hmm. And there was definitely no sign of an intruder?"

"Nope! Nothing like that and in any case, she's got that great big dog in the house hasn't she?"

"Perry? Yes and I've seen him with strangers – no he wouldn't let anyone in that's for sure. Another pint?"

"No, got to get back now. Anyway, nice to see you again although these are sad circumstances. You missed the funeral." This was said with curiosity rather than reproach.

"Yes, I didn't find out about all of this until I got back from settling some business matters – a cremation then?" He felt the sense of guilt and regret at having been absent at such an important time.

The doctor nodded. "Yes it was in her will as was your inheritance and, by the way, a generous donation to my practice. I must say your existence caused a bit of a stir. Even *I* forgot about you and your wife – how is she?"

"She died, I'm afraid, – cancer," replied Steven. A fleeting memory of Ginny, smiling.

Dr. Hammond said, "Oh, sorry to hear that." He paused, as though deciding whether or not to ask more questions but then said, "So you'll not be staying then. Selling up?"

"You're the second person to ask me that," replied Steven. "No I'm staying on – settling down – another Grockle takes root." He sipped his pint and then became aware of someone standing close to him. He turned to see the young bearded man, Dan, and his companion. Steven felt a little prickle run over his scalp, something he always felt as a portent of danger.

"Well, you said it, Grockle. Another bloody incomer – taking our houses, jobs: why don't you stay where you belong?" Dan's tone was highly aggressive and he stood challenging Steven who slowly put down his pint and then turned to face the two men.

He felt a sense of irritation as he looked at the young man – so confident and arrogant. "Yesterday I told you to get off my land and now I am telling you straight. Get out of my face, sit down somewhere and leave me to get on with what is, after all, a private conversation." He said this in a soft tone but there was an underlying threat in his voice, which should have acted as a warning, to anyone with the sense to listen.

The move, when it came, was sudden but totally predictable, Dan launched a clumsy overarm swing at Steven's head only to find empty air and his wrist caught in a strong grip. Using the momentum generated by the punch, Steven pulled the arm down and round sending Dan spinning away in a violent movement which landed him, sprawling, across a table. Sensing movement from Dan's companion, Steven continued his body movement and swung towards the man sending a stunning forearm smash into his unprotected face. The man gave a grunt and fell to the floor clutching his bleeding nose. Dan had staggered up and seizing an empty beer bottle he broke it against the ledge and launched himself and the jagged weapon straight at Steven's face. Steven swayed to the side, caught Dan's wrist and twisted it. Dan screamed in pain, the jagged bottle falling to the floor from a now limp wrist. The other man stumbled to his feet and ran for the door with Dan fleeing after him clutching his injured arm.

It was over in a moment – so fast that the landlord barely had time to put down the pint he was pulling. "What the hell," he burst out. "What's going on?"

The doctor intervened. "Its OK Ken, those two started it – real troublemakers as you well know, and Steven here finished it."

"Sure," said Steven, "sorry about that but I had no choice."

Ken nodded, seemingly satisfied and said, "OK, sorry about those two." He continued to serve the rather astonished customer who was eyeing Steven with a mixture of admiration and concern. Paul Hammond turned back to Steven. "Are you OK? God, I've only seen that sort of thing on TV. What is it – Kung Fu or something?"

"Something like that – a mixture of Aikido and Karate, something I've learned over the years. It comes in handy sometimes." His mind was calm and clear. The measured response to the attack had left him unruffled.

The doctor nodded. "Handy, yes, I can see that and Dan Wade isn't going to be using his hand for some time by the look of things. But they picked on you deliberately. Do you know them?"

Steven told him about the encounter in the field. The doctor looked puzzled. "Hmm, strange, I wonder what they were looking for?"

"Who are they?" asked Steven. "You seem to know them."

"I know everyone in the village – part of the job, you know. They work for Jane Trethowan – in fact she owns the land next to yours so, whatever they were looking for, they were searching her land first. I wonder if she knows?" He picked up his glass and drained the last dregs but declined a further drink.

Steven said, "The Trethowans – are they a local family?"

"Yes, been in the area for years. They go way back and have properties all over the South-West. Jane is the only survivor though. Spends time between here and her other properties but, lately, she seems to prefer Porlock. She's a bit strong on local issues, politics and all that. A bit of a fanatic about the rights of local people against incomers. She feels that people moving in are changing the culture of the area. I don't agree fully with that although there are some merits to her case. However, without incomers, many of the villages would die and, in any case, most businesses are owned by incomers. But there you are. I suppose you might say she is on the extreme right in politics."

"What, Nationalist Party you mean?"

"Oh no, no, it's far more focussed than that. She's after creating a sort of pan-Celtic state incorporating Wales and the South-West, a form of independence. Other nationalist groups won't have anything to do with her – I think they see her as being a bit crackers. She's written about it. You'll find things in the library – its all well argued though. Harps back to ancient history and the destruction of Celtic customs first by the Romans then the Anglo-Saxons and Normans. She rails against landowners who claim descent from William the Conqueror. She likes all that Holy Grail stuff – King Arthur, that sort of thing. She's into folk customs as well; you know, the Hobby Horse and so on. A bit 'New Agey' for some but I find her quite nice. You ought to meet her, you'd like her. Perhaps she doesn't know what those two are up to." He looked at his watch. "Must go, surgery calls. Nice to see you again. We must do this again some time only without the entertainment." He left and Steven turned to the landlord.

"Look, I'm sorry about that unpleasantness – they left me no choice and nothing's broken."

"Only Dan Wade's wrist by the sound of things," replied Ken. "Anyway, they've been asking for it. You watch out for them although I think it more likely they'll watch out for you." The landlord gave a chuckle and turned to serve a new customer.

Strolling back to Hawkwood, Steven went over the attack in his mind. In a way he regretted having been placed in a position where he had to use force and he considered whether or not he could have dealt with the matter in a different way. A few years ago, he would have laid into the two men with much more lethal intent. However, he had now learned to control this violent disposition. At the heart of all martial arts was the need to avoid conflict where possible and to only use the skill when there was no other option. Could he have reasoned his way out of the situation? But, no, he was experienced enough to realise that Dan was determined to confront him no matter what; it was unfinished business. Without Perry's intervention, Steven now had no doubt that the two men would have attacked him in the field. His initial defence against the man's attack had been measured and should have been enough but Dan's use of a broken bottle and the intervention of his companion had forced upon Steven the need to be more forceful. He had not broken Dan's wrist, just wrenched it badly. No, his assessment was correct – there had been no other way.

He wondered about Jane Trethowan and if she knew about their activities on his land. He decided that it might be a good idea to contact her on his return to Hawkwood for a neighbourly chat.

When he got home the answerphone was winking at him; he pressed the switch and a cultured voice came from the recorder.

"Hallo Mr. Downs, this is Jane Trethowan. We are neighbours. I am sorry about your aunt. Perhaps we could meet for a drink. I am having a few friends over tomorrow night and it would give you an opportunity to get to know a few people. About 7.00 p.m. Will that be OK? Give me a call." She left a number which he jotted down.

He dialled the number and a man's voice answered. He asked for Jane and there was a pause, a click and then she was on the phone. Her voice was strong and clear with no trace of a West Country accent. Obviously a product of a good public school.

"How nice of you to call back so soon," she trilled. "Would you like to come up for a drink tomorrow night about 7.00 p.m? A sort of 'get to know you' thing. Anyway, I'd like to meet you. We could have a neighbourly chat."

Steven muttered a few pleasantries and accepted the invitation. It was strange the way things happened he mused. He had only been thinking of her and she was on the phone. Even used the same words 'a neighbourly chat'. At least it would give him an opportunity to raise the matter of the behaviour of her two employees.

That afternoon he drove to Taunton Crematorium and visited the area where Rita's ashes had been scattered. He took the opportunity to re-acquaint himself with the pleasant county town strolling around its shops and along the riverside.

On his way back to Porlock and driving along the high winding road through the Brendon Hills, he pondered the strange turn his life had taken since the sudden death of his wife. The decline of his office equipment business had been gradual but inexorable and had brought him to the edge of deep despair. But then, out of the blue, the death of his aunt had changed everything. He was a wealthy man, the owner of a fine house and land and placed within one of the most beautiful parts of England. True, Porlock was a bit isolated from major cities and the drive from the village to the motorway necessitated good planning before any excursion could be undertaken but that isolation had preserved this part of Somerset from the scourge of too much tourism. The villages, the winding roads bounded by high hedgerows, the leisurely pace of life all harked back to a by-gone age, and this Steven loved. In fact, on the long drive from the South-East he got the feeling that he was travelling through time, from the hectic hub-bub of city life to, what was for him, a rural idyll.

The only cloud darkening his horizon was the behaviour of the two louts, so unusual in a genteel village and carrying with it echoes of big city life. He was puzzled by their behaviour and aggression. He hoped that his action towards them could now end the trouble and they would leave him alone. He wasn't scared of them, just irritated that they had bothered the tranquillity of his new life. Now that the doctor had revealed that the two men worked for Jane Trethowan it made him consider raising the matter with her. Certainly their digging activities might not be known to her and, in any case, they should not have been on his land. On that score alone, he might have cause to bring it to her attention.

Crossing the moorland between Dunkery Hill and the sweep of Robin How and starting his descent to Webbers Post, he pulled over and gazed at the magnificent view that spread before him. The green covering of trees descended the deep coomb of the Horner Valley and, to his front, the wide open stretch of the Bristol Channel led his eyes towards the low horizon line of Welsh uplands on the other side. There was a misty haze obscuring his view of the distant Welsh landscape but, as he looked, the sunlight broke through sending a shaft of pale light onto the shadowy hills across the Channel. It was as though the light was a beacon, he found himself thinking, a beacon pointing the way to some mysterious future. The thought was fleeting and was gone as quickly as it came, vanishing from his mind as swiftly as the sunbeam vanished in the, all enveloping, mist. He looked over to his right. Hurlestone Point jutted out to the sea and below Selworthy Beacon, the little white painted church at Selworthy gleamed against the dark green woodland. He felt pleasure at the sight, then started up the engine and drove on down through Horner and so on to Porlock.

He wondered about Jane Trethowan and whether she was young or old. It had been difficult to tell from her cultured voice. He hoped they would get along and that the trouble between the two men and him would not cloud their meeting. Tomorrow he would find out.

CHAPTER 3

He spent a leisurely day going around the house sorting out Rita's possessions and clothing which he bagged up ready for local charity shops. Despite her undoubted wealth, Rita seemed to have lived a relatively simple life. The house was furnished with a hotchpotch of different furniture, none of it of any real value and she seemed to have spent most of her life either in the library, the kitchen or her bedroom. The library was only that in name as it had very few books on the shelves. These contained a few novels, a selection of Rita's own works, a set of encyclopaedias which he liked browsing through, a thesaurus, several magazines – mainly local, an atlas and some cookery books. There was a typewriter – she had never mastered a word processor – and a bundle of papers showing the workings of a new novel in its early stages. So Dr. Hammond had been right about her still producing work and this certainly demonstrated that her mental faculties were not impaired

Steven bundled the papers together and put them into an empty folder. He would keep them as a memento or, perhaps, they would have some interest or value to some of her many fans. Glancing at the works on the shelves he realised, with a slight sense of guilt, that he had never read any of her novels, but a brief look at the synopses of her books confirmed that he would not bother to do so. They were typically romantic mushy works, 'womens' books', he felt dismissively. Nevertheless they would continue to provide him with income as the royalties from her books were part of his inheritance.

He picked up an envelope addressed to her and within it was a terse note in a bold, flashy, ornate hand.

"I have attempted to discuss the sale of your land to me but you do not reply. Could we meet for a drink and a neighbourly chat. Please contact me.
    Jane Trethowan."

There was Jane Trethowan's phone number at the top of the note which was written on a parchment-like paper, bordered by ornate, Celtic designs. Her signature was elaborately extravagant.

"A neighbourly chat," he mused aloud. So Jane Trethowan had been trying to buy Hawkwood, hence her invitation to him for this evening. He felt a sense of irritation at the thought. Why did she want the land? Perhaps Dan and his companion were digging on his land with her knowledge after all. He would have to clear this up tonight and stop this speculation about whether or not he was going to sell the house.

He pondered about what to put on for the meeting with his neighbour, not certain if it was formal. He settled on casual countrywear and then strolled around to the Trethowan property, an extremely grand mansion in a setting even more stunning than his own. It was set amidst well landscaped gardens with a sweeping driveway up to the front door. He rang the bell and the door was opened by, of all things, a liveried butler. Steven felt himself thinking that it was a bit over the top although not particularly out of place, judging from the grandeur of the mansion.

"Good evening, I'm Steven Downs. Miss Trethowan invited me."

"Yes, I know, do come in." The butler stepped back, took Steven's coat and motioned him to an open door from which could be heard the murmur of conversation. Steven crossed the extremely large hallway and entered the room. He noticed Dr. Hammond and Colonel Simmonds, another couple unknown to him and, to his surprise, he saw Dan Wade's companion serving behind a bar. He was sporting a black eye, the result of his abortive encounter with Steven in the Royal Oak. A tall woman who had been talking to a rather imposing looking man detached herself from her companion and came over to him.

"Hallo, you must be Steven Downs. I'm Jane, Jane Trethowan."

He shook hands surprised at the strength of her grip. She led him towards the bar.

"Do come over here and have a drink. Ray, give Mr. Downs whatever he wants. I'll be with you in a moment." She smiled at him in a friendly welcoming manner and walked back to the man she had been talking with. Ray showed no signs of recognition as he asked Steven what he wanted. Steven settled for a whisky and was given a generous shot which he topped up with water.

"How's the eye?" asked Steven, not one to hold grudges.

"What do you think?" replied Ray in a mumble and then turned to serve the doctor who had approached the bar.

"Hallo Steven, nice to see you again". They chatted for a time and then Jane joined them.

"So, you two know each other," she said lightly, "and here I am inviting you on a get to know you basis."

She turned as Colonel Simmonds joined the group. "Oh yes," he said, "Steven knows a few people down here. Been coming down for a number of years to see his aunt, haven't you? Must say, though, completely forgot about his existence."

Steven nodded. "That's so but I never really mix in the village. I've met Dr. Hammond and Colonel Simmonds, slightly, through their contact with my aunt, but, otherwise, I'm just another city boy."

"Ah, I see, that explains it then," she said, as though musing aloud.

"Explains what?" asked Steven curiously.

"My not knowing anything about you," she replied and taking him by the arm she led him away from the others and over to the imposing figure with whom she had been in conversation. "This is Sir Roger Martin." They shook hands. Steven remembered seeing photos of the man in the papers. He ran a large industrial complex near Bristol.

"You're down from London?" said Sir Roger. "Must be a real culture shock for you. This part of Somerset has maintained much of its '50s character, some say pre-war even. Still that keeps too many visitors from spoiling the place. Too far from the M5 you know."

"Not at all," said Steven. "I've been coming down regularly. I'm used to Porlock." He felt that he was sounding a bit defensive – the new, incoming city dweller, keen to show that he was a part of the village scene.

"Ah yes, but I suppose you'll soon miss the bright lights and bustle. Visiting Hawkwood as a weekend haven or will you sell up?" Clearly, Sir Roger was determined to pigeon-hole him as a typical weekender.

Steven paused before replying. He was quite a private man and didn't like discussing his affairs with complete strangers. Still, it would be impolite not to reply and, in any case, it didn't really matter if he laid this constant question to rest once and for all particularly as he now knew that Jane was interested in the property.

"On the contrary," he said, "I intend to move down and settle here. I've given up work for the time being and I can't think of a better place to settle down and take stock – can you?" He looked at both of them and noted that Jane's expression of polite interest did not change.

Sir Roger chuckled. "No I certainly can't think of a better place but the constant influx of incomers is certainly altering the demographics of the area, pushing up house prices too, but in your case, that's not an issue. Don't you agree Jane?" He turned to her and she smiled.

"Oh don't lets go into all of that now Roger. After all Mr. Downs, or may I call you Steven?..." She went on with her conversation without waiting for his affirmative reply, "...Steven's just moved down. He's lost his aunt and is settling her affairs. Let the dust settle a bit before making any long term decisions, eh?"

"My condolences", murmured Sir Roger and moved off to talk to the couple who had just joined up with the doctor and colonel.

"So," she again took his arm and led him over to a corner of the room, "how are you settling in now – was it awful going to the house and all that? It must have been a shock for you. Rita never mentioned you though."

"Did you know her well?" asked Steven although he knew the answer. Rita was very reclusive and never had visitors.

"Oh yes, we were good friends," she replied to his surprise. "In fact she was talking about selling up and moving into something smaller."

"Really?" He looked at her with some uncertainty. If that was so, why the rather terse and formal note from Jane to Rita he had found in the library? "I didn't know that."

"Still," she went on, "that doesn't matter for now does it?" Without waiting for his reply she continued, "I love this area, its so very special. My family have been in the region forever, in fact they helped to develop many of the farms and towns across the South-West from Somerset to Cornwall. I feel so in tune with the land, it's hard to explain it to outsiders – not that I am saying you are an outsider but, well, you know what I mean. So many incomers, old customs forgotten, people take little interest in the very ancient past. All they want is a good deal on a house, a garden to potter around in, a trip to the garden centre, a game of bowls – so bloody insular, no sense of what was here or what the land means to the people who were here for centuries. And the Government tends to ignore us – everything goes to the Home Counties and London. Roger and I are trying to do something about that..." She paused, "I'm sorry, you'll have to stop me when I start off about the land and politics."

Steven smiled at her. "Not at all," he said, "I like enthusiasm in people." He was warming to her. She was not particularly beautiful, more one of those women termed handsome with a rather long face, a pronounced patrician nose and dark brown eyes. Her black hair was cut in such a manner as to take away the length of her face. She was dressed in black with a fine lace working around the neckline and shoulders. She wore no jewellery around her neck but the sparkle of diamonds flashed from her earrings and from several rings on her rather shapely fingers. He went on, "I'm sure it will be an interesting time for me. I'm looking forward to exploring the moors again. I can certainly understand your love of the area."

"Oh, can you? Good." She smiled again. "Perhaps I can show you areas you don't know."

"I'd like that. Yes, certainly, I'd be delighted." He smiled at her and she looked into his eyes returning his smile.

"How about tomorrow then?" she said. "I'll come for you, say, ten o'clock. We can get some lunch later. Yes?"

He was surprised at her invitation which was more a statement that would brook no refusal. "Fine," he sipped his drink. "This is a lovely house. How old is it?"

"It actually goes back to the 15th century in parts but it was remodelled in the 1800s and has had extensive modernisation since then. All mod cons you know. Do you want a tour? Oh look, let's do it tomorrow. We'll go for a walk around the area and then have some lunch here. OK?"

"Sounds brilliant." He smiled at her again, glad that they were getting along so well.

"Do you know Sean and Fiona Thurlow?" She gestured towards the couple who were engaged in conversation with Sir Roger.

"No – never met them," he replied.

"Sean! Fiona!" Jane called across the room and the man and woman turned towards her. "Come and meet Steven."

Sean was a man in his fifties and his wife was about the same age. She must have been really stunning when younger, Steven found himself thinking, and, indeed, she still was. She looked familiar, he thought and stood up as the couple came over.

"So," said Sean, "You've got Hawkwood, eh? A legacy too – here, here's my card."

Before Steven could comment the man had produced a card. Steven accepted it, trying to hide his feelings. How many people knew of his bequest he wondered? He glanced at the card and saw that Sean was a financial consultant, with an office in Porlock. "Thanks, but I've got my own ideas about investments," he said, hoping he was not being too rude to this rather affable man. He looked at Fiona and said, "Forgive me but you look familiar."

"And so she should," interjected Jane. "She's been on every fashion cover you can name."

"A long time ago," said Fiona, smiling.

"Oh God," said Steven, "of course – sorry."

"Nothing to apologise for," said Fiona. "Time marches on."

"Not in your case," said Steven, in an attempt at a compliment and keen to make amends for not recognising this household icon.

"My, my. What a charmer, eh?" said Jane. You'll have to watch out Sean, now that Steven is here."

Sean shrugged his shoulders. "Fiona's her own mistress. I've just been along for the ride."

"And what a ride, I bet," said Jane, much to Steven's surprise at the coarse tone she used and at the obvious double entendre. Sean and his wife both laughed at the rather crude joke. They continued some inconsequential, social chatter until Steven said, "I'll head back now – got to take the dog out."

"See you around," said Sean.

"Yes, I suppose you will." Steven turned to Jane. "Thanks for the invitation."

"You're welcome," she replied. "I'll see you tomorrow at ten." She accompanied him to the door.

Steven waved farewell to the doctor and colonel and said, "I'm looking forward to it." He gave a little salute to her and stepped out of the door. She smiled and closed it behind him.

He heard it close and he started down the driveway which was lined with high fir trees and rhododendrons. As the path curved away he looked back at the house admiring its rambling form and location. He found himself looking forward to seeing Jane again. Strange, in a way, as he had not found her particularly attractive yet there had been something about her which sent a vague half remembered excitement through him. He had been out with no one since the death of Ginny and had felt no particular inclination to do so. Perhaps it was time to break up his loneliness and, in any case, wasn't he getting ahead of himself? He had just met her and all they were doing was meeting as neighbours for a stroll and lunch; all very neighbourly. It was strange also, how she had demonstrated a sudden coarseness but, perhaps, this indicated a 'fun' side to her personality which had seemed to be a bit intense.

On arriving back he took Perry out for a short walk around the garden. He reminded himself that he ought to set about hiring a gardener to get some order into the place; perhaps Jane would know someone. He wandered up to the wild area with its small stream and stood in the grove. It was getting quite chilly as the late afternoon sun dipped away to the west and it was really quite gloomy as he passed into the trees. He had hardly ever been to this part of the garden. The stream was tinkling and splashing in front of him and he looked at where it emerged from the jumble of rocks. These were tumbled and jumbled, half buried in soil which had built up against them over many hundreds of years. Steven liked studying rock formations and was always on the look out for fossils. He studied the rocks closely and saw that the jumble was the result of some sort of landslide from the higher ground above, which had, obviously, occurred centuries ago. He quickly saw that there would be no fossils at this location.

The dying sun sent a shaft of light through the trees and lit up the grove and rocks for a moment, bathing the stone blood red. He shivered, felt a fleeting sense of unease and looked to see if Perry was near. He wasn't. In fact, he wasn't anywhere in sight so Steven turned and walked out of the grove and back into the garden where he found the dog sitting waiting for him. Another strange quirk; won't go out of the kitchen door, won't go into the grove. He had heard that animals did tend to avoid certain places and he knew that many people considered them to be very aware of 'atmospheres'. Steven also knew about energy lines and he considered the possibility that Hawkwood was on a ley line. He would try to find out; perhaps Jane knew or perhaps someone else in the village might know something about the area. Jane – that was the second time he had thought about her. Perhaps she had made a greater impression on him than he realised and, again, he found himself looking forward to seeing her.

CHAPTER 4

The next day dawned bright and sunny. He was glad about this as Exmoor could often be misty and wet at this time of year so the promise of a fine day and his outing with Jane set him up in a happy mood. At 10.00 a.m. on the dot she rang the bell.

"Hi," he said opening the door. "Come in. Would you like a coffee or something before we go?"

"Oh, yes, OK." She stepped in and he took her through to the kitchen. She was wearing a hooded coat and walking boots – obviously expensive. He felt she looked extremely elegant.

"It's quite a big house, isn't it?" she observed. "How are you going to manage it all?"

He pottered about making coffee as he answered her. "Well, I might get someone once a week to do a general cleaning and I think I will certainly do something about the garden. That really is a problem; too long neglected you know. Rita wasn't really interested and, in any case, couldn't do it as she got older. Do you know anyone?"

"Yes – probably." She looked around as Perry entered the room and came slowly over to Jane who patted him on the head. "Wow, he's big. What's his name?"

Steven replied, slightly puzzled, "Perry, but you must know him – when you visited Rita."

Jane seemed momentarily flustered but quickly recovered. "Well, yes of course I have seen him but she always let him out when I came in. As soon as I sat down he used to growl at me, so Rita always let him out into the garden", she gestured at the kitchen door. She took the coffee, refused sugar and settled back in her chair. "Yes, it is quite a big garden. I might be able to find someone to help you." She paused, took a sip of the drink, put the cup down and said, "I've brought you a little gift, a sort of a welcome gift if you like." She took a small box from her pocket and laid it on the table.

"Well, that's kind of you." He opened the box; it was a crystal pendant on a leather thong. He picked it up – it was beautifully carved and heavy. "Thanks very much, but you didn't have to you know." He slipped it over his head and tucked it inside his shirt.

"I know I didn't but, well, the usual thing is a bottle of wine or flowers. You didn't look like a flowers man to me and I'm not sure what you really like to drink. I saw the pendant and I felt it would suit you. You don't mind do you? You don't mind such things? I am sure you were into that sort of thing when you were younger and all that," she paused as if embarrassed.

Steven laughed. "No, its great – nice and chunky. Thanks and, yes, I had the beads, flares, all of it you know, even played in a band – drums, singing – a bit of pop, late night stuff." He sat down opposite her, the table between them. It was a nice gift and he felt the chunkiness of the stone against his chest, warm and friendly.

"Really – how exciting. Were you well known?" She picked up her mug, cradling it in her hands.

"No, but I was never out of work – so couldn't have been that bad. Where are you taking me?" He never dwelt upon his musical career which had been relatively successful. There was something sad about older musicians who harped on about their glory days.

"Where would you like to go?" she asked as she sipped her drink.

"Oh, I don't know; I'll leave it to you. I usually go up to Granny's Ride or the Centenary Path, sometimes to the beach."

"Well, I know a really secret little valley – very mysterious; you'll love it and always want to go back." She smiled at him. "Tell me, what do you intend to do down here? I mean, Porlock is not the most exciting of places, beautiful though it is. You've come down from London and I don't see you joining the local bowling club. Do you ride, hunt?"

Steven disliked hunting. He was not a vegetarian and he certainly enjoyed a good piece of venison. It was the unfairness of organised hunts that he disliked. One man, a dog, a rifle – fine but, twenty riders, forty hounds, all chasing one animal seemed intrinsically unfair to him. However, he knew enough about local politics not to get involved in a pro or anti hunting debate. When in Rome and all that. He did ride but felt it better to say, "No, I don't. I don't ride."

"Do you object to hunting?"

The question was casual but it startled him, coming so quickly on his thoughts. He sensed that there could be an argument if he said the wrong thing. He opted for diplomacy. "No, no particular objection – people can do as they want as long as they don't hassle me."

"And you're not a man to be hassled as Dan and Ray can attest. Yes, Dan works for me as well and you've put him out of action for a while." There was a smile playing around her eyes.

He looked at her, "I'm sorry, but they did go for me," he said. "Anyway, its not as bad as all that. His wrist isn't broken, just badly sprained."

She laughed. "Yes, I heard all about it. It's all over the village. What happened?"

Steven told her of his encounter with the two men in the field and in the pub.

She looked puzzled. "Hmm! I don't know what they were up to. In my field as well you say? Well... hmm. I'll look into it. But enough of this, what about you? You've come down here – inherited all of this – do you have someone, a partner? Am I being rude?"

He shook his head. "No not at all." Then he went on, "There's no one at present; I lost my wife a few years ago – cancer. No one since. No inclination but now I'm in a new situation. A different time, different place, different circumstances. In fact, I feel a lot more relaxed of late – people are very kind, very welcoming."

He raised his cup in a toast to her. "I've been quite lonely I suppose. Never realised it, I've been so busy and then Rita's death and all that."

He was surprised how much he was opening up to this complete stranger but she seemed to exude an air which encouraged confidence. She sat there smiling at him saying nothing. He continued, "Yes, I was very close to my wife – someone to share one's life with you know, and then – all gone suddenly, not just her, the business, everything. Then Rita and the sudden change. Out of the darkness and into the light? And now, new house, new way of life, new friends?" He ended in a query raising his eyebrows at her.

"Yes, friends, sure," she said putting down her cup. "We can be and should be good friends, being close neighbours as we are and, I must say, the social life down here could certainly do with you. So there – OK, let's go." She got up suddenly and he found himself obeying her with some alacrity.

As Jane had indicated a possible problem between her and Perry, he had decided to leave the dog in the house. He got his coat and joined Jane who was standing by the door. They walked into the village and up towards Hawkcombe. She led him off onto a high path into the woods and then darted suddenly up a scarcely visible steep path which led upwards and then dipped down into a deep and beautiful valley down which tumbled the inevitable stream. It was a silent, mysterious place indeed, well away from the usual marked routes. The leaf-strewn path lay alongside the stream and was bounded on one side by a dry stone wall green with moss and age.

"Very few people come here," she said. "It's my special valley and now it's yours. You must come here – enjoy it. You see," she pointed to some new leaves, "I'm bringing it all alive for you. Soon, all of this will be alive." She swept her arms around her as though she was conducting some silent, spiritual symphony – imposing her Will upon the scene.

He stood listening to the stream and the occasional cry of birds. The valley rose steeply on either side in tree-covered slopes. The two of them walked along, climbing at times where the path became rough and high and the water gushed down in white sparkling falls. Soon they reached a point where two paths intersected. She pushed her hood back and he saw her cheeks glowing with the effort of the climb.

"That one takes you back to Hawkcombe and that one up to Ley Hill," she said, "but as we want some lunch, I suggest we go back along the Hawkcombe route," and she turned up a pathway to her right. "The path above us takes a higher route. This one's best; it's a lovely walk and you never meet anyone. Perry will love it. I expect you to use it now I've shown it to you," she chided.

"OK, I will, I assure you." He laughed and said, "You're right. It's lovely."

They climbed steadily with the sound of the stream coming up from below. The path took a high turn then a gradual descent, bisected another path and so down to the path which led back to Hawkcombe and Porlock. They passed several rather lavish houses and then by some cottages and on down into Parsons Street and the village. In a short time, they were at Jane's house where the butler had prepared a light lunch in a large Victorian conservatory.

As he sipped a delicious white wine, Steven looked around hoping for some ideas which could help with his own conservatory. The furniture was obviously expensive as were the fine array of plants, some very mature. Set around the room were classical statues and at one end, there was a particularly impressive statue of a Roman or Greek god.

"Who's he?" asked Steven. He got up and walked over to the statue to examine it more closely.

"Oh, Zeus, Jove, Jupiter. That's a copy of Jupiter Optimus Maximus taken from one in the Vatican Museum." She came over and stood looking at the statue.

He surveyed the room. On one of the walls was a Gorgon-like face. "That one's familiar. It's from Bath, isn't it?"

"Yes. It's a cast from there. The attribution is uncertain but I feel it's a depiction of a solar deity – Bel or Belanus. That would fit in with the thermal nature of the springs – you know, linking the heat from the earth with the fire of the sun."

Steven nodded then said, "I've seen lots of marble statues in situ and in museums but they're always in their natural state. Why are these all painted?" He gestured at the statues all of which were pigmented with bright colours. In some cases this contrasted oddly with the more sober black and white chequered floor.

"Well," she said, "in ancient times, temples and statues were very colourful. You see that one, well that's Athena. The colours of her cloak are taken from actual archaeological evidence, traces of colour found on ancient statues."

"I didn't know that. It looks pricey," he said, indicating Jupiter.

"Oh it was," she answered, "but, if you want something you've got to have it. I always get what I want." She looked at him boldly then turned and sat down again at the table.

Her movements were fluid, as though she had been a dancer, he thought. "And what is it you want?" he asked her, feeling excitement growing in him.

"Oh, lots of things," she said. "I want a great many things and I have a great many things. But what I want most I never seem to be lucky with and that is someone special, of my own, you know, someone to share everything with," she tailed off and poured some more wine for them both.

"Isn't there anyone then?" he asked. "I mean, you seem so set up, so in control of everything." He drank some more of the wine, put the glass down and helped himself to some pâté.

"Oh, there have been men – that's easy but I want a proper relationship – someone of my own; you know, you've had it with your wife. I envy you." She took a mouthful of smoked salmon and chewed on it. He found himself watching her mouth as it moved – the red of her lips contrasting with the white flash of her small, perfect teeth.

"Yes, I do know what you mean. When Ginny died I was devastated, lost, in despair. I felt I couldn't go on." He finished his food and drank some more wine. It seemed to be going to his head; he felt relaxed and comfortable with her. He hadn't felt so comfortable with a woman before – even with Ginny. It was strange indeed. He looked at her and she held his gaze. Then she lowered her lids slightly and he was taken by the curling length of her lashes. There was a warmth within her eyes which set up a strange longing for her.

"And now," she asked with a light smile, "how do you feel now?" Her lips were red, moist and he found them to be alluringly beautiful.

He put down his glass. "I feel good, peaceful, at ease. As though I've known you for years." He got up and moved round to her. She remained seated but lifted her head holding his gaze. He moved close to her, bent his head and kissed her full on the lips which parted. They were soft – like petals, he found himself thinking. He held the kiss for a while then stepped back. She rose and went to him; they embraced, kissing again. He did not know what was happening. It all seemed so quick yet dreamlike. Soon he found himself climbing the stairs and then they were in an extraordinarily lavish bedroom. In a haze he undressed and then they were both naked and clasping one another in a frenzy of passion. When it was over he lay back against the soft pillows and she was leaning over him, her breasts pressed against his chest.

She said, smiling, "You needed that I must say."

He looked up at her still panting. "Yes, yes I did. God!" His words were stopped by her kiss. He felt the weight of her as she leaned over him – the warmth and vitality of her body.

They lay back on the bed together and then she said, "I'm so glad you've come down here. I always say we could do with some new blood. Well, you're certainly going to make life interesting."

"More than just interesting, I hope," he said. "I've never felt like that before, not even with Ginny." And it was true. At this moment Jane filled his mind and he ran his hands along the side of her thigh.

Jane smiled. "Oh you were just frustrated – no sex for years and then, here I am."

"No, no. It's not like that. This was special," he said earnestly. "I want to see you again and again." He leaned up on one elbow and looked down on her.

"Don't be so extravagant," she said, "and stop being so serious. Come on, it was good sex, that's all." She was looking up at him in a teasing manner.

He was dismayed. "Good sex, yes but God, Jane, it was more than that, at least to me it was. I've never felt so close to anyone before. I'm going to need you now. When can we meet again?"

She got out of bed and he watched as she went over to the window, her naked form silhouetted against the light, her movements fluid, lithe – like a cat. "I've got some business to attend to over the next few days. I will call you when I get back." Her tone was soft, musing almost as though she was thinking aloud.

"Business?" he asked. "What kind of business?" He felt disappointed. He wanted to see her as soon as possible.

"Land buying," she replied. "I try to acquire as much as I can; a family tradition you know."

He remembered the note to Rita. "Oh yes. You were wanting to buy Hawkwood."

"Yes that's right – did Rita tell you?" She turned and stood framed by the window. He could not see her face.

"No, but I read a note you sent her." He lay there looking at her.

She said, "Will you sell Hawkwood to me, Steven?" She came over to the bed and stood provocatively next to his face. His eyes rested on the curve of her hips, the mound of pubic hair and up to her breasts. She leaned over him, her nipple brushing his mouth. He gasped and reached for her pulling her onto him. He was in her and she was riding him. She was fierce and she grasped his wrists holding them flat above his head as she rose up and down faster and faster. He exploded into her and she continued to her own climax and fell sprawling to the side of him. They lay gasping.

"God," he said, "you're amazing." He held her closely to him, stroking the nape of her neck, drinking in the scent of her hair.

She was silent for a long while then said, almost in a childish voice, "Sell me Hawkwood Steven, go on, its too big for one person. You don't really want it. I'll give you a good price and you can buy a nice little cottage. Go on… go on…" She was prodding him playfully, giggling.

He laughed, leaned up on one elbow and looked down at her. Her eyes were looking at him, mischievous and playful.

"My God, you're like a little kid wanting a toy. I hope you didn't sleep with me just to get your way," he said, teasing her.

She became serious, a look of distress on her face. "Oh no. Oh, of course not. Don't be horrid; I wanted you – couldn't you see that?" She looked crestfallen, hurt, a tear in her eye. She raised her hand and brushed the tear away.

He felt immediately contrite and anxious to please her. "Yes, yes and I wanted you. I want you now – always." He kissed her and she nestled against him then said, "I didn't mean to pressure you. It's just that I've always wanted that land and I thought that with Rita gone I would be able to bid for it. It meant a lot to me, that was all. I'm sorry, I didn't mean..." She tailed off and sighed.

He kissed her. "OK, OK. I'll think about it."

She said, "Will you? Oh thank you – that's all I want you to do."

"OK, I will, I promise. Now, when can we meet again?"

"Tomorrow," she said, "come here tomorrow at around 11 o'clock. OK?"

"11 o'clock – yes, I can't wait."

He kissed her again and she got up. "I'm going to have a shower," she said, "There's one next door as well."

Back downstairs she gave him coffee, made small talk then said she had to see someone. It seemed as though she was in a hurry and, in no time at all he found himself bundled out of the house and walking back to Hawkwood. His mind, though, was full of her and he was constantly assailed by images of their love-making. Gradually his mind cleared and, that evening, he went over and over the events of the day. It was strange. He remembered clearly the walk through the woods and the lunch or, at least, part of the lunch. Then everything seemed to change and became blurred. He remembered the love-making and felt a strong sense of guilt at his feelings of disloyalty to Ginny. And then, the question of the house sale; a strange time to bring it up, almost crass, and what had he said? He couldn't remember clearly. Did he say he would sell it? No, no, he recalled saying he'd *think* about it but, of course, he wouldn't sell his house. What had happened to him? She seemed so desirable, irresistible, yet she was nothing special. Frustration and drink, that was it. Now that he was away from her he could think more clearly. He'd have to watch the drink, that was for certain.

CHAPTER 5

He approached Jane's house the next day in some confusion. True, he was eager to see her again but unsure about it as well. After all, only yesterday, they had been making passionate love and he had felt overwhelming feelings for her yet she had changed, almost in a flash, from passion to a sort of indifference; no wonder he was bewildered. Steven was conscious of his loneliness and she had awoken long hidden emotions with her evident abandoned passion; again, a twinge of guilt at the thought of Ginny. And then the sudden talk about the house sale. There was something nagging at his mind. Jane had said that Rita had been a friend and that they were discussing the sale of the house, yet Steven knew that this was unlikely because of his aunt's reclusive behaviour. In any case, if Jane was such a friend why the note requesting a meeting? Still something nagged at him. What was it?

He went over in his mind Jane's visit to Hawkwood. Yes, that was it, Perry – she didn't know him and the dog didn't know her, that was evident. Also, that bit about him growling at her and Rita putting him out via the kitchen door – that was it! Perry *never ever* went out of the kitchen door and would not, in any case, growl at a welcome guest in the house. So Jane was lying about the sale and her relationship with Rita. He rang the bell and was shown into a large sitting-room by the butler.

"Miss Trethowan has asked me to tell you that she will be with you in a moment. Can I get you anything?" The butler's voice was as pretentious as his appearance.

"No, no thank you," replied Steven. The butler left the room.

Steven looked around, got up and walked over to the window. He could see the front driveway and the ornamental gardens laid to the front of the house. He heard Jane's laugh and a deeper voice as footsteps passed by the sitting room door. Then the voices were at the front of the building. A car was driving up to the front of the house. Jane, accompanied by Roger Martin, stepped onto the drive. Clearly she had been in some sort of meeting with him but then, to Steven's astonishment and sudden distress, he saw the man turn to Jane and hold her in a far from formal embrace, kissing her on the lips. Steven's distress was caused, not only by the nature of the embrace but also by the way Roger Martin's hand was caressing the curve of Jane's buttocks. He stepped back from the window and sat down. Only yesterday he had been holding her; they had seemed so close; his mind had been full of her, but now… The butler came in and he was taken into another room where Jane sat with an elderly man.

The Moon Temple

"Oh, hallo Steven. How are you? Would you like a drink? Do come and sit down." Despite this invitation, she made no effort to get up or to get him anything.

Steven stood looking at her totally dumfounded by her cool casual manner. It was as if they had just met and yesterday's closeness had never happened. He muttered that he didn't want a drink.

"This is Geoff Twindly, he's my solicitor, handles all my business deals. Geoff, Steven Downs." The solicitor did stand and came towards Steven. They shook hands and Steven sat down as Twindly returned to his seat.

"Well, Mr. Downs, I was sorry to hear about your aunt. Still, an ill wind and all that, eh?" Geoff Twindly was busy clicking open his attaché case. He continued speaking as he drew out papers. "So, selling up, eh? Well, I don't blame you, it's a very big property for a single person. The market's not that good down here but I have got a rough valuation and Jane is ready to meet your price." He held out the papers.

Steven didn't take them. He turned to Jane, bewildered, the memory of Roger Martin still fresh in his mind. "What's this all about, Jane?" he asked angrily.

"Why, darling," she said with a little laugh, "I know we had a lovely time yesterday but I didn't think you'd forget so soon. The house dear, Hawkwood, you said you'd sell it to me." She continued smiling at him, her gaze open.

"No, I haven't forgotten our day, how could I? But I certainly did *not* say I'd sell. I said I'd *think* about it. Well, I have and I'm staying. I'm sorry Mr. Twindly, there will be no sale. There's been a misunderstanding." As he said this he felt a sense of consternation as though unwilling to disappoint her.

Jane said nothing and her face, no longer smiling, showed no emotion as she turned to her solicitor. "Oh dear, Geoff," she said, "I've obviously got it wrong. Sorry about that."

"No problem," said Twindly closing his case. He got up and left the room with no further acknowledgement of Steven's presence. The front door closed and Steven and Jane stood facing each other. She was looking at him in a way he could not interpret but he began to feel that he had, somehow, let her down.

"I'm sorry, Jane," said Steven almost in a placating tone. "I really didn't say I'd sell; don't you remember? Oh come on, it doesn't matter at this time does it, really? Anyway, we're just getting to know each other, plenty of time for other things. I've just met a really great girl and I intend to take her to lunch so come on." He was so lost in his anticipation of being with her that he didn't see the coldness in her. All memories of her behaviour with Roger Martin had vanished.

"I'm sorry as well. No, I can't come to lunch, I'm going away on business, remember?" Her voice was flat and terse.

"Oh!" He was disappointed. "When you get back then?"

"I don't know. I don't think so. I'm so busy." She looked away from him and it was as though she had loosened a link between them. He felt deeply hurt and foolish at her evident rejection of him. She went on, "And there's no way you will consider selling up?"

He felt more in control and his tone hardened. "I'm sorry, no. I'm afraid you and I are destined to be neighbours for good or ill."

"Yes," she said softly as though lost in thought and led him to the front door. She looked into his eyes and said, "Goodbye." He was confused. What was happening? All so quick – as if yesterday had never happened. She closed the door before he could speak and he stared foolishly at the dark panels.

As he walked down the driveway he turned and looked back at the blank doorway. He felt as though she was still standing there behind the closed door.

He remembered the strange look in her eyes and the almost thoughtful way she had said the word, 'goodbye'. There had been a finality in her statement and he felt a sense of emptiness and loss. He carried on down the pathway remembering Jane's eyes and it was as though her eyes were following him, watching him, all the way to his house.

The rest of the day was confused and he seemed to be in a low state of mind. Jane's change of manner from the passionate lover to the cold business-like woman had his senses reeling and he felt like a rejected schoolboy lover for he was, indeed, absolutely head over heels in love with Jane Trethowan, this he knew beyond doubt. He didn't care about her behaviour with Roger Martin, who was probably her lover. Perhaps she had many lovers, and why not? He was startled by his thinking. He had never been a man who was prepared to be just another string to a woman's bow but now, well, if that is what it meant to be with her then he would be her lover as well. Anything to be with her. He picked up the phone and called her number. The phone was answered by Jane's butler who told him that she had left for a business trip and would be away for a few days. Bitterly disappointed he sat in the armchair as the evening gloom darkened the room.

Why had she been so giving and then so suddenly rejecting of him? He went over the events of the day before and for the life of him he could not remember clearly anything that had happened. One moment they had been having lunch after the walk and then they were in bed and next he was walking home. The more he thought about it the more blurred it became. It must have been the drink but, then, he had drunk very little, just some wine, surely? As for the love-making it was a kaleidoscope of images that flashed through his mind; her eyes, her breasts, the warm moistness, the passion, the eyes, again the eyes kept coming back. He felt his stomach full of butterflies as though he was in love for the first time. Then the memory of Roger Martin's groping hand came to him and he felt hurt, humiliated and desperate to see her again.

That night he slept badly, tossing and turning, his mind full of her. He must see her. The house, that was it; she wanted the house and the land. Well then she could have it, yes that was it. He'd let her have the house and then she would see him again. There now – Roger Martin could go to hell.

The clear light of day showed the world in a different way. He looked out of the window at the scenery and realised how much he loved the area. What on earth was he doing thinking of selling, or even giving Jane his house? What on earth was he thinking? Had he gone mad? Over breakfast he took a much more cool look at the whole matter. True, he had enjoyed the sex but Jane was not *that* fantastic, not even particularly good looking. In any case she had revealed her true purpose when she had made an immediate play for the house. It was a clumsy move, crass, lacking in any subtlety. Then, clearly, she had been lying; she did not know Rita well, if at all. She had not been to the house and had made an error when she had told him, or indicated, that Perry went out of the kitchen door. So what was it all about?

As the day wore on he began to recover his sense of proportion. True, he had felt, and still felt, wounded by her rejection of him and her obvious attempt to manipulate his emotions to her advantage but, at least, now that she had gone away he was beginning to see things more clearly. He *must* have been drunk, surely that could have been the only explanation. Feeling better, he whistled for Perry and soon the two of them were walking out towards the place to which Jane had taken him. He remembered the way and the two companions, man and dog, enjoyed a walk alongside the stream along the quiet valley floor. It was beginning to grow dark so forsaking that path which took him towards Hawkcombe he retraced his steps vowing to return and complete the trek another day.

Back home again he felt shivery as though coming down with a temperature. He took two Paracetamol and sat down to watch TV but he could not find any channel of interest and he flicked up and down for a while. He felt a growing sense of unease but could not place any reasons to feel so. Was that a noise in the hall or someone at the door? He went out into the hall and opened the door but no one was there.

"Must have been Perry," he mused aloud and went to look for the dog but Perry was curled up asleep behind Steven's chair. Out of the corner of his eye he saw a movement in the dark corner of the hall; he went over to it but it was only the shadowy shape of a coat hanging on a hook. He went back into the lounge and switched on the TV again but once more he found nothing of interest. There was a sense of someone watching him and he spun round – nothing.

Steven began to feel irritated with himself and realised that whatever he was feeling had to be the result of a bug and he decided on an early night. As he went upstairs to his bedroom he felt an overwhelming sadness hit him and he longed to see Rita again. How sad to have missed her funeral and not to have been able to say goodbye properly. If only he had called her and spoken to her, perhaps he could have helped her more. Steven opened Rita's bedroom door and looked in. He saw the empty bed, now remade and tidy, with no signs of the dreadful prelude to her untimely death. He closed the door and went into his own room where he was soon lying, tossing fitfully, as yet another bad night dragged on.

He awoke, suddenly, to the sound of wind and with rain battering against the windows. He was trying to drift off when he heard another noise coming from the stairs, a scraping, dragging noise – Perry! Usually, the dog would thump and clatter his way up to Steven's room each morning but it was still dark and this was a dragging noise. He put the light on, went to the door and looked out into the dark corridor. The scraping noise was on the stairs, no doubt of that. He went to the head of the stairs and flicked the switch.

It wasn't Perry on the stairs, it was Rita. His eyes and his mind tried to comprehend what was before him and his heart began to hammer in absolute terror. Rita, dressed only in her nightgown which was soaked by the rain, was crawling painfully up the stairs, her torn hands clawing at the stair treads. Steven was rooted to the spot. He felt dizzy. This could not be; she was dead, dead, cremated but no, here she was, crawling up, up towards him. Her grey and thinning hair, also soaked and clinging to her pale skull-like head, hung around her as she slowly raised her white, dead, face towards him and he looked into round, staring, terrified eyes which held him in a deadly compelling gaze.

Involuntarily, he felt himself drawn towards the crawling form and began to move to the head of the stairs.

There was a noise from below. Perry, aroused by Steven's walking along the corridor, had come to investigate. Steven saw the dog at the foot of the stairs and realised that Rita's apparition had disappeared. The dog clattered up to him and Steven came to, his heart still hammering. What was he doing here, why?

"A nightmare," he said aloud. "A bloody horrible dream."

He recovered himself and went back to his room accompanied now by Perry; he was grateful for the dog's friendly normal presence. He lay back in his bed, his mind re-running the dreadful dream and the eyes of Rita seemed to merge into those of Jane Trethowan as he drifted into a deep slumber.

He awoke to a grey and rainy day which lent an air of depressive heaviness to the overwhelming feelings of loneliness now enveloping him. Steven remembered the events of the night but attributed the vision of Rita to a feverish illness. He felt his limbs to be heavy and he had developed a pounding headache. The house seemed to be closing in around him and he could not rest. He put on his coat and went into Porlock where he did some shopping and purchased some more cold remedies. The day was one of those dank, cold, wet days where everything seemed to be dripping and no amount of protection prevented water from seeping in. It was down his neck, in his face, soaking his coat and it even seemed to gust into the shops whenever he opened a door. It was as though he was carrying his own personal bad weather system with him and he was grateful to return to Hawkwood but there it was cold; the heating system was not on.

He went to the cupboard and looked at the system – it was switched off. Steven thought this was strange because it had been perfectly all right until then, or had it? After all, so far he had experienced only good weather so perhaps he hadn't noticed the system before. He switched it on but soon realised that it would make no difference as it was a storage system and would only take in electric power overnight. So, he went into the lounge to light the fire but found he had run out of fuel for that. Everything was going wrong. He felt unwell, cold, in despair, sorry for himself, angry, fed up, depressed, sad, melancholy – in fact every possible bad combination seemed to be coming at him as the dank day continued through its remorseless endless grey cycle.

He attempted to meditate, as he had always done whenever he had felt low but it was to no avail. Every attempt to calm his thoughts was interrupted by persistent visual pictures of Jane; her naked body, the warm closeness of her embrace, the scent of her. At one point he opened his eyes startled by the very real sense that she was next to him. The physical presence of her body seemed real, almost touching him as though she had entered the room and was standing behind him. He turned, words of pleasure and welcome on his lips but the room was empty.

Steven felt disturbed by the sensations, tried once again to calm his mind but it was no good and he gave up in a real sense of depression. He found himself longing for Jane again and again and, at one point, found himself weeping in an absolute state of maudlin self-pity, abandoned by Jane, by Ginny and by Rita. Here he was all alone, rattling around in this great house accompanied only by a dog; how pathetic.

He took his medicine and went to bed but not without first searching the house thoroughly and ensuring that all perimeter access points were secure. Again, that jumpy feeling of being watched and, several times, he spun quickly because he thought he had caught a glimpse of someone but always there was nothing. He drifted off to sleep and soon he was walking in the wooded valley with Jane and Perry. The valley was lined with dark twisted, watching trees and Perry bounded ahead disappearing around the bend. Steven held Jane's hand as they scrambled over the rocks; she tripped and he felt the pull on his arm. He turned to help and found that he was holding the shrunken arm of Rita's corpse – he screamed and awoke and lay, trying to dispel the image – but it was persistent. The room seemed to be closing in on him, the shadows heavy around him and then he felt something on the bed, the weight of someone sitting near his feet. It moved onto him, crawling along his legs and pressing down on his chest. He saw eyes – half opened slits, and then there was a wetness across his face and he felt his mouth clamped in a wet, smothering kiss. He forced himself to a gasping wakefulness out of yet another nightmare. His body was drenched in sweat and he felt really hot. He got out of bed and noticed that the heating was now on so he stripped a covering from the bed. He took two more Paracetemol, gulped down the water, as he felt completely parched, and then went back to bed falling, soon, into another dreaming sleep.

Perry and Steven were walking in the valley again. Perry bounded ahead and disappeared around the bend. Steven called for him and turned the bend in the path to find Perry lying on the ground covered in blood. He bent down and saw that the dog's throat had been torn out by some other creature and it was out there somewhere close waiting, coming near, nearer. His heart was hammering as he willed himself to waken. Something dark in the trees pursuing him along the valley – something – he awoke with sunlight streaming into the room. He lay for a while listening to the birds chattering and greeting the bright day. He felt better and got out of bed, the memories of the nightmares beginning to fade.

He noticed that the melancholia of the day before had lifted as though the bright sunlight had driven it away. He began a series of exercises in an attempt to balance himself again after, what he perceived to be, a virus attack. Soon he was deep into a lengthy series of Tai-Chi movements and he felt himself growing stronger and calmer as the Chi began to course through him. As he swayed and moved his body through the intricate and ancient moves, he felt his mind beginning to settle and the dark sense of melancholy lifted.

Perry came clattering up the stairs and waited in the room as Steven got ready. He spoke to the dog, "Oh, I do feel better – yes I am. We'll go for a walk after breakfast, eh? Yes, good boy." He patted and stroked Perry's head. God, what dreadful dreams, what on earth was it all about? All mixed up – Jane, Rita, death, melancholy thoughts. He looked out of the window at the glorious view. Only yesterday he had been so down that he had even considered giving up and going back to London. Jane could have had the house, he would almost have given it away but, now, with the bright light of day and the prospect of a good walk ahead, all of those desperate and sad thoughts had vanished.

Downstairs he prepared a hearty breakfast and then the two of them set out for a walk in the moors. He decided to avoid Jane's valley; it had figured in his nightmares and, in any case, it would only make him unhappy as he recalled the enjoyment he had felt whilst with her. A fresh direction and fresh air would help to lay a few ghosts and dispel the sad memories.

CHAPTER 6

Steven and Perry made their way up Hawkcombe and turned off through an iron gate, they crossed a stream and were soon walking on the path which led, eventually, to Hawkcombe Head high on the moor. He avoided the steep path which led to Jane's valley and continued along enjoying the sense of freedom and the exercise. The path twisted and wound its way along the side of the hills and opened up in a wider series of coombs, each one fed by a stream. The ground was difficult in places and he diverted off on several occasions. He mounted a rise, turned sharply left and found himself walking along the trail he and Jane had walked upon only a short time ago. Steven paused, shrugged his shoulders and entered the valley which had played such a part in his nightmares and yet, at the same time, held the promise of his memories of her.

Jane – she figured so high in his mind now but why? He had felt the cleansing power of the Chi exercise flush his cluttered thoughts and, for a time, he was able to view his situation and his feelings in a more rational manner. True, Jane had been seemingly passionate towards him but then there had been that sudden cold change. The appointment and her behaviour with the solicitor and her apparent relationship with Roger Martin had been a startling revelation. Surely it could not be that she had seduced him merely to get the house and land? His vanity would not accept this yet there seemed to be no doubt that this was exactly what she had done. So why did he yearn for her so? As he tried to analyse his feelings he felt the sense of melancholy return but dispelled it quickly.

For a time he distracted himself by observing the way the water splashed down between the rocks and he sat back against the dry stone wall lining the path and studied the valley. It was, indeed, a beautiful place with its stream and steep wood-covered sides mounting towards the higher moor – Jane had been right about that and he had a sudden memory of her, smiling. The valley seemed timeless and he could envisage the past when prehistoric hunters searched for game perhaps stopping at this very spot to drink, ever conscious of the waiting predator lurking in the shadows. He rose, startled at the thought. Predator? Yes, this was indeed the sort of place, lonely, remote, untouched by hikers, where a predator could hide away waiting for that time, that moment when unwary prey ventured into its kingdom. He shook his head and said aloud, "Oh, stop it". He'd be seeing the Beast of Exmoor next. No sooner had this thought come into his mind than he felt an incredible sense of vulnerability and frailty.

The sun, which had been sending bright beams of light into the valley, had gone, lost behind clouds and the surrounding slopes took on a sombre, brooding atmosphere. It was all so different from when he had been there with Jane. He remembered her talking about bringing the place alive, as indeed it was. This time, though, there was not that sense of spirituality he had felt when the wind had stirred the dancing trees. Instead, he became conscious that there was a constant battle of life and death going on all around him. The trees with their twisting, writhing branches seemed to be locked in a titanic struggle with each other, striving for the light, for the very air. He felt, or rather 'saw', that same battle continuing all around beneath his feet as each tree fought for the moisture in the ground, roots reaching, gripping, strangling other roots of other trees. How could he see this; it was too much, too depressing a picture and he cursed himself and told himself to get hold of his thoughts. He called to Perry and they turned up from the path to a higher route leaving the stream below.

He felt apprehensive, vulnerable, but could not pin the sense down. The feelings of vulnerability and total helplessness grew and Steven had a sudden, chilling, perception of how it must feel to be prey, to be a deer lost in the woods. But, unlike a deer, he lacked its sense of smell, its superior vision and, above all, its speed in flight. Instead, he was merely a clumsy, stumbling human from the city, with no idea of the nature of the countryside and its perils – so real to him, now. What was going on? His rational mind attempted to overcome the rising fear within him for he knew he was here, walking in a beautiful valley on Exmoor, in England – not in the far and savage wilds.

Soon they were walking along a path which was eerily familiar to Steven. It was the same path he had seen in his dream, or at least it seemed similar; but how could that be? He had never been here before. Jane had not taken him this far and yet it was, somehow, familiar. Perry bounded ahead and disappeared around a bend leaving Steven alone and then he knew there was something behind him, along the pathway, stalking him. He spun round. Nothing – but then predators knew how to hide, to be silent and still, waiting for the moment to pounce, to rend and tear. His heart began to hammer. He tried to call Perry but he could not. "Don't run," he found himself muttering aloud. But it was there, close, near, ready to spring out of the shadows. Suddenly he heard a branch crack and something clutched at his leg and he gasped; it was only brambles. Where was Perry? He turned the bend and the dog lay quivering in the pathway, whining and trembling in utter terror.

The all-pervading sense of menace was almost on him but there was nothing there that he could see. Panting now in fear he bent over the dog. Perry showed no signs of injury but lay quivering and whining as though trying to grovel his way deep into the ground. Steven attempted to rouse the dog but to no avail. Whatever was out there after them was close; he could almost hear it, see it. Was that a moving shape in the shadows? He felt his heart jumping, hammering. He was now in a blind panic and leaving Perry he began to run, stumbling along the pathway conscious that the beast was almost on him. He staggered, tripped and fell heavily but hardly noticed the pain of the fall nor the blood beginning to run from a cut hand. The path descended steeply and before he could recover himself he tumbled again rolling down the pathway to end up, breathless, at the feet of a woman who was ascending the path from the other direction.

"Oh my goodness! Are you all right? Wait, I'll help you." The woman leaned over him and Steven looked into concerned, grey eyes. The sense of menace, pursuit and danger had vanished and Perry came following down the track and fawned around Steven.

"Hallo," said the woman to Perry who began to wag his tail at her. She turned back to Steven. "Are you OK? That was some tumble you took and, oh, your hand is bleeding. Here let me help you." She assisted him to his feet and he leant back, panting, against the tree.

"Stupid of me. Going too fast and lost my footing. Ouch, that hurts!" He rubbed his hip and then took out a tissue to staunch the cut hand.

"Look, that needs attention. I live just below near here. Come on, I'll help you."

"Oh, really no, no thanks. I'll be OK." He stood up straight but slumped back feeling weak and nauseous, still shaken by his experience.

"I insist, you look terrible. That was a really bad fall. Come on, its just down there; we'll see how it is – you might need medical attention."

She supported him and, no longer protesting, Steven allowed her to guide him down to her cottage at the bottom of the pathway. He had not had time to take stock of her but felt her strength as she supported him. As they walked she chatted to him. She had a soft West Country lilt to her voice. "I'm Marian Hall and who's this?" She looked down at Perry who was looking up at her, tongue lolling as though in a big smile.

"He's Perry. I'm Steven Downs. Do you mind dogs in your house? Not everyone does."

"Oh, I love 'em but Tanith might not be so kind."

"Tanith?"

"My cat – she's a sort of mixed Persian tortoiseshell, something or other," replied Marian.

They passed a few large houses and then stopped outside a cottage. "Here we are." She opened the gate which led around the side to a door. She opened it and they entered into a large stone-floored kitchen. She turned on the cold tap in the sink and told Steven to run the cut hand under the seemingly icy water. He did this and flinched at the sting of the water on the cut which, he saw, was not too bad. Marian came over, turned off the water and dabbed the wet hand dry with paper towel.

"Hmm! Not deep then." She fished around in a box and pulled out a plaster which she placed over the cut. Her red hair fell across her face and she flicked it back in order to see better. "I think that will do. Have you had a tetanus shot recently?" He nodded. "Hey, you look a bit peeky. Come, sit here." She pulled up a chair. Indeed he did feel shaken and a bit queezy; gratefully he sat down. He was finding it difficult to concentrate.

"You're very kind," he said. "I'll be on my way in a minute – just a bit shaky. You came along at just the right moment."

"What moment was that?" She was pottering around filling a kettle and had her back to him.

"My fall," said Steven. "You came just at the right moment."

She turned and looked at him. "Yes, your fall, but it took more than a fall to give you the sort of expression that was on your face. You looked as though you were running from the Devil himself, not that I believe in *him* but it took more than a fall for you to look like that. I heard you crashing towards me you know. What was the matter?"

He could not read her expression but it was clear, from her tone of voice, that she was voicing genuine interest and concern. He felt tempted to tell her but what could he say to this young woman, a complete stranger? "No, I lost my footing and thought I was going to break something. Really." He thought he could see the scepticism on her face but, then, realised that her expression had not changed and he felt that she had accepted his explanation.

"Here," she said, "have a cup of tea," and she handed him some hot sweet tea. "Good for shock."

He took the drink and sipped at it slowly. A cat came into the room, saw Perry and arched its back, hissing. "Stop it, Tanith," said Marian. "Be polite. We have guests." The cat leapt up onto a high cupboard where it stood glaring down at perplexed Perry who had had very little contact with cats. "She'll settle in a minute." Marian went over to the cat and stroked the animal until it settled down. "There now, that's better." She came and sat down again and continued, "So you're new down here?"

"No, not really." He gave a brief outline of his relationship with Porlock over the years.

Marian expressed her condolences about Rita and then said, "Well, you've certainly gained a reputation down here already. What was that all about in the pub – you know, the fight?"

Steven marvelled at the bush telegraph that seemed to operate in villages. "Oh, a couple of idiots – a bit worse for drink no doubt."

"That wasn't what I heard," she said, "come on, tell all, we country folk lead very sheltered loives." She had put on a strong exaggerated West Country accent this time. She sat back in her chair holding her cup and looked at him with seeming anticipation of a good story.

He laughed and realised that he was feeling remarkably relaxed in her presence.

"OK," he said and, soon, for the second time he found himself opening up to a complete stranger. She listened as he spoke about his wife's death, the business collapse, Rita, Dan and Ray, Jane Trethowan and then he paused startled at the fact that he had been so open.

"I'm sorry," he said, "I must be boring you. I didn't realise I was going on so much." He was embarrassed as he said this but she was not smiling now.

"It's all right," she said softly, "you seem to be in need of a good talk."

He looked up at her, studying her as she held his gaze. She was of indeterminate age, thirty something he supposed. Her grey eyes were set in a pale almost childlike face framed by deep copper-red hair which hung in thick heavy waves to her waist. She was above medium height with a strong looking sturdy build as though she had worked on the land – very Celtic he found himself thinking. A stone pendant hung at her throat and various rings adorned her fingers.

"You have a lot of grief to work through. These things take time and sometimes a shock, such as your fall, can trigger emotions." Marian got up and came over to him and put a hand on his head gently. He was unsure how to react but then he felt a warmth run through him and he relaxed as his initial uncertainty vanished.

"Lots of tension and fear. Fear? Why?" She was talking to herself as she stood behind him and she placed another hand on his shoulder. He felt comforted instantly and then, to his alarm, tears welled in his eyes and ran down his cheeks. Feeling foolish he pulled out a tissue and wiped his eyes. She stepped away from him and, moving to the other side of the table, she sat down again.

"What is it? What's wrong, you can tell me?" She was speaking softly to him and then he was talking about Jane and his yearning for her and of the depression, the waves of melancholia, the jumpiness and fear within the house, the sinister sense of watching, waiting forms, the beast in the woods. It all came out in a wave of gasping, terse sentences and then it was done and he felt the relief that can only come when a great burden has finally been discarded. It was as though the gloom that had assailed him over the past days had been dispelled by a great golden beam of sunlight.

"I'm sorry," he said. "You must think I'm off my head. A grown man running from ghosts, shadows." He felt extremely embarrassed. He had *never* spoken, so openly, about his feelings to anyone and certainly not about ghostly fears. What would she think of him?

"No, not at all," she said, then was silent and seemed to be thinking to herself.

Steven needed to break the silence. "Now I can understand my aunt. Poor lady, she must have had a similar sort of experience in the house and ran out at night terrified, to die on the moor. Perhaps the house is haunted. What do you think? Oh, you must think I'm crazy but I can't explain it otherwise. What do you think?" He tailed off and took another drink of his tea, draining the cup.

The Moon Temple

Marian said nothing, only looking at him in a way Steven did not understand. She seemed to be looking not at him directly but at the totality of his being, his physical and spiritual self. He felt something within her that he could not place but which tugged at deep, atavistic memories. For a moment he felt uneasy. The kitchen was alternating between sunlight and shade as clouds, pushed by high winds, crossed the face of the sun. It was as though the room was spinning in its own space, divorced from other earthly attachments.

Then she spoke. "No, not crazy or silly – very real, all of it – and deadly."

She got up again and made another pot of tea, as he pondered her words. She poured out two more cups and pushed one over to him. He lifted it and took refuge behind its rim sipping the warm fluid. She put a log on the kitchen fire stoking the red embers into a flame.

Putting down the poker she came back to the table. "Not silly at all," she said. "What do you know of witchcraft?"

He was startled at the question but responded quickly, wondering what she meant. "Only what I've seen in films, TV, read about. Dennis Wheatley, that sort of thing." He paused then said, "Are you saying this is it? This is what's happening to me? Who? Why? Oh come on, surely not. I'm not closed to the idea, after all I've been around long enough to know there are many strange things which can't be explained away; but who would want to? I don't know anyone who would want to hurt Rita or me. Not even Dan or Ray, they're thugs, not witches."

"What about Jane Trethowan?" The question said quietly, seemed to crackle in the room.

He was shocked. "Jane? Why? What for? Oh come on, we were only making love…" He paused, embarrassed again. "Sorry, shouldn't have said that. But no, why would she? A witch, Jane? No." It was a preposterous suggestion – surely?

"Jane – yes! She's a well-known occultist you know…" – Steven remembered the doctor's words, 'A bit New Agey' – "written books about it all as well. She's a most powerful occult practitioner. The Craft tradition has been in her family for years as it has been in mine. Yes, mine. I'm what you would term a witch although it's not a term *I* use. Some of us use our powers to heal, do divination, that sort of thing; others use the power to get power and they can and will do anything to get their way. You said that she wanted your property and that she had got nowhere with your aunt – so Rita dies in mysterious circumstances. You – well, she first seduces you then she tries to frighten you out, or to death. Is it so strange? I know about your martial arts. Some would consider high practitioners of those arts are magical as well. Look what you did to Dan."

Why did this seem so matter of fact, thought Steven as he took in her words? He nodded for he had seen martial arts masters perform seemingly impossible feats.

"That's true but that's physical – magic is to do with the mind, the intangible isn't it?" There had been numerous articles about the occult in periodicals throughout the 1960s and '70s, when New Age ideas had come into prominence, so none of this was entirely surprising to him.

"You understand and use Chi energies don't you?" she said. "That's not exactly what you would term physical in the usually accepted understanding of the term."

Steven agreed, "True, the ability to raise and use Chi – the life force – is an essential component in all forms of martial arts."

She went on, "OK – that makes you sensitive, psychic even. That's how Jane got at you and perhaps your aunt – she was very artistic, sensitive, yes? Open to things and, therefore, open to psychic attack. You have been, are being, psychically attacked." She said this in a straightforward tone as if it was an everyday occurrence.

"I've heard of that sort of thing – never really sure about it though. However, I don't see myself as being psychic…" he paused, "…although I have to say that, as I developed my skills and became more adept, I found that I could anticipate the moves of an opponent. It was almost as though they were moving in slow motion or I could perceive what they were going to do before they did it. But what you're saying is that witches can send a power to do something – it's not physical. Mine you can demonstrate – yours is inexplicable."

Marian leaned forward, animated by the discussion. "Inexplicable maybe but that doesn't mean the use of such powers is impossible. You understand Chi or Ki, what about healing – Reiki?"

He pondered this. Yes Reiki masters could 'beam' power to heal over a distance and spiritual healers, no matter of what faith, could do likewise. "Yes, you're right. I see where you're going with this."

"OK, look, there's been quite a lot of scientific exploration into energies such as electro-magnetic impulses, about their effect on people. Do you know they were doing an experiment in a so-called haunted house? They put some people into a dark room and passed a low frequency pulse through the room, you know, beyond human auditory range. Well, most felt something as though someone had touched them; some felt frightened. It's the brain you see, it tries to interpret things and, if it can't explain it, then it finds the nearest equivalent thing – creates images – so, some people see, say, a form – a ghost."

He nodded, "Yes, I saw that on TV. Go on."

"Well, every living thing has a basic reflex, 'a sense of fear'," she made quote signs, "even a single cell organism will show some sort of reaction to attack. It can't see but it can sense. They did an experiment with someone with Parkinson's Disease – I can't remember it exactly, but she showed sadness when they passed a current of electricity through her brain. Her expression became sad and later she felt the emotion. Energies are weird but they can be used, in experiments, to cause things to happen. Magicians, witches, whatever you want to call them, use energies as well. They can focus their minds to achieve a desired end. With a determined and directed application of the Will, changes can be made to occur. In fact, the occultist Aleistair Crowley defined magic almost like that. We use our power to sense, transmit, make changes, make things happen. Science today is beginning to understand that there are other forms of energy beyond what is generally known. Concepts of Time and Space are being altered due to a greater exploration and study of quantum physics."

"You said Jane was an occultist – does that mean she's a black magician, that sort of thing – using these strange powers to harm me – a psychic attack, as you called it?"

Marian gave a wry smile. "Well how she uses her power is up to her. One could argue that *all* use of magic has an effect on others. Look, you want something someone else wants and you do a spell to get it. That's good for you but bad for someone else. One could say that there's no black or white magic, only shades of grey. It's a neutral force, how it's used is the issue. All action has a re-action. Occultist? Well, occult merely means the hidden or the veiled; so fortune-tellers, mediums, crystal healers, dowsers could all be said to be using occult powers. What Jane is doing, and I'm sure she is, what she's doing is bad 'cos she's deliberately hurting others to achieve her own ends. When I laid my hands on your head, you felt something didn't you?" She held her hands out.

He nodded. "Yes I felt warmth, comfort, peace – yes, peace." He said the last word almost to himself.

She nodded. "I used my power to help you to get well not to hurt you – you see what I mean?" She went on. "There are those practitioners who use power solely for selfish ends. It would be like you using your skills to beat up other people, a total misuse of a great gift. There are people who actually revel in the idea of being black magicians, Satanists, for example. The press lump us all together. Modern pagans, like Wiccans, don't acknowledge Satan – it's a Judaeo-Christian concept. That dark angel tempting people and tormenting souls for all eternity has no place in the modern pagan mind. I don't worship the Devil neither does Jane Trethowan but she, unlike me, will conjure up dark energies, negative power, something like anti-matter – and this will form images in the mind; despair, melancholy, suicidal feelings, ghosts…"

"The Beast of Exmoor," he interrupted.

"…Exactly – did you notice that as you thought of something it manifested in your mind?"

He remembered the words 'neighbourly chat'.

Marian said, "Somehow she's tapped into you. Look I know its personal but you said you were making love – you meant making love, sex, yes?" She raised her eyebrows in query. It was a direct and personal question but seemed entirely acceptable in view of the circumstances.

He replied, "Well, yes, of course, that's the euphemism for it." A memory of Jane's pliant, willing body, came to him.

Marian seemed to be pondering his response. "Hmm! Very close. That's probably it; she may have kept something of you, your essence, you know, body fluids."

She could have been speaking of some inanimate object, so casual were her words.

He looked startled. "Oh, ugh! Really? That's gross." Again, the memories of his sexual encounter with Jane were there – insistent.

She looked at him. "Not really, its very natural and very ancient. Blood, semen, sweat, body hair, nail clippings, all of these have been used in witchcraft. We'll have to see what happens next." Marian made it all sound somehow normal.

He slumped. "You mean its not over? I feel so all right now. Surely that's it?" He couldn't go through that terror again, he told himself.

She smiled. "Yes, you do look better, but that's probably because you're with me and here. Bad vibes will have difficulties penetrating here. It's protected."

Steven was trying to accept her statements but, then, rationality crept in. It all seemed so preposterous. Here he was with a complete stranger, sitting in a cottage in Exmoor, talking about witches and black magic. Surely it was all ridiculous? Yet, he couldn't explain the dreadful feelings of the past days nor the events in the woods nor the fact that he felt so different in Marian's company.

"OK" he said, "I'm finding it difficult but I think I do believe you." He pushed aside his rational thoughts and had a fleeting memory of Jane's lips on his – so real – so moist and soft.

"The sign of a good healthy open mind," Marian was saying. "There's another way she can get at you – your innocence."

He hardly heard her. He could feel the lips, warm and soft, on his.

Marian was watching him closely. "You must try to think of other things. Don't think of her. Don't dwell on what has happened."

He was startled. Could she read his mind? The feeling of Jane's lips vanished and he pulled himself together. "OK, OK, but you're forgetting one thing. I felt strangely attracted to her from the outset..." he paused; – "Yes?" she encouraged, – "...Well, yes, I must say that was a bit strange. I mean she's all right but I did feel extraordinarily attracted to her from the very beginning. I mean, well, do you know her? She's not *that* attractive is she? Oh God, that sounds so terrible but, well, it doesn't make any sense. I'm too long in the tooth to get carried away like that and yet..." again he paused. Why *had* she seemed so desirable?

As though answering his unspoken question, Marian gave a little laugh. "But that's easy to explain," she said. "She merely used an old trick. She was using what we call 'the glamour' to trap you. Do you know that I could make you fall in love with me now – no, don't look alarmed, I wont, but I could. Basic witch practice really." She shrugged her shoulders and made a dismissive gesture with her hand.

"A useful trick then. You could bottle it and make a fortune." This was all crazy, he found himself thinking.

"The trouble is, it doesn't last, only temporary I'm afraid." She laughed again and then became serious. "But that's how it is and that's what she did. She trapped you, bewitched you and, no doubt, would end by killing you like she did Rita. It's not over, Steven, of that I'm sure but at least now you're on your guard. So, if you start to feel low, depressed, phone me – here's my number." She scribbled the phone number on a piece of paper and passed it to him.

"It's possible that she might give up?" he queried. He was feeling a growing sense of unease at the thought that the horrific experiences would return.

"Perhaps, we'll have to see – phone me if necessary no matter what time. I might be able to help you. The puzzle though, is this. Why is she doing it? What is so special about your house and land, Steven?"

CHAPTER 7

The blazing log crackled and burst into bright flame sending up a shower of sparks which hovered in the rising heat and wafted up the chimney. He considered her words. "I really haven't the foggiest idea unless it's to do with some sort of coin hoard. After all, those two idiots were going over the land with a metal detector. I certainly don't believe it that Jane didn't know about them. Perhaps someone local might know, a historian or a local archaeologist."

"You may be right. There are all sorts of stories and legends but I've never heard anything relating to your house or land. Do you know that Jesus was supposed to have been at Culbone? King Arthur slew a dragon at Dunster, that sort of thing but not on your land, nothing. Unless, yes, now wait a minute." She disappeared from the kitchen and he heard her clattering about in the next room.

This was ridiculous, he found himself thinking, and he wondered if he ought to leave but it couldn't hurt to stay a while longer; it was cosy here and his hip still ached. He looked down at Perry who was curled up in front of the fire. The cat had settled down on the cupboard top but was keeping a watching eye on the dog. Marian came back holding a book.

"This is an old local history book compiled in the 1800s by a local vicar. It seems that there may have been some burials, ancient ones, on your part of the moor but they were grubbed out long ago by farmers. Still, I suppose something could have survived. At least it's a start. Perhaps you ought to scout around, buy a metal detector yourself and have a go; why not?" She closed the book and laid it on the table.

"Yeah." The idea appealed to him. "I could get one. Don't know much about it though but I might turn up something although by the look of Dan's efforts it doesn't look very promising."

"Good," she said and smiled at him. "That's more positive." She changed the subject. "Are you hungry? I could knock up a tuna sandwich if you like." She got up and looked at Perry who lazily stretched and also got up as she moved.

Steven realised that he felt ravenous and said, "That's kind of you but Perry will be hungry as well."

"I could give him some cat food if you like." Perry nuzzled at her licking her hand. "Oh, he likes me, don't you – yes, yes you do." She ruffled the dog's head and his stubby tail began wagging furiously. "He's lovely. Didn't he do anything to protect Rita though – you know on that night?"

"Well that's a puzzle I must say. I don't know where he was or how he reacted but he was certainly assertive with Dan and Ray, so I'm sure he would have had a go at anyone threatening Rita. No, I don't think it was an intruder, at least not a physical one. I think Rita was driven out of the house by the same sort of activity that's been bugging me. That confirms your ideas about psychic attacks. Poor old Rita, horrible the whole thing." He felt a growing sense of guilt as he remembered his aunt and how he had failed to contact her over the final weeks. As he was talking Marian was opening up a tin of cat food and this was soon gobbled down by the dog. Tanith had sat upright like an Egyptian cat and she looked, with seeming curiosity and disdain, at the slurping dog below her. As Marian prepared some sandwiches, Steven asked to use the bathroom and was directed upstairs. Outside of the kitchen he could smell the faint scent of incense. It reminded him of childhood – of being in church. Mounting the stairs he noticed a variety of strange pictures lining the walls of the staircase. The bathroom was neat and clean and when he came downstairs the sandwiches and another pot of tea were ready.

"This is really kind of you," he said. "I feel I'm imposing on you." He sat down by the fire feeling strangely pleased that he would be remaining with her a bit longer.

"Do you hear me complaining? Oh come on, I'm sure you would do likewise if the situation was reversed." She handed him a lap tray which held a sandwich and a cup of tea.

He munched at his sandwich. "So what do you do with your time when you're not rescuing bewitched and hungry hikers?"

"Oh this and that. I do part time lecturing at the local community college – anthropology, religious studies, whatever. I also write articles for the local press and a few obscure academic magazines. I don't need much really. I'm pretty self-sufficient, grow my own veggie stuff. I own the cottage so no mortgage. I sometimes do a few hours at the Visitors' Centre. A bit of this and that plus a bit of money left by my parents, they're both dead."

"You're alone then? No partner? – sorry, a bit personal that." He had seen no sign of another person in the cottage.

"It's all right, no, no one now. I did have a long relationship but he moved on a few years ago. I think I was too quirky for him."

Steven laughed, "I can understand that. Oops, sorry," as he ducked a crust flung at him by Marian.

"Now now, I can always send you out again to be devoured by the creatures of the night," she paused – "no, that's not really funny is it?"

In response to further questioning, Steven learned that Marian had studied anthropology, obtaining a bachelor's degree. She had included a module in religious studies and had taken a particular interest in cultures which had not been overly influenced by, or converted to, any of the major faiths. In return he told her something of his own past and his flirtation with Eastern philosophies. "That's why I don't find the things you're saying so weird," he said. "There are so many strange things in the world, so, I suppose, anything is possible." There was a silence between them for a while then Steven said, "Do you think she'll try again?"

"I really truly don't know. I'm afraid it's one of those things that can only be judged if and when it happens. Look, you're welcome to stay here overnight if you like. I can make up a bed for you." Her open generosity was something that Steven had not experienced before and his city mind felt an immediate suspicion, but he could see her openness and lack of guile.

He said, "That's really very kind of you but I've got to face this whatever it is. Perhaps it really is all in my mind. Grief, tiredness, that sort of thing." He did not sound convinced and he began to wonder if he should accept her invitation after all.

She attempted to lift the mood. "Yep, you could be right but remember what I said. I'm on the end of a phone." She became serious, "No, do it, phone me, I mean it. If I'm right you *will* need me." She stopped and looked at him intently then smiled. "More tea?" she asked, lightening the mood instantly.

"No, I'm fine, thanks. I've taken up far too much of your time and I think Tanith would like to reclaim her place by the fire. I'll be in touch with you regardless if that's OK with you?" He realised how much he had enjoyed being in her company and felt reluctant to leave her. He got up and Perry stood also, tail wagging.

"I'd like that. Anyway, I'd like to see this mansion of yours that's causing all the trouble." She was ruffling Perry's neck and then she, too, stood up.

He leapt at the opening. "Tomorrow, how about tomorrow? How are you fixed?"

"OK, yes, what time?" She seemed genuinely pleased at his invitation.

"Come for lunch. I'll rustle up a pasta or something. Errrr, you're veggie are you?" He had come across many of these New Age people; almost inevitably they avoided meat.

"Not at all. Meat, veg, anything. If it moves or grows I'll eat it I can assure you." She bared her teeth, "Umm! Fooood, as Homer Simpson would say."

"Aha! You like The Simpsons." The long running TV series was one of Steven's favourite shows.

"Oh yes, very profound and uplifting." She laughed. "OK I'll come around noon. Is that OK?"

They agreed the time and then, calling Perry to him, he left Marian's house. As he walked back towards Hawkwood he went over the whole morning in his mind. From the narrow pathway leading back to the main village he could look up towards the wood-covered hill where he had experienced such terror. It looked peaceful, harmless and he found himself wondering if it had happened. In fact, the closer he got to his house, the more he felt how unreal and, indeed, ridiculous the incidents had been. He went over his meeting with Marian. She was nice, no doubt of that, but a bit weird really. One of those lonely 'cat' ladies – eccentric perhaps. As for being a witch well, she would be wouldn't she? Why were these sort of women always witches or spiritualists or something? How *could* Jane Trethowan be a witch? She was a well-known landowner, a respected member of the community; the whole thing was preposterous.

By the time he had reached Hawkwood he had convinced himself that Marian was a friendly, helpful, slightly cranky but lonely woman with an over-ripe imagination. Perhaps he should cancel the lunch but then, that would be impolite and, in any case, he did owe her some hospitality after her kindness. Show her around the house and where the metal detecting had taken place, a drink, lunch and then that would be it. Duty done and no more obligation.

He opened the door to the house and went into the lounge. The place seemed unthreatening and this confirmed his view that his meeting and conversation with Marian had been absurd. He went upstairs and decided on a shower to freshen himself up. As he undressed and removed the pendant from his neck, a pang of memory hit him and he remembered Jane's face and body. He fingered the pendant, sighed and then laid it on the dressing table. Back downstairs, he fell asleep exhausted in his chair and woke to the sound of rain hitting the window – it was dark. This time, though, instead of a feeling of melancholy, Steven felt much lighter in his mind. He put on some 'Fleetwood Mac' and poured himself a whisky as the throbbing beat of 'The Chain' filled the room.

He thought about his experience in the woods and now it seemed distant and ridiculous. He couldn't think why it was that he should have felt so frightened. Perhaps he *had* been ill; perhaps he was finding the changes which had taken place, the loss of his business, the death of Rita – perhaps these things were causing him mental strain. But, then, what about Perry's behaviour? Well, perhaps the dog had been spooked by some animal – maybe a stag.

The evening passed pleasantly and he felt as though the fever had finally lifted. Probably the shock of the fall, he mused and then remembered Marian's grey concerned eyes. She was nice, he thought to himself and it would be fun to see her tomorrow. In fact he found himself positively looking forward to it and he was in a much happier mood when he went to bed, passing an uneventful night.

The next day was still gloomy with a driving rain. He got up, showered and dressed. The crystal pendant caught his eye. He picked it up and put it on and, again, a memory of Jane came to him – her face as she had given him the present; the little smile; the uncertainty in her eyes as she had wondered how he would react to the gift.

Downstairs, he found the house to be cold; the electricity had failed again. He cursed, found the fuse box and tripped the circuit breaker; the lights came on but then he remembered that the storage system would not work and the house was becoming more and more chilly. He cursed again and felt a growing irritation. Marian was coming to visit. "A fire, must light a fire," he said aloud. He went outside and found some old logs which were damp due to the fact that a window of the shed had been left open and the driving rain had got inside. He rooted about, found some coalite in a bag and returned to the house. It took him more than thirty minutes to get a smoky, reluctant fire going and he felt his irritation reaching a peak. "Bloody country houses," he shouted. "No central heating, a bit of rain and bloody disaster. Typical bloody hick town." He banged his toe against a chair and was hopping around on one foot when the bell rang. God, was that the time already? He went to the door to let Marian in – it was Jane.

He was startled to see her. "Hi," she said. "Oh! Are you all right?" Her tone was one of concern as he hobbled on his injured foot.

"Yes…sure," he replied. "Oh yes, I'm OK. Come in. I thought you were away." He wondered what she wanted; their last meeting had ended so badly. Yet, now she was here. He felt a sudden hope.

"I was and now I'm back. Brrr, a bit cold in here isn't it? No heating?" She looked around her and at the smoky, reluctant fire.

He explained about the electricity and asked if she wanted anything. He felt a growing sense of longing for her but tried to maintain an indifferent manner.

"I just thought I'd call by to see how you were getting along. Are you enjoying the country air and all that?" She removed her coat and flung it over the back of the chair. She looked elegant, lithe, her movements fluid. She had a lovely mouth, he found himself thinking and her hair had an almost ebony sheen to it. He was about to answer her when he remembered his strange conversation with Marian. Some latent sense of caution tugged at the back of his mind. He had a fleeting memory of Perry and Tanith by Marian's fire.

"Oh yes, fine, no problem. Perry and I are real old ramblers. Up hill, down dale, you know, a man and his dog." He gestured to a chair by the smouldering fire. She was back again and he felt a growing sense of pleasure and excitement – his stomach full of butterflies.

She sat down. "Oh, and have you been to the place I took you – it's a lovely place?" She raised her hand to brush back a strand of hair. Her hands, he noted, were long and slender, her movements, graceful. Again, he thought of her as a dancer.

He sat opposite her. "Yes, I was there yesterday. A really pretty valley that and we'll do some more exploring later." God, she did have absolutely magnificent eyes; he hadn't realised they were so large.

She said nothing and Steven wondered if she really had been hexing him. It was all a bit silly really but then why had she lied about Rita? Again, a fleeting memory of Marian and his conversation with her – but Jane was speaking.

"I'd love to go back there with you Steven," she was saying. "I feel things went a bit wrong between us the other day. I got a bit over enthusiastic about the house but I can see that you're happy here and I shouldn't have pushed you to sell. Am I forgiven?"

She leaned towards him and he was suddenly conscious of the swelling of her breasts and the moistness of her lips. He felt his stomach lurch and the old feelings coming back. He coughed as he spoke. "Yes, of course. I'd love that." He stood up and moved towards her with mounting feelings of physical longing.

The doorbell rang. Marian – he'd forgotten she was coming. He looked at Jane. There was an expression on her face he could not read. The aura of compelling desire had gone.

"Visitors?" Jane asked. "Pity. Oh well, I'll be in touch." She rose and went with him to the door. That brusque manner and coldness again. He wondered, briefly, why he had considered her to be so desirable. Now, she seemed tetchy, her manner abrupt and rude.

He opened the door and Marian said, "Well here I am – what's cooking doc?" She stopped as she saw Jane standing behind him.

"Hallo Marian," said Jane. Her tone indicated a surprise which she quickly hid. "I didn't know you knew Steven." She turned to Steven and said, "You're full of surprises aren't you?" Her manner and voice had changed; harder, colder. Was there an underlying tone of anger?

"I'll give you a call?" he asked as she stepped past Marian.

"No, I'm away I'm afraid. Won't be back for a month or so. See you." She didn't look back. As she walked across the driveway he found himself looking at her retreating figure with a mixture of disappointment and relief.

"Was I interrupting something?" Marian stepped inside and he closed the door without answering her, his mind still focused on Jane. Steven led Marian into the lounge where the fire was just beginning to splutter into a definite more warming form.

"It's cold in here." She walked over to the reluctant fire and poked at it.

Steven was thinking about Jane. Again, that sudden change of mood, friendly, sexy, then cold and hard. Yet she had seemed so beautiful, desirable, inviting. They could have been…

Marian knocked on the table. "Hallo! Is anyone there?"

He came to and seemed to be suddenly aware of her as she stood watching him. He pulled himself together. "I'm sorry – just thinking of something. Look, its freezing in here. The heating has packed up overnight. We could go to the pub." He was beginning to feel a bit more in control again.

"Yep, fine with me but I'd love to come back and have a look around if that's OK with you?"

He collected his coat. "Sure, no problem." He put another log on the fire. "Should have warmed up by then."

They left the house and were soon at the Castle tucking into a bar meal. A roaring fire lent the pub a cosy, welcoming ambience and he found himself relaxing in Marian's friendly chatty company.

"So you know Jane as well," he said, "you didn't say so yesterday. Clearly she doesn't like you. Is there history between you?" He was wondering if that was why Marian was saying such weird things about Jane.

"Well, Porlock isn't exactly London. Of course I know her and she knows me and she knows that I know about her wicked ways. Not too complicated that sentence, was it?"

"What is it, some sort of feud?"

"Not at all. She does her thing and I do mine. I'll tell you something. Now she'll be wondering what the hell I'm doing with you – I can be sure of that." She went on, "Tell me, what did she want?"

He realised that he didn't really know *what* Jane had wanted. All he knew was that he had felt a strong attraction to her again.

"I'm not sure it's your business," he said tartly but then apologised. "Sorry, I shouldn't have said that." He felt immediately contrite and churlish. What the hell was the matter with him?

"No offence taken – you don't have to tell me anything." She finished her meal as she said this and looked up at him. There was something in her eyes he could not read but he sensed real concern. The feelings of warmth and companionship were suddenly back again and he said, "I'm not sure what she wanted. To make up, I think."

"What did she say, do? Think carefully. It might be important."

"Well, she just came by to see if I was all right and then she asked me if I had enjoyed the country air and had I been..." he paused, "...had I been into the valley where she had taken me? Hmm! Yes, and then she said she'd love to go there with me again and then it all became a bit hazy. If you hadn't arrived when you did I think I would be upstairs with her and back to square one." He stopped talking and went over it all in his mind. He was bewildered and looked at Marian who said nothing. She stirred her coffee, put down the spoon and took a chocolate mint out of its wrapper.

Steven said, "Bloody hell – this is weird. I mean, I wouldn't normally want to jump into bed with someone who had just knocked me back. It's weird." He rubbed his brow, puzzled and then remembered what Marian had said about 'using the glamour'. "Bloody hell," he said again. "She bewitched me."

Marian finished her chocolate and then, as though confirming something in her mind, she nodded. "OK, you're getting there – how did you pass the night?" she asked.

"No problem at all. Nothing. No ghosts, no bad feelings; in fact I felt really great, that is, until this morning."

"Why, what happened?"

"Well everything and nothing. No electricity, no heating, no dry fuel, bloody miserable thoughts. I was so fed up with the place. All those feelings again." He drank his coffee.

She pondered about this for a while then said, "Look, stay with me on this, OK? You came back home, you had a good night, no problems at all. Then this morning it all starts to go wrong and then madam appears. Don't you think it's all a bit too neat?"

"But what would she want, then?" His mind was racing through a kaleidoscope of images.

"I think she expected something to happen to you yesterday. She doesn't know why it didn't so she tried again last night. For some reason it didn't work so she came round, in person, to check you out and, perhaps, finish the job."

"Oh come on, please! This is stretching it a bit." He felt Marian was exaggerating – going too far. He scratched at his chest and a button popped open. The pendant glinted.

"What's that?" she asked and pointed at the crystal. "It looks nice."

"Oh, Jane gave it to me," he said tucking it back inside his shirt. He felt the heavy chunkiness against his chest. He remembered her face as she had handed it to him.

"Did she now, and you've worn it all the time?" Marian leaned across the table, resting her chin on her hands.

"Yes – no – I took it off last night." He remembered laying it on the dressing table.

"And had a good night's sleep. You put it on again this morning and, hey presto, all's wrong again, eh?" She sat back in her chair, a look of satisfaction on her face.

He was startled. It was true he had taken it off when he'd had the shower. The evening had been pleasant and relaxed and he had slept like a top. "But what's it got to do with anything?"

"I think it's a tool she's using – no body fluids, only the crystal. Can I see it?" She held out her hand. He took it off and she accepted it from him. She held it in her hands and closed her eyes then after a while said, "Yes, this is the means to get at you. You mustn't wear it anymore at least not until I've done something to it. Will you let me have it for a while?" She raised her eyebrows in query.

He nodded. "Of course, you're welcome to it if you think it will help but wait a minute, what about Rita, she didn't have anything of Jane's so how did she get at her?"

Marian shrugged. "It's not always necessary to give someone something, it just makes it a more powerful spell if there's a direct link." She put the pendant in the pocket of her coat.

Then he remembered. "The note – there was a note to Rita from Jane. I found it in the library." He sat upright, startled. It had flashed into his mind, suddenly.

"Do you still have it?"

Back at the house, he went into the library and returned holding the note which he handed to Marian. She studied it. "Yes, look, here. Do you see below her signature, in the flourish, there are some signs, very tiny, and in the surrounding Celtic design. It's a sigil. This is not just a note, it's a spell."

He looked carefully and sure enough within the flourishing signature and Celtic border designs there was a strange woven pattern of words, very tiny and very well disguised. "My God, you're right. What do I do with this? Take it to the police?"

"Hardly, they *would* think you were completely off your head." She was studying the writing and holding the paper up to the light.

He nodded. "Yes, true, but if you're right then it's horrible. What do I do now?" Why was he believing her? Yet, the signs were certainly there.

"Well, this." She took out a pen and made some signs on the back of the note then she took it over to the fire and placed it in the grate. It smouldered and burst into flames and she poked at it until it vanished. "I wrote a counter-spell on it and destroyed it. Without the counter-spell the original curse would have remained even if burned."

"Will it be OK now? Is it finished?" He looked from the fire to Marian. Was he being a fool? This all seemed preposterous.

"Again, I don't know. We'll just have to wait. She can still get at you but she may back off now that she's seen me. Without doubt she'll think that her attacks on you have failed 'cos of me and that's partly true. She may assume I've discovered the pendant and give up or she'll try again. Look, why don't you come back with me? I can give you a haven." Again, that generous, open offer.

"But not forever, can you?" he said. He sounded depressed and he felt confused. Could all of this be true? But the marks *had* been there.

She sensed his doubts. "Steven, I *can* help you properly but I need to get some things ready. I'll go home and get what I need."

She started to put her coat on but he stopped her. "I know you're sincere about this. To be honest I believe you – sometimes – and then I don't know what to think. When you talk about it, it all seems to make sense, if anything like this can make sense, but then when I'm on my own it all seems stupid. I don't want to upset you; I know that you believe all of this. I do and then I don't. I don't know. Oh, it all sounds so feeble." He stopped and sat back in his chair looking dejected.

She took off her coat. "I know. Don't worry, I'm not offended. I *know* it's real but I can certainly see why you wouldn't believe it all. Will you do this for me? Stay in this room tonight. Keep as much light burning as you can; stoke up the fire; keep Perry with you. Don't leave the room no matter what. If tonight goes OK then, perhaps, she will have given up – I've got the pendant now. If not, then we'll do something about it. Will you promise me that? Oh, and if you're in trouble, phone me. Is there a phone here? Yes – keep it near you and phone me any time."

"OK I'll do what you say." There was no harm in following her rather strange instructions

"Make sure you're warm; get blankets, food, water, a pot to wee in but stay here. I'm going to do some protective signs, OK? Indulge me, I'm a crank; it will please me, OK?" She was looking at him in an earnest manner as though willing him to comply.

He nodded and she went out into the kitchen returning with a bowl of water. "Salt water, very effective. Do you have incense? No, of course you don't. Go and get your things and don't forget food and drink and candles. Do you have candles? Good – get them and matches."

He went out and was soon back with all the items.

She circled the room splashing salt water around and then she made certain signs at each corner. It all seemed bizarre and theatrical, he thought, but she was nice – a bit weird – and it could do no harm. She put her coat on. "I'll let myself out. Remember, stay here, promise?" Her tone was firm and serious.

"I promise," he smiled. "Don't worry, I'll do as you say. Go on, go. I'll phone you if I need you. OK? Look, I've got a good book." He sat down by the fire. "See, nice and comfortable. You go and I'll see you tomorrow."

She waved and then she was gone and he was alone with Perry.

CHAPTER 8

As he stoked up the fire Steven thought about Marian and about Jane. The two women were so different. Jane was sophisticated whereas Marian was more rustic. In fact, the more he thought about the two women the greater the contrast seemed to jump out at him. For a moment, he again considered the possibility of some sort of rivalry, some feud between them but then he dismissed this. However, it had been Marian who had brought up the matter of Jane using witchcraft against him. Jane had never mentioned Marian but, then, why would she? He felt a sudden yearning for Jane but quickly pushed this aside and picked up his book.

He noticed that it had grown dark so he lit some of the lamps. Perry had settled by the now blazing fire. Steven's mind drifted back to Jane. What would have happened if Marian had not arrived? No doubt about it, he would have been upstairs with Jane. She would have been in his bed, in his arms, panting, warm, soft, giving, on him, kissing him, holding him hard, lips against him, kissing, kissing…

He woke with a start. He must have fallen asleep for the fire had burned down and two of the lamps had gone out, perhaps the bulbs had blown. He looked for Perry and saw that the dog was standing facing the door growling softly. Alarmed now Steven got to his feet and went over to the dog. "What is it boy?" The dog looked up at him then back at the door, alert, watching. Steven listened then heard a soft sound and a clinking of glass.

"Burglars – bloody burglars." He was angry, all of Marian's entreated warnings forgotten, and he stepped over her imaginary circle and turned the handle of the door softly, quietly, and looked into the dark hallway. Silence but then another clink from the orangery. They'd got in that way. He crept out towards the orangery, the dog following, and stood outside the glass double doors. He could see inside for the moon was shining and casting a pale light into the room. Empty. He went in and began checking the windows. One was open at the top and a soft breeze, blowing in, was causing a loose bamboo pole, stuck in a pot, to rattle against a glass shelf. He shut the window and looked into the moonlit garden.

The eerie light was shining through the trees and bushes casting strange pale shadows and the soft breeze was making those shadows dance and sway, lengthening and shortening. He turned away then spun back quickly. Something had moved in the deeper shadows. He stared fixedly at the point. Was that a shape – a man? He strained his eyes and then the moon disappeared behind a cloud and Steven became conscious of the shape coming towards the windows, vast and empty, a black void. As he watched it, with mounting terror, a fleeting memory came to him. He remembered standing in Rita's room and feeling that echoing sensation of deadness. But now the void was here.

He felt sick and overcome by a state of deep melancholia. The 'thing', whatever it was, pressed against the glass which seemed to bow inwards. There was the sound of something clawing at the glass as though trying to break through but nothing was there, only the terrible darkness of the void. Steven was utterly terrified, fearful and overwhelmed by a sense of horror. He jumped back from the glass, conscious of its seeming fragility. Perry's growling had become a long continuous rumble mixed with whining, every muscle in the dog's powerful body was tensed for attack. Steven's eyes tried to see through the black void. A terrible stench filled the room and he vomited violently and fell retching to the floor. He remembered Marian's warnings and tried to get up, or to crawl towards the door, back to the lounge where she had urged him to stay but he could not move that way. On the contrary, he found himself moving slowly, inexorably, towards the patio doors leading out to the garden. He felt pressure pressing against his ears and a dreadful moaning as though a million souls, trapped in Hell, were crying to him. Behind this sound he could hear the scraping of claws on the glass and Perry barking, barking and, with difficulty, he opened his eyes to see the dog running furiously back and forth, barking at the darkness beyond and hurling himself up at the bowing windows.

Steven felt a dreadful sense of despair and desolation, of his utter helplessness and lack of worth. Why was he here, a stranger in Porlock, an incomer, an outsider, not wanted? Why stay? Why fight it? Go – better still, die. End it all, out there in the darkness. Death, oblivion, peace. Death beckoned, opening welcoming arms out there, high on the moor. It was as though he could sense an insistent whisper deep within his soul. "Come to me Steven – come to Rita – come!" He was close to the patio doors, his hand reaching for the handles. It seemed as though he was in a timeless void lost forever. Only death could end it. His hand grasped one of the handles.

The phone rang, jangling and the pressure and darkness vanished instantly. The phone shrilled on and on. He recovered his sense of purpose and staggered to his feet unsteady and swaying, still feeling nauseous. He found the phone in a dark corner, led by its insistent summons. He picked it up.

"Steven!" It was Marian. "How's it going? I was worrying about you – is everything OK?" There was anxiety in her tone.

He held the phone as though fearful that the contact would be lost and gone forever. "Marian," he gasped trying to breath normally. "Marian." He was finding it difficult to gather his wits. The void, the deadness, the horror, was filling his mind.

"Steven, what's wrong? Hallo! Hallo! Steven, are you there?" Her voice had risen, her anxiety now plain to him.

"Oh God, Marian, horrible, horrible." He could only gasp, he felt faint. He needed her here, now. He felt himself beginning to tremble.

"I'm coming over." The phone went dead and he looked at it, bewildered, lost. Had she abandoned him? No, she said she was coming. "Make it soon, soon," he muttered.

Steven stumbled to the door taking fresh strength from the sound of her voice. He knew he had to get back to the lounge – had to hold on until she came. There was a deadness hanging in the orangery, a memory of what had happened and it was getting stronger; it was coming back. He had to get out to the lounge. His legs began to drag as though something was holding him, slowing him. He felt a sense of anger rising within him and his memories of martial arts contests sprang to his mind. Summoning up his Chi he turned to the dark beyond and yelled, "Fuck you!" punching at the air with his closed fist and, for a brief moment, it seemed as though the pressure of the alien force recoiled.

He started to regain some control and forced his way out across the hall and into the welcoming light of the lounge. He scrabbled around for candles and lit several to enhance the light of the one remaining bulb. He poked at a smouldering log and it crackled into flame. Perry was beside him but facing the door still growling and whining. At last the bell rang and Steven dashed out of the room, across the hall and flung open the front door.

Marian rushed in. "My God! Steven, what?"

He looked in a state of severe shock. He was pale and trembling and seemed utterly broken in spirit. She took him in her arms and felt him cling to her like a child in terror. Back in the lounge she went over to the lamps and flicked the switches, they came on.

"I don't understand," he said, with a puzzled tone. "They were on and then they went out." He looked confused, pale and smelled of vomit.

"What happened? Tell me? Wait, I'll get you a drink." She moved towards the door.

"No, don't leave me, don't, please stay, don't go out there," his voice pleading, terrified.

"You went out of the room didn't you? Where to? What happened? Tell me." Marian held his arms and made him face her and soon she had the whole story. She sat back against the wall. "My God, she's powerful – and determined. I honestly thought she would back off. I feel responsible, I should have protected you." She looked dismayed, worried.

"Look, don't say that. I didn't listen to you, didn't really believe I suppose. But I sure as hell do now. God, it was awful, terrible, the worst experience I have ever had – terrible. I wouldn't have believed it possible. Do you know, I wanted to die. I wanted to run out into whatever it was out there, up there on the moor. I wanted, would have welcomed, death. Horrible, horrible," he tailed off and then found himself beginning to weep uncontrollably. The memory of the void was with him, in him, enveloping him.

Marian put her arms around him. "Oh Steven, Steven, there let it go." She was rocking him and murmuring soothing words of comfort. The sobbing lessened and he straightened, pulling away, embarrassed and ashamed of the weakness shown to this kind woman who was barely known to him.

"I'm so sorry, sorry." He wiped his eyes and looked into the fire. "I don't understand what's happening to me. Why is she doing this? I've done nothing to her." He began to cry again full of self-pity and, yes, self-loathing. What was the matter with him? He couldn't understand any of it. He had never felt so wretched.

Marian got up, stood behind him and placed her hands on his shoulders. He stiffened but then relaxed as a wave of warmth radiated from her hands. "There, there, shh... Be still... Breath slowly. Use your meditation, draw in the warmth, the light; see the darkness leaving you. Breath, deeply."

Soon he felt a calmness returning and after a while she lifted her hands away and he remained in a meditative state whilst she went out of the room and into the orangery.

He came to slowly and was aware of Marian sitting in front of the fire gazing at the flames. "Phew! God, that's better. Thank you, thanks Marian, I'm so sorry. I didn't really listen to you. Now I know it's all real. What can I do? I feel so useless. I can't fight her. It's too much. I'm going to go back to London. I'll sell up. She'll no doubt get the place on the open market but I don't give a damn." The words tumbled out and he looked at her, waiting for her comment.

Marian continued to gaze into the blaze and then said softly, "Steven, yesterday when we were in my cottage I studied you. I could see that you are a strong man physically but, more than that, I could see your spirit, some say aura – I could see your spirit self. You are strong, so strong, a warrior and magical too."

"Magical, what do you mean?" He was puzzled and cast his mind back to their time together in the cottage. He remembered that strange moment when he had felt her studying him.

"It has been said that all women are witches. If all women are witches then so are men or, perhaps they're magicians. You, my Steven, are a magician too – a Merlin perhaps. Do you know that Merlin was actually a title?"

"I don't feel magical nor magician-like and certainly not a Merlin. I feel like shit – useless, cast away, dead almost." He felt so worthless. What on earth was she talking about? Why was he feeling like this?

As though reading his mind, she said, "Look, you have been assaulted psychically. You understand physical assault, look what you did to Dan and Ray. Well, psychic attack is the same sort of principle but instead of hitting at organs, the body, broken nose, no teeth, etcetera, it hits at your mind, your spirit, your Will. She has sought to destroy your Will, to drive you crazy, out of your mind and so out of the house, out of Porlock or, literally, out of your body. Your death would accomplish all of these of course, just as your aunt's death seemed to create an empty property for her to bid for."

Steven listened but felt helpless, useless, unable to grasp the enormity of Marian's assertions. The black void was there, filling his mind. He became morose again, depressed. She tried to rouse him out of this growing and obvious depression. "Steven, you're strong, a warrior; you can, you must fight her or she'll win."

She stopped as it was clear that she was getting nowhere. There had to be some deeper reason for his condition for, despite what he had gone through, Marian knew him to be a fighter. Marian considered the situation which she could see was dire. If he continued like this, he would sink deeper and deeper into a black depression and, perhaps, madness. Even here within the bright room protected by her magic circle and with the alien force held at bay by her presence, the dark heaviness of the void seemed to be closing in. She had gone into the orangery and, psychically, had built a protective shield; this was holding and must hold until dawn but because of her need to assist him, her abilities to fight the menace were being weakened.

Marian pushed an unprotesting Steven over to the fire, sat him in a chair and put a circle of candles around him. Then she used salt and water to strengthen the circle linking the candles one to another. She took her own pendant and hung it around his neck. Throughout all of this, Steven sat in an apparent catatonic state, unseeing, unfeeling. She stoked up the fire, lit more candles to create more light and then, kneeling beside him, she began a series of mental exercises designed to raise her power. The pressure on the atmosphere around the house lessened and Perry, who had remained throughout all of this on guard at the door, relaxed and came over to her, settling by her side. And so the rest of that terrible night passed and Marian was never so grateful as when the first glimmers of daylight heralded the rising sun and the blackness vanished.

She went over to Steven and saw that the catatonic state had changed and he was sleeping deeply but naturally. She opened the curtains and the door of the lounge allowing the freshness of the morning to circulate around. Marian was deeply puzzled. True, Jane was powerful but then, so was Marian herself. She had removed Jane's pendant – it was back at the cottage – and had discovered and burnt the paper curse. So what was allowing such power to enter and affect Steven? There had to be something else.

She went to the orangery where the attack had manifested. She stood silently, eyes closed, questing psychically. Yes, there was something, something close by, malevolent and deadly. She circled the room and detected the force and power coming from a spot near the patio doors. She opened them. A noise behind her caused her to turn and Steven stood there bewildered and confused.

"What are you doing here? How did you get in? I can't remember why you're here," he staggered to a chair and looked at her. "God, my head, it hurts. What happened?"

"Steven, you don't remember anything?"

"No, why?" He was puzzled. What was she doing here? When did she arrive?

Marian came to him and placed her hand on his hot head. The pain lifted suddenly and he looked up at her, memories coming back.

"Yes, now I do. God, the darkness and the horrible night. Oh God, what happened?"

She went over everything and he remembered it as she began recalling the events of the night.

"Yes, I remember up to the point when it all went blank. Oh, I feel so terribly depressed. I just want to get out – for this to end." He sounded deeply dejected.

"I know but we're going to fight it, fight her." She stood in front of him, hands on hips, looking determined.

"Why, what's the use, you can't protect me or help me. No one can. She's won. I'm getting out of here today. Hey, what are you doing?"

She had turned away and was walking briskly across the room. He stopped and watched as Marian, who had opened the patio doors, went down on her hands and knees and began scrabbling about in a large container which stood by the door. She did not reply but tugged at the remnants of a bush pulling the root ball easily out of the pot.

"This has been disturbed recently. See how easily I pulled this out?" She began groping into the container. "Yes, yes, I thought so." Triumphantly, she pulled out an object – it was an earthenware bottle.

"What's that?" he asked. He came over to her and stood looking at the earth-encrusted bottle.

Marian undid the canvas stopper and as she lifted it a dreadful smell wafted on the air. "Errgh!" She took the bottle onto the patio and tipped the contents onto the stone floor. Steven followed her and looked at the mess lying there. Amidst the very obvious brown sludge of faeces was the dead mouldering body of a rat. He felt bile rise in his throat as he recognised the smell. It was the same foul odour he had smelt in the orangery during the attack.

"What is it?" he asked. The smell was terrible – all pervading.

"A present from Jane. A Balarmine, a witch bottle; an ancient way of raising malevolence. A curse, a spell but a horrible one. This may have been put here to drive out your aunt and I'm inclined to think that it's been used to get at you, as well."

"What do we do with it?" This was bizarre, horrible.

Marian went inside and threw some more wood on the fire. She took up the ash shovel and scraped the mess off the patio, then she flung the whole lot deep into the white heat of the fire, at the same time uttering incomprehensible words which sounded to Steven's ears like Welsh. He saw the rotting flesh of the rat twist and turn in the heat and then watched it seemingly come alive and try to pull itself out of the flames. Was it a trick of the light caused by the flames, the smoke? All reason told him that it was a product of a tired and wounded mind – a delusion and the twisting shape was merely the result of the heat as the fire dried out the flesh and took hold.

Marian held it with the poker pushing it deep into the fire and Steven watched as the thing gradually shrivelled and turned black. Marian held it until the black scorched object crumbled away into ash and this she poked into the deeper recesses of the fire. She then went into the kitchen, boiled up a kettle of water and washed away any last signs of the mess that remained on the patio. She smashed the container and buried it.

"Now you will be free here, Steven, but not free of her, not yet. You have seen what she's doing to you, has done to you and to Rita. Do you still want to leave, run away?" She stood before him, hands on her hips, determined and, to his eyes, suddenly unearthly and powerful, her pale face framed by her copper hair.

He looked at her and then back at the glowing fire. "No, I'll not run away. I want to get her, grind *her* into ashes. I could kill her." He felt his anger rising but then suddenly it waned again and he slumped back into the chair. "But what can I do against that," he gestured at the fire. "She's winning and will do so, unless you can really help." He realised, with fear, that he was up against an enemy who was using methods beyond his comprehension.

Marian smiled. "I could see a glimpse of the warrior then but, yes, I can and will help you and we *will* beat her. But you've been so psychically drained that I will have to cleanse you of the spell and awaken the magician within you. I *will* do that but we'll go back to my cottage. We need the power and protection of the Moon Temple."

At the Portal

CHAPTER 9

In a short time and under Marian's cajoling, Steven had gathered some clothing and toiletries, some dog food and money. He packed these in preparation for his move to his temporary base in Marian's cottage. It was as though he were moving in a dream; everything seemed unreal yet flashes of memory, flitting across his tired brain, confirmed how dreadful and dangerous the whole experience had been. She checked around his house, turning off appliances and securing windows. Then she took her car keys, loaded her car and soon the three of them were driving the short distance to her cottage.

Perry seemed totally unconcerned and trotted into the kitchen where, to Tanith's annoyance, he cleaned up the remnants of food that remained in the cat's bowl. She hissed and arched her back but then decided to observe events from her usual lofty perch on the cupboard. Marian took Steven upstairs to a small bedroom which had a single bed. It was a bit cluttered but he was uncomplaining and put his clothing away, then joined her in the kitchen where she had made him a cup of coffee.

"There, get that down you," she said passing the cup towards him. It tasted of whisky and he drained it gratefully.

"A little pick-me-up. Won't do you any harm. Now, what about some breakfast, muesli OK?" She didn't wait for an answer but busied herself preparing two dishes one of which she pushed to him across the table.

"Well, here we are then. Now, a plan of campaign I think," she smiled at him. He looked at her morosely and didn't answer as she continued speaking. "Jane said she was going away so, if that *is* so, we'll have a breathing space. No reason to think she hasn't gone, after all, if last night's shenanigans had worked and you had, well, died then she would want to be far away. Not that any police could or would link your death to her but, well, you never know. Better safe than sorry I suppose but, later on, I want you to phone her; make an excuse about her visit yesterday, if she's still there. One way or another we'll know if she's gone."

He nodded, "OK, but what then?"

"Then we take some time out to prepare you. I think there's something much deeper going on here. We must try to find out what it is, starting with the metal detecting. But I have another idea. I've a friend who lives in Glastonbury. She's clairvoyant, very sensitive, past lives that sort of thing. I want to bring her here to go over Hawkwood if that's OK with you?"

Steven shrugged. "It's all up to you. I don't know about these things. To be honest, I just want it all to end. Do whatever you think." He felt extremely low, lacking in any vitality.

Marian was not the least bit disheartened. She knew that his attitude was the result of the psychic battering and she also knew that his strength would return as the day went on, particularly now that he was away from the house and the curses had been removed. The pendant was, of course, now in the cottage and in proximity to Steven but she was confident that her own protective powers had nullified its potential for harm.

"Steven, I'm going to give you back your strength but we'll do this tonight in my Moon Temple. Today you'll relax, go upstairs and rest. You must be exhausted. I'll wake you later – go on, go and lie down."

"What's the Moon Temple?" he asked.

"I'll explain later – go and have a rest."

He obeyed her and was soon sound asleep. Marian got up and went out of the kitchen across the hall and opened the door which led into a large room. The room was strange. The floor was of chequered black and white tiles. One complete side of the room, facing the garden, consisted of huge picture windows giving a panoramic view of the garden, the stream and the rising wood-covered hills. The ceiling, too, was mainly glass, like a conservatory. One of the side walls had a doorway leading out to the garden and the other walls were adorned with paintings and with stone or wooden carvings. The general theme was to give a sense of the classical ancient world but two of the pictures were, clearly, specially commissioned works with an occult theme. One depicted a young woman, with flowing dark hair, crowned by a crescent moon. The other was of an athletic man wearing a crown of antler horns. Both were naked. There was another large painting of a seated woman, clearly a Goddess, surrounded by myriad shapes and forms.

In each corner was a small table holding an ornate silver candlestick. In the centre of the room was a square table covered with a black cloth on which were woven many astrological planetary symbols mixed with pentagrams and lunar symbols. Upon this altar, for it was an altar, lay a sword, a cup, a crystal wand, a dagger, a glowing candle behind a red glass holder and, in the very centre, a large carved statue of a woman wearing a lunar crown of the crescent moon. The Goddess was sitting cross-legged and was naked but for a stone carved pendant around the long neck. Her breasts were well formed and jutting; the eyes were slanted, large and feline and the moulded hair curled, like snakes, down the statue's back and over the exquisitely sculpted shoulders. The statue gave the impression of great strength and seemed ancient.

Marian looked around the room checking that all was in order. Then she went to a small cupboard set in one of the walls and took from it a black box. She laid this on the altar and placed on top of the box a piece of parchment upon which had been written some words and signs. She took a silken cord and wrapped this tightly around the box fixing the parchment to it. Then she lit some charcoal and when it had spluttered for a while, she sprinkled incense onto it. As the aromatic perfume filled the room she went out, closing the door.

She stoked up the embers of her fire and soon a warm blaze was heating the lounge. Marian sat back in the armchair and went over the events of the past days in her mind. Certainly this had to be the worst experience of bad magic that she had ever encountered. In herself, she was confident of her own considerable knowledge and that she would be able to fight Jane but Steven posed a complication. All of this was entirely new to him and Jane could use his ignorance. Yet, despite his seeming outward innocence, she had seen deeper and knew that his training in martial arts and his deep understanding of meditation techniques and the ability to raise and utilise Chi made him more than capable of meeting the magical threat posed by Jane if this knowledge could be channelled correctly.

Marian's task was, first, to cleanse him of the oppressive nature of Jane's actions and then re-attune him so that he would, in effect, become a partner to confront Jane and her powers. She felt a deep sense of compassion for the wounded innocent man who had stumbled into this evil web and she felt a strong and growing desire to assist him to overcome the darkness that was closing in. There was a memory from her early years – a memory of actions long regretted. Now she was being presented with an opportunity to redress the karmic balance. There was also something else – unknown, strange and powerful. It was as though something from the distant past was trying to get through to her, that she had to help, that much depended upon her involvement. There was a task to be accomplished, as yet unknown, and she and Steven were destined for this path no matter what the peril or outcome. Whatever was hidden in her psyche was calling to her, giving her a sense of purpose which she did not, as yet, understand. All Marian knew was that she had to help him and would do so. She quietened her mind and was soon asleep with Perry lying contentedly before the blaze.

Some time later she awoke to the sound of clinking cups in the kitchen. She went in to find Steven, looking much refreshed, rinsing cups in the sink. "Hi," she said, "feel better? Did you sleep?"

"Oh yes. Much better and thank you – thank you for all of this but I must go back, I can't presume on you again." He put the cups down, allowing them to drain but it was clear from his tone that he would be reluctant to leave.

"Later, much later," she said. "Tonight we have work to do then you can go and, more to the point, you will want to return to your life and action. Action, Steven, that's what you're good at." She went over to Tanith and stroked the cat then patted Perry, who had sat up, tongue lolling. "OK, leave those things." She beckoned him to follow.

They went into the lounge. Steven had not been in there and looked around with interest at the variety of bric-a-brac, statues, crystals, dream catchers, wind chimes, which seemed to adorn every possible space. Bookshelves were filled with various tomes of many types and sizes. In the

The Moon Temple

fireplace was a bronze hare on one side whilst on the other side a giant statue of a black cat sat staring at the entrance door as though on guard. The whole place, although a bit chaotic, looked homely and inviting and, above all, safe.

"Wow, I'd hate to do the cleaning here," he said.

She looked around her and gave a little shrug. "Well, I get around to it, eventually. Now – phone, over there. Give madam a ring. If she's there you'll have to make some excuse say, about her interrupted visit. If she's not then it doesn't matter but don't say who you are. At least we'll know." She folded her arms and leaned back against the wall as he dialled Jane's number. The butler answered and informed him that Jane was away and would return in a few days and could he take a message? Steven refused to leave his name or a message and rang off.

"She's not there – a few days at least."

"Good, that certainly helps. At least you'll feel that she can't do any harm and that's what counts."

Marian went over to the window and looked out. "I think we should go for a walk up there." She gestured towards the pathway where they had first met. "It's not raining and the fresh air will do you good. Holistic healing – blow away the cobwebs from your mind by taking in some good fresh air. On top of that I want you to walk the valley where Jane took you and where you had the bad experiences."

Steven looked doubtful and said, "OK, a walk I agree but couldn't we go down to the beach… nice and open, fresh?"

But she was adamant. "Who's the healer here? Doctor's orders you know." She stood in front of him hands resting on her hips in what he now recognised as a characteristic pose. She appeared strong, purposeful, and, he sensed, within her a desire to help him that was genuine without any guile. He stood up and got his coat. Perry leapt up, tail wagging, causing Tanith to rouse from her reverie, looking startled. She surveyed the scene and saw that it did not involve her. The cat settled back on the dresser top.

"Well, *he* knows what's good for him," Marian said patting the dog. She put on a hooded coat and boots and soon they were setting off up the pathway where Steven had stumbled and fallen.

It was all so different. He could not believe the sense of lightness he felt as he walked up the steep path to the level walkway high above the stream – the place where he had sensed the predatory beast. Perry showed no signs of fear and bounded back and forth sniffing here and there, running ahead, running back to see if they were following and then bounding ahead again. They walked in silence and then stopped to rest high on the hill and sat on a fallen tree trunk.

"It's really lovely here," he said. "It seems ridiculous that I should have been so fearful." Then a shadow crossed his face. "It's not real though is it, this sense of freedom? After all you're with me; I'm not alone so I can't really tell if I'll be OK, can I?"

"Do you want me to leave you here?" she asked him. But he hastily said that he wanted her to stay.

"I'm not sure I feel *that* secure yet, not yet, perhaps tomorrow – I don't know." He looked at her, "You must think I'm a wimp but I can't help it. I've never felt so scared as last night." His face had taken on a haunted, drained look.

She touched him on the arm in a gesture of reassurance. "Steven, tonight we'll go into my Temple and I *will* cleanse you of the filth that's invaded you. Then we'll find out exactly what it's all about. I'm not sure how. Tomorrow we'll go to Glastonbury to see Vivien – you'll like her, she's *really* weird."

He was unsure. "Do we have to, I mean, well, does she have to know about this? I feel really embarrassed you know." The thought of involving another person in this bizarre affair really concerned him.

Marian saw his distress. "Vivien's a clairvoyant, she's into all of this and she and I have worked together before. She's not like me, doesn't practice magic but she's so sensitive. I really think, no *I know*, she will help you, help us and we may need her in our fight. Jane is extremely powerful, far more so than I realised. Do you know she asked me to join her once but I turned her down? Something didn't seem right. Her vibes were all wrong. I declined, politely of course, said I was a loner, no good in groups, that sort of thing."

"Does she have a group, what do you call it – a coven?"

"I'm not sure what she's got." She paused then said, "Covens are a bit of an invention you know. The media and movies love them. Neo-pagans do form into groups of thirteen and then split off into other covens but it's really a medieval invention. The idea of a group of thirteen people assembling together came out of the medieval witch trials, thirteen being seen as an unlucky number, you know, the Last Supper. So a coven, which in the eyes of the Church *must* have been a group of Satanists, became the accepted norm for witches and their kind. Witch trials were held for a variety of reasons – political, to grab land, to get rid of rivals. If you could get someone to incriminate others – under torture of course – then what better way than to say that there's a group of them, eh? Actually, if you think about it, it's difficult to get two or three people able to work closely together and in secret, never mind thirteen."

He nodded. "That's true, you only have to attend a Board Meeting to see how people act in groups. However, to be fair, some groups can be a good thing. Not all of them are destructive. They can be supportive – if you have the right balance – comforting, enfolding and can engender a sense of belonging."

"True," she said. "Mind you, I'd hate to be in one with someone like Jane."

"I see what you mean," he replied. Then, "Do you think she's a loner like you?"

"Could be but then she does have her minions like Dan and Ray. I don't know their role." She got up and they resumed their walk chatting together. "Thirteen people could also be linked to Arthur and the Round Table – you know, twelve knights plus an empty seat, the Siege Perilous, and thirteen is actually a lunar number," she said. "Thirteen moon cycles per year. Used to be the way the ancients measured time. In the past, pre-Christian that is, there was a greater sense of balance, of polarity, male and female, dark and light, sun and moon. Investigations at Stonehenge have revealed that it served not only as a temple of the sun but of the moon as well."

"Stonehenge – Druids you mean?"

"Well, modern Druids go there to acknowledge the sun but I've not seen them paying equal homage to the moon – a few, I would say." She bent down, picked up a piece of stone, examined it and then put it back. "I'm always looking for fossils, arrow heads, that sort of thing."

"So do I," he said. "Never had any luck, though."

They reached the stream at a point where the water tumbled steeply down a rock fall. The place was dramatic and beautiful and Steven felt his heart lift in a sense of joy. He hadn't come this far with Jane. "Oh, this is great, lovely and so beautiful," he said.

She turned to him. "Yes and this is a special place and you sense it to be so. Do you have a coin?" She was rummaging in the pocket of her coat.

He felt in his pocket and pulled out a 50p piece. "Here," he said, holding it out to her.

"No, you, you throw it in – a token, a gift to the Spirit of the place." She gestured towards the stream and smiled. There was an expression in her eyes he could not read.

He looked at her and then tossed the coin into a spot where the water seemed to gush out in a white plume from a dark hollow. They stood there silently whilst further down Perry lapped at the cool, clear water. Then they started back and, in silence lost in their own different thoughts, they climbed along the pathway and so back to the log where they had rested earlier.

"How do you feel now?" she asked him. Despite the effort of the walk she was breathing easily and he realised that she must be extremely fit.

"Relaxed. Peaceful. Much, much better." And, indeed he did – as though the stream and its rushing force had cleansed his mind.

She smiled. "There, I said fresh air would do you good. So, tell me what you felt at the stream?"

He pondered this and then said, "It was beautiful and peaceful. Powerful too if that's not a contradiction."

"You can have peaceful power – the power of silence. Listen and be still." She placed a finger against her lips and gestured around them. He heard the breeze rustling the branches and the birds calling to one another, some near, some far away. She seemed like a Nature Spirit in her hooded coat, he mused to himself.

Jane, too, had acted in a similar way but he knew that it was different with Marian. She really *was* a part of this. Whereas Jane had been misusing the power of Nature, Marian was in harmony with it and he knew she could utilise it if she wanted to, but that it would be to benefit not to harm.

They sat quietly until she moved and then he said, "Why did you ask me to throw a coin? Was I supposed to make a wish, like a wishing well?"

"In a way. In the end you do whatever you feel. The offering is sometimes enough." Then she went on, "Wishing wells are only a folk memory of our pre-Christian past. In those times, ancient people were aware that we were not alone on this planet. I don't mean animals, I mean that they were aware of other energies, other forces, entities. You felt that at the stream."

Indeed Steven had felt a sense of something else at the stream but it had not been the same as the horror chasing him through the woods. This time he had felt a sense of freedom, joy, pleasure, beauty, as though he could tap into the very spirit of the gambolling, bubbling stream. He said this and she nodded smiling.

"I said you were magical. Yes, that *is* a special place and there *is* a Spirit there. The coin is merely a token to show an acknowledgement of its presence, very ancient." She continued, "In the distant past, people would go to a special place and invoke the power of the Spirit or God, whatever they called it. They might make a wish for healing, for good fortune, or, perhaps to curse someone and, if successful, they might make an offering, something valuable to them – like a sword, perhaps, or make a sacrifice or raise an altar. In Roman times altars were raised, many surviving in museums, raised to a particular deity, say, Silvanus, and then they might add an inscription – 'to the Spirit of the place'. They knew, you see, knew there were other energies. Have you ever seen those strange carvings of little hooded beings – genii cuculati – hooded Spirits? No one knows what they're meant to represent but I think they are Spirits of the place." She swept her arms around and he followed her movements. For a moment he could imagine little hooded faces peering out at them from the shadows. It was all so alive and, with her hooded coat, she seemed very much part of it. He had a memory of Jane, in her hooded coat, standing in the valley – but it was so different now.

"All wiped out by the Christians?" he queried, trying to bring the conversation onto a level he could grasp.

She responded. "Well yes and no. They just changed the system. Instead of it being sacred to a Spirit, a particular place might have a shrine raised to St. Theresa or St. Anthony – in the end it's all the same." She paused then said, "You'll notice that not every stream, lake, hill, glade is sacred, only some and some of them don't seem particularly dramatic. Then, of course, you have your holy wells. Most are pre-Christian in origin. The Christians just changed the focus to St. Agnes or Our Lady's Well. Here, do you want one?" She pulled out a packet of mints. He took one, unwrapped the sweet and popped it into his mouth.

He savoured the taste then said, "Hmm! Interesting but weren't ancient people very bloodthirsty? Druids slaughtered people."

Perry stopped snuffling around and came and sat next to Marian. She patted him as she continued speaking. "Well, they have had a bad press. Don't forget that history is written by the winners. All we know of Druids comes mainly from Roman historians and they had a vested interest in painting lurid pictures about the people they were conquering. However, I'm not one of those pagans who sees the ancient pre-Christian worshippers as benign, flower power hippies. I really get quite irritated by modern pagans who see Native Americans as being wise, peaceful, tree hugging folk. No, the ancient world was brutal, as the world is today, of course. The peoples of Europe and, in particular Celtic tribes, practised head hunting and there are also plenty of bog bodies indicating ritual murder or sacrifice. Sacrifice of animals was common and what greater sacrifice could there be than to offer the body of a human being. All that fear and power generated by the act. Just read the Bible." She pushed the hood of her coat back and the breeze lifted some of her hair so that it floated, serpentine, in the air.

He looked at her. "And you agree with that sort of thing?" he asked warily. After what had happened to him nothing would surprise him.

"Of course I don't but," she paused and then went on, "there are people who do. There have been ritual murders carried out in Europe and the U.S.A. and it's still relatively common in parts of Africa today. No, I don't agree with raising power that way but it's a quick way of releasing the energies required. It's a short cut, if that's not too ghastly a pun but not one that I follow. The idea of sacrificing a living being, beast or man, is very ancient, particularly in the sun worshipping cults – so is cannibalism. No, don't worry, I'm not one but cannibalism was seen as a way of consuming the 'spirit' of a person, of an enemy, perhaps, or even of a relative who had died. Don't forget the concept of sacrifice which lies behind Christianity. Look at Catholics – don't they consume the body and blood of Christ at Holy Communion?"

"Yes, but not in reality." He had always found that concept hard to grasp and he remembered the priest intoning the words, 'This is my body; this is my blood'.

"No, of course not," she was saying, "but the central point of the Mass is when the bread and wine become the *actual* body and blood of Christ, isn't it? So, yes, I know it's not real but *the idea* is still there – a remnant from a very ancient past in which pain, death and the eating of flesh were an integral part of magic and religion." She continued, "Self-flagellation, the mortification of the flesh, was a common practice of religious mystics of many faiths. Pain, the infliction of pain, alters the mind energies. Pain, death, all paths that have been used, but not by me." There was a silence between them as he pondered her words. Again, he had a strange feeling that he was not a part of the modern world. That he was, somehow, divorced from Time. He had a sudden vision of his aunt fleeing in panic from Hawkwood.

"Do you think Jane does?" he asked softly.

"Could be. After all, I *am* sure she killed Rita and now she's trying it with you. Of course, she may not be using the deaths as a means of raising power; she's demonstrated an ability to do that without deaths. Causing death is another thing." Once more, Steven noted that Marian had seemed to pick up his thoughts. It made him feel uneasy. What did he know of her?

They got up and continued along the trail and so, finally, back to the cottage where they were soon sitting comfortably ensconced in chairs before the blazing fire. Perry, tired out by his walk, stretched out full length enjoying the blaze. Tanith, fed up with her high place on the cupboard and determined no longer to be deprived of the warmth, descended and cautiously circled the prone dog who remained still, eyeing her. The cat finally decided that the dog was harmless and sat down in front of the fire where she began washing herself.

"Ah, peace reigns," said Marian. She handed Steven a toasted teacake and they sat munching them. Perry's powerful, strong bulk was in marked contrast to the slender, graceful movements of the cat, Steven found himself thinking. Tanith stretched her lithe body, her claws extended, as she sharpened them on a lump of wood. It reminded him of Jane and, as he watched the cat, Tanith met and held his gaze. A memory of the predator came into his mind but it was fleeting and then the cat settled down, tucking her paws under her body and closing her eyes.

CHAPTER 10

Steven looked up from the resting form of Tanith and said, "I wish peace would reign in my mind." He leaned towards Marian and touched her hand, briefly, in a gesture of companionship. "Thanks for today," he said, "but are you sure you *want* to get mixed up in all of this? After all, we've seen that Jane can be dangerous. Clearly, there's something very, very wrong with her. Do you know, I find her rapid changes in mood very disturbing as well." He bit into the buttered tea-cake, savouring the spicy, familiar taste which reminded him of summer days with Ginny. He felt a sense of warmth and friendship towards Marian as he looked at her sitting, comfortably, beside the fire.

She gave a little smile. "Yes, I *do* want to get involved. Apart from the fact that I now regard you as a friend..." Steven noted the continuation of his own thought processes, "...I would want to help you as a friend but it's more than that. There's something dark and dangerous going on. It's not just that she wants your house and land, there's more to it. Not treasure trove even – she's extremely wealthy – no, there's something else and it's to do with my world, the magical world. That makes it my business. I'm for the Light and she's obviously working for the Dark; a true old battle – Gandulf against the Dark Lord, that sort of thing; not that I look like Gandulf[*], I hope."

He laughed. "No, certainly not." Then, serious again, "But you say you're for the Light – what is that? What do you believe in?"

Marian put down her plate and took a sip of tea as she pondered his question. "Hmm, difficult to say. I've always had a problem with this. You see, I don't believe in God or, should I say, I don't believe in God as perceived by the Judaeo-Christians and followers of Islam – People of the Book as Arabs say. I'm not religious, in that sense, you know, devotional. Religions, what are *they* all about? I find them too controlling, demanding this and that from their followers and, in many cases, spilling over into secular matters, as well."

Steven remembered his Roman Catholic upbringing and nodded. "Yes, you may be right but they do provide comfort and guidance don't they?"

"True," she said. "But that guidance also spills over into social control in many cases. OK, they provide a focus for people and give some meaning and an explanation behind their lives but they also become a crutch for many people."

---

[*] "The Lord of the Rings" – J.R. Tolkein

He recalled an old friend who had found help and support from a religious organisation when rehabilitating from a drug dependency. "OK," he said, "I can see what you're saying but offering a crutch to people isn't necessarily a bad thing." He told her of his friend.

"No, of course not and sometimes that may be essential. The problem comes when people exchange one dependency for another and then they forget how to stand alone."

It was clear that Marian had very strong views about organised religion. Steven put this down to the fact that she was pagan in her outlook. He knew that there was considerable antipathy shown towards New Age thinking by some sections of the Christian Church. However, he enjoyed this sort of discussion and thought that he ought to pursue things further. It would be interesting to see where they went with this. Also, he liked Marian very much. He found that he felt comfortable with her and he wanted to know more about her. He was surprised at this thought and a memory of Ginny came to him. But Ginny, too, had enjoyed such discussions. No doubt she would approve.

He returned to the subject. "I understand that," he said. "But, because a few needy souls act that way doesn't negate the fact that religious groups *do* provide a great deal of comfort to many, in a variety of ways."

"Such as?" she asked, leaning forward and clearly enjoying the exchange.

"Well, apart from ministering to people's spiritual needs, they bring enlightenment; they inspire works of art. Look at the great cathedrals – that sort of thing." He had always been impressed by the skill, devotion and sheer hard work that had gone into the building of the great medieval cathedrals.

Marian nodded. "Don't forget the great stone circles. People of the past built monuments as well, you know. Of course, we don't know if they were the product of *organised* religion. Anyway, to go back to your cathedrals, when they were building those magnificent structures, people lived in hovels, were starving. Great lords built them not always to the glory of God but to show their own power, wealth and status, as well as to gain an Indulgence from the pains of Purgatory."

"Yes, you're probably right about that, but Muslims built their great mosques as a demonstration of their faith."

"And to show status and power as well," she said. "You can't deny that."

Marian picked up the poker and pushed a smouldering log deeper into the glowing embers of the fire. As she prodded at it Steven watched her hair fall across her face, masking her profile. For a moment, he had a sense of other women, long ago, stoking the tribal fires. "Keepers of the Flame," he found himself thinking and wondered where it came from; then she sat back, resting her hands in her lap. The impression was gone and he said, "But religious people are good to the poor. They encouraged – encourage – the quality of mercy and the notion of charity, don't they?"

She nodded. "True, but mercy and charity are not the prerogative of those who are religious. Such qualities are present, also, in those who don't follow any religious practices. Just look at Humanists. Don't forget that, throughout history, religious adherents have shown themselves to be merciless to those who don't follow their faith. I accept all people's beliefs providing they're willing to accept mine but, even here, in this village, I've been ignored and, a couple of times, vilified by so called Christians because I'm seen as a bit weird – a pagan – a witch. This has happened to my mother and grandmother – she told me – and, as I understand it, we only escaped persecution in the seventeenth century because this place was remote and because we were good at healing and at helping women in childbirth. Do you see?" She was talking about the past and present as if they were interwoven in the here and now.

Steven wondered why he did not find this to be strange. "Yes, sure. You do feel strongly about all of this, don't you? But, as a pagan, don't you worship nature, the moon, the sun – that sort of thing? I knew some guys when I was playing music, they were into that sort of thing. Isn't it like that?"

"Not worship – no. Acknowledge – that's a better word. I respect them. 'Nature'," she made quote signs, "is all around us. We're part of it. It's part of us and, yes, the sun, the moon, the planets and stars all have an influence over our lives."

"What – you mean, astrology? I've never gone along with that."

The reluctant log started to burst into tiny flames along its length and Marian said, "Ah, good. No, not your newspaper astrology. There are effects, though, from the alignments. You can judge people's characters – you know – some of these star sign characteristics do seem to correlate – like, fiery types, earthy types. I bet you're a fire sign – Aries, Leo?"

"Aries," he said surprised.

"See," she said. "Magic – I read it in the flames. No, just joking – but, to go back to religion, religion is about certainty and faith. I'm never certain about anything. Certainty leads to a closing of the mind to other possibilities. I don't know if there is a God or Gods. This may seem strange to you 'cos, clearly, there are inexplicable things going on which involve unknown forces. You see, when human beings can't find a satisfactory explanation for something, they tend to attribute the inexplicable to some sort of divine or supernatural intervention." She began twisting one of the rings on her fingers. Steven noticed that she was also wearing a silver bangle on her left wrist; it had been hidden by her long sleeve.

He settled back in his chair, his mind re-running the terrors of the previous night. "But, if that horror I experienced wasn't to do with the supernatural, what the hell was it?"

"Supernatural, yes, meaning that it was beyond what is normally considered to be natural. But it wasn't anything to do with a God or, for that matter, the Devil; it was a direct projection of an energy force unleashed upon you by Jane Trethowan. OK, I can't explain it to you but I could do the same thing, using certain techniques. If both of us can turn that energy on and off then it can't be truly what is considered to be supernatural, can it? It merely means that, at the moment, only a few of us know where the switch is." She raised her eyebrows at him and then smiled. "Do you see?" she said again.

"Yes," he replied. There was a lot of what she was saying that made sense to him. He knew how to focus his mind, in combat situations, to the point where he could act with intense force and speed to overcome an opponent.

"Good," she said. "I told you that I didn't believe in the usual accepted concept of God but I believe there is a Life Force – a universal Life Force, if you like, that permeates all things and is everywhere. Everything, every atom is interlinked. Christians believe that their God was, is and will always be; I say the same about the Life Force."

As Marian spoke about the Life Force permeating all things, Steven recalled his early flirtation with mysticism and New Age ideas. He remembered a little about the Kabalah – the idea of a great, unknowable but eternal vastness – the beginning of all things – which could only become known to mankind, in part, through a series of emanations, a constant flowing force depicted, superbly, in the glyph of the Tree of Life. He raised this with her, drawing the comparison.

She nodded. "Yes, the Tree with its roots in Heaven; an important and useful concept and it can be used for a variety of practices, from magic to divination and to meditation. But, you implied a flow, or emanation, from above, from Heaven to Earth. If you *do* study Kabalah, remember that no one Sefirah is more important than the other. The energies are all inter-related, in balance – as above, so below, it has been said. Just as that flame can't exist without that piece of wood," she pointed at the log, "so the Tree can't exist without its component parts."

"Oh, no," he made a dismissive gesture with his hand, "it's all too complicated. I'm not interested in it now. It was just something that I and some friends dabbled with. But, what you were saying about the Life Force, wouldn't such a thing be the equivalent of what others term God?"

She paused, before answering, then said, "Well, yes, I suppose so, except God, as perceived by most religions, barring, I think, Hinduism, seems to be not only the creator of all things but the judge and jury as well. If you don't obey *my* rules then that's it – finished, kaput – for ever and ever, amen. Think of it – all those aeons of time; millions and millions of years of evolution all designed by a creator to culminate in *us*? Created in His image? Look at all the other complex life forms around us, some more complex than us even. Think of the Universe. No, its all too silly, too egocentric. As if a creator of all things would bother about our wrong doings and punish us forever. I can't accept that and this is where my concept comes in." She looked up at him, "You've been waiting for this haven't you? I can see your eager anticipation."

"I'm all ears. Carry on O Great One," he bowed his head before her in mock humility.

Marian laughed. "I'll smite you in a minute," she said, then continued, "I think *we're* responsible for everything we do. We build up a sort of balance sheet – you know, good works, bad works, that sort of thing. If the bad works outweigh the good then we're paid back in some way. There's a way out though. We can do works that don't cause harm to others. We can come back – try again – try to make it right. Finally, and this is similar to Hinduism, we achieve a way of life that is, I suppose, blessed and then that's it. We merge into the universal Life Force.

He said, "I see where you're coming from but how does all this link in with Jane and what you both do? What about magic? How does it fit in with your ideas?"

She nodded. "OK, I'll try to explain. By using magical practices we can alter events in our own, and in other people's, lives, either for good or ill. Light and Dark you see and we may have to pay back for that intervention. That's my karma, if you like. I have these strange skills which I can use to help or harm others. The choice is mine but, whatever I do, it always has an effect upon the lives of others – so, I have to pay back in some way – so will Jane."

"But, how do you know you did wrong in a previous life?" he asked. "It doesn't seem fair otherwise."

"Conscience," she replied, "that little nagging voice inside. Most of us know when we're doing wrong. Most people recognise evil. It's a sort of darkness of the soul, if you like. It's a lack, a conscious lack, of care and feeling for others; hurting others when you know you're doing it. It's the opposite of progress; it's everything that's negative, against life. I'm not talking about psychopaths – they're ill. I mean those people, like those torturing dictators, who live off the suffering of millions in order to gratify their own needs."

"Like the Nazis did?"

"Well, yes. They knew *exactly* what they were doing. But, then, here's the problem. Good is recognised because of the existence of evil. The Dark allows Light to be seen. Out of evil deeds, or events, can come good deeds. There's much suffering in the world but look at the people who give up financial gain in order to work amongst the poor and the sick. Out of the Second World War came the United Nations – not perfect, I admit, but heading in the right direction towards a world of peace."

"So, no Heaven, no Hell, just reincarnation?"

"No Heaven, no Hell. That's too simplistic. Reincarnation, at least, gives you the chance to achieve some sort of completion. I think Hell is manifested in the sort of lives people have to endure. Look at the dreadful conditions and horrible illnesses that inflict so many. It's like the Hindu concept of karma – pay back. But, if you can recognise your faults and weaknesses, if you can rectify them, then there's the chance to rid yourself of your karmic debt and you can strive to bring things back into balance. It's all about balance, polarity – the Tree of Life, if you like." She sat back. "Does it make any sense?"

He nodded. "It's similar to Hinduism and Buddhism in a way, but who is organising all of this? Who are you paying your debt to if there is no God?"

"Aha! You've got me there." She laughed then said, "Well, some of us think that there are higher beings – Karmic Lords if you like – a sort of vetting panel, who judge you and decide your fate."

"But, that's the same sort of thing as God judging you, isn't it?" He felt her ideas were a bit muddled.

"Yes, but fairer, don't you think? Anyway, I'm not sure they're actual Beings. I think it's a way that the human mind can understand things – you know, humanising metaphysical concepts. No, everything is made up of atoms and molecules, small particles, vibrating at certain rates, within a great sea of energy, to create seemingly solid objects, like this table, you, me. Through all of this flows the Life Force – maintaining balance. When we die, nothing is lost. Our bits break up and are dispersed into the great sea of energy."

He interrupted her. "And your soul, what of that?"

"The soul – yes – our spirit – life force. It goes on – I know it goes on – and it inhabits something, or someone else, who is due to be born. We return, if that is the Will of the Lords of Karma. We try again but it's not the Will, or the whim of one divine being in the sense of the God in the Bible. If you like, the Lords of Karma are a way of expressing the complex, total purpose of the Life Force because dark and, what we term, evil deeds upset the universal web's ability to maintain harmonic balance. So it has a way of achieving balance and, in our case, this manifests through the idea of a karmic jury."

"So, you do your best not to do wrong, is that it?"

"Yes," she replied. "I try not to do harm to others – try to live a balanced life. Modern pagans, Wiccans, have a saying, 'an' it harm none, do what ye will'. I try to go along with that."

He nodded. "Didn't Jesus say, 'Do unto others as you would have others do unto you'?"

"Yes, He did. You see, we're all striving for the same thing in the end."

"'No man is an island – everyone part of one continent' to paraphrase Bunyan," said Steven.

"Oh dear," she chuckled, "we are getting literary, aren't we? Anyway, do my ideas seem silly?" She sat back waiting for his reply.

"No, not really – no more so than anyone elses. No more so than an Eternal Divine Being."

"Good, I like my ideas. Anyway, they aren't mine – they're my family's and other occultists, of course. That's how it is and always has been and will be."

"Amen," he said. "Complicated isn't it?" He paused, then said, "How do you know it all goes on?"

"I've had glimpses," she replied. "Flashes of the past, if you like. But I'm not that practised at it; some people are more adept at it, more advanced perhaps, like my friend Vivien or," she paused then went on, "or, it's a safety valve."

"What do you mean?"

"Well, as I told you, occult merely means 'hidden' or 'veiled' so, when you practice in the occult world, you learn how to part the veil – see beyond it into other dimensions. Sometimes, though, the veil can't be closed and the result is madness. So, maybe, when I died in a previous incarnation, I set up a safety valve – protection if you like – to stop me from going too far. Perhaps I'm not ready." She gazed into the fire and seemed lost in thought.

He looked at Perry reclining in a deep sleep and wondered if dogs came back; what did Perry dream about? "Well, I've never had any experiences like that," he said.

She looked up at him. "Have you tried?"

"No."

"Well, you have to open yourself to it. You'll see in time." And with these mysterious words she fell silent again until she said, "It gets worse." She paused and looked up from her contemplation of the fire. "You see, I *do* use God Forms in my practices." The log burst into bright flames sending a spattering of sparks into the room. One landed on Perry. He opened his eyes, lifted his head, shook it and then flopped down again.

Steven bent forward and flicked the ash off the dog. The fire was well alight now and the flames were beginning to roar and crackle in a truly, merry blaze. "Go on," he said. He noticed Marian's shadow, a black, dancing shape on the far wall.

She got up and switched on a few lamps, then settled back in her chair. "It's difficult to explain. I use the ancient Greek Goddess Hecate – traditional goddess of witches, even Shakespeare knew that – and I might invoke Isis, or Pan, or Belanus, or Ishtar – it depends on what I'm doing. Now, that might sound confused and contradictory, particularly in the light of what I've just said about a divine being. What I use, though, is an energy and it can be focused in a sound, a name, a word of power, if you like. Names, words, what are they? Only vibrations on the air, but, if used in a certain context with meaning and in conjunction with other things, then they help to alter the psyche – open pathways, gateways, to another dimension. Hecate, in particular, does it for me."

"Hmm, yes, I think I understand that. In martial arts a powerful strike is often accompanied by an expulsion of breath in the form of a cry or shout. It adds force." He got up and walked across the room and poured himself a cup of tea. "Do you want one," he asked?

She shook her head. "It'll be cold."

He tasted it. "Nope, still warm." He sat down again. "Why Hecate? Why that one?"

"Tradition, family tradition," she replied. "Of course I can't know when they first used Her but She's pretty ancient so must have come into the family centuries ago. Perhaps it started at the time of the Romans. They were here for almost four hundred years and, yes, I know before you say it, the Romans would probably have used Diana or Luna."

He put up a defensive hand. "I wasn't going to say anything. The Classics are not my scene."

Marian shrugged. "Sorry. Anyway, Diana, Fortuna, Artemis, Isis – the Roman Empire was a good time for Goddesses and for priestesses as well. They were very eclectic you know; good and clever politics really. They didn't impose anything other than have an expectation that the people they conquered honoured the Roman Gods and the Emperor. Do that and you could keep your own form of worship. In fact, they were interested in all religions, particularly those that were very old, like Judaism or Egyptian and Persian mystery religions."

"They didn't like the Christians." Steven recalled some Hollywood movies.

"Ah well, you see, the Christians were accepted at first. The Romans thought they were just another Jewish sect. It was when the Christians refused to obey the rules, to honour the Roman Gods, well, this offended conservative Roman society. The Christians were seen as enemies of Roman order. Anyway, Hecate – well, she wasn't widely, openly worshipped although statues were sometimes set up at crossroads. She was depicted as a Triple Goddess, which was an ancient way of denoting great power."

"Like the Trinity?"

"Yes – yes, I suppose so. It's difficult for the human mind to comprehend, or explain, a great force so, yes, it's the same idea. Like Hindus depict their deities with lots of arms. Our little minds can't grasp the idea of this great unknowable force, hence the tendency to humanise it – you know, God becomes human – like Egyptian Pharoahs, Divine Emperors, the Messiah, Avatars in India – that sort of thing. Then we give human attributes to the Force, or component parts of this Force, and call them Gods – Goddesses – Jupiter – Hecate. Anyway, people would leave offerings at Her statues. After all, when you set out on a journey, physical or spiritual, you never know what will happen, do you? There were temples to Her – there's a ruined one in Turkey but, in general, She was mysterious – not really a Greek Goddess at all – much older, a Titan, an ancient, very old deity."

Marian got up and went over to a picture which was hanging in the shadows. She took it down and brought it to him. It was a photograph of an ancient statue, a Triple Goddess. "That's Hecate. This statue is in the British Museum. She was mysterious, hidden, presiding over life and death – childbirth, a dangerous time for women – and so She became a special deity for them. Then it becomes that She presides, not only over such mysterious matters, but over everything that is dark and dangerous, the night, for example. She becomes Queen of the Night and takes on aspects of other lunar deities. Queen of the Night, of the Moon – and look how mysterious that eerie little planet can be; ever changing, sometimes full, sometimes scarcely there and, for a time, not there at all during the dark phase. So She becomes the ruler of all things hidden, all things occult – magic – witches – the whole thing."

She finished speaking and sat back in her chair, looking at the picture. Then, in the sudden stillness of the room she began reciting softly,

"Mystic Goddess, dost thou want me?
Here I stand, defenceless, take me;
Take me to that hidden world
Where secret splendours lie enfurled
Beneath thy cloak of midnight hue;
Enfold me there and take me through
To all the wonders I desire.
So, now I swear, by sacred fire,
To serve Thee well, great Hecate,
And walk the paths of night with Thee."

She looked up from the picture and stared into the flames. In the ensuing silence only the crackling fire could be heard and, as Steven sat back in his chair watching her, he felt that, once again, he was in ancient times and that it was not Marian he was seeing but many women – women who had sat around the firelight, in the deep of night, and who had invoked elemental Spirits out of the flames. Women who had followed the ancient, dangerous and secret path of witchcraft.

CHAPTER 11

There was a powerful stillness in the room as if Marian had, by speaking the name, invoked the very presence of the ancient Goddess.

Steven felt a tingle run up his spine and shivered involuntarily as he moved his chair closer to the fire. Marian stood up and placed the picture back on the wall. "However," she said, "Hecate was also known as the beloved of Zeus – so, She couldn't have been that bad, eh?"

This last sentence seemed to break the spell and Steven relaxed, surprised how his body had become so tense. He felt the heat of the fire and moved back again. "What was that rhyme?" he asked her.

"Oh, just one of my family's traditional invocations to Hecate."

He nodded, accepting her statement as naturally as she had said it. Then he asked her, "When you were speaking about re-incarnation and all that, you said that I would 'see' in time. What did you mean by that?"

"Well, as I said, I know we come back and inhabit something or someone else. That's how we are able to link back across Time, scry in the spirit, contact with ancestors, travel on the astral…

"Whoa! Hold on. You're talking to a novice, now."

She laughed. "Oops, sorry, but it's *because* we're all linked in this gigantic web of energy that we're able, some of us at least, able to manipulate it, to cause changes. Anyone can learn to do it but only a very few bother, or have the potential and imagination, to apply themselves to the training. You have."

"Me? Why? How do you know?" He wondered what was coming next but he noted a feeling of pleasure at the way she was beginning to include him, or enclose him, in her strange world.

Marian looked at him with a very direct gaze, her eyes holding him. He noticed the flicker of the fire reflected within the moistness of her grey eyes. She spoke softly but firmly. "I know it. I have read you." He was about to question her as to her meaning but she was continuing and her voice had returned to a normal conversational tone. "In practical terms, you've demonstrated your capacity to study and attain, not only a high level of physical skill in your use of martial arts, but you've also developed your spiritual side. Meditation is an essential component in what you do?"

He nodded. "Yes, I find it particularly helpful. It stills the mind – clears it if you like – ready for combat."

She nodded. "Yes, and that skill opens up a pathway, which can be developed, and then you will be in touch with a different reality – another dimension divorced from Time and Space. It will enable you to walk between the worlds of Matter and Spirit."

He considered her statement. In some vague, distant way, he felt that he understood her, as though she was voicing a memory, echoing down a long corridor.

"You understand what I'm saying, don't you?" she said. "Something is awakening isn't it?"

He nodded and was silent but he was startled at this demonstration of her perception and, again, felt uneasy. Could she read his mind? He had a sudden memory of Jane – intrusive and tangible – a memory of her hands on his body. He pushed it out of his mind, and said, "How will all this help me to battle Jane? What is she? You said she was an occultist. What was it you said, 'The Craft'? Is she a witch – that sort of thing?"

"To be perfectly honest, I don't know what she is. I've never bothered with such definitions. She doesn't have to *be* anything. All those terms, such as witches, magicians, Satanists, are all somewhat silly. At the end of the day, it's the ability to utilise the energy to a particular end that's important. True, the terms denote particular styles of working."

"That curse in the bottle – what kind of practise was that?" He felt his stomach turn at the memory of the dead rat.

"Look," she said, "don't worry about what kind of magic or practice; it was bad, malevolent and that's what's important. Too many practitioners lose themselves in the workings and teachings of their groups – like organised religions. That's why I've avoided groups, in part, and also why I turned down Jane but as to what she is, I really don't know. Obviously, she knows her craft. Perhaps she's like me; it's been in her family, you know, going back into the distant past. Druidic, even."

Steven looked up from studying glowing pictures in the fire. "Druidic? You're a Druid? I thought people said you were a witch."

Marian smiled. "Aah now, that's my point. Labels, you see. What's in a name? We used to be called 'cunning women' or 'cunning men' as well. No, not a modern Stonehenge type Druid – that's all new. My family tradition does state that we carried a knowledge from the time before the Romans were here. Perhaps that knowledge was druidic, we've always been here in the West Country – same as the Trethowan family. In fact, there was a family tie, some generations ago, cousins of our two families married as I understand it, but that branch died out."

"You don't mean you're related to her, do you?" He was suddenly anxious at the thought.

"No, don't worry. I said, cousins and a long time ago at that."

His anxiety lifted and he looked back at the glowing embers. "Do you have any other family?"

"Yes, I've a cousin in Wales and I suppose there must be others around but we've lost touch. No, just me and me liddle cat – aren't we, eh?" She reached forward and stroked Tanith who rolled over and dabbed at her fingers. Marian sat back in her chair and continued. "So, anyway, knowledge was passed on but much of this would have altered and would have adapted to changing ideas following the advent of Christianity and subsequent historical changes. But memories, teachings, continue – it's probably where my karma thing comes from – my grandmother talked about it a lot. It certainly predates the Victorian interest in Eastern religious thought, you know, the Theosophists, spiritual mediums, that sort of thing. I know because I have manuscripts written by my ancestors, going way back into mediaeval times. That's where that invocation came from. Historians confirm that the Celts had a belief in re-birth. Anyway, as I said, I avoid other groups. There's nothing wrong with them, it's just that it doesn't suit me. I think some of their writings are pretty good – very spiritual – and it's an alternative to mainstream religions. A Goddess and a God – so at least they're looking to balance things – and a bit of magic as well."

She put both hands out in front of her as though miming scales. "Balance – it's all about balance – maintaining stability. That's where some major religions have gone wrong. Christians have got into a mess over the Virgin Mary and look how some of them feel about women priests. Islam has no female deity and look how women are perceived. As for the Jews well, if you read the Bible, you'll see that they had consistent problems with Canaanite Goddesses. So they did away with Goddesses and they took Yaweh as their one God. It was left to Jewish mystics to find their way back via the Kabalah when they changed the Shekinah – the essence of God – and made it correspond to a Divine Goddess."

"But if you are using Hecate and the moon, where's your balance, your polarity?"

"Aah, well, I said to you that Hecate does it for me. It appeals to me as does the whole thing about Lunar magic. The moon draws me as it does the tides of the Earth. However, I do utilise the energy of the sun. Without the sun there would be no life so I do acknowledge it, and utilise its energies through Belanus or I might use natural forces of the countryside through Silvanus, Faunus or even Apollo, another solar deity. Here, on Exmoor with its woods and wild life, the image of the Horned God, Cerne or Cernunnos, is strong. And then, I have my own guardian in the form of Pegasus, the winged horse, a sun symbol. So, balance you see. Oh dear," she said, "I must stop this – I do go on – I get carried away."

Steven didn't comment on that but, instead, said, "Those manuscripts, they'd be of great historical interest and value."

"Oh, I know that but they're private and will remain so although, if you're a good boy I might show them to you."

Steven laughed. "I hear and obey." He noticed that it had grown very dark outside. "When do we start and what will we do?"

Marian looked round towards the window. "The moon's full tonight – a good omen. It'll be quite high by around eleven o'clock so we'll do the ceremony then. What will we do? Well, you'll have to go with the flow. You'll do nothing at this stage. No, you could light the candles when I indicate for you to do so; some participation will help."

"Where do we do it? Here? What is this Moon Temple?"

She got up and beckoned him to follow. They went over to the doorway which led to her Temple. He looked inside, astonished by the sight that greeted him. "Wow! The real thing, just like the movies. I didn't really expect it." The smell of the burnt incense wafted to his nose and he felt a thrill run through him. "Err! What do I wear? I mean, is it in the nude?" He had seen enough films and read books and, although he was not particularly shy, the thought of prancing around naked, in front of a strange woman, did not appeal.

Marian laughed. "Do you want to be? I don't mind. After all, down 'ere on Exmoor, us folks live quoit uneventful loives an' if you, a big city boy wants to dance around in all your naked glory, who be oi to stop 'ee?"

He looked at her warily but her use of the exaggerated accent indicated that she was certainly teasing him.

"Oh don't worry," she said with a chuckle. "I've got something for you to put on. My ex had a robe made which should fit you." She eyed him up and down as she said this, nodding to herself.

They went in and he looked at the paintings. Pointing at the horned man he said, "Is that the Nature God?"

"Yes, Cerne or Herne. The horned image is very ancient – back into the palaeolithic even. It represents the wild power of Nature but was corrupted, as an image, by Christians equating it with Satan."

"And what about the woman?" He gestured at the painting and at the statue on the altar.

"The Goddess. She has been in all cultures from – well – forever. Known by many names. This one represents Lunar power. Really though, equating the Goddess with an actual woman, as some pagans do today, is silly. She doesn't represent earthly women. Instead, she is a force, a power within women and also within men. All powers balance out. Problems arise when there is too much emphasis one way or another. Lunar magic taps into the hidden secret soul and is linked also to Earth powers. Solar magic is more active and, uncontrolled can be destructive. In fact, both can be destructive if used unwisely. It's always important to retain a sense of balance."

"What do you do with these?" He indicated the implements which were laid out on the altar top.

Marian picked up the dagger. "This represents the masculine side of human nature – the force of the Will – action, and is used to cast and banish circles. It's forged in fire, in flames and is a Solar implement. The wand is a traditional implement of all who work magic and also represents Will. It is also associated with the element of Air for it accompanies invocations. It is used to direct energy, power and is, therefore, a very personal implement. Some are made of willow or hazel but mine is crystal – it's a personal choice – what feels right for you. The cup, a feminine symbol, is used to hold wine or water. It is deep, containing hidden depths and is Lunar, associated with water and the tides of the Earth. It is a nurturing symbol and is indicative of sharing hence it's often used in blessings and consecration within the Rite. The sword, well, that's similar in its use to the dagger. It's unlikely that a simple country woman would have possessed such an important status object but swords are a mystical tool and figure in all legends. Anyway, I like it. Remember, though, none of these things are necessities. Magic is from the mind, the spirit. These are just aids, triggers if you like, and, anyway, are good theatre. The altar itself is an extension of the ground upon which it stands, out into the cosmos and its attribution is to the Earth – stability. The black and white floor represents balance between Light and Darkness."

Studying the room, Steven recalled Jane's conservatory, with its statues and chequered floor. He wondered if that room had a similar use.

Marian continued, gesturing around the room, "The whole Temple should be viewed as a sphere for, when I cast the circle, I do so to create a total sphere of Light which not only offers protection, but also concentrates the energies of the working and places me at the very centre of the cosmos. The power is then 'flung out'," she made quote signs, "onto the aether. At each corner we light a candle. The Eastern quarter," she indicated it, "represents the element of Air, the South is Fire, the West is Water and the North is Earth. The practitioner represents Spirit – the life force. Four elements were all the ancients knew about. Nowadays we know there are more but those four essential elements encapsulate them all, so it doesn't matter. In fact all of this," she swept her arms around the room, "is not entirely necessary to the practice of magic but when faced with a big problem, it helps, psychologically, to stand in a place which is special and sacred. Stone circles, churches, mosques, temples all serve the same purpose – a place to concentrate the energy of the mind, commune with the Spirits or Gods, the place *where power is strong.*" She stood, silently, and he wondered if she was praying. They left the room and returned to the lounge. Sitting down in her chair Marian said, "All of these things are aids to get us out of a mundane existence. Candles, incense, music, drumming, chanting, words said in a particular pattern-like rhyme, strange words and sounds, all vibrational energies you see, all designed to alter mood and so, Time and Space are altered as well. Believe me, it works."

He nodded, "I believe you, I certainly do and I can see what you mean." He paused then changed the subject. "I'm feeling really eager for this – and hungry – how about some food?"

She studied him. "Yes, I can see you're up for this and that's good. I know you're hungry but we'll have something after the ceremony. Now I suggest you sit quietly, read something – here." She handed him a book about modern witchcraft. "Have a read of that, it'll give you some idea of what's going to happen. Not the same but something of that sort. We'll get ready at ten o'clock. OK?" She smiled at him and touched his cheek. "Relax for a bit, OK?" She left the room and closed the door.

Steven looked at the book which had a rather lurid cover depicting a goat with an inscribed pentagram between its horns. It was one of the many popular books that had been published around the 1970s and '80s and purported to give insight into the workings of a typical Wiccan coven. He leafed through it looking at the pictures of nubile young women and, usually, older men demonstrating various aspects of their calling. He spent the next hours reading about the religion, for it was quite clear that there was a religious agenda in the writing, a determination to convince the reader that the practice of modern witchcraft was merely a revival of an old religion that had been universally practised across Europe from the Stone Age. It had been largely wiped out by persecution except for isolated areas where it had gone underground. Thus it had survived, in Tuscany for example, and had remained as a practice across the whole of Europe in some families. This seemed to confirm Marian's assertions of a family tradition.

There was a great deal about the revival of the Craft following the repeal of the Witchcraft Act in the '50s and there was a blossoming in the liberated free-thinking era of the 1960s and '70s. From that point Steven perceived a significant change, a growing eclecticism, with the Craft of Gardener and Valiente becoming a hybrid of other esoteric practices. As far as Steven could see, later practitioners happily absorbed the Kabalah, Egyptian magic, Tantra, Yoga, Celtic magic, Nordic magic, Shamanism and there was a great emphasis on Native American practices.

He read through a ceremony to do with casting a circle with much 'Summoning of the Lords of the Watch Towers' and then felt he had had enough. Putting the book back he marvelled at the range of subjects on Marian's shelves. There were books on anthropology, sociology, several of a religious type, comparative religion, fortune telling, Tarot, crystal healing and a whole series of books dealing with ancient history, the classical past and archaeology. Mixed in with these learned subjects were novels, with a number dealing with ghosts, vampires, science fiction and the inevitable works by Tolkein, Rowling, Rice and Wheatley. She also had a range of gardening books, cookery books and works dealing with conservation and wildlife. There were some videos and DVDs predominantly by Attenborough, so the environmental theme was carried into the visual medium.

He looked at her tapes and discs and saw, with pleasure, that she favoured Super Groups of the 1970s and '80s. There were a number of New Age music discs, some of which he had himself, and it pleased him to see that their musical tastes were so similar. He heard her come into the room. "I see you like Fleetwood Mac," he said.

"Yes, I think they're brilliant, at least, from the time Lynsey Buckingham and Stevie Nicks came into the group. It all changed then."

"You're right – I love Stevie – she's a great poet. She can really turn it on. Take 'Edge of Seventeen' – brilliant – and 'Beauty and the Beast' – and have you seen the video where she does the final song, 'Sisters of the Moon'?"

She was delighted by his evident enthusiasm. "Oh yes, 'The Mirage Tour' I've got it." She plucked it off the shelf and handed it to him. "Stevie's song publishing company is called, 'Welsh Witch Music'."

"She certainly weaves a spell on me when she performs," he said handing the video back to her.

"That's because she's pretty. I don't know many men who aren't obsessed with Stevie Nicks."

Steven was amazed at how relaxed he felt in her company. He wondered about her seemingly lonely life then realised he was assuming 'loneliness'. She had said there was no partner but that didn't mean that she had no relationship with anyone and he realised he was being presumptuous. Then he wondered why he was thinking about her in this way. She was a bit young for him although it didn't seem so when they were together. As though reading his mind Marian said, "So what do you do with your time when you're not beating up louts in the village pub or escaping from slavering beasts. Has there been anyone – is there anyone, since you lost your wife?"

He was slightly taken aback by the direct nature of the question, particularly as it had come so quickly on his own train of thought. Perhaps he'd have to find a way to guard his mind. "No, no one. To be honest, I've not felt like meeting anyone. It's taken a while to get over her loss and then the business bust up. No one – except, that is, my stupid lapse with Jane." There it was again, this time quite vivid, a memory of Jane – no, more a real sensation of warm, moist lips upon his.

"Oh come on," Marian said. "We've been over that. You didn't stand a chance. That wasn't real – at least I hope, for your sake, it wasn't real." She was watching him intently. "It isn't real," she said, strongly, and he felt his head clear and the sensation of Jane vanished.

He shook his head. "Don't worry, I can see what happened or I think I can, although I still find it difficult to grasp. It all seems so hazy." He mused about it and said, "It *was* weird and then that sudden switch of mood..."

"Dark and Light – back to polarity, eh?" She changed the subject. "Did you look at the book?"

He nodded, "A bit of a read I would think. Interesting though. So you would be an hereditary sort, yes?"

"It would seem so. I've met some of those people," she pointed at the book, "some I can relate to but others seem more interested in their own sense of importance. Too much emphasis on hierarchies, you know, high priestess, high priest, king of the witches, gathering followers, I can't take all that. Also, I don't like the way some of them are becoming dogmatic and exclusive. I said to you earlier, organised religions are not for me although I do understand that many people need them. As soon as you get 'religious' you get 'certainty'," she made signs in the air, "and, as I said, I'm never certain of anything. I even doubt myself sometimes. Sometimes I think I'm deluding myself – that it's all nonsense but then, sometimes, like now, something serious and definite happens and I know it's all real. Sometimes you meet a Jane Trethowan." She fell silent and looked at him thoughtfully.

Steven touched her hand. "There's nothing wrong or weak about self-doubt. It's healthy to question things." He dredged back into his former Catholic childhood and remembered his scripture. "Didn't Jesus doubt Himself at one point? If He could then *you*, a mere little witch in the middle of the woods, can have a few doubts as well. There, my Catholic education left something behind."

She smiled. "You can't equate me with that great teacher but yes, yes, I know but, still, sometimes I do," then quickly, "but I don't doubt now. No, this is all very, very real as we know. Anyway, that's why I avoid religions – all too sure, full of faith to the point of blindness and bigotry. I don't dislike Christians but most of them won't accept me. I'm of 'the Devil', I'm suffering from possession. Well, perhaps they're right but I'd rather be possessed by whatever I experience than be stuck in their bigotry and the narrowness of their vision. As I said – not for me."

Steven was about to say that he felt she was being as dogmatic as the people she professed to despise but then thought better of it and remained silent as Marian continued. "We have spoken about me but very little of what you believe in. A Roman Catholic, eh?"

"Oh, not now. I left all that long ago."

"What then – nothing?"

"No, not exactly. I tried the mystical East bit but couldn't get into it all. I suppose there's nothing really for me. I understand your bit about the sea of energy – I feel that – Chi, that sort of thing – an understanding of other energies. But, no, I don't have any real beliefs in God. Still – all of this Trethowan thing has got me really wondering." He stopped and said, "Can we start soon? I'm really curious."

Marian looked at the clock. "OK, let's get ready. I suggest you have a shower, not because you're smelly or anything, just good preparation; an outward cleansing before your spiritual cleansing. Then, on your bed, you'll find a robe and white cord; put them on, OK? I'll see you down here when you're ready." She got up and he followed her upstairs.

On the landing, he stopped outside his door and said to her, "You know when you were talking, well, I got a strong impression of Jane. I could feel her near me."

"I know. I felt she was questing around but it's OK, she can't get through now; I've stopped it. Don't worry, it'll be OK." She squeezed his arm and then went into her room.

When he had showered, Steven looked at the robe which reminded him of a priest's cassock. Not sure what to do, he put his underwear back on and pulled the robe over his head then tied the white cord around his waist. She had left him a pentagram pendant and he put this on as well. He heard her moving around in the next room then heard her footsteps descending the stairs. He popped back into the bathroom, felt the need to urinate, did so and then looked at himself in the mirror. He looked quite dramatic, he thought to himself but still felt foolish as he went downstairs. Tanith and Perry were curled up together in front of the fire, asleep.

"My, my, Gandulf himself – no, you look good. I thought it would fit." She was wearing an identical robe and her long copper coloured hair was set off to advantage against the black material. The three quarter length sleeves revealed a heavy silver bracelet around her left wrist whilst a bracelet of stones adorned the right wrist. Around her neck she wore a large silver pendant shaped into a silver disc adorned on each side by a crescent; obviously a depiction of the moon's phases. She looked taller and, he thought, powerful and, yes, magnificent. He could well imagine her as a druidic priestess.

"OK," she said. "Now we've admired one another..." He laughed and she continued, "...now we'll go inside. Just lend yourself to what is going on, I'll be saying quite a lot. At those times try to visualise my words; much of magic depends upon creative visualisation, mind pictures which then impress themselves upon the aether. Thus, when I speak the words describing the Temple, this impresses the image. Through constant repetition the Temple can be summoned at Will. In fact, it's always there, in vibrational terms. In other words it is a sacred space, my sacred space, the same as a church or a mosque or a stone circle."

"Or sacred shrine?" he asked.

"Exactly. The vibrational energies, generated by practice and by worship, permeate the astral plane. That's why, sometimes, you can feel atmospheres in a particular place. The vibrational energy remains. That's how psychics can read them. OK. So when we go in just watch what I do. I'll tell you if there's anything I want you to do or where to stand, kneel and so forth. OK?"

"OK," Steven replied feeling a bit nervous now as well as a little excited.

"Think of it as though you were entering a dojo," she said suddenly. "I was trying to think of the word; that's right, isn't it?"

"Yes, dojo, a place where martial arts are practised." He had a sudden image of a Japanese temple he had once visited – the peaceful expression on the face of the Buddha.

"Good." She touched his face, serious suddenly. "This will work, Steven, I know it will. You're feeling much better now but you're still vulnerable to her. After this, you will have the strength and power to resist. I'm going to awaken your magical self. You and I have a great task ahead, this I now know, and you will be priest to my priestess. No, say nothing. I know you don't fully understand but you *do* have the power within you. I've seen it, sensed it. This will be like an initiation – you've certainly passed your ordeal.

Metamorphosis

CHAPTER 12

With a mingled sense of trepidation and excitement, he followed her into the Temple lit now by the solitary red light and the pale glow of moonlight, which entered through the glass roof and gleamed off the magical tools lying on the altar. In front of the Goddess statue was an incense burner and next to it lay a box with a piece of paper tied to it. Looking up he could see the white orb of the full moon.

"This is a good omen," Marian said to him, pointing up to the moon. "Now stand there," she indicated a spot in front of the altar, "and breathe deeply and regularly to quieten the mind. Try to focus on the altar. Oh, why am I saying this to you? Go into a meditation state." Marian came and stood alongside him as she said this.

Steven nodded and began a series of breathing techniques, which would allow him to reach a place deep within his own spirit. Before entering the Temple, Marian must have turned on a disc for a strange, haunting, rhythmic sound of music filled the background.

He allowed the atmospheric music to wrap itself around him until he felt her touch his shoulder. He watched her as she made a symbol which at first he took to be the sign of the cross, but then saw it was very different. Her words rang out clear and firm in a tone of command.

> *"Powers of Light be with us,*
> *Guard and protect us,*
> *Be merciful unto us*
> *Through Time and throughout Eternity."*

Marian brought her hands together in a sweeping motion of completion then lit a taper, and ignited a small votive candle on the altar. She placed some incense into the burner and a pungent, aromatic smoke wafted into the air. As Marian handed the taper to Steven she said to him, "Follow me around, and when I point to the candle, you light it." Picking up the crystal wand, Marian walked over to one of the corner tables and pointed the wand towards it crying out:

"*I call unto me the force of the wind that my voice might carry to the throne of The Most High. Come, O Sacred Spirit of Air."*

She inscribed a pentagram in the air then pointed at the candle set in the ornate silver holder on the table. Steven stepped forward and lit the candle. He noticed a small stoppered glass bottle on the table. She said to him, "Try to visualise the elemental power of the air. Create it in your mind." He nodded and stood beside her and imagined the free flow of the wind, the power of storms and then the image of the dancing trees came to his mind and he held it there.

With her wand pointing at the floor as though inscribing a mark she moved on to the next corner and made the pentagram sign. Her voice rang out clear, firm, powerful:

"I call unto me the burning brightness of fire that this place might be sanctified and protected in the name of Our Lady. Come, O Sacred Spirit of Fire."

This time Steven conjured up the fierce heat of fire. The image of the burning body of the rat came as a flickering momentary picture and then he saw the comfort and security that fire could also produce and he was suddenly back in the armchair, resting before the blazing logs of Marian's fire, with Perry and Tanith curled up asleep. He noticed a round, glinting stone upon the table.

They stood at the next quarter and, again, she made the sign:

"I call unto me the power of rushing waters so that our spirits will be cleansed in the sight of the Exalted Ones. Come, O Sacred One of the Deep."

An image of the sea in its full power passed through his mind and then he was suddenly back in the valley and the chuckling stream was glittering in and out of pale moonlit pools. He understood the destructive force of water yet saw it balanced by its cleansing, soothing, life giving properties. Upon the table, sparkling in the candlelight was a bowl of water.

Finally, they reached the last corner. As he lit the candle he saw a container full of soil resting on the table. Marian faced the quarter and called out, her voice echoing in the still room:

"I call unto me the strength of the earth that we may walk with fearless steps before the Mighty Ones. Come, O Sacred Spirit of the Earth."

It was easy for Steven to visualise the surrounding hills and the forest which covered them. But then he saw, also, its fruitfulness, its nurturing power and, in a flash, he saw how integrated the whole system of the planet really was; a thriving, throbbing, web of life eternally changing renewing itself. He understood the concept behind the eternal Earth Mother Goddess.

As Marian completed the circumambulations of the room and reached the starting point, she said, in a firm voice, *"Thus do we complete the circle"*.

Placing her wand back upon the altar, Marian took the taper from Steven, pinched out the flame and sent him back to his original position. They stood facing one another across the altar as she spread her arms out wide. The fullness of the sleeves of her gown hung loosely and he was reminded of wings. In the candlelight, and with the smoke of incense rising in front of her, she looked like an ethereal spirit about to rise into the heavens as she cried:

"From flame to flame, let there be a sphere of fire and shining light around us. Let the Spirits of the Elements be joined around the circle as

about us flame the pentagrams and all around, above and below, is the glorious power of Light."

Marian placed her wand upon the altar and took up the dagger. Standing in the eastern quarter she made another sign, which Steven realised was a circle and two crescents. Using the dagger as though carving the symbol onto an invisible surface she called out:

"Thus do I inscribe Her sign in the East."

She went to each of the quarters carrying out the same task, South, West and North then, placing her dagger back on the altar she circled round in a clockwise direction whispering, with emphasised breathing, the names, *"Artemis, Selene, Hecate,"* ringing a bell as she passed each quarter. She returned to her place beside Steven and said to him, "Now I will create The Moon Temple. Listen to what I'm saying and visualise as much as you can. Your visualisation will attune you to the vibrational energies of my sacred space and enable our spiritual harmonies to coalesce together." Marian stood behind Steven and he could sense her growing quieter as she breathed in and out in a rhythmic pattern. Then she cried:

"I stand at the portal, I, Sela, your priestess. I stand at the portal and call across Time. Hear me, I, Sela, your priestess. To you do I call, Great Mother. Hear me, I, Sela, your priestess."

She moved around the circle in a prowling manner as though searching for something. Steven wondered at the name, Sela, but then remembered what he had read. Practitioners often had a magical name so, clearly, Sela belonged to Marian. She stood behind him and then she began to speak softly, almost to herself.

> *"Feel now and sense within the quiet of mind*
> *Then shape, within these bounds of sacred kind,*
> *A place of marble stones and wooden beams*
> *That guards the hidden, secret world, of dreams."*

She moved to the front facing away from him her arms moving as though sketching a picture in the air.

> *"And in this place of silent mystery*
> *The smoke of incense rises, twisting free,*
> *To curl around the rafters of the room*
> *And carries whispers through the moonlit gloom."*

His mind began following her words and he visualised a classical Greek temple on a hillside, similar to one that he had once seen.

*"For here in this Temple, open to the air,
Selene's radiant light is everywhere;
And moonbeams dance and glint in darkness deep,
Awakening shadowed forms, as from a sleep,
To writhe and prance, with elemental glee,
Around the portals of this sanctuary."*

She matched her gestures to the words as though conjuring up phantoms and spirits around the room which, to Steven's mind, had become hazy and ethereal. He really did feel that he was in an ancient temple. The insistent rhythm of the music transported him to a timeless world and he could not tell where they were. It was as if they were between the worlds of Matter and Spirit, a glowing sphere of light pulsating with energy.

*"Upon an altar, cup and dagger lie
Gleaming bright, beneath the velvet sky;
And flickering candles cast a gentle glow,
Across the chequered floorway there below."*

She came alongside him and pointed towards the door.

*"Now see and sense, across this marbled floor,
Behind the altar's shape, and open door;
And in that place a mighty form appears
Which stirs within the soul such nameless fears."*

His heart began to pound as he followed her pointing hand and, indeed, it did seem as though there was a shape standing there.

*"But fear it not, look well, for it is She;
The Silver Shining One, Great Hecate!"*

She ended her invocation with a shout and he thought he heard the name echoing across centuries of Time. His heart was beating fast. He felt a pressure of energy as though a great hand was pushing him down and he went to his knees feeling giddy. The pressure eased and then he was breathing normally again. He gasped, and climbed unsteadily to his feet. Her hands helped him.

"Are you all right? Don't be alarmed. You felt the energy of Hecate; you are truly special." She smiled, "OK?" There was a look in her eyes that he could not read but he sensed that she was pleased at the effect of her words.

"Yes, OK, I'm fine, yes." He felt as though he had experienced an electric shock.

As Steven recovered his composure, she continued, *"Thus do we prepare the place of ritual. The intention of the rite is to cleanse Steven of the curse that has afflicted him; to give him his strength; to enhance his own latent powers. I, Sela, ask this of you. Hear me Great One, give us your power. Lead us in the path of light and wisdom for we are your children."* She sprinkled some more incense on the burner and then said, *"Accept this burnt offering, Great Triple Goddess; thus do I call upon you, Artemis, Selene, Hecate."*

She called the names loudly and rang the small bell which echoed vibrating on the air. *"This Temple is sacred to Hecate but from the dawn of time She has been known by many names. She who has been called Hecate, Ishtar, Isis, Inanna, Cybele, Bride, Kliba, Disha, Pomeru, Shabi, Daclo, Merupi. Sela calls you; Sela calls you; Sela calls you. Aid me in my task; give me your power; grant me your strength; cleanse my friend; grant him strength and protection; show us the way; guide us; guide me, I, Sela your priestess."*

She threw more incense on the coals then turned to him and told him to rest upon the floor. He knelt back on his heels. Sela, he now thought of her as Sela, picked up the box and, with her dagger, cut the cord. She took up the parchment and burnt it upon the hot charcoal, waiting until it had blackened and crumbled away. Then she opened the box and Steven saw, with a start, that she was holding Jane's pendant. Taking a piece of cord, Sela wrapped it around the pendant which she then held in the smoke of the incense. Her body was masking the altar so that Steven could not see everything that Sela was doing but he saw her lift a small bowl to her mouth as though to drink from it. She held the pendant at arm's length and blew a spray of water at it with a loud expulsion of her breath.

Sela walked around the altar so that she was now facing Steven and, picking up her wand, she pointed it at the crystal pendant crying,

"I cleanse this instrument of malevolence and charge it with my own Will."

Putting the wand back upon the altar she took up her dagger and cut the string, at the same time saying,

"I free the Spirit within. Let it now serve my Will and only my Will."

Sela held the pendant over the incense burner again and began to chant, in an eerie, whispering voice,

> *"I call you, I call you*
> *Come forth now, come forth.*
> *I bind you, I cleanse you, I free you*
> *Come forth.*
> *You're mine now, you're mine now*
> *Come forth now, come forth.*
> *To the Temple, my Temple*
> *In the moonlight, come forth."*

At the end, she pressed the pendant to her breast and then held it to her forehead before placing it back upon the altar.

There was a long pause during which Steven noticed that the music was fading away until there was a still and pregnant silence in the room. Sela bent and picked up a small round drum upon which she began to tap out a rhythmic, triple beat, at the same time swaying her body from side to side. She started to turn on the spot and then, still spinning, she danced slowly to the furthest corner of the Moon Temple. As the drumbeat quickened, Sela continued her spinning dance, circling the room in, what Steven perceived, was a spiral pattern towards the altar. He heard her voice, soft at first, chanting out strange words which became louder as she whirled around the room. Steven felt his pulse quicken and, once again, he had that feeling of looking into the very ancient past as Sela danced her dervish dance, hair flying out around her shoulders, her feet stamping on the black and white floor of her Temple to the rhythmic beating of her drum.

She whirled and whirled towards the altar, her voice becoming breathless as she chanted out her spell and then she collapsed before the altar her body quivering and shaking as the drum rolled from her hands.

Steven had felt himself rooted to the spot, mesmerised by the seemingly demonic figure. Now, alarmed, he went to assist her but she rose suddenly to her hands and knees, a wild figure, her hair covering her face. She motioned him back, stood up and stamped her foot three times and, holding the pendant in her hand, she circled around the temple until she stood beneath a bright shaft of moonlight, holding the pendant within it as though studying it. Then Sela began to speak in a whispering voice:

> *"Once again, the current stirring*
> *Eddies and spiral twists*
> *Its potent way across the aether.*
> *Into his frozen soul*
> *The moving force has come;*
> *Starting his pausing breath,*
> *Quickening his bloodless heart,*
> *Freeing him from crystal web*
> *Woven by Jane Trethowan;*
> *She of night fears and dead thoughts,*
> *The harbinger of grief and sorrow."*

Steven felt a surge of emotion rush through him as the memories of Jane and the dreadful events of the past days surfaced. He listened to Sela's words as she raised her voice.

*"Now a new moon rises,
Casting clean light into the shadows.
Silver and deep blue waken the gloom
Where night things walk their secret ways,
Sighing soft songs to the stars."*

A vision of Sela's grey, concerned eyes and her great compassion brought a sudden sense of closeness to her as though their spirits were merged.

*"The serpent wakens too, beneath the stone,
Shedding the dead thrawl of it's skin,
Darting out its questing, probing tongue,
Testing and tasting the life force of the moon
As ruby red the blood glows in its eyes."*

At these words he felt the memories of Ginny changing becoming less tinged with sadness and the sense of powerlessness at his relationship with Jane, lifted. He felt a sudden surge of joy, of liberation and a desire for a new life and he found himself watching Sela intently. There was a rush of energy running through him and he felt it shiver up his spine and reach his loins, causing an erection.

*"The Magus treads, once more, on sacred earth;
Lifts his eyes towards the silver moon,
Invokes the power of that eternal stream,
Whose gentle current bathes with healing light,
His tired enfeebled form."*

He found himself on his feet and by her side, standing in the moonlight. He took the pendant from her and looked at it. It could not harm him now, this he knew, and he handed it back to her as she continued speaking:

*"Taking a fragment from his crystal cell,
Shaping a pendant from the shattered stone,
He waits as footsteps sound outside the circle,
Marking the advent of a new beginning.
The Priestess steps within the sacred place,
Accepts the gift of crystal, freely offered,
Sees the moonlight caught within its prism
And takes the Magus by his outstretched hand."*

Sela took him by the hand and looked into his eyes as she continued her flowing words. She led him back to the altar. He felt uplifted, renewed, cleansed, the tears running freely down his face, yet he was smiling now, with a deep sense of inner peace.

> *"The moon's glow bathing both with eerie light,*
> *Its potent softness flowing through their bodies*
> *Twists and eddies, snake-like, in their souls*
> *As, stepping out beneath the stars of Heaven,*
> *The Priest and Priestess walk their mystic path."*

She held his hand a little longer then turned to him and kissed his wet cheek. "I am your Moon Sister and I vow to aid and protect you. There, gone, gone, yes?"

"Yes, gone, thank you. Oh thank you." He wiped his eyes on his sleeve, the sense of elation coursing through him. She held the pendant and offered it to him.

"No – I don't want it. I'm not frightened of it. I just don't want it now. I want one from you. Yes?" Suddenly, he wanted to be with her, be like her. He wanted to be closer to her. To have something from her.

"Yes," she said, "OK". She placed it back on the altar. "Right now, let us have a period of contemplation." She knelt back on her heels and he followed suit and began deep breathing until he was lost in meditation. After a short while, he felt her move and rise and he did likewise, opening his eyes and looking around at the room – so different, now. Different, special and, yes, sacred.

She spoke. *"We give thanks O Great One and, as a token between us we share this cup."*

Sela took up the cup and passed it to him; he sipped it, tasted wine and passed it back to her. She drank from the cup. Again, Sela said, *"We give thanks O Great One;"* then added, *"go now in peace but if ever I have need then hear me, Sela, and return to me."* As she said this she held the cup high, as though in offering, then she placed it back on the altar.

Sela took up her dagger, went to the northern quarter and stabbed her dagger at the air. *"Vashte,"* she cried. She did the same at the other quarters, placed her dagger on the altar, then returned to the northern quarter and said,

> *"Spirit of the North; Spirit of Earth; Spirit of Light*
> *We thank you for aiding us in this rite.*
> *Go now in peace, with our gratitude."*

She moved to the west and said,

> *"Spirit of the West; Spirit of the Waters; Spirit of Light;*
> *We thank you for aiding us in this rite,*
> *Go now in peace, with our gratitude."*

Again, Sela repeated the process at the remaining two quarters with their attributions of Fire and Air. Then she took up the sword and stood midway between the north and east of the circle. Holding the sword, by its handle and blade, high above her head she cried, *"There is no part of mankind that is not of the Gods."* Then in lower tones, *"But let us always remember we are but an insignificant part of a great oneness. Therefore we give thanks to you, O Great One and to the Spirits of the Elements. Go now in peace but if ever we have need of you then hear us and return to our aid."*

Sela stood still for a while then lowered her arms. *"Let it so be,"* she said and gestured for him to repeat the phrase, which he did. *"Let it so be"* he said. Still holding the sword she said, "I'm going to banish the circle now. Follow me around and pinch out each candle flame as we leave each quarter."

They went to the northern quarter where she made a sign of the pentagram with the sword and cried, *"I banish this sign in the North. Yet, as it fades, let it take away all forces that would do us harm."* He pinched out the candle and followed her to the western quarter. She kept the sword pointed at the ground until she reached the quarter where she inscribed another pentagram. *"I banish this sign in the West, yet, as it fades, let it leave only feelings of companionship, trust and love."*

They moved to the southern quarter. *"I banish this sign in the South, yet, as it fades, let it leave only feelings of cleansing peace."*

Finally, at the eastern quarter, she cried, *"I banish this sign in the East, yet, as it fades, let it take away hurt, fear and grief. Leave feelings of strength and purpose, courage to fight the Dark and boundless compassion."* He pinched out the last candle. The Temple was now illuminated only by the red flame, the votive candle on the altar, and the moonlight.

Sela placed the sword back on the altar, stood for a moment, and clapped her hands together three times crying, *"The rite is completed."*

After a lengthy period, during which Steven noted a sense of disappointment that the ceremony had ended, she turned to him. They embraced and then they left the temple in silence. In silence he returned to his room and changed and, again in silence, his mind ablaze with the images he had seen, he sat in the lounge as she busied herself in the kitchen. She appeared with a tray laden with food.

"Well?" she said when he had filled his plate. "How do you feel?"

"I feel," he paused, "I feel cleansed, strengthened, renewed, great, wonderful." He laughed. "I don't know. It's as though a great burden has been lifted. Thanks, thanks Sela – I may call you that?"

"Not in public – it's my magical name – after a Moon Goddess. Try to stick to Marian." He nodded but he knew that he would always think of her as Sela – the memory and power of the ceremony was too strong.

"So many questions. What was that I felt when I collapsed?"

"A rush of power – energy – Hecate if you like."

"What, really the Goddess Hecate?" He was stunned at her casual words.

"No, I think that is what the ancients thought; but power, yes. I call it Her, Hecate. I also feel energies if I use the names Cybele, Isis, Pan, Belanus – some slightly different in intensity. Quite clearly, I'm channelling a potent unknown energy source but I don't think they're actual Gods and Goddesses – remember what we were talking about? However, I like the concept and the ceremonial overtones. It enables me to tune in; it's all a trick of the mind really." She helped herself to some salad.

"But, surely this proves the existence of God or Gods and Hecate must be real." He took a sip of wine. His mind was full of the images and impressions of the rite and he could still feel his body tingling from the power rush of Hecate.

"No, because if She was an actual entity, Goddess, then She would manifest universally as Hecate and there would be no doubt in anyone's mind, no Christianity, no Islam, no Buddha – only the Silver Shining One. But, instead, different cultures feel that power but name the power Loki, White Buffalo Woman, Krishna, Jesus, perhaps. It's an energy. What, though, I don't really know. I channel it and it can help me to cause changes. My brain utilises the imagery of ritual to create the link between the power and me." She saw the puzzlement on his face. "Oh, look, perhaps She *is* real – I don't really know. All I know is that by using that name I can open many strange pathways. Maybe you're right."

He nodded accepting her statement and then asked, "Why did you choose Hecate and not, say, a local deity of ancient Britain?"

She took a mouthful of chicken and chewed on it for a while and then said, "Well, as I told you, it was a tradition in my family, like those Tuscan witches discovered by Leland; you read about that? They had Aradia and Diana; my family had Hecate but then you can sometimes find something that pushes you in a particular direction. Well, back about twenty years ago I was wandering around an art fair and casually flicking through some old posters, when I came upon this astonishing painting of what was, quite clearly, a depiction of an ancient Goddess. She was surrounded by creatures of the night but there was also an incredibly strange beauty about Her. I loved it and decided to buy it. When I pulled it out of its holder I looked at the back and it said "Hecate". That was it – that was enough for me. It was as simple as that. It's on the wall of my Temple. You should go and have a proper look."

He finished his meal and was silent for a while then said, "Tell me, you said a few things in another language; what was it?"

She laughed. "No, not another language, although perhaps it is – after all, what is language but a series of sounds, vibrations. No, the Kliba, Disha bit was merely a compilation of initials of a variety of goddesses. I got a number of them and put them together to form words. Vashte is a sort of shorthand for "make the Temple vanish". It's all part of a mind trick to alter what is ordinary, like the incense, music and implements. After all, nowadays, why use a sword as a weapon? Why not a Colt 45? Well, of course, swords are magical. The way they're made; think of it. You first get the ore and then it's smelted, forged, polished and lo you have a magnificent deadly thing which denotes power, can protect, can kill. From rock comes a sword – the sword in the stone. I think Arthur was a smithy and drew the sword from the stone, not in the way they put it – you know, a haft sticking out of a rock – but he literally created a sword out of rock; a magical sword." She stopped. "I do go on don't I?"

He smiled, "I love it – its all new to me but what about your spell? That was fantastic. I, well, I felt so moved, so energised." He didn't mention the surge of power to his genitals.

"Well, it was actually a poem I wrote. I call it 'The Resurrection of Merlin.' For 'Jane Trethowan' it should say the 'Dread Morgana'. Do you remember the Arthurian story? Morgana steals Merlin's secrets and traps him in a crystal web. They made a film about it, with Helen Mirren. The legends are a bit confused. Some say it was Vivian, others, Nimue, others that Vivian and Morgana are the same. The film had it as Morgan or Morgana – I felt there was a parallel. For Morgana read Jane; for Merlin read you."

"I'm not a Merlin," he protested.

"Oh, you are – believe me – I know. And in our coming battle with the dread Jane Trethowan and her crew, you will need all your powers believe me."

She was serious and her voice was very firm with no banter. He felt a shiver run through him. This time there was no fear any more, just a strong desire to come into combat with whatever was seeking to destroy him.

Seemingly picking up his thoughts, she nodded and said, "Yes, it will happen soon." Then, "You could tell that you have an intuition about all of this, perhaps a past life memory. You reacted to the spell; you rose and came to me."

"Yes, I did, I don't know why I did but it just seemed as though I was impelled. Also, well, look, don't misunderstand me, but when you were speaking about the serpent, I felt a shock of energy run through me – it, well, I got a physical manifestation." He tailed off embarrassed.

She laughed, "You mean you got a hard on. Oh don't look so shocked – I have been around you know. No, seriously, that was good; it was the Serpent Power, Kundalini – very potent and used in magic, particularly Tantric magic. You'll have to read up on it. But no, that was what I expected – it's in the poem for a reason. Also, the serpent represents knowledge, wisdom, eternity. The biblical representation of the serpent in the Garden of Eden means that Adam and Eve were tempted by the acquisition of knowledge – hence the so called Fall from Innocence or Ignorance – depends how you look at it. Don't forget that Lucifer means Lightbearer, you know – bringing light into darkness, just as Hecate is often depicted carrying a torch to light the way through the underworld. She is sometimes seen as a prelude to the dawn – the Bringer of Light, you see."

Perry wanted to go out so she led him to the garden door and let him out. Tanith got up and followed him. "They're getting on all right," he said.

"Well, of course, Tanith is a real lady you know. Who could fail to love her – even Perry can see that." As she said this, he felt a wave of affection for Sela. Was he falling for her? But he dismissed it and returned to the subject of the ceremony. "But, that bit about the 'life-force of the moon' – see I remember – what did it mean?"

Sela picked up her glass. "This is like a chalice – a feminine symbol, yes? Well, in magical practice the chalice is also a representation of the vagina. Women, in ancient times, were seen as magical because life came from their bodies and also because they bled, regularly, without a wound. That blood, the blood of the moon, was seen as magical, sacred and, at that time of the month, priestesses were considered to be oracular. A priest could become oracular as well, if he drank the blood of a priestess – 'tasting the life-force of the moon'."

Steven nodded, "I've heard of that," he said.

"It's all tied up with fertility rites, you see. That's why some societies and, later on, religions, saw women as being 'unclean' at the time of menstruation. It harks back to the time when women had power and were, therefore, feared. They still are, hence the attitude of men towards women and the objections to women priests."

"I see," he said. "So the Christian thing of drinking Christ's blood isn't so strange, then."

"Exactly. It was merely an extension of existing practices in Mystery Religions except, in the Christian rites, actual blood wasn't used. The magical bit was the belief that mere bread and wine had changed into Christ's flesh and blood."

"Yes, I get it. And blood is seen as special – hence blood rites; pacts written in blood and so on – yes?"

"Yes," she said.

"And the box, that paper you burned, that strange drumming chant, that whirling dance – what was that? God, you seemed so pagan when you did that – strange, as though from a time long ago."

Sela looked into the fire as though reading something mysterious within its glowing heart.

"I was raising power – a cone of power. I was creating a vortex in Time and Space – a swirl of energy so that I could focus the intent of my Will. As for the pendant spell, well it goes back to ancient times. The Romans were very successful in their wars but it was not only in military terms; they were also adept at psychological warfare, particularly against towns. Do you know what they would do? Well, when laying siege to a town they would set up an altar outside the walls and then their priests would perform a ceremony of Evocatio. They would summon the deity of the town to them and promise the deity a better service if you like. Can you imagine the fear and distress of ancient peoples when they saw the Romans summoning their Gods. It could destroy the Will of the people. Well, I did something like that. I bound the Spirit of the Pendant, its force if you like; I then freed it and, through a counter spell and promise, I took its energy and then closed the portal by burning the sigil written on the paper."

Steven shook his head, "I don't get any of this. So that's why it can't hurt. What, an actual spirit in the pendant?"

She smiled, "Well, yes, in a way. Remember what I said about energies, forces – like a charged-up super battery if you like – almost alive, like a virus."

"Will Jane know?"

"Not yet but when she returns she will. She'll realise that you aren't dead. She will try to activate the pendant in an attempt to re-establish control over you. It won't work, then we'll have to see what she does next. By that time I hope we've discovered what she's after. Psychologically, we'll have attacked her. We have a possession of hers. It might help to undermine her confidence." She stopped and looked at him with concern, "Oh, you *do* look tired."

Steven felt tiredness engulf him and he stifled a yawn. His brain was spinning, filled with a confusion of images.

"You must be exhausted. Why don't you turn in? We're off to Glastonbury tomorrow. An early start. Go on, go to bed."

She got up and went to the door to let Perry in. Tanith decided to stay out but the dog quickly ensconced itself back by the fire. Without further words, Steven went up to bed his mind full of the evening's events. He could hear Sela pottering about below and then he fell into a deep sleep.

The Stars of Heaven

CHAPTER 13

He awoke to an insistent shaking and was conscious of a hand on his shoulder. He spun up quickly nearly knocking the cup of tea out of Sela's hand.

"Wow! Jumpy! Sorry, but I did call you – you seemed dead to the world. I was thinking of setting a charge of dynamite under your bed. Wow! When you go off to the land of nod you really take a trip." She was standing by the side of his bed dressed in an oversize bathrobe.

Steven sat up. "I'm sorry. Phew, I was really out of it. No I don't usually go off so deeply. Thanks," he took the tea. "What time is it?" He sipped the hot, sweet liquid, as he tried to gather his thoughts.

"Seven-thirty," she said. "We need an early start. Takes about two hours from here; we're meeting Vivien at one o'clock so if we leave at nine we'll get there about eleven, time for coffee and a browse around. I've been in the bathroom, its all clear for you. Breakfast in thirty minutes, OK?" She bustled out of the room.

As he drank the tea, his mind re-visited the events of the previous evening. He felt extremely well and very conscious that the gloom and depression of the previous days had definitely disappeared. In a short while he had showered, shaved and dressed and was soon downstairs. Perry came to greet him and they had a five minutes tussle on the floor.

"You're covered in cat fur now," said Sela coming into the room. "I need to vacuum that rug – here." She got her clothes-brush and quickly brushed his back. "That's the trouble with pets, or, should I say, the trouble with a fluffy long-haired cat. Looks like I need to brush her as well."

They sat in the kitchen to have breakfast and chatted about the trip; he found that he was looking forward to it although he was still uncertain about involving another person.

"Shall we take Perry?" asked Sela. The dog was sitting beside her chair waiting for tit-bits. Clearly, he had taken to her.

"No, I'm sure he'll be OK. I'll leave him the shirt I was wearing yesterday just in case but he looks comfortable here – or no, I tell you what, we'll drop him back to Hawkwood. It's on our way." And this they did. He entered the house with some slight trepidation but there was nothing of the sinister atmosphere anywhere and Perry was soon gobbling a plate of food and was left to guard the house.

The two friends drove the winding road to Bridgwater with a good rocking tape of 'Various Artists' pounding out an accompanying beat. Steven took the alternative cut across the Quantocks, because he enjoyed the wooded hills, and then back onto the Bridgwater road and through the town. As they travelled high above the Levels, Sela pointed ahead. "There's Glastonbury Tor." She indicated a strange, conical hill which seemed to rise out of nowhere, for there was a mist covering the ground around. Steven had never been to Glastonbury. All he knew of it was they had an annual Rock Festival and that it was supposed to be a centre of psychic phenomena. He had always meant to go to the festival but had missed it on each successive year.

"What will we do before meeting Vivien?" he asked.

"We'll have a browse around the shops. Anyway, I'm going to get you a pendant to replace Jane's – you asked me, remember?" They drove into the town's outskirts. "That's Wearyall Hill." She indicated high ground to her right. "In legend, Joseph of Arimathæa came here with the cup containing Christ's blood. He stuck his staff in the ground and a thorn tree grew; the same thorns that were used in the Crown of Thorns, or so they say. Actually, the thorns *are* a type found in the Middle East but were probably brought back by a crusader."

"Why would Joseph come here – I mean – how did he get here – why bother?"

"Well, this whole area was once marshland, hence 'The Isle of Avalon'. We'll go up the Tor and you can see that the ground would have been covered in water in the past. As for him coming here, why not? Britain was such a mysterious magical place. This would have been just before or, perhaps, during the Roman invasion which was 43 A.D., so it's entirely possible that he did come here. Remember, I told you that Jesus was at Culbone. No reason why He shouldn't have been. People travelled widely in the ancient world, look at St. Paul in the Acts of the Apostles. People engaged in trade and Britain traded a great deal with the rest of the known world. It's all possible. Do you know that Diodorus, an ancient historian, spoke of a triangular island to the north where there lay a great temple to Apollo – Stonehenge? After all, Apollo was a Sun God and Stonehenge is a Sun Temple as well as a Moon Temple, incidentally."

"Yes – you said so yesterday – I remember; but the Druids honour the sun and Midsummer's Day."

"Yes, modern Druids do that. I'm talking of a time before even the Celtic Druids. I'm talking of when Stonehenge was built, nearly 5000 years ago. The ancients honoured the sun, yes, but they also honoured the moon. If you build a great structure like that, you make sure it balances in terms of its spiritual meaning. In the ancient world the moon and sun were equal but different. Each was powerful in its sphere of influence; after all, the sun might rule through the long hot summer but what about the long, cold and clear nights of winter? Who rides high in the sky then, eh? Have you never heard of the phrase, 'hunter's moon'? Hunter-gathering peoples, like other predators, hunted in packs, at night, under the light of the full moon. *She* had to be honoured."

The image of a panther creeping along in the moonlight came to him. "I suppose that's where we get our fear of the dark."

"Probably – yes," she said. Then she continued, "Ancient peoples were not as primitive, or superstitious, as modern man might think. If you take stone circles, for example, they were often aligned like a calendar, to denote particular seasons. So, for agricultural peoples, this could have been important. Artefacts have been discovered showing the importance of such knowledge. In other words, so-called primitive beliefs had a far more practical input to ancient societies than, say, modern-type religions. Ancient people actually *lived* their lives within a total context of interaction between man, nature and the Gods."

They drove into a car-park by the ruined abbey and were soon enjoying a coffee in a small teashop. Sela continued to tell him about the town and its legends. "Anyway, Joseph of Arimathæa is supposed to have buried the Cup or Chalice – the Holy Grail, under Chalice Hill, hence the name. There's a well there which has red water flowing from it – the Blood of Christ. Actually the well is older than Christianity and the red water is caused by minerals but it's a good story. We'll go there – drink up. We'll go to the well – a good pun, no?"

"No," he said.

"Oh, well, I do try."

They wandered in and out of several shops specialising in crystals, incense and various types of magical paraphernalia. He saw several statues which took his liking and some crystal wands similar, but not the same, as Sela's.

"I think that pendant would suit you." It was a triangular shaped quartz on a leather thong and she bought it for him. He reciprocated by purchasing a ring she liked. "An exchange of gifts – lovely – seals our friendship." She seemed childlike in her pleasure. He ended up buying a goddess figure, some incense, a few crystals he liked the look of and a crystal wand, which was skilfully carved and set with other stones.

"My place is going to look like yours soon," he said.

"Oh, you're just an old hippy at heart. You'll be wearing flares soon."

"Well, I did have my moments you know. I even had some beads once." He mused about his music days, wishing he had managed to get to, at least, one of the Rock festivals.

"You devil," she said, "I bet there was no stopping you."

They walked back to the car and drove through the town, making for the road leading to the Tor. As they climbed the steep hill towards the access point, Sela pointed to some of the houses. "Dion Fortune lived up there. She was a famous occultist and author; wrote some strange, but interesting novels – I'll lend them to you." She approached a pathway which led to the rising Tor beyond.

He looked at the unusual shape of the Tor and at the terrace-like lines around it. "What are those?" He indicated the ridges.

"Some say agricultural terraces, others say it's a spiral path – a serpent pathway. I favour the latter, not because it appeals to my witchy mind but because terraces make no sense. Look around you, there's enough agricultural land even without going down to the marshland area. In any case, the monks of Glastonbury Abbey drained all the marshland so they had plenty of areas to plant crops or to graze their cattle or sheep. No, it's a mystic maze pattern."

Soon they were puffing their way up and stopped to rest. Sela pointed to the surrounding area. "See, this is a landmark for miles so it would almost certainly have had some mystical significance. And, look up there," she pointed at the tower crowning the summit. "St. Michael's Tower; Christian's always put a monument to St. Michael on top of an old pagan sacred site to hold the Devil down – for 'Devil' read 'Earth Energies'."

They continued up to the summit which provided a magnificent view of the surrounding countryside now that the mist had lifted. "As I told you, this is still known as the Isle of Avalon," Sela said. "In legend, King Arthur was brought here after he was mortally wounded. It's said that he lies here, beneath the Tor – ready to come back and save us all." She swept her arms around, "You can see how flat the land is, making this high ground and Wearyall Hill, over there, proper islands if you remember that, prior to land reclamation, this was all watery, boggy marshland." She pointed to a distant mound. "Brent Knoll, an Iron Age hill fort." She turned and indicated another rise of ground in the distance. "Cadbury Castle – another hill fort. Did you know that it was re-furbished in the 6th century? Somebody powerful lived there – some say that, if a King Arthur had really lived, then that was his Camelot. The river Camel runs by it. Come on, down we go to Chalice Well."

"Do you think there was an Arthur?" he asked her.

"Oh, sure," she said, "but not like in Malory or the films. Most likely he was a Romano-British leader – you know, after Rome withdrew help. Someone held the line against the Saxons, that's for sure. Myths, legends, often have a basis in fact."

They scrambled back down the steep steps and path onto the road and so down to the gardens surrounding the well. On the way, Sela repeated the tale of the Holy Grail. "But Dion Fortune, you know, the one who lived near the Tor – she said that the well is an ancient sacred well, pre-Christian and, of course, that would be right. The well never dries up and its water is red so you can see that it would be a focal point for worshippers. It's supposed to have healing properties, spiritual as well as physical."

Inside the gardens, Steven remarked, "This must be a pretty place when all the leaves and flowers are out. It's got a lovely atmosphere now."

She smiled and stopped beside an ornate waterfall spouting from the mouth of a stone lion's head. She was silent and Steven sensed something special was about to happen. Sela bent and took up a glass, left there for visitors, into which water was splashing. She filled it and held it, one hand around the top the other cradling the base; she had held the altar cup in the same way Steven recalled. She handed it to him and bade him take a sip. He took the cup and holding it in the same manner, he sipped the water which had a strange taste and handed it back. Sela drank some of it and put the cup down again.

He felt as though he had taken part in a rite that was, indeed, very ancient. She said nothing and walked him further into the garden to a spot where she lifted a wooden covering which carried an ornate design. Beneath it was a stone well.

"This site alternates between being a pagan and a Christian shrine," she said, "but really you can't confine something that has a universal meaning to one religion." They made their way back to the car and again, in silence, drove back to the car-park.

They sat in a café and soon Sela said, "Ah, here she comes," and a small woman, slightly older than Sela, slim-built and with raven black hair, came over to them. She was wearing a hooded coat made of suede. She looked very Gothic with a pale face and dark eye make-up in contrast to rather wide, red lips.

"Hi there – mwah, mwah," – this sound accompanied two kisses to Sela's cheeks.

"And you must be Steve. Mwah, mwah." There was a faint smell of an exotic expensive perfume. "Well, what have you two been up to? Do tell." Vivien had a rather arty affected way of talking as though she had once been an actress. She reached into her bag and took out a packet of cigarettes. He noticed her slim fingers and well manicured long fingernails, painted a dark red. She wore a silver ring set with a ruby stone.

"Ah," said Sela, "wouldn't you like to know? Well, I won't beat about the bush; Steven's got himself into a real mess and I want you to help him and me." She launched into a synopsis of the story. Vivien listened and lit up a cigarette, coughed, then took another drag. She said nothing as Sela spoke only turning her eyes now and then to Steven. When she did this she looked at him in a way that made him blush.

Sela finished, "Well, there you are. Can you, will you, help?"

"But of course I will. I've heard of the Trethowan bitch – read one of her books. Very strange views, extreme right wing and all that; you know, to the right of the Nazis. Combine that with magic and you've got problems indeed. Are we eating?" They chose something off the menu and continued their conversation. She asked Steven about his background and he filled her in with the full picture.

"So," she said, "all alone, eh?" and again she gave him a look which left little doubt as to her intentions. She had a way of lowering her lashes and glancing sideways at a person which gave her a mysterious appearance.

Sela said firmly, "Now Vivien, this is deadly serious; no time for any of that. Can you come to Porlock?"

Vivien took another thoughtful drag on her cigarette. "I can, in a few days maybe." She fished in her bag and took out a diary. "Maybe, oh yes, but not 'til Friday. Is that OK?"

"Fine, yes, excellent," said Sela. She seemed very pleased and Steven wondered if it was with a feeling of relief at finding another ally.

The food arrived and they tucked in as Vivien continued to ask questions about Steven, the house, Rita, Jane then back to the house.

"I really don't know much about the land," he said. "Marian," he remembered to call her that, "Marian found a book which mentioned burials but I don't know, I've not seen anything."

Vivien pondered this. "Well," she said, "if there was anything I'll find it, I'll know."

"How?" he asked, puzzled.

Vivien put down her knife and fork, rested her chin on her hands and said, "Vibrations my dear, good vibrations as in the song, or bad vibes. Ugh! Not nice – nasty, nasty hobbitses." She lapsed into a peculiar voice, looked at him, became serious and said, "Gollum – Lord of the Rings – you know?"

He laughed, "Oh yes, I know. But seriously, can you really tell if something's there?"

"But of course I can. My God, sometimes I feel positively faint – depends on the energy. I can't go in some of the shops here, positively awash with ley line energies. Drives me mad sometimes but then, perhaps I am. Do you think I am, sweet little friend of mine?" She batted her eyes at Sela and began eating again.

Sela laughed. "Yep, mad as a proverbial hatter – but then in this case, we need someone who is a complete nutcase. Who else would bother? So, the day after tomorrow; bring your things – I don't know how long this will take. Will it be all right with whoever you're living or sleeping with?"

"There's no one. No, *really*, there hasn't been any one for six months. Don't look at me like that. It's absolutely true. No sex, nothing – *for six months*." She turned to Steven, "Can you believe that?" Again she stared at him an open invitation in her eyes.

Steven was not sure what to say, so said nothing but smiled uncertainly. Vivien lowered her lashes and gave him that sidelong glance and then returned to her meal as the three of them continued their lunch.

As Sela and Vivien chatted, inconsequentially, Steven allowed his mind to dwell upon the visit to the Well and he was startled when Vivien said, suddenly, "Did you like the Well?"

"Yes – very spiritual," he replied. Good God, could she read minds also?

As he didn't say any more, Vivien turned to Sela and said, "He's nice. I like him. Strong and silent type. OK then you two. I must get back – got a reading at three p.m. so au revoir. Until we meet again," she said theatrically and got up. "Mwah! mwah!" to Sela. "Mwah! mwah!" to Steven and she was gone, her hooded figure seemingly disappearing into the shadows of the room as she left them.

"Phew!" said Steven, "are you sure she can help? I mean, she's a bit, well, over the top isn't she?"

"Don't be fooled," said Sela, "if anyone can help she can. Viv's extremely good at what she does. Very sensitive, teeters on the edge of sanity because of it. She's had a nervous breakdown. Actually, she had been in a long relationship, very unusual for Viv. Lasted a year or more but then her partner left her. She was a right cow. Just dumped Viv and went. Viv was in a terrible state, took lots of drugs and ended up in hospital."

"She? Oh, so it was a lesbian relationship. I thought she liked only men," said Steven, "the way she looked at me." The memory of that sidelong glance was strangely compelling.

"Men, women, Viv is eclectic in her tastes; all shapes, sizes, ages, all genders, even me once."

Steven looked at her. "You had sex with Viv?"

"Well, yes but it didn't go anywhere, too complicated, and anyway I didn't really enjoy it. Not that Viv isn't nice; I just don't feel comfortable with same sex sex if you see what I mean. You should always try these things out – you never know." She picked up a napkin and dabbed at her lips.

"*I* know what I like," said Steven, "and I can't say I'd ever fancy a man."

"He who doth protest…" said Sela teasing him.

"No, really, I've had offers, just not interested."

She nodded and shrugged as they sat in silence for a while with Steven contemplating the rather exciting image of the two women but, then, he quickly dispelled the thought.

Sela returned to the subject of her friend. "Well, anyway, she took a while to recover but it seems that her psychic abilities were heightened by her experience; near to death I suppose. She's very sensitive, artistic, very special. Look," she said, "I'll give you an example of her abilities. Her brother, who lived in Canada, died a few years ago. Viv had a premonition. There were some jackdaws nesting in her chimney and one of them got trapped and flew down into the lounge. I was trying to get it out – it was fluttering all over the place, leaving sooty marks on the walls. I asked Viv to help but she'd gone white and sweaty. Anyway, I eventually got it out and asked her what was wrong. She told me that she knew her brother would die and he did – an unexpected heart attack. Somehow, the bird had triggered something in her mind, in her psyche. No obvious connection – but there you are, it was true. Yes, we need her, believe me."

Steven nodded, "OK, that's weird, I must say. A bit creepy, really – OK you know best but she did make me feel uncomfortable."

Sela laughed, "Vivien has that effect on men. She wants something and goes for it – so watch out."

Steven studied her face now in profile, as she looked over at the counter. He realised, suddenly, that he did want someone himself and that it was Sela he wanted. Their relationship was progressing so naturally and in such a relaxed manner that it was hard to realise they had known each other only a few days. He wondered if there was any likelihood of the relationship blossoming into something more intimate but realised that this was unlikely; he was thirteen years older than her. She looked round and caught his glance.

"OK?" she asked.

"Yes, fine." He wondered if she knew what he was thinking. He was finding it all very strange. Could *they* all read minds – Jane, Vivien, Sela?

She held his gaze in a disconcerting way and then said, "We'd better get back. Our four-legged friends will be chomping their way through our respective houses."

During the return drive Sela spoke of her friend, the daughter of an eccentric couple who had married late in life to fulfil family convention. Otherwise they had lived a rather strange, bohemian life, part artists, part poets, bad actors and even worse parents to Vivien. She had grown up equally eccentric and had manifested psychic gifts early on in life. She would often 'correct' a medium during her mother's interminable séances and this became highly disconcerting to all when it was seen that many of Vivien's statements struck chords with the bereaved relatives attending the séance. Her parents vanished whilst on a trip to Turkey – a mystery never solved – and Vivien came to live nearby to Sela and her family. The two girls became close. They parted during their university years, with Vivien doing a humanities degree and Sela doing anthropology. However, the two friends remained in close touch and met regularly. Vivien had assisted Sela once or twice in the past and had demonstrated an adeptness at managing, and channelling, the tricky matter of past-life regression. As Steven suspected, Vivien went through men in the way that a mincer takes in a solid object and leaves it broken, mashed up and in pieces. A trail of broken hearts and marriages littered her past. No wonder, now that she was becoming older, she had no one in train; there was hardly anyone left, at least in the Glastonbury region.

As they came to the end of the Bratton Straight, the panorama of Exmoor stretched before them, hidden, in parts by mist and rain, a tableau of greens, soft greys and almost purple-like black.

"I love the weather when it does this," he said.

"So do I," she replied. "Living here you can really feel and measure the passage of the seasons, of nature, the whole cycle of creation. Look at those lambs, a bit early. I always worry about them in this sort of weather. Oh look, they've got raincoats on."

Steven glanced over to a passing field and, indeed, the lambs were wearing black and yellow coverings. He felt glad but didn't know why. After all, many of the lambs were due for slaughter quite soon; still, no reason why they shouldn't be comfortable. "A short life and a merry one," he remarked as he steered the car through an absolute downpour of heavy rain into the village. "Want to come up for a coffee?" he asked and was disappointed when she declined and said she would have to get on home.

"I've got a lecture to prepare. The material world does, at times, encroach on the spiritual you know and I've got me and one hell of a hungry cat to support. But, as they always say in the movies, I'll take a rain check." This, in American accent.

"Sure, no problem. I'll give you a call." He stopped outside her cottage.

"No need," she said, "I'll come over tomorrow at ten o'clock. We have much to do, to prepare. Anyway, I want to have a look around that vast place of yours – we didn't get round to it the other day. I might pick up a clue or two."

"Sure, ten will be fine." He felt pleased.

"Do you want to come in?" she asked pausing before her dash to her door.

"No, like you I've got a hungry dog awaiting me."

She was suddenly serious, "Steven, it'll be all right – you know, back at the house."

"I know. No, really, I know. I feel totally freed from it all and certainly strong enough to handle anything. Thanks," he leaned over and pecked her on the cheek, "Mwah!" mimicking Vivien. Sela laughed and dashed out of the car, through the rain and into her house.

He drove back home with the rain bucketing down and up to the front door. There was an overwhelming gloom all around but this was due to the weather and he entered the house to be greeted by Perry. This time it really was different. He felt completely relaxed and he cheerfully prepared a meal, put the T.V. on and settled back for a restful evening. He found his mind wandering constantly to Sela. He felt strongly attracted to her and, for a moment wondered if she had 'glamoured' him but dismissed this. What vanity anyway. She had nothing to gain unlike Jane. He felt a pleasant anticipation over the prospect of seeing her again. He thought about Vivien and realised with a shock, that he quite fancied her as well. From a state of virtual celibacy since the death of Ginny, he had found himself in bed with Jane and now fancying two women. He put it down to frustration and concentrated on the T.V. for the rest of the evening. At 10.30 the phone rang. "Are you OK?" she asked.

"Yes, fine, no problems. Thanks, thanks for the trip – for everything."

"Good – glad you liked it. I knew you would. See you tomorrow." She rang off – he felt elated.

CHAPTER 14

Following an extremely good night's sleep, untroubled by any nightmares, Steven awoke with a sense of purpose and anticipation. He looked at his watch and was amazed to see that it was almost 9 o'clock. He had never slept so long and realised that Sela would be arriving in an hour. He got ready, had a light breakfast, let Perry out of the front door and was just calling him in when Sela drove her little car up the drive and parked it alongside his.

"Morrning zur," she drawled in her overdone West Country accent. Then said, "I've just realised our cars are Japanese; they can have a chat; share experiences."

They went inside. "This is a lovely house," she remarked as he showed her around. "Aha! The Master Bedroom." She went over to the windows, "Oh what a wonderful view." They went downstairs. "I was particularly taken by your conservatory," she said, "make a lovely temple you know." She stood at the bottom of the stairs, hands on hips, surveying the entrance hall.

"Orangery actually, although to be honest, I'm not sure of the difference but, yes, I thought of it last night. Do you think I could use it as a temple? I'd like to learn more – do what you do – can you teach me?" He began to guide her away from the hallway towards the kitchen.

"There's not much to teach really," she replied. He looked surprised but she went on, "Magic is a state of mind – a trick, if you like, a way of changing your mindset to achieve results." They went into the kitchen and sat down with some coffee. "The words I use are mine, derived from my family it's true, but largely mine. Take that poem I used, 'The Resurrection of Merlin', it all fitted with what I wanted to do. The *magic* was that you responded intuitively and aided the spell by your actions. Likewise when I was building the Moon Temple, I wrote the words because I wanted to create a visual picture – creative visualisation; I love using poetic words, metre, that sort of thing." She sat back in her chair.

He shook his head. "No, no it's more than that, it's got to be. What about the power rush, that was real?" He could almost feel that strange force again, and the power that had pushed him to his knees.

She nodded, "Yes. All I'm saying is that there is no set formula. That's the problem with ceremonial magicians. Yes, you need to use techniques to get you from one level to the next but then they become too complicated. In the end you can't work *their* magic unless the time is right, the planets are in the right place, the right colours are used for your robes and temple things, the right tools, the right incense, and the words have to be said in a special way –

all too much. You get lost in the process, the actions, and lose the essence, the intuitive nature behind the purpose of the rite." She took a sip of coffee. "Do you see?"

"Yes, I can see what you mean. That was partly what put me off Kabalah – all too much for my brain, perhaps. I can see how it would suit some though; but what about all those books and what about the training of shamans, that sort of thing – that book you gave me to read?"

"Well, what are the books? Much of what is written down derives from a particular man who claimed initiation from a traditional coven then each successive writer changes it here and there, takes out a bit, adds in a bit. In the end you have something which purports to be the correct way to do things. Nothing particularly wrong with that providing it doesn't become like dogma – 'only this is right'."

"You mean like the Christians, mainstream religions. *They* have the correct message from God."

"Yes, *they're* right, everything else is error. They all get lost in process, the correct way. They lose sight of the intrinsic spirituality of mankind, the spirit within that seeks to unite with the Great Spirit, or universal energy, all around. Magic should be for all – free – eclectic, ever changing and growing. Like I said to you, it's all a great sea of energy and we're all part of it but you don't need to say things by rote to get into it or, if you forget the words, that's it. That's all too silly. Just stand alone, in the middle of a forest at night, and feel the power of the Earth and the cosmos around you. Then your mind can soar – your spirit fly and then words mean nothing – just feelings – that's what counts."

He pondered her words. "But you said certain words, words chanted, drumming, and so on, all helped to lift you out of the mundane. What about your family traditions – the manuscripts?"

"Yes, I did but that doesn't mean that all of those things have to be done in one particular way; that would limit freedom of expression, of intuition, of the need to demonstrate the power of the spirit, if we were all so constrained. If it was so ordained, then magical words would *have* to be pronounced only in a special way as laid down by the original person who made the spell. Of course, that can't be so. I do different things to Jane, or to Wiccans and my spells work. That means it must be something other than the actual process doesn't it?"

He said, "Yes I follow you. But your family traditions – what about them?"

She shrugged. "Yes, I was taught traditional techniques but no one said it *had* to be that way. I was always encouraged to improvise – discover my own ways as well as traditions." She went on, "We don't speak in the same way as people did a hundred years ago let alone fifty thousand years ago. Look at the variety of accents in Britain today. We don't know how the ancient Britons spoke nor how the Romans spoke Latin, the correct pronunciation that is. The

Bible is supposed to be the Word of God yet scholars argue about it constantly, particularly about its translation and interpretation. Muslims have passed on the words of the Prophet as revealed to him by Allah and even they have arguments about interpretation. There are schisms amongst their followers. Same thing amongst the Jews, Hindus, Buddhists – everyone arguing – thinking they're right." She sounded exasperated.

"What we're doing in magic is to attempt direct intervention in the laws of Time and Space. It's not the same as passing on moral teachings as all religions seek to do. Magic is outside conventional mores, although most practitioners can, and do, adhere to society's norms and values. We seek to 'Feel the earth and walk the storms; Play with phantoms, nameless forms; With elementals of the night; With satyrs, nymphs and elven sprite'. Sorry, one of my poetic efforts, 'A Hymn to Pan'. You should read Crowley's book – absolutely brilliant and, oh, does he capture the essence of magic. In magic you have to be a bit mad," she paused and gave a little laugh. "Here I go again – stop me next time I start."

"Phew," he said, "I'm not going to take all of this in." He felt she tended to dart around in her arguments but he got the gist of her statements.

"Yes you will. All of those things I said – chanting, drumming, vibrating the words of power, whispers, yells even, anything that helps *you* to break out of the ordinary world. It *can* happen in organised religion, of course it can, but that's devotion not magic. I'm merely saying that's *not* the only true way." She made a clenching motion with her hand. "You can't chain, constrain the spiritual impulse and say that only by doing something in *our* way is right; look at the differences between Catholics and Evangelical Christians."

"True," he said. "I see that."

"So, now, can I teach you? Well, I can show you what I do and you can learn what I do, learn my words, my poems, my invocations but, and this is the point, my way is no more correct than anyone else's, no better, no worse but, for me, it works and probably will for you." She scratched her ankle. "Hmmm! Must have got bitten by something." She continued speaking, "Having learned these things, or any other rites, then comes the magic bit. That means you have to find a way to let your psychic self come through; the sudden shift from just saying the words by rote to feeling and projecting them. That's something I can't teach you. When it happens you'll know."

Steven understood her. "Yes, in martial arts a person can learn the moves but then there's always a crossover from student to adept. Breaking a brick with your hand needs a sudden switch of the mind, not just hard hands."

"Exactly," she said and continued: "Equally, you could look at any other rites but don't get bogged down in slavishly following others. That way you stifle your own creative, intuitive powers and without that and your ability to focus your own spiritual mind, you'll get nowhere. Even Aristotle, who sought to comprehend the Universe through logical reasoning, understood that, once you moved into the world of the Spirit then emotions, feelings were more important than fact and logic. So, you see, you have to summon up the flame that lies within yourself. It's no good always looking for the answer elsewhere. The power comes from *within* and is then *focused*. All the gurus or books in the world can't help. You find it inside of yourself – perhaps that's the way to know God."

"The Kingdom of God is within," Steven interjected, remembering his early religious education. "Jesus said that."

Sela paused, then nodded. "Yes, you're right. He did say that – the same sort of thing, I suppose. I'd forgotten about that. Perhaps the whole Pentecost thing was a way of saying that the Apostles had found the way to ignite *their* inner flames – some say that Jesus was a magician – it's all the same thing."

She finished her drink, carried the cup to the sink, rinsed it and after placing it on the draining board she returned to her chair. She continued speaking, "Once you've learned how to ignite the flame then you can move forward, if that's the right term. By igniting your inner flame, you're able to draw back the veil, if you like, and see into other levels of consciousness. You become more aware; your channels are open and then, and only then, will you become truly capable of channelling, directing and using, your powers. It's when you part the veil that you can use magic to cause changes or you develop other psychic abilities. Remember what I said about Hecate lighting up the darkness?"

"What about shamans though? Are they the same, you know, like witches, magicians?"

"They use different techniques for different purposes. Their path moves into one that is far more linked to a time when mankind functioned in a more nomadic lifestyle. There's an emphasis on oral tradition, herbal medicine, contact with the vibrational energies of the land and the ancestral past. There's an acceptance of the close link between mankind and other living things on the planet; totem animals, that sort of thing. As for shamanic training, well, that includes the use of mind changing drugs, contact with ancestors and healing with plants. Clearly such skill requires long training. The use of drugs to achieve altered states of consciousness and the ability to deal with the trips, spirit vision, requires careful detailed training so that sanity is maintained. That's different from the sort of magic that I do. Vivien knows a bit about that. You will have to ask her."

"Does she? Yet she seems so vague, spaced out." he said.

"Oh, don't be taken in. I've told you, she's very skilled."

"Isn't there a danger of psychosis, though? How does she know she's not deluding herself – you know, hearing voices in her head?"

Sela nodded. "Yes, I can see how that could be the danger – but not in Vivien's case. She has an ability to differentiate between the sort of gabbling voices that many psychotic people experience and the channelling of a spirit voice. She *does* have a way into the spirit world."

Steven considered her words and then said, "What did you mean about 'contact with ancestors'? You've mentioned this before."

She considered this then said, "It's a complex matter which requires training, and it doesn't necessarily need drugs. Have you heard about certain techniques, used by esoteric practitioners, called Path Workings?"

"Yes – it's used in Kabalah, I remember."

"Well, yes – something like that. However, long before the more formal religions developed, ancient peoples were much more in touch with life and death. Did you know that they would bury their dead beneath the floors of their houses? Continuity you see, no bar between the living and the dead. Burial chambers were also built in the style of long houses which could be accessed. So, a person could enter there and commune with their dead ancestors. Modern esoteric practitioners can still do this. It's not confined to shamans – I've done it."

He was startled. "What, you mean you've talked to the ancient dead?"

She shook her head. "No, not literally but through something similar to Path Working, guided spiritual tours if you like, a person can enter through the portal of the Underworld and invoke an archetypal figure – a priest perhaps, a king, which is a projection or a culmination of all the vibrational energies that have permeated the place for thousands of years."

"That's astonishing," he said.

"It's good if you can go to actual sites but you can do this at home. Using meditation and creative visualisation you can access that which lies deeply hidden within your psyche – atavistic memories. It can put you deeply in tune with the land – the soul of the land if you like. It's a way of developing your spirituality, a personal link, if you like, between you and the soul of the planet. No intermediary, no religious hierarchy, just you and – well – God, the Godhead, whatever you want to call it." She stopped and looked at him, that questioning look on her face again.

"That's remarkable." He went on, "I think I might like to study that sort of thing. I've always had a strong feeling for the land, the environment, the relationship between us and other living things. I've been involved in some campaigns, you know, and I get really fed up with the way the big companies are ruining everything and upsetting the balance of things, as you would say." He looked at her thoughtfully then said, "I will ask Vivien but I think you're underestimating your own powers."

"Good," she said. "I'm glad you're doing practical things to help the planet. Too many occultists concentrate on healing the land through the spirit world. They forget the real world. As for me, well, I'm not a guru you know," she laughed. "It's probably because you've not been in contact with this sort of thing that you feel the way you do. I can't stand the way some people set themselves up as something special. There have been very few *true* teachers."

He shook his head. "No, you're wrong. It's true I don't know a lot about this but I know people and I've met people of power – in my training you know." He got up and poured some more coffee. "Biscuit?"

"Ooh, yes please – any choccy ones?" She took a chocolate biscuit. "I never buy these – got to watch my figure."

He smiled then went on, "You're selling yourself short, you know. I was incredibly scared by what has been going on and I'm not easily frightened. You've dispelled that. Remember, I've experienced things I didn't know were possible and now, thanks to you, it's gone. No, you have enormous skill and power. Perhaps you've been locked away down here too long to realise what silly people there are out there. When I was a musician, I met lots of different types. I came upon some who made a great thing of being fortune-tellers, psychic healers, that sort of thing. I didn't meet anyone who impressed me the way you have and, for that matter, the way Jane Trethowan has. No, you have power and, clearly, so does she. You two are the real thing and, boy, do I need you to believe that." He looked at her earnestly and repeated, "Believe me, I was never so scared."

She nodded, "I hear you. Don't worry, I know what she can do and I know what I can do but don't put me up there on some sort of pedestal."

Steven smiled, "Why not? No, OK, but I've seen people in my world who talk a lot but can't act. I know what real power is and you've got it. OK, maybe you're not a guru but you're the nearest darn thing to one I've ever met."

She was silent again, as though thinking carefully before speaking. Then she appeared to come to some sort of decision. She looked away and said, "I've not been entirely straight with you." She walked over to the window and stared out into the garden.

"What do you mean?" he wondered what she was going to say.

She continued to stand at the window staring out at the trees beyond. When she spoke it was in a quiet tone, almost musing. "I told you that I was for the Light against the Dark, remember?" He nodded and she went on, "Do you remember our discussion about evil? I said to you that evil was when people set out to harm others in the full knowledge that what they were doing was wrong. I know this 'cos I've been there." She turned back towards him and sat opposite him. She was toying with the pendant around her throat.

"What, you're saying you're evil? Oh come on – look at the way you're helping me against Jane. *She's* evil, not you."

She gave a little shrug. "Yes, she is but I also said that there was no black or white magic as well, didn't I? That it's a neutral force and that its use depends on the intentions of the practitioner. When I was younger, I was full of it – of a sense of power and self-importance. The problem with having my sort of ability is that there is always the temptation to use it – because I can, if you see what I mean. It's tempting to try things out – to bewitch others or to interfere in their lives. Oh yes, I did use my powers to help others, became quite a good village 'wise woman'; but once, just once, I used it to harm another person."

"Well, no one is perfect. After all…"

She stopped him. "No, listen to me. A friend of mine was seriously abused and injured by a boyfriend. She was subjected to a brutal sexual attack and she came to me for help, so I fixed him – hexed him."

"What happened?" he asked softly.

"There was a car accident and he was badly crippled. In a wheelchair for life, now. She was happy and left him. I go and see him now and again to help him. I felt terrible about it and I vowed never to use the dark art again. But my conscience isn't clear. You, now – well, you've given me a chance at, well, a sort of redemption."

He touched her hand in sympathy. "Oh, once, one mistake. Come on, no one is perfect believe it or not. Look, when *I* was young I did some terrible things; gangs, that sort of thing. We used to go 'queer' bashing – beating up gays. Terrible, yes. Then one night we picked on a lad who stood up to us – no chance at all but he was so brave – made me feel small, stupid. There was a look in his eyes that shamed me. From then on I channelled my violence through martial arts training. So there you are you see – God, your guilt is almost Roman Catholic – are you sure you're not one?"

She gave a sad smile. "Yes but it's more to do with my karma. There will be a reckoning. There always is." Again, she seemed lost in thought.

"Well, I still say you're the best thing that could have happened to me in all of this horrible affair. You're helping me and that's good enough for me – so maybe it *will* all come out right in the end."

She said nothing and finished her coffee then, after a while, "Thanks, thanks for that. I'm not trying to be modest you know. I just find it hard to believe that anyone would want to learn anything from me."

"OK," he said, "I do – so there; now let's go out and look at my domain." He held out his hand and pulled her to her feet. She gave a little laugh, and said, "Yes, OK."

He opened the kitchen door that led onto the side of the house and then went back to Perry and let him out of the front door.

"Why did you do that?" she asked. "Why can't he come this way?"

"He won't. Never goes out this way – never comes near this part of the house or," he paused as if thinking, "or, indeed, he never comes to this bit of the property, even though this part of the garden becomes wild and continues onto the moor."

"Really – now that *is* interesting. Animals are very psychic you know. Perhaps he can sense something here. Let me try although I'm not that good at it; Vivien is the one for that sort of thing."

She stood silently for a while. "No, I can sense nothing here but maybe further out." She walked to the end of the patio and continued questing.

"Actually," said Steven, watching her, "you may be right about animals. I remember, when I was young, when I was still living with my parents, we had two little terriers. Well, I was alone one evening, just reading, when I became aware that something was worrying the dogs. They were both sitting very alert and watching something. I couldn't see anything – thought it might be a spider but I couldn't see it anywhere. Anyway, they were, quite clearly, following something with their eyes. They both got up and went over to the door where they started growling. I opened the door, even though I was scared stiff, and they rushed out into the hallway, barking. Then they chased the 'thing', whatever it was, upstairs. I was only a kid and, believe me I was bloody terrified so I ran back into the sitting room and shut the door. Luckily, Mum and Dad came back and Dad went all over the house but there was nothing and the dogs settled down. God knows what they were seeing."

She continued trying to sense the energies, then shrugged. "Well, there you are then. They can see things we can't, just as a bat can hear things beyond our range. We have quite limited senses, in general. Let's continue the tour, shall we?"

They wandered out of the patio area and into the more formal gardens. She remarked upon their potential as they walked towards the side of the house where the garden became wild, merged into the trees and so on up to the moor. They entered the grove, the stream sparkling ahead of them.

"Pretty," she said. "Now if I owned the house, this would be my favourite spot." She pointed to the rocks around them.

"Funny, it's mine too now, although I felt uneasy originally. I prefer wild places. I never really understand this human obsession to impose order on Nature. Have you seen some of the gardens in the village? You could play billiards on their lawns – so neat and tidy; too clinical."

"You're only saying that because you don't like gardening, I bet."

He laughed. "Well, it's true I don't like gardening but that doesn't mean I don't like pottering around and having some tidy areas. I'm one of those instant gardeners; I buy plants from the garden centre and just stick them in. Voila! instant colour and no fuss."

Sela laughed. "Well, there you are. At least that's better than someone else I knew. They put plastic daffodils in their garden – in January. People kept stopping to look – couldn't understand how the daffs had come out so early."

She stood looking at the rocks, lost in thought, then said, "I like this jumble of rocks. Now I do feel something here – this is like an old sacred place." She held her hands over them and said, "Wow! These are buzzing. This is *really* special."

And indeed, it did seem special, particularly now that she was standing there, he caught himself thinking. The jumble of rocks, out of which the stream seemed to emanate, was set off, to advantage, by rhododendron plants and trees and he could see the beginning of buds all around. The rain of the day before had given Nature that extra boost and leaves were appearing everywhere.

"Have you a coin?" she said. "I'm always asking you that."

"Here," he pulled out a small silver coin. Sela took it and climbed up onto a long rock shelf. The breeze ruffled at her hair causing it to swirl about her and, as she stood contemplating the scene, he felt that she looked like a pagan priestess with her bangles and beads and flowing dress. He had that strange feeling again, that he was looking into the ancient past. She was silent for a moment then threw the coin into the water crying, "For the Gods!" She looked startled, turned to him and said, "Now, why did I say that? There you are, you see, intuition." She surveyed the grove. "You should make this your special place – you know – raise a statue, it's lovely and I do feel something here. It's strong but I'm not able to identify it. We'll get Vivien to have a prowl around. Where were they digging?"

He helped her down and they walked to the other part of the garden, through the gate and out onto the fields. "And this is all yours? My, my. Oh, is this them?"

"Yes," he said, "and here, and there."

"Hmm, strange," she said, "and they've not been back?"

"No, at least not that I know of, although I wonder who put that thing in the pot." He shivered involuntarily at the memory of the dead body of the rat.

"That would be, would have to be, Jane. She would have done it either before you were here or when you were out. Where's her land?" He pointed to the next field and Jane's house, the top of which could just be seen above the trees. "Yes, it would be easy for her to do it – any time really." Sela studied the location again and then they went back inside. "Yes, Jane could have done it easily. From the state of the rat's rotted body, it must have been already prepared. Perhaps she did it to get your aunt. Perhaps she tried with the note first and then with the Balarmine. Then she re-activated it when her pendant curse failed. Preparing such a powerful curse takes time. We'll never really know." For a short while she was silent, as though considering what to say. Then, in a musing tone, "Perhaps it was Jane, herself, stalking you in the woods."

He was startled. "But, there was nothing there. Just a sense of something horrible – like a panther or something."

Sela nodded. "Perhaps she shape-shifted… a sort of change of her form. Some of us have the skill, you know."

"What, like a vampire?" He eyed her, his voice nervous.

"In a way, yes. I use Tanith – a use of the astral body…" She saw the look in his eyes and hastened to re-assure him. "Don't think about it for now. It's a technique – I'll tell you more later – when you're ready. Are you sure you *want* to learn about this sort of thing?"

He nodded. "Yes, sure – absolutely. Apprehensive, but – yes."

"I tell you what," she said, "we'll reciprocate. I'll teach you, no, show you, otherwise I'm contradicting myself, show you a simple opening ceremony – casting the circle, yes? Some psychic self-defence. In turn, you show me some simple Karate-type self-defence – never know when a girl might need it."

"OK, fair enough." He laughed. "But couldn't you just zap someone?"

"No, not like that. It's not like the films you know. I don't just point a finger and a bolt of lightening flashes out. I could hex them though, but that wouldn't be any good for me if I was being mugged would it?"

She followed him into the orangery. "This is a brilliant room. Look at this chequered black and white floor as well – great!"

For the next hour she showed him how to prepare himself for a ceremony, similar to his own meditation practices. She explained about the elemental quarters and the use of creative visualisation and she wrote down some details.

"I use the image of Pegasus at the quarters," she said. "It's a beautiful image and it also provides me with balance, polarity, in my Moon Temple. Pegasus is a symbol of the sun, solar power; the winged horse was a very popular sign in Iron Age Britian. Balance, you see, sun and moon. I love the great white winged horse and I visualise him flying through the air in the eastern quarter or rising, phoenix like, from the fire in the south. In the west I have him splashing through a river and, in the north, I picture him galloping across the earth. Everyone does it differently. The common one is to visualise guardian angels. That's more to do with Kabalistic magic."

Standing in the centre of the room Sela made the sign of a cross saying, *"Ateh, Malkuth, Ve Geburah, Ve Gedulah, Le Olahm, Amen."* She then made another sign in the air, which he recognised as a pentagram and pointed her finger at it, crying out a word he did not understand. She did this three more times so that she had faced all of the compass points then, standing with her arms outstretched she cried aloud, *"Before me Raphael, behind me Gabriel, on my right Michael, on my left Uriel".*

"What was that?" he asked.

"The Banishing Ritual of the Pentagram," she said. "A ceremonial magic technique in which protective guardian angels are invoked. I use the pentagram but add a moon symbol and say something else. It's a way of opening the gateway if you like and, psychologically, it's very reassuring – gives a sense of protection. So, you see – many of the techniques have a similarity, no matter what system is used."

"Why do you use a pentagram?" he asked her.

"It represents the four elements plus spirit."

"But, why is it depicted as evil if it's upside down – you know, you see it associated with Black Magic?"

She sighed. "Yes, I know. It's just ignorance and sensationalism. Look!" She held out her finger upon which she was wearing a ring with an inscribed pentagram. "Which way up is it?"

"The star is upside down," he replied.

"To your view, yes – but to my view it's the other way up. It's all about interpretation, and there are many but it is an ancient sign and has nothing to do with Satan as the movies would have you believe. It is a symbol of Light and protection but, in the end, it is only a symbol. The intention and meaning lies within the mind of the practitioner."

Steven nodded then said, "It's funny but when you said that bit about guardian angels, I remembered that when I was young, and still a Roman Catholic, and if I got scared of ghosts or something, I used to visualise either St. Michael the Archangel or the Virgin Mary."

She clapped her hands and laughed. "Oh excellent, excellent, I said you were special."

"What do you mean?"

"St. Michael is a very powerful occult figure. Remember what I said at Glastonbury? Drives out the demons – and the Virgin Mary, well, there you are – an archetypal Goddess if ever there was one."

"But she's the Mother of God," he said.

"And who better to be a Goddess than the *Mother* of God? Look, Mary is only mentioned a couple of times in the Gospels and Jesus Himself refers to her as 'woman'. Mary was not seen as anything special until she was created 'Mother of God' at the Council of Ephesus – incidentally a long time centre of Goddess worship. You see, early Christians were following Judaic practices. Women weren't seen as important religious figures. In the Roman world as I told you, there was a plethora of practices, not the least the worship of the Goddess Isis. Do you know she wore blue and white, as well? I digress, anyway, when you can't change people's allegiance, change the deity to match their needs. For Isis read Mary. Look at the Madonna and Child then look at statues of Isis suckling Horus. So you're just an old Goddess follower after all. That's why Roman Catholicism has been so successful in the New World. The spirits and gods can be easily absorbed, equated if you like, with saints. All that ritual, robes, incense – brilliant. It's not surprising that many ceremonial magicians were once Catholics. Lapsed Catholics make wonderful pagans you know – and why not? They've been steeped in a sense of the spirit world, of another reality, from their very earliest years. What better initiation into the Mysteries could there be?"

Sela walked over to one of the windows and stood silently for a moment with her back to him. "Actually, I was just thinking," she said, turning round to look at him, "...those books which carry on about Jesus and Mary Magdalene – you know, the Merovingian blood line, descendants of Jesus and Mary – well, you couldn't have people walking around descended from Jesus if he really was divine, could you?"

"No, I suppose not," Steven replied. "He'd have to be only half a god, wouldn't he?"

"That's right. That's the trouble with all this desire to equate humans with the Divine. The vanity of humanity – hey that rhymes!"

"A poet and you don't know it," he said laughing.

"Oh, puh-leeze," she said, laughing as well. "Anyway Jesus would have had half of Mary's DNA, so it can't be – unless, of course, He just appeared on the scene at around thirty years of age and all the virgin birth stuff was just added on by the early Church in order to compete with other mystery cults."

He sat down on the floor looking up at her as she talked. She was always so full of enthusiasm about her subject and he found himself wanting to learn as much as he could from her. "You know when you were doing the ceremony, well, I understand about the elements but what was the bottle at the eastern quarter?"

"Ah, well, I thought to myself, Air, how can I represent it? So I got an old glass perfume bottle, cleaned it out and put the stopper back in. Air enclosed in a glass bottle; not bad, eh? The stone at the southern quarter is a meteorite, so that accounts for Fire; the other two, Water and Earth are obvious, yes?"

"Yes." He watched her as she walked around the orangery. In a way, Sela was a bit of a throw-back in her dress style. So far she always wore flowing skirts and T-shirts over which she wore a long sleeved three-quarter length knitted jacket which fell below her waist. With the numerous rings, bangles and pendant she would certainly not have looked out of place in swinging, hippy London. Suddenly he felt an overwhelming desire to be with her and said, "How would you like to go for a meal tonight?" No harm in asking her that, surely?

She seemed taken aback but pleased. "Oh! Well, yeah, OK. Where?"

He named a small restaurant in the village. "Will you have to go home to feed Tanith?" She said she would but not until around 4 o'clock. He looked at his watch, plenty of time for a walk so he suggested a stroll to the beach.

They wandered down the high hedgerowed lane and found themselves out on the vast shingle ridge that swept along the whole of Porlock Bay. Beneath the enormous sweep of the misty sky, the furthest limits of the shoreline merged with the hazy forelands, which jutted out into the grey and white surf. There was a coming and going of sound coinciding with the ebbing and flowing of the constant waves, as they pushed and pulled at the shingle barrier. Sela stood upon a high point which, Steven saw, was the remnants of a wartime building of some sort.

She folded her coat closer around her body, a protection from the stiff, cold, breeze but she did not raise her hood, allowing her red hair to flare around her in billowing, copper waves. As he looked at her standing there in her green-coloured coat, he recalled how she had invoked the elemental forces of Air, Water, Fire and Earth in the Moon Temple. Steven began to understand, more fully, Sela's close affinity with the powers of Nature. In the woodland valley he had perceived this link but, out here beneath the sky, with the rolling hills of the moor embracing them; with the surging power of the sea engaged in its everlasting quest to reclaim the land; with the pale sun lighting her hair so that it glowed like copper fire, Steven saw the elemental powers coming together. He felt that Sela *could* take these forces and, somehow, blend them together within herself in order to utilise their stored potency as an expression of her Will.

"You should come here just after a storm," she said. "It's amazing."

He came out of his reverie and helped her down. "Oh, I have. I sometimes bring Perry here – he loves it."

"Does he try to go in the water? It can be very dangerous you know."

"No, Perry just rushes up and down along the edge of the waves. He's not very adventurous."

"He's lovely," she replied. "Clearly he dotes on you."

"Well – yes but I feed him, don't I?"

"No," she laughed, "it's more than that. Animals know if you really care or not and, unlike some humans, they'll always be loyal to you."

They continued their inconsequential chatter as they made their way from the beach back towards Porlock. The walk was enjoyable to Steven. Sela knew so much about the countryside, about plants, birds, country life. She was a veritable mine of information. "I'm just an old hedgewitch," she said. Clearly she felt relaxed with him but did this mean he was in with a chance of a more personal relationship? He was surprised at his thoughts. It was as though something was driving him down a path. There was an inevitability about it all, as though they had to be together.

That afternoon, when Sela had returned home to Tanith, he went over in his mind what she had shown him. He went into the orangery and practised casting the circle and calling up the elements, referring now and then, to the notes that she had provided for him. It was strange, though, that whenever he tried to visualise the elements, as she had told him to do, the image of Sela kept coming into his mind and, from that time on, he knew that he would always associate those elemental powers with her. He would not use the imagery of Pegasus, as she did. He would use, instead, the image of Sela, standing there upon the beach, between earth, sea and sky, like a pagan priestess of Nature and of Mother Earth. Feeling energised he went through a series of martial arts exercises, telling himself that he must get back into training again. In this way he passed the time until he was ready to pick up Sela.

CHAPTER 15

She had obviously taken time to get ready and was wearing a red and black outfit which made her look extremely attractive, he found himself thinking. He was glad that he, too, had made an effort and felt he looked quite good in his suede leather jacket, beige trousers and tan shoes.

"My, my, you dress up well," she laughed.

"I should be complimenting you," he said. "OK, so we've both made an effort. Let's hope the food matches our hard work."

"What do you mean 'hard work'? Are you saying I generally look a mess? No, don't answer that." She put on a strong country accent. "Down 'ere we gets an ol' sack and shoves it over our 'eads. A good ol' pair of gum boots and we'ze ready, arrh!"

Steven chuckled. "You sound like a bad take-off of 'The Archers'. Funny though, your accent isn't that strong. I think the West Country accent is fading away. Take Jane; very public school." They walked down to the restaurant along the quiet road. There was not a soul in sight and the lights of the restaurant were warm and welcoming. There was one other customer in the room.

"Hallo Steven, hallo Marian," said Paul Hammond. "Try the moules meunière – delicious." The doctor was just paying his bill. "How are things at the house?"

"Fine," Steven lied. "Everything's just perfect."

"Oh good, and how are you, Marian?" asked the doctor. "Still brewing your potions?" He said this with a slight chuckle, eyeing her with evident amusement.

Marian didn't laugh. "Well, at least mine don't cause dependency like some of the stuff you give out." Steven noted the hostility in her voice.

"Oh dear, tetchy, tetchy." The doctor put on his coat and said, "Perhaps you need to read the runes or something – help find your way, ha ha!" He left the restaurant. They sat down.

"Well, what on earth was that all about?" Steven asked.

"Oh, he's one of the old type of doctors. Doesn't agree with complimentary therapies. Thinks its all mumbo jumbo. I've had some serious disagreements with him – doesn't like herbal treatments or healing by touch – that sort of thing."

"Why? Did you give one of his patients something?"

"Yes, and she got better, much to his annoyance. Said it was all in her mind – these doctors won't accept new practices." She paused. "Actually, I'm being a bit unfair. The village G.P. *does* encourage complimentary

The Moon Temple

practices and there's a big practice in Minehead which does, as well. Some of them are a bit more willing to try alternatives but most – *most,* don't. They think only they have the answers – like some occultists remember? Do you know him?"

Steven nodded. "Well, he treated Rita. I've met him a few times. He knows Jane as well. He was at the cocktail party she invited me to."

"Well that's not a surprise. He's lived here forever. Everyone knows everyone here and everyone *knows* about everyone. You can't have a secret – look at you and your trouble in the pub – everyone knew about it." They opened the menu. "Are we having starters?" she asked.

"Yes, anything you like. Ah, they've got avocado with prawns; what about the moules?" He pointed to the menu board on which were written some specialities.

"No, I don't like the idea that they're alive when put in the pot. Same way I can't eat lobster. I know it's a bit inconsistent 'cos I like fish and meat but, well, they're killed differently."

"Well, it's all pretty sick really isn't it. I mean everything is alive, unless you're one of those vegans, you know, those ones who only eat things which have dropped off trees."

They studied the menu sipping gin and tonics. In the end, she had soup followed by venison steak; Steven had the avocado and also had the venison. He complimented it with a good red wine and soon they were tucking in.

"Umm, this is a nice wine," she said.

"Yes, it is. It's a Merlot blended with Cabernet."

"Oh, do you know a lot about wine? I rarely drink it 'cos I don't go out much and I never buy it; I make my own."

"No, I don't know a lot about wines. I think there's quite a lot of pretentiousness about the whole thing. I just like certain wines; but you said you make your own." He was genuinely interested and continued, "I've always fancied doing that but never got round to it; what do you make?"

"Oh, rhubarb, elderflower that sort of thing. I do an occasional sloe gin."

"Aha! I'd like a drop of that." He was silent for a while and then said, "Do you like the music they're playing?" The voice of Nina Simone was crooning gently in the background.

"Yes. She's very soulful; lots of feeling – she was quite political as well – African-American rights. I admire her."

He looked at her and said, "And are you political?" He thought it might be a good idea to see where she stood, especially now that he knew something of Jane Trethowan's political leanings.

She shook her head. "No, not really. I would be, I suppose, if there was a viable Green Party down here."

"What about Jane Trethowan's views?"

Sela gave an exasperated gesture. "No, too extreme; all that separatist nonsense. I don't go with that. Lots of people seem to support her though, even Sir Roger Martin – you know, the local big-wig, seems interested. She attracts those who have other axes to grind, like some of the pro-hunting lobby who think she'll protect their interests."

He remembered the groping hand of Roger Martin on Jane's body, noting that the unpleasant memory no longer upset him. "You're against hunting I take it?" he said.

"Yes, but I do like meat. It bothers me, you know, the way things are killed. I suppose I'm a bit of a hypocrite really – you know, let someone else do the killing. The trouble is, it tastes so good." She continued, "I do wonder about it all – that we kill to eat. The whole mystery of the creation thing bothers me. Look, if you were an omnipotent Being would you make it so that the only way to stay alive is to kill other things? I mean, why can't we just gulp air or something or why do we need anything at all?" She looked at him, earnestly, "It all seems so cruel."

He nodded. "Yes, if you look at those nature films, things are always killing other things or having sex. I wouldn't want to be a gazelle. Everything, but everything is after you – or a wildebeest." He sliced into his venison steak, thoughtfully.

"It's all about 'the Great Divine Plan'," she made quote signs. "We're all, in the end, consuming energy – sunlight. Everything needs sunlight in some form or another. Plants need the sun, animals eat the plants, we eat the animals or the plants – all converted into sunlight-generated energy." She put down her knife and fork as she spoke and took a sip of wine.

Steven considered her words then said, "What about those shrimps that live deep down in the sea around those thermal vents? They're not living on sunlight."

"Well, in a way they are, if you consider that the planet was probably converted out of stellar matter which eventually coalesced into our sun."[*] She was silent for a while and then said, "It's a nice place, do you usually come here?"

"Not often. I used to come here with Ginny and sometimes with Rita; nice little place. It's changed hands since I was last here, though. The menu's more varied and the music is certainly better."

They munched on through their meal mainly in companionable silence interspersed with general chit-chat. He felt more and more comfortable with her and she seemed to be enjoying his company. They talked about films, music, T.V., books and had similar, but not identical, tastes in many areas although in terms of music she liked a lot of the more recent groups.

"It's interesting isn't it?" he observed. "People tend to be fond of music that has a special meaning at particular times in their lives."

"Yes, Bowie was big when I was a student."

"Well, I like him also – a real original talent."

---

[*] The Last Hours of Ancient Sunlight – Thom Hartman

He returned to the matter of Jane Trethowan. Her attack on him had caused a sense of confusion in his mind. If everything Sela had said about Jane's psychic attack was true and if she was responsible for the death of his aunt, he had to try to understand what lay behind her motives and of these he had only a vague idea. "Look," he said, "this Jane Trethowan thing – her wanting my land, is it all linked with her politics?"

"I don't know." She looked at him thoughtfully and continued, "She's got this thing about self-determination for what she terms are the 'true people' of Britain and there are those who will follow her. I went to one of her talks in the village hall; Roger Martin was there, giving his support. He's quite odd you know. Anyway, it was a bit silly – at least, I thought it was. She wants a pan-Celtic state incorporating all the West Country, Wales and she even has contacts with people in Brittany. I don't know what she's doing about Ireland – not that she'd stand much of a chance with that lot."

Steven said, "OK, but are you sure it's so bad? There's nothing wrong in wanting to promote a certain type of culture – a Celtic culture, is there? Haven't the Welsh and the Scots got devolved government?"

"Devolution is one thing; total independence is something else. Anyway, what *is* Celtic? There's a whole debate about that you know; it's very confused. The Ancient Greeks talked about Keltoi, a particular tribe of people, but it doesn't mean that *all* the people of Europe, apart from the Germans, were of the same group. There were similarities in weaponry and artwork in some but not all. In any case, the so-called Celts came to these islands not as one invading force but over centuries and found an indigenous population already here – the ones that had raised the stone circles. So who does she mean by 'true people'? The whole Celtic thing only came about in the nineteenth century, a sort of Romantic movement.

"But there is a recognisable form of Celtic music, poetry, art, that sort of thing isn't there?"

"Well, I suppose so, yes, but it's the term 'Celt' that's wrong. A great many of the Irish and people of Scotland have Norse blood in their veins and as for the British race – well, what race? These islands are made up of so many incoming groups – over centuries and centuries. It's all ridiculous; even the royal family is German, I think."

"Hmmm! Yes – confusing isn't it?" He took another sip of wine.

"Anyway," she said, "I suppose I'm what would be termed as typically Celtic aren't I?"

"It was my first impression when I saw you," he said, "– the hair."

"Ah, yes," she replied, "can't do much about that.

There was a lull and then she asked him about Ginny. "Only if you want to talk about it though."

"No, it's OK. It's been a while now. God, it does go fast doesn't it? But at the time it was terrible. She got breast cancer, had a mastectomy but it spread and then, suddenly, she was gone – just like that. Terrible and so, so sad. She was full of life, funny, intelligent – all gone just like that." He paused then went on, "I was devastated, lost, almost gave up – I didn't think I'd manage." He remembered the two of them, sitting with Rita, in the same restaurant – seemingly so long ago, now.

Sela nodded in sympathy. "Yes, when you lose someone it's so devastating isn't it? I know it's not the same thing but when Chris left me I felt as though the world had collapsed around me."

"What happened?" He poured some more wine for them both, finishing the bottle. "Shall we have another?" he asked.

"No, I'm fine," she said, then continued. "Oh, he was married. Had two, no three children but was unhappy – no, really he was – I knew them both. She had MS – in remission for a while then she got really ill and he had to go back; duty and all that. One day he was there then gone."

"How did you cope?"

"You have to, don't you? God, why do we love? It's like an addiction, a terrible need and then it ends and you fall apart." She drank her wine, put the glass down and continued her meal.

"So," he said, "both of us – wounded and still here."

She smiled sadly and nodded, "Yes, still here."

Again he wondered about her life, up there in the valley, just her and a cat.

"Do you get lonely?" he asked, then regretted it as, clearly, this implied an assumption that she had little social life.

She paused, before replying and picked some candle wax off the side of the holder. "Being alone doesn't mean that I'm lonely. I *like* my own company." It sounded like a reproach and he was about to interject, to apologise, for the implication behind his question but she went on. "Being alone, up there, with all of Nature around me, helps me to pursue my spiritual path without too much distraction. God, that sounds pretentious doesn't it? I don't mean it to, only you need peace if you're going to follow my path." She paused then said, "That doesn't mean I exclude all other things and I did have Chris – but he didn't really follow my way of thinking. When I look back now, I don't know how we stayed together – just physical, I suppose, but he was very egocentric; childlike at times."

"Do you still miss him?"

"Sometimes – you can't be with someone for a while and not miss them can you? As I said, you have to cope."

He remembered lying in bed with Ginny and nodded, "Yes, you're right; you just get on with it."

"Anyway…" she went on, still moulding the wax into little pellets – she pulled the candle closer to her and began picking off other solidified waxen chips. "…Anyway, being alone gives me opportunities to achieve a sort of inner peace. Where I live is really beautiful and I don't need much to enjoy it all. So, I'm not really alone, am I? I've got it all – my cottage, my cat and Mother Nature watching over me."

He saw the flame flickering and dancing with the breath of her words, the light glinting on the rings of her fingers. She put the wax pellets into the holder and pushed it from her into the middle of the table. "In any case," she said, "I do go out with friends, occasionally." She seemed defensive.

"Oh, yes, yes, I'm sure," he said. "I didn't mean to imply that you never went anywhere." He tailed off, feeling foolish.

She laughed. "Why, are you interested?" Very bold and direct.

He was taken aback and stammered, "Well, I didn't mean to imply…"

"So you're not. Oh woe is me." She rested her head in her hands in a mock gesture of despair.

"No, no, I mean, yes, I would like to see you a bit more but… Oh, I don't want to mess this up. I'd like to be, well, more than just friends – if you see what I mean." He hoped he hadn't ruined things now. He felt really anxious. How would she react? Would she see him as too old?

As though answering his unspoken thoughts, she said, "No, it's OK." Then she feigned a serious tone, "I'm not looking for a father figure you know, even though you are quite old – you make too much of that you know." She laughed, "Yes I'd like us to go out. I feel that we get on really well, don't you? Anyway, we have a strong mystical bond now. We're spiritual friends, soul mates."

Relieved, he smiled, his face lighting up.

"Aah," she said, "that's nice. That's the first really proper smile I've seen on you."

"Well, I was a bit worried about the age gap, thirteen years is quite a lot.

"I'm older than Time," she said, softly, gazing into his eyes. For a moment he looked at her realising that she might, indeed, be right, at least in the things she knew. Again, he felt that strange atavistic tug at the back of his mind. Sela had the capacity to seem completely otherworldly, at times, and this could be unsettling.

They decided not to have a dessert but to have coffee with a liqueur. As she was uncertain about what to drink, he suggested Strega. "In Italian, Strega means witch," he said, "this is supposed to be a witch's drink."

"Aah – very apt," she said, laughing.

"I've really enjoyed this evening," he said. "This is the first time I've really been out for ages." He savoured the sweet liqueur and toasted her. "Thanks," he said and he finished the drink.

She smiled, seriously this time. "I'm glad, no, I really am." She reached over and rested her hand on his. He put his other hand over hers cupping it. They said nothing but she didn't remove her hand and he felt a sense of excitement and desire run through him. She looked down at their cupped hands and said, "How about getting the bill?"

Walking back slowly through the village in silence, she stopped and said, "Look, don't take me home – no," seeing the sudden disappointed look on his face, "no, I mean, let's go back to Hawkwood. Tanith can look after herself – she's out most of the night but Perry needs to be tucked in." She reached up and touched his face, gently. He pulled her towards him and they kissed. As they pulled apart she said, "O zurr – oi'll be the tahk o' the village."

Back at Hawkwood Steven saw to Perry's needs, locked up the house and then turned to Sela embracing her. They kissed, again, and then she said, "I don't want coffee, I'd rather visit that great big Master Bedroom of yours." She moved away from him and before he realised it she was halfway up the stairs. "Race you," she called over her shoulder giggling.

"We'll see about that," and he was soon after her.

They tumbled onto the bed and, in a flurry of clothing, embraces and kisses, Steven found himself making quick, urgent love to her. It was as though all the fear, anxiety and tension of the previous days coalesced into a driving burst of exuberant energy and the two of them were soon lying together panting for breath and smiling at each other.

"Wowee!" she said, catching her breath.

He leaned over her and kissed her, gently stroking her face and running his fingers through her hair. "God, I haven't felt like that for years" he said. Then, remembering Jane, he added, "Well, not like *that* anyway. I felt I was sixteen again."

"Yep – not bad for a wise, old, Karate master," she smiled at him. Then, "I know what you're thinking – about your encounter with Miss Trethowan – well, don't. It's not the same. You had no control over that. I told you – it's a witch trick."

"No, you're right. This *was* special." He kissed her again and looked at her as she lay with her copper hair spread over the pillow, framing her pale face. "You look like a Celtic princess." He caressed her shoulders and traced the outlines of the tattoos, visible on her upper arms. "What are these?"

She pointed to the one on her left arm. "This one is the triple moon, a symbol of Lunar power, and this one," she indicated the unusual design on her right arm, "this is a triscalis, a symbol of the sun, or Solar power. Do you think they're common, you know, like an old dock worker?"

"No, I think they're sexy – very wild and pagan. A bit butch though. Still, I know you're not that even if you did go with Viv." He lay back on the pillow.

"What, gay you mean? No, I like – love men – any man, old – young – dying – dead – anything, as long as it's a maaaan!" She grabbed hold of him hard.

"Ouch!" he cried.

"Sorry – I get a bit carried away – Vivien's influence, I think."

"I hope not." He held her to him and felt himself becoming aroused again. Instead of responding to him, she disengaged herself from him gently and then said,

"No, not here, this is special. I want us to go into the orangery. I have a feeling about this Steven – something special – you and me against the Dark."

He looked at her, not understanding but ready to go and do whatever she wanted. She got out of bed and wrapped the bedcover around herself like a cloak. He got up and put on his dressing gown and followed her down the stairs to the orangery.

The moon was shining into the room and she went and stood in the moonlight letting the cover slip to the floor. She had her back to him facing out into the moonlit garden and she raised her arms up towards the round, shining, orb. She was silent for a while and he stood looking at her still, white, form, which was partly concealed by the thick waves of hair flowing down her back. He was about to go to her but stopped as, suddenly, she said in a firm strong voice,

"I call to you, my Sister of the Night,
As from the void and darkness all about
Descends a silver rain of shining light
To fall upon this place and seek me out."

He watched her, aware that something potent was taking place and he felt a feeling, similar to pins and needles beginning to prickle over his body as she continued her invocation.

"My soul is set afire like burning flame
As, from the depths of earth a force has come
To tear my spirit free from mortal frame,
To leave my body empty cold and numb."

She turned to face him and stood, legs astride and arms raised at her side, palms towards him in an Egyptian-like pose.

"And so, transfigured, tasting my rebirth,
I wing through space across the aeons of Time,
With all the elemental powers of Earth,
To take that silver crown and make it mine."

She opened her eyes and looked directly at him. He could see the glint of reflected moonlight within her eyes and, with some of her hair coiling over her shoulders and over her breasts in serpentine folds, he was reminded of the image of the Goddess statue he had seen on her altar.

"For I can feel the cosmic power in me;
A force and brightness fiercer than the sun;
Immortal, now, I face my destiny,
Thus, Goddess of the Earth and Moon are one."

She finished in a high shout, paused and then knelt on the bed covering, raising her arms towards him.

He felt an incredible wave of desire engulf him and he went to her and lay on her, entering her as she writhed and bucked beneath him. He was lost in her, in the magic of her and then he felt her move and twist and then he was behind her beast-like, caught in the frenzy of rampant sexuality. He seemed inexhaustible, lustful, potent beyond his understanding, full of the joy of truly liberated sexual congress. And then he felt her moving, bucking, writhing; heard her moaning and panting and then she gave a long cry as, together, they reached an overwhelming, all encompassing peak of fulfilment, uniting them in a seeming burst of cosmic energy. Spent, he collapsed to the ground beside her as she lowered herself and nestled her back against him. He held her close, both of them breathing heavily and he kissed her neck and her hair. She turned to him and he kissed her lips and her closed eyes. She opened them and he looked into their depths seeing his image reflected there. The sense of having been one with her came to him again and Steven knew that their love-making had been more than a mere union between a mortal man and a mortal woman. It had been a momentary merging of two Spirits and he knew he had been, for a brief time, within the realms of the Gods.

They lay together, exhausted, until their heavy breathing subsided. Sela leaned towards him and kissed him then said, "Brrr – getting chilly." She rose, gathered up the cover and padded out of the orangery and back up to the bedroom. She dived into the bed and snuggled against him as he held her tenderly, his mind re-running the images of the orangery.

"Tell me," he said, "what was that – that poem – what we did?"

She smiled. "It's a way of helping you to meet the Goddess; it's known as 'Drawing Down, or Calling Down, the Moon' in Wiccan circles but it's a very old technique – very powerful and magical. If used in a ceremony and with purpose then, at the moment of orgasm a spell is flung out – the creation of what has been termed a 'magical child' or, if you like, an outcome. Enormously effective but, in this case, I wanted you to meet the Goddess and for you to feel your own earthly power. A possession, in your case, by Pan, if you like. I wanted us to seal our relationship, make us closer. Did you mind?"

"Mind? God, no, wonderful." He kissed her and lay back holding her in his arms.

After a while he said, "I feel absolutely amazing; you haven't hexed me I hope, because, if you have, I don't care."

She leaned on one elbow and looked at him. "Do you seriously think I'd do that to you? No, no need to, my beauty and charm speak volumes without all of that witchy hexing stuff." She lay back down and snuggled into him again.

He was silent for a while and lay stroking her body. He said, "If this was an old black and white movie we'd be puffing on cigarettes. Do you smoke?"

"Nah," she said, "don't like it." He could feel her breath against his shoulder as she spoke.

"What about pot?" He asked.

"I've tried it in cakes, that sort of thing. Doesn't appeal to me. What about you?"

"No, don't smoke. Like you, I tried it in cakes and chewed some resin. I had too much, once and had a bad experience so I didn't bother any more. Too introspective; I prefer drink but that caused problems for me."

She nodded against his shoulder. "Yes, I understand; alcohol can cause a lot of problems."

They lay silently together and he was conscious that her breathing was becoming deeper and more regular. He felt his arm getting cramped and moved to ease it.

She opened her eyes, kissed him and then said, "Oh, I'm exhausted." Suddenly she was asleep.

He listened to her soft breathing as she nestled against him. He marvelled at his good fortune then remembered the reasons that had led to their meeting and the shadow of Jane's memory clouded his happiness. He looked at Sela as she lay against him, her face peaceful in repose, and, with that image in his mind and the memory of her giving warmth, he, too, was soon asleep.

Steven awoke to her soft caress and her head nestling in on his shoulder and so, as the sunlight poked its busy inquisitive fingers between the gaps of the curtains, they melded into each other's physical and spiritual selves and he knew, for the first time since Ginny, the wonderful power of love between two people who cared deeply for one another.

CHAPTER 16

They passed the next days in blissful enjoyment of each other's company, engaged in a mutual journey of discovery. As they wandered the moors and valleys of Exmoor, his already awakened sense of the spiritual blossomed like a tree bearing the promise of fruit. She was delighted at his capacity to grasp hold of the ideas she expressed. "Yes, you see, I said that you had great power within you. You seem to belong here."

"I belong here because you're here," he said and she kissed him. He looked into her eyes. "I feel as though you've awoken things that were sleeping within me. You've made me see the world in such a different way – you make the whole forest and the hills vibrate, come alive in a way I've never experienced before." He paused then said, "You're a very spiritual woman, you know."

"Why thank you, kind sir," she said. "The trouble is I tend to lose myself in the spiritual side of things, the mystical, and lose sight of the necessities of material life as well. Like I said to you, being alone isn't always a bad thing but then you get a bit lost. I forget to maintain a sense of balance – something I'm always supposed to be striving for." They were half-way up the side of a wooded hill and she stopped, as she said this, turning to face him. "Perhaps now you're with me I'll achieve that."

He shook his head. "No, you certainly intervened on the material plane when you offered your help to me." He put his arms around her and felt her relax against him so that he could feel the beating of her heart.

She looked up at him and said, "That was all to do with the spiritual, psychic world. It was fated that we should meet but for what great purpose I don't know as yet. Let's hope Vivien can give us some clues." She pulled back from him and kissed him again.

They climbed to the top of a high, moorland hill and Steven gave an exclamation of pleasure. "Ah! So beautiful and wild. Sometimes I feel I could just lift off and fly to the heavens – sounds silly doesn't it?"

"No, not really. Perhaps your spirit self remembers another existence. Perhaps you could fly, once."

He looked at her puzzled. "What do you mean?"

"We all have spirit animals – totems if you like. Mine is the white winged horse – yours, well, yours is a hawk; I've seen it, sensed it. You are the hawk. It will protect you – help you. It will come to you when you are at your lowest – it *will* protect you – remember what I said about shape-shifting?"

He was puzzled. "I don't understand."

"You will – one day." She didn't add to this enigmatic reply and continued down to a lower stretch of moorland.

"God, this is lovely, isn't it?" Steven said, looking at the rising moorland behind them down which they had just scrambled. The moor divided off into separate coombs, each one covered with dense forest. Where they were standing was like an amphitheatre and he remarked on this.

"You're right," she said. "This is a sort of natural temple – we'll have to come here again." She looked around her and nodded. "Yes, we'll come here again and you're right, it is lovely. You can feel the earth's power here, can't you? Let's ask for a sign, shall we – something to bless us – yes?" She looked at him earnestly and he wondered what she meant.

"OK – whatever you say."

Sela held her arms out and cried, "Mother Earth, Mother Earth – we honour you, give us your blessing – we are part of you, born of you. We are your children." She stopped speaking and stood with her arms spread wide and her eyes closed.

Steven, uncertain of what to do, waited as a breeze rose and swirled around them. He felt his pulse quicken. Was that it? Had she raised the wind? He heard a rustling from nearby and the movement of heavy bodies. Heart pounding, he turned to see three Exmoor ponies climbing up out of the coomb. Sela opened her eyes and gave an exclamation of pleasure. "You see. She heard us. Three horses. I said that my totem was a horse didn't I."

"Well – yes, but you said a white winged horse – these are a sort of dull brown."

"Oh, don't be so literal. After all …" She stopped, as from out of the bushes stepped a large white horse. It was not an Exmoor pony. Quite clearly this was a well-groomed horse and it had a halter with a trailing lead. Sela went to it and stroked it. "Oh, isn't it beautiful? So, what do you say now, Mr. Sceptic? A white horse – see?"

There was some more rustling and scrabbling and a rider appeared on a black horse. It was Fiona Thurlow, looking elegant, if a bit dishevelled. It was obvious that she had been in some sort of accident for her riding clothes were muddy and she had a graze on her cheek. "Oh, hallo again," she said. "Thank goodness – you've got him. I took a tumble and he broke loose. I've been trying to get hold of him for the last hour."

"Are you O.K?" asked Steven.

"Yes, no problem," replied Fiona. She did not acknowledge Sela but took hold of the halter. "Come, Pegasus," she said and trotted off down the trail.

Steven watched them disappear and turned to Sela. "OK," he said. "You got your white horse."

She said nothing for a while, only staring down the trail to the place where the rider and horses had melded into the trees. Then she turned to him and smiled. "Well, then. There, you see – my white horse. But it's more than that. Didn't you hear what she called him? Pegasus, she called him Pegasus."

"Yes – so?"

"Pegasus is the name of the white winged horse in the legend – my totem and my Solar guardian."

"Yes – yes, you're right." He looked at her in astonishment. "Is that a sign then – I suppose it must be?"

They began to descend the trail and Sela said, "Yes, a sign – a blessing and a reaffirmation, if you like. We have been blessed as Children of the Earth Mother and of the living sun." She negotiated a tricky slope then said, "You seem to know that woman. She looked familiar to me but I couldn't place her."

"Oh, that's Fiona Thurlow. She used to be a top model."

"Ah – yes, I thought I recognised her but couldn't remember. But, do you know her?"

"I met her at Jane's, that's all – and her husband."

Sela said nothing more and, as they continued down towards Hawkwood, Steven considered the event. It had been a strange occurrence he had to admit but he felt a little uneasy. The sign, the blessing, as Sela called it, had been marred by the intrusion of Jane in the form of Fiona but, as Sela had made no further comment, he felt it couldn't have been important. He dismissed his feelings of unease as they arrived back at the house.

That night, as they were about to go to bed, Sela said, "Have you ever been out on the moor at night?"

"No, I've never had the time. Anyway, it's difficult to see and, if I'm honest, I'd probably find it a bit spooky being a city boy and all that."

She laughed. "Let's go out now. The moon's still bright and you'll love it. You're with me – I know my way. Come on, I dare you."

Taken by her evident enthusiasm and not wanting to be seen as a wimp, he agreed and soon the two of them were ascending a stony moonlit path which led to the open moorland where they had seen the white horse. The moon was high in the sky and it's light was enough to form strong shadows against the varied shades of grey and white which marked out rocks and vegetation. They stood on a high point of the open ground and Sela gestured around her and up at the sky. "Look, look at it all. I said we'd come back here. Isn't it just the best thing in the world? And the silence – no cars – nothing. What do you think?"

He looked all around and then up to the canopy of stars above them. "You're right. You never see these in the city. Do you know what they are?"

Sela sat on a rock and pointed out various constellations, she then pointed at the moon and said, "She's on the wane now. Some say that it's a time to work bad magic or to banish things that are harmful. Again, it depends how you look at it. It could be taken as a movement towards a new beginning for everything is a cycle – death and rebirth. Like I said, what's good for some could be bad for someone else."

"Do you work up here – in the moonlight?"

"Sometimes, yes. Of course, I've got my garden and Temple – but here, under the stars it's different."

"What do you do? The same sort of thing?"

"Yes, but without all the tools. Just a fire – perhaps some incense and candles and a wand. You don't need all the other bits and, oh yes – perhaps a small drum to accompany a chant."

"What sort of chant? Do you mean a spell?" He had a memory of her standing in the moonlight, naked, turning to him in the orangery.

She nodded and said softly, almost in a whisper, "Yes, naked in the moonlight, I weave my spell."

He was startled, once again, at her ability to link into his thoughts. She continued to speak, softly now, as though to herself. "I'd light a fire, say, here…" She rose from the rock and knelt down on the ground, indicating a small circle of stones in which were the charred remains of other fires. "I'd take my drum and start my chant, to make the spell come through – perhaps one like this."

Sela knelt back on her heels and started to tap one hand on her lap, in an insistent rhythm. She closed her eyes as she continued to beat her hand on her thigh. Then she opened her eyes, looked up at the moon and began to chant;

"In the deep of night, Selene,
Shining, silver, ghost of light,
Artemis and wild Hecate
Call to me upon this night.
Come, then, powers my brain is reeling
Let your arrows pierce me deep;
Come, then, powers let savage feelings
Stir my soul from waking sleep.
Oh, you forces come, release me
From this dull and lifeless world;
Stir that place so hidden, deadly,
Where the Serpent Power lies curled."

She rose from her heels into an upright kneeling posture and began a sinuous swaying movement of her body.

"Through my body, twisting, turning
Mounting swiftly, rising free;
Till my blood runs hot and burning
With the heat of ecstasy."

As Steven watched her and listened to her he felt a prickling sensation running through him and up his spine.

> *"Ah! My body yearns for pleasure,*
> *Find me, grasp me, make me shout;*
> *Delve and taste the hidden treasure,*
> *Stroke and touch within, without."*

She looked from the moon to him and he felt caught by her compelling gaze. He moved towards her filled with that same wild passion that had taken him when they had been together in the orangery. He knelt in front of her and there was a faint smile on her lips as she looked away from him and back up at the moon, continuing with the chant, her body now moving in a serpentine manner.

> *"Now my mind with wild thoughts raving*
> *Roars and flames with lustful fire,*
> *Greedy for you, drunk with craving,*
> *Drowning in this mad desire.*
> *Blend now find yourself inside me,*
> *Join and feel the power flow,*
> *Through my moist and writhing body,*
> *Draw it out and let it go."*

Her words became faster and her voice rose

> *"Speak the words of mystic meaning,*
> *Set your thoughts upon the goal,*
> *Fling them out unto that gleaming*
> *Symbol of my secret soul.*
> *To the realms of wild Hecate*
> *Turn my eyes to Her until,*
> *All the power that lies inside me*
> *Forms and flies to do my Will!"*

As she came to the end, she flung her arms up to the moon and then opened them to him, her eyes bright, her lips moist. She looked alien, wild, as though it was not Sela before him but some strange, elemental, moorland Spirit who had, somehow, taken her place. Mixed feelings raced through his brain in rapid sequence, as he knelt before her – feelings of raging desire and fear, yes, fear – the fear of the unknown; ancient memories; atavistic memories; the fear of the witch. Steven knew that Sela had raised the Serpent Power, Kundalini. She had bewitched him, as she had bewitched him in the orangery – given way to that temptation which was always there in magic. But it didn't matter now for he also knew, instinctively, that the magic had been in him as well, there all the time, Sela had merely evoked it and awoken it.

He said nothing as he took her in his arms. She responded to him and gave herself to him there and then, upon the damp, stony, moon-shadowed ground of the moor – and it was the most natural of things for they were wild creatures, part of Nature and of the earth on which they lay – Children of the Goddess. He was potent and she was passionate beneath him and, then, on him – and the moonlight was in her hair and in her eyes and the stars were a jewelled crown around her head.

When it was over and they made their way back to Hawkwood, neither said anything. It was as if each understood by silent, mutual consent, that nothing *needed* to be said. But he remembered her standing in her Moon Temple and then the last lines of her pendant spell came to him as though she was speaking to him, in his thoughts.

> *"The moon's glow bathing both with eerie light,*
> *It's potent softness flowing through their bodies*
> *Twists and eddies, snake-like, in their souls*
> *As, stepping out beneath the stars of Heaven,*
> *The Priest and Priestess walk their mystic path."*

He knew, then, that the spell was complete and that he was truly in union with Sela.

The Cycle of Eternity

CHAPTER 17

Too soon, it seemed to Steven, their time together drew to an end. Today Vivien would arrive and Sela needed to see to Tanith and prepare a room for her friend. It was agreed that they would come over to Steven after lunch, allowing some time for the two women to catch up on things. Before she left he asked her, "Are you going to tell her about us?"

"Of course, do you mind? She'll ask me anyway and will have assumed we had a thing going on. Vivien would never believe that men and women could be just friends."

"Do you think they can?" he asked.

"Of course, don't you? I had a very good male friend and we went around together – no sex. It just didn't arise and, before you ask, he wasn't gay. Was married and had a mistress or two. It wasn't anything to do with me not fancying him or him not fancying me – it just didn't occur to us. Haven't you ever had a woman friend then?"

Steven thought for a while. "Well, no, not a close friend but Ginny did have a friend, the wife of a neighbour, and I used to get along with her fine. Yes, you're right; no sexual attraction, we were comfortable together. I used to help her with the D.I.Y., her husband was useless and I would often be alone with her. No, you're right, no sex, just companionship."

She nodded. "Yep, I think a lot of sexual attraction is due to pheremones, you know, those subtle scents. How else can you explain the madness of lust or obsessive desire for someone who may be horrible from a character point of view?"

"Yes," he said, "you may be right. I was once attracted to a right selfish little bitch – horrible personality but there was this terrible attraction – moth to the flame syndrome. Would have been a total disaster for all concerned. She had two kids as well. I hope you're not saying that *our* relationship is due to pheromones." He was suddenly anxious.

She laughed, "Well, you are pretty ugly – what on earth am I, a lonely innocent maiden, doing with you, a rich, widower and landowner – heir to a great house?" She came over to him. "Of course I don't think it's just pheromones, although they play a major part," she teased, then continued: "No, my sweet Stevie, I think I *love* you if you don't mind."

"Mind? No, no I can't believe my luck. I think you're wonderful. Even if it *was* just temporary lust, I'd take that and make the most of it." He reached for her and held her to him looking into her eyes. She put her arms up around his neck and kissed him. "See you later," and was gone.

He went upstairs to his room and looked at the tousled bed. The memories of their love-making flooded back and then he realised that he no longer felt a sense of guilt. He looked at the picture of Ginny smiling at him, wondered if he ought to put it away but then decided to leave it, confident that Sela would not mind.

After cleaning up, he took Perry for a walk into the hills. He looked at the rolling panorama of woodland and, again, contemplated his good fortune. Would it last though? Could he be so lucky? Would there be a future for him and Sela? He offered a silent question to the air around him, remembering Sela's talk about entities. If there was anything, would it, could it, bless him? He asked for a sign.

At that moment the sun went behind a cloud and he shivered in the sudden chill wind. He saw movement on the brow of the hill and a stag stood looking at him. They stared at each other and then the stag turned and disappeared behind the hill. Was this an omen? If so, what did it mean? He thought about it as he continued his walk. A stag was a symbol of Exmoor National Park so, perhaps, it was a sign that the moor was accepting him, welcoming him. Yet, if so, why did he feel a sense of unease? He shrugged his shoulders and walked back down into the village to do some shopping.

In the village he saw Dan, outside of the Lorna Doone Hotel, talking with two men. Dan's arm was resting in a sling and Steven was conscious of the men looking across at him but he ignored them. He was pleased with himself, at this ability to control his feelings for, once, he would have challenged them directly with the usual, "What're you looking at?" That was a while ago now, at a time when he had been young and violent. As he was about to cross the road a car tooted him. He saw that the occupants were Jane's friends Sean and Fiona. They waved to him in a friendly manner and he acknowledged their greeting as they drove past. Back at Hawkwood he ate a sandwich and was putting things away when the crunch of tyres on gravel announced the arrival of Sela and Vivien.

"Hallo again, mwah, mwah," the usual pecks on cheeks were exchanged and Vivien swept into the house. "Ooh, lovely – what a lovely place. Now, before we go any further, slip the kettle on and let's have a coffee and a spliff." She followed him into the kitchen, ensconced herself in a chair and started to prepare a roll-up cigarette. She fished in her bag, took out a penknife and began shaving bits of marijuana resin into her tobacco. Sela looked on in amusement as Vivien turned to Steven, "Do you want one? Now tell me about that big dog of yours – won't go out the back, eh?"

"No, I don't smoke," said Steven declining the proffered cigarette, "but you carry on – oh, I don't have an ashtray use this." He pushed a saucer over to her as Perry came over and sniffed at Vivien's legs.

As Sela made coffee, Vivien puffed at her cigarette. Steven told her about Perry's reluctance to go out of the kitchen door and also the fact that the dog avoided a certain part of the garden.

The Moon Temple

Vivien nodded to herself. "That's obvious then. He *knows* there's something there, animals always know. We used to have that ability once, some of us still do, me for instance. I don't think there is anything magical about it." She drew in a deep drag of tobacco smoke, held it and let it go continuing, "It's just a natural ability that modern town-dwelling humans have lost."

"But you live in a town," he said.

"Yes, that's true. Oh, don't get complicated darling, I don't know any more than anyone else. All I know is that I sense things, most people don't." She took another drag; Steven looked at Sela, a query in his eyes.

"Don't worry. Smoking pot heightens her abilities. Here's your coffee Viv," she said.

"OK," said Vivien. "First I'll have a look around your house – its lovely. Got a spare room for a friendly lady like me, darling?" She fluttered her eyelashes at him and gave him the sidelong glance.

"Errr," he hesitated, not sure what to say, "Well…" Why did she have this maddening capacity to unsettle him?

"Oh don't worry, sweetness, this is all a bit too 'Cold Comfort Farm'* for me. I like people around me."

"You mean you like lots of men around you," said Sela; she continued, "well there are some big bucks down 'ere, me dear."

"Ooo! The thought of a lusty swineherd clasping me to his sweaty, hay covered chest really does things for me," said Vivien. "What are the milkmaids like?"

"She's not joking," said Sela to Steven who was watching Vivien with some uncertainty.

Vivien kicked her under the table. "Don't be bitchy it doesn't suit you. Anyway, you're doing all right, eh?" She winked and nudged Steven, "Eh? Getting it on, eh boy?"

"Oh stop it Vivien," said Sela. "Leave poor Steven alone. Now, where shall we start?"

Steven gave her a tour of the house. Vivien made a couple of obvious remarks about the bedrooms and was ecstatic about the views and then they went into the orangery. She paused as though listening and then said, "Whew! Lots and lots of energy here. Good… now… underlying memory – bad, bad." She was speaking softly to herself. "But good, clean… now clean."

They went outside and, again, she paused standing on the patio. "Strong energies, very strong." Vivien pointed towards the wild part of the garden. "There, strong, strong." They walked towards the trees and into their shade. The tinkling sound of the stream was all around. Vivien stopped at the rocks and fell against them. Steven thought she had stumbled but then saw that her

---

* Cold Comfort Farm – Stella Gibbons

face was drained and beaded with sweat. He went to help her but Sela stopped him as Vivien began to speak.

"Aah! Strong power, the light of sun; the dark of death; the flash of light; the power of the sun; the wheel of fire and the horns of the moon. Sorrow, anger and despair, pain and the end of battle… death awaits…" She tailed off and was asleep, lying on the rocks.

Steven went over to her. He looked down at her and then turned to Sela, "What the hell was all that about?"

"She's had a vision, spirit vision. She'll be all right in a minute. Just let her recover. Do you remember what she was saying 'cos she won't?"

"I got the gist of it but…"

There was a snort from Vivien and she opened her eyes. "Got a ciggy?" she asked blinking at them.

Back at the house, the three of them sat in the lounge in front of the fire.

"OK," said Vivien, "tell me what I said."

"Well, you caught me by surprise so I wasn't really concentrating but I got some of it. What about you Steven?" Sela asked.

"Same, I thought you'd fallen over or that you'd fainted but I got a bit of it. Something about the sun and the moon."

"The light of the sun, the wheel of fire and the horns of the moon," said Sela. She continued, "Lots about power and death. Oh yes, something about the end of battle."

"Yes, I remember that bit and 'sorrow, anger'…" he paused. "No, nothing else. What does it mean?" he asked Vivien.

"Search me," she said. "That's the trouble with this sort of thing – it's rarely clear." She puffed at her cigarette, sending clouds of blue smoke into the air which wafted around her like a genie.

"So, you can't help then," said a disappointed Steven. Without really realising it he had begun to put a lot of faith in this strange, quirky woman.

Vivien raised an eyebrow, "I didn't say that. It's just that sometimes you get a sudden rush of images, too much sometimes and then your brain cuts it out like a circuit breaker, otherwise I'd go mad. But, now I know what to expect, we'll go back – now." She got up, stubbed out the cigarette and they followed her across the garden and back into the glade.

"Will she be OK?" asked Steven anxiously.

"She knows what she's doing," said Sela. They entered the shadows. Vivien was standing by the rocks her eyes closed as though listening. She said, in a strange voice, "Here she lies resting. Do not fear. No harm, no harm." It was as though she was talking to someone. "No harm, we respect the power," she was whispering.

Then suddenly there was a coldness but not of the wind. The whole area became cold and there was the sense of a presence. A dark shape seemed to materialise in front of them as though a hole had opened up in the air itself. Steven looked in utter disbelief and considerable fear, as a dark, man-like animal shape rushed at them. He had an impression of pointed ears, a featureless face, a padding of paws on the ground and a terrible coldness as the 'thing' closed with them and went right through them. He gasped and felt dizzy and then Sela was pulling him back into the sunlight.

"Vivien, where is she?" he asked. She emerged backing slowly from the trees and then turned to them. "A Guardian Spirit. Something very special is there."

"A Guardian Spirit?" queried Steven. "What are you talking about? Is that what you mean, 'Spirit of the place'?" he asked Sela.

"No, no, this is different. Rare but not unheard of. Come let's go back to the house."

They left the grove and returned to Hawkwood in silence, each of them lost in thought. To Steven the incident had been extremely nerve shattering. Back inside, he poured them all a shot of whisky. Sela turned to him. "Is that like anything you've experienced here or around the house?"

"No, different. I didn't feel it to be evil, not like that horror of the other night. Frightening, yes but then it's not every day you come face to face with a shadowy beast-man who rushes right through you. What the hell was it?"

Sela sipped her drink. "I remember reading about an archaeologist who found something up near Hadrian's Wall. She took the object home to study it and was assailed by a black shape with pointed ears. She took the object back and wasn't bothered again. A Guardian Spirit was often invoked to protect graves etcetera from robbers. I've never seen one before. Strange but not harmful."

"Bloody frightening though," he said.

"It's meant to be," said Vivien. "Keeps intruders away."

Steven said, "But I've been going in that part of the garden for ages – my favourite spot. We were there the other day," he said to Sela.

"Yes and I said it was special."

"So why didn't he, it, appear?" he asked.

Vivien lit a cigarette. "Because of me; I was questing, psychically and obviously activated it. Like a hologram I suppose – you know, in those sci fi films. A projection, probably what visions are. Haven't you ever wondered about those appearances of the Virgin Mary? They are probably Guardian Spirits but peasants give them Christian attributes. It would be interesting to investigate such sites," she mused. "They happen all over the world. Some people think they're time travellers or aliens. Great, isn't it?" She looked pleased with herself.

"Well then, what do we do now?" asked Steven. "Doesn't that finish it for now?" He felt reluctant to stir up the strange spirit again.

Sela turned to Vivien, "What do you think, Viv? What do you think we should do? This is your area of work."

Vivien puffed thoughtfully at her cigarette then said, "That explains the dog's problems then. He knows the Guardian is in there. Now why is it there, *that's* the

The Moon Temple

question? We'll have to find out and I'm going to suggest two things. First, I think that we should do some scouting around the area using the metal detector." She saw the look of surprise on Steven's face. "Oh yes, Marian asked if I could get hold of one in Glastonbury. Well, I knew a couple of guys who are always searching for the Grail – actually crazy really. The Grail is an 'ideal' but there you are. They're always searching – drives me mad but they just won't listen. Actually," she said, "the whole Grail thing has spawned virtually a new religion. There's the Church of the Holy Grail; the Order of the Holy Grail; there are rituals based upon the Sacred Blood – theories linked to the Merovingians – you know, descent from Jesus who married Mary Magdalen – conspiracy theories, masons – it's madness I tell you. Well, anyway, let's have a *practical* search first; might find something straight away – treasure darlings; just think, a veritable pot of gold, with the emphasis on 'pot'". She fished around in her bag and pulled out cigarette papers, resin, tobacco and her knife and began preparing another drug-laden cigarette.

"You use a lot of that, don't you?" said Steven, watching Vivien as she rolled the mixture into a cigarette shape.

"I do indeed – do you disapprove? Am I being a naughty girl? Do you want to *punish* me?" She gazed at him with a wide open, childlike look then bent down to finish the roll-up glancing sideways at him again with a slight smile on her face.

He laughed. "No, you do what you like. It's your body. I just wondered if it would impair your thinking, that's all."

Vivien turned to Sela. "My *thinking*? Poor dear, doesn't he realise I *can't* think unless I have this?" She became serious suddenly. "Look, don't worry; this is resin. I'm not using super skunk, which could be a problem – too much THC[*]. No, this just lifts me – opens my mind. Don't worry, I'm OK. Believe me."

"OK," said Steven, "and, if we don't find anything, what then?"

Vivien took a deep drag into her lungs. "Aah! Aah! Well, then we move from the material plane to the spiritual level. Now Marian, I suggest we try psychic questing possibly in the spirit vision, yes?"

"Yes, yes why not," said Sela with evident enthusiasm.

"Hold on," said Steven, "what do you mean?"

Sela looked at Vivien, "You explain, it's your field."

Vivien took another drag, held it and then blew out the smoke. "Well, darling, it's like this. You know about meditation, OK? I know about that as well but some people like me can go beyond it onto a level of existence where the mind can access things outside of normal Time and Space. For what *I* do, I take a drug – no not this, something else used for centuries by our ancestors. It helps me to fly out of my body and access a different dimension…" she paused. "Understand?"

---

[*] THC is Tetrahydrocannabindl – The psycho-active ingredient of the cannabis plant.

"Not really," he said. "Aren't you just using hallucogenic drugs, that sort of thing? What's the difference between that and what you do? I mean, what about all those hippies, rock stars, are they all accessing the spirit world?" He was genuinely puzzled.

"No, not the same thing. Yes, you can have a mind-altering experience using LSD for example or magic mushrooms. It's what you *do* with the experience – moving beyond colours, lights, distorted images. It's finding the way through and then it all becomes different out on the astral. I can't explain it any more than I can explain the fact, the *fact*," she emphasised the word, "that I *am* psychic."

Sela said, "Just go with the flow babes, it does seem odd but it does give results. When shall we make a start?"

"Oh, tomorrow, I am too hazy and tired now," said Vivien.

Steven muttered to himself, "I'm not surprised." Vivien seemed to have a capacity for drugs and drink which would have put him under the table by now as he watched her puff at her cigarette and empty her whisky glass. They decided to eat out and went down to the village, returning back to Hawkwood at 9 p.m.

By this time, Vivien was beginning to show signs of intoxication, having finished off the best part of a bottle of red wine and rounding it off with a double Tia Maria. She lit up yet another cigarette and settled back in the armchair.

Steven put on a disc by the group, 'Dead Can Dance', and they sat nursing drinks and listening to the mournful rhythmic music.

"OK Viv, time to go," Sela said. But Vivien was deeply asleep in the armchair.

"Oh well, she'll have to stay here overnight I'm afraid." She turned to Steven, "Sorry, no choice."

Steven looked alarmed. "Oh really? Oh no! Can't we wake her up?"

Sela laughed. "What are you frightened of? She's just a little man-hungry, gothic, vampiric-looking lady in some distress at present. No, I've seen her like this. I'd never get her in the car let alone out again and into my house. No, you're stuck with her."

"Can't you stay as well? I'd love you to spend the night with me," he pleaded.

"Oh sweetheart, I'd love to, you know I would if I could but I can't. I've got clothes in the machine, a paper to prepare, a cat to feed – we'll have lots of time when all this is done."

"But, oh well, OK but…" he tailed off.

"But what? *You* can't be held responsible for *what might happen between you.*" She whispered the last words nudging him.

"Oh come on. I would never take advantage of someone in her state."

"No, but *she* might," said Sela. "I'm off. I leave you with my sexy, drugged little friend, lover man. I'll be 'round at 9 o'clock. OK? Tanith awaits." She kissed him on the lips and he watched her car drive off, feeling lonely.

CHAPTER 18

Steven locked up then went into the lounge. The now snoring Vivien had slid down the armchair and was half way onto the floor. He hoisted her up, balanced her against him then lifted her across his shoulders in a fireman's lift. Upstairs, he pushed open the door to Rita's room and dumped Vivien on the bed; he covered her with a quilt and left her.

Later, in the night, he heard her snort awake, mutter some words, then begin to snore again. He was next woken by the sound of his door creaking open and, to his alarm, saw a half dressed Vivien stumbling around saying, "Loo, where's the fucking loo?" He took her arm and guided her to the en suite in her bedroom and sat her down; she was wearing only her top. He went out, heard her pass water and then the sound of snoring again. This time he decided to leave her there; at least he wouldn't have a soiled bed.

In the morning, he knocked on her door and heard a startled, "What the hell?" He peered in. Vivien had obviously got off the toilet and had made her way back to the bed but had only got half-way before slumping to the floor. She was coming to in a state of bewilderment and she was saying, "Oh no, not again!" He saw that she was displaying far too much flesh so did not go in. He closed the door and then knocked again.

"Oh God! Just a minute; hell – bugger! Oh, OK."

He opened the door and Vivien was in bed. "Good morning," he said. "Would you like a cup of tea?"

"Coffee, black coffee and a ciggy. Oh hell, I bloody well disgraced myself. Did you put me to bed?"

"Well, I put you *on* the bed," he said.

"And undressed me, eh? Did you have your wicked way?" she leered at him.

"Certainly not." He was outraged that she should say this. "You undressed yourself."

"Oh, don't get all starchy. Hell – I woke up on the loo and don't know how I got there."

"I put you there – you came into my room."

"Oh bugger! I'm sorry I'm always doing something like that. God, I'm thirsty and I need a smoke. Be a darling and get my ciggies."

Steven put a cup of black coffee, a glass of water and some cigarettes on a tray and took them to her. "Oh you angel." She drained the water, lit a cigarette and then lay back against the pillows. She looked dreadful. Her eye make-up had smeared and she was as pale as a ghost. She patted the bed,

"Come on, sit here or, better still, why don't you join me?" She pulled aside the cover exposing her naked thigh.

"Thank you, but no. I'll make some breakfast. Marian will be here soon – the shower's over there." He hurried out.

When she came down she was dressed and made up. "Looking better, eh?" she said. "I could see why you didn't want to get into bed with me; I wouldn't have got into bed with me either."

Steven laughed but then realised that Vivien was serious. She had actually expected him to join her and assumed that her terrible appearance had put him off. He was about to make some statement about his new relationship with Sela but then thought it better to leave the matter. Vivien sipped her coffee and, as though reading his mind said, "So Stevie baby, you and my red haired friend are getting it on, eh? Well I don't blame you. You're a bit old for her but, then, I always preferred older men; they take their time; know how to please a girl. Oh come on, don't look so prudish. We're practically related now."

He changed the subject. "Where's the metal detector? Do you know how to use it?"

She got up and went into the hall returning with a long bulky bag. "No, I've never used one but Gary said there was an instruction book." Steven unzipped the bag pocket and took out an instruction manual.

The bell rang and Perry barked. "Hi you two," said Sela.

Vivien rushed over to her. "Oh Marian, Marian, thank God you've arrived. The man is an absolute monster – *a monster* I tell you. He, he…" she paused at the top of an hysterical sounding note, "…he came into my room with the most awful cup of coffee I've ever had in my life." She collapsed over her friend sobbing dramatically. Steven, who, for a moment had wondered where this was going, laughed with relief.

"Yes," said Sela, "I know he's a bastard but what's a country girl to do down 'ere." She winked at him.

"Needless to say darling, I completely disgraced myself. Ended up half naked in his room; then he sat me on the loo and then he had me crawling all over the floor. I warn you, no good will come of it." She shook her head and wagged a finger at them.

Steven raised an eyebrow, "I'll explain later. Now back to the detector. You make yourself a drink while I have a read. In fact, I'll take it outside and practice." He left the two women and after half an hour or so he had a fair idea of the possibilities of the machine.

They wandered down to the field and showed Vivien the excavations. She was silent, standing with her eyes closed. She opened them and turned, with a shrug of her shoulders. "Hmm, odd, nothing here; I can't sense anything here," she said.

The Moon Temple

Steven passed the detector back and forth around the holes – it beeped and he investigated but it was only a bit of metal piping. Vivien said, "Look, the place where there is something is in the grove. That's where we should look."

Back in the shaded grove, Vivien shut her eyes again as Sela did a binding spell to prevent the Guardian appearing.

Vivien continued her psychic questing. "Yes, power, lots of power. Sweep the thing around those rocks, Steven," she said. He obeyed. Nothing at first and then a 'beep'. He focused around and then there was another 'beep'; two different places close to the stream.

As he held the buzzing detector over a spot, Sela dug using a trowel. "Yes, look." She held a muddy object in her hand. She rinsed it in the stream; it was an encrusted silver coin.

She studied the coin which had something inscribed on it. "It looks like a horse – look, the legs and some words but I can't read them." Steven took it and tried to decipher the inscriptions but gave up and continued using the detector. In a short time they found two more all with the same design and indistinct words.

"Must be Roman," said Sela, "but I don't recognise the head, a bit primitive." She passed the coins around but neither Steven nor Vivien could recognise the coin type.

"Something more, over there," said Vivien, "under the rocks. I can feel it – very, very strong. I felt it when we came here before. There is something very, very special there – I know there is."

Steven clambered up and swept the detector back and forth but could pick up nothing. "Perhaps the rocks are too much for it," he said. "Let's get back to the house."

Vivien had gone pale again and was keeping away from the location. She nodded, "Yes, let's."

Back at the house Sela rinsed the coins in water and gently removed the grime and mud as much as was possible. Now it was clearer. There were three silver coins, all with a stylised horse inscribed on one side with jumbled letters – CE … C … EN. On the other side they could make out a portrait bust on one of the coins but on the other two the bust was not so clear.

"What do you think?" asked Steven.

"No idea," said Sela, "but if there are three there may be more, yes?" She looked at the other two friends.

"You mean there might be a hoard?" Vivien asked.

"Yes," replied Sela. "It's possible and what you sensed could indicate that."

"Hmm! Yes, but what I was sensing was an energy hard to pin down. Very, very powerful. And the Guardian – what about it? A Guardian wouldn't be put on a site unless something incredibly important was there. Pity you're not an archaeologist," Vivien said to Steven.

"An archaeologist – yes – that's what we need," said Sela, "and I've met Timothy Hutchins. He's a local archaeologist and, what's more, he's into Earth Mysteries. He'll listen to us without thinking we're nuts."

"He wouldn't think that, not with the coins," said Steven.

"Coins are often found. I sometimes think Romans went around with holes in their pockets. No, I mean the detector isn't picking up anything else so an archaeologist wouldn't necessarily be that interested. However, if I say that Viv has *sensed* something he might be interested."

Vivien pondered for a while and then said, "Look, we'll try psychometry first using the coins. I may be able to get something from them."

"Psychometry?" asked Steven.

"Yes, a sensitive can pick up impressions from objects say, like that ring you're wearing. Objects absorb the energies and vibrations, the life energy if you like, of a person or persons who have been associated with them." Vivien paused, looked over at Sela who was studying the coins and continued, "For example, I will know who held them last," she nodded over at her friend, "even if I had not seen her with them. The trick will be to try to sense beyond that – to the time when they were lost or offered up."

Steven shook his head. "But that would have been centuries ago."

Vivien continued talking as she got up and went over to Sela. "No, it's not like that. It's to do with vibrational harmonies. Everything vibrates at a particular rate – these coins are vibrating now – it's partly what gives them their shape, their form, their substance. That is never lost as long as they exist. I try to tune into them, to match my harmonies with theirs. Don't worry your head about it; I can't explain. Now we need to create a mood. Do you have incense, soft music, and, yes, do you have a recorder?"

Steven gathered the items and said, "Will this do?" He had a small dictaphone.

"It'll do," said Vivien and she went on: "I've got a feeling about the grove, something special, deeper, more intense. I'll try with the coins first to see where it leads; I might sense who held them and threw them down."

"But shouldn't they have been actually in the water, not where we found them?" asked Steven.

Vivien nodded. "Yes, you're right. That's why it's possible they may have been dropped and were not votive offerings. We'll try to find out."

Sela looked up. She had been half listening to them whilst studying the coins with a magnifying glass found in the kitchen drawer. "Oh, but they were in the water. I did some geology when I was doing my degree. We found these lying in gravel and pebbles. Clearly the course of the stream has changed over time. Also there were established rocks, obviously the original, but overlaid, in part, by a jumble of rocks which must have slid down from the bank above; some sort of landslide I suppose. This must have changed the course of the stream. If you look again you'll see the original channel coming out of the stones from below. So, I'm sure – yes, these were *offered* – a votive offering just as we threw a coin into the stream," she smiled at Steven at the memory.

"OK, then," said Vivien. She turned to Steven. "Do you have some nice, moody music, non-intrusive?" He showed her a disc. "This is a piece I use for meditation; it's a piece of Reiki music."

She listened to it for a while. "Great, just the thing – now some incense – let's create a nice witchy-type mood – all ethereal and spoooooky – ooooh!"

Steven lit some 'Night Queen' and a couple of candles which he had purchased in Glastonbury, whilst Sela drew the curtains to darken the room.

Then she said, "We should create a special working environment. A sacred space in which to carry out the search."

"I don't usually bother with all that," said Vivien. "I just do it but, OK, you do your spooky bit if you like. She's *very* theatrical, you know." This to Steven.

Sela said, "Yes, and usually it doesn't matter but I think there is something special going on and remember Jane Trethowan hovering in the background. I want to be sure she can't scry us. I want us to be cloaked. OK?"

"OK, sure – you're probably right," said her friend.

Sela circled the room invoking the elemental spirits and inscribing her pentagrams. She stood silently for a while, the others watching her, and then she spoke an invocation to Hecate.

"Where are you, Lady? Come, for I call you
Deep from your demon world, come, for I need you.
Lady of Darkness secret and hidden,
Guardian of fantastic wonders forbidden;
Death bringer, life giver, always so distant,
Storm riding Devil Queen spare me one instant.
Mystical Goddess, Mistress Immortal,
Be with me now as I stand at the portal.
Lead me on through to the depths of my being,
Freeing those senses, all knowing, all seeing.
Come to me now in your mantle of midnight,
Great in your splendour, crowned with the starlight;
Wraith-like enchantress, Spirit eternal,
Come here to me from your dark realm infernal.
Out of the depths of my soul's long time yearning,
Waken the memories, past lives returning.
Here to me, here, in the glow of the fire bright,
Mother, Creator, Queen of the Moonlight;
Ruler of Spirits in mist world concealing,
All things are known to you, yours for revealing.
Grant me the power I seek then, Great Huntress,

> *Stalker of souls, lissome seductress.*
> *Make me the ruler of things vain and mortal.*
> *Now, make it now, as I step through the portal."*

She opened her eyes and looked at them and said, "All right, let's get on with it."

Steven said, "That was all a bit dark, wasn't it? All that about infernal worlds and devil queens."

"Yes, well when you seek to delve into the deeper parts of the mind you need to remember that there are many sides to human nature and to the psychic world. It's not all fairies and pretty rainbows you know."

Sela handed the coins to Vivien and the three of them sat down allowing the soft music and the scent of incense to waft around them. After a while, Vivien, who was sitting with her eyes closed, said, "Yes, I can see Marian with the coins – you do love Steven don't you?"

Steven looked over at Sela who raised her eyebrows at him giving a shrug and a smile. Vivien was silent for a long time then she said softly, "Yes, great sadness but hazy, clouded, a woman, young, grief and yes, some fear." She gave a sudden cry, "For the Gods." There was a long silence then she opened her eyes and looked at Sela saying, "I can't go beyond this. There's so much more but it's not for me, it's for you. You must do this – you, Marian. Something I've seen, not clear but it must be you."

Sela said, "But you know I'm not good at psychometry. If you can't sense anything more then how can I?"

Vivien got up and put the coins down. "I'm not talking of psychometry – I'm talking about past life regression."

Sela looked at her, perplexed. "Why, why me?"

"Because I got a glimpse of the past but it was hazy, unclear but I know you are linked in some way. I don't know what. No, it definitely *has* to be you."

Steven was puzzled. "Past life regression? Oh yes." He turned to Sela, "We talked of that; wasn't there a book? Why, though, do you want Marian to do this? Is it safe?" He had heard of people losing their minds when delving into aspects of occult practice.

"*My dear*," said Vivien, "you're dealing with me and your own personal little witch lady. Don't worry, it's safe, *if you know what you're doing* and I do."

Sela was doubtful. "You've tried to hypnotise me before – it didn't work"

"Yes, yes, I know but I'm going to get you to take something this time – help you to fly out and flit around on the astral; you'll love it." She saw the doubt on Sela's face. "No, I *do* know about all of this you know – I *do* and I'm certain that this concerns you. Trust me. We do want to get to the bottom of all of this, don't we?"

Sela was silent, pondering, then said "OK, let's do it. Anyway, I've never tried this, strange as it may seem. Yes, I know about it, met people who have done it but never me. Yes, why not?" She was suddenly enthusiastic. "What will you use?"

Vivien got her bag and began fishing around inside. She pulled out a small pouch and opened it, tipping some small packets onto the table. "Now, I've thought about this – no really, I have," she said, looking at Steven. "I *do* take this sort of thing seriously."

"Are they all drugs? God, it's a good job the police haven't picked you up," he said.

"Oh, don't be stuffy." She went on: "Now we'll do a combination of things. The music – it's nice isn't it? The music and the incense, together with Marian's own meditation skills will all help. She's right though, I can't hypnotise her without other help. She's too powerful for my little brain to overcome. Alas, what could I not do if I could overpower her – "

"Oh get on with it, Viv," said Sela, anxious to press ahead with the quest.

"Tut tut, patience my love. OK, we can't use LSD or magic mushrooms; too long-lasting. You don't smoke, so pot's no good and even if you did, it would take a while to act. No, we want something quick and not long-lasting so that you'll be OK in a short while. So," she picked up a small packet, "we'll use this. It's from Brazil and contains something known as DMT[*], mixed with something else – don't ask me the chemical name, I'll be buggered if I can remember it. It's very effective in getting you out into the spirit world and you'll be all right in an hour or so."

Steven was about to protest but then saw it was no use. The two women were into this now and nothing he said could stop them. In any case, he was curious to see where this would lead. Then he remembered when he and Sela had been in the grove. She had stood on the rock shelf and thrown a coin into the stream and, as she had done this, she had cried "For the Gods". These were the very words Vivien had used. Perhaps this was what Vivien was picking up.

He mentioned this and Sela, remembering, nodded. "Yes, I did call that out but I didn't know why."

Vivien looked at both of them and said, "Yes – but that's the point. I wasn't holding *your* coin. I was holding one of these – so I couldn't have picked up those thoughts, could I? That's why I *know* it's to do with Marian – something I saw in the spirit. We must do this – believe me – OK?" She had

---

[*] DMT is Dimethyl Tryuptomine, a powerful hallucinogen with a distant, chemical relationship to LSD. It is incorporated in a drink, known in Brazil as ayahuasca and is used by sorcerers of the Amazon forests. Because DMT breaks down rapidly in the digestive system, when taken orally, it is combined with other plants which contain the drug Harmaline. This prolongs the effects of DMT and is used to promote visionary and trance experiences. Shamans of the Amazon use plants containing Harmaline as a 'guide' into the world of the spirits. DMT is illegal in most countries and should not be used without medical or shamanic guidance.

become very serious and intense and this feeling was communicated to the others.

"OK, sure," said Sela as she settled herself on the sofa reclining back, her hands resting on her lap.

"Have a good trip," said Vivien, then became serious, again. "Now listen, it'll work in a short while – that's why it's used a lot – as a sort of businessman's tripping drug – they're getting fed up with cocaine. You'll get lots of colours, distortions perhaps and then I'll try to put you into a trance. If it doesn't get us anywhere well, no harm done. You'll have had an interesting experience. I envy you."

"You do it then," interjected Steven, still anxious.

"I told you, this is not for me. Look, I know that you think I'm off my head, though, for the life of me, I can't see why but I *do* know about these things. I am *sure* she has a big part to play in this. Something I saw, felt, when I held the coins; trust me." She reached out and patted Steven on the arm in a gesture of reassurance. For a moment the carefree, clown-like Vivien disappeared and a look of caring compassion came into her eyes. Then it was gone and she turned to Sela. "Now sweetie pie, are you ready? OK, take this… Good girl. Just a short while and you'll begin to feel it, see things. You tell me, us, what you are seeing and then I'll try to put you under. OK? Now, start your meditation thing, just let the music carry you away. OK Stevie boy, switch on the recorder."

CHAPTER 19

There was a period of silence. Steven, unsure of what to do, sat across the other side of the room so that he could watch the two women without getting in the way. Vivien sat alongside the reclining form of Sela who was now in a state of meditation. The music filled the silence with its gentle rhythmic patterns and the aromatic smoke of the incense in the shady room lent the scene an unearthly quality.

Suddenly: "I can feel, no, I can see the music." Sela was smiling. "I can see it, yes, see it, beautiful colours." She was silent again.

Vivien spoke softly, "Can you go outside?"

"Yes, outside, I'm there… Ahh! Beautiful colours, flowers, trees, grass, all dancing to the music… the music of love."

"Walk to the grove, Marian. Tell us what you see."

There was a short silence then, "The grove, the rocks and the stream. It's silver, gold, silver, gold, beautiful colours. It's singing."

"What's singing?"

"The stream is singing and laughing at me."

Vivien picked up the coins and placed them in Sela's hand. "Do you feel these? Tell me what you sense. Try to sense them. Try now."

There was a long silence. A look of puzzlement came across Sela's face and she frowned. Then she started to twitch, her whole body moving in spasms.

Alarmed, Steven rose but Vivien held up a staying hand. "It's all right Marian, you are with me, Vivien – and with Steven. Breathe slowly, breathe – yes, take deep breaths, slowly, slowly, good, yes, good." Sela stopped twitching and her breathing eased.

"Can you see the grove still?" asked Vivien after awhile.

"Yes, of course I can." The voice was different, deeper and with a strange lilt. "I must be here to fulfil my task."

"What task is that?"

"The offering to the Gods." The tape hissed softly as Vivien and Steven exchanged glances.

Vivien contemplated the reclining form of her friend. "Why must you do this?" she asked.

"She will not rest. I… we, have buried her now and I am sad, so sad." Sela's face crumpled as she began to cry but then she stopped and was calm again.

Vivien motioned to Steven and he followed her out of the room. "Should we be leaving her?" he asked anxiously.

"Don't worry, it's OK but something odd has happened."

"Odd, what do you mean?"

Vivien looked back towards the room. "She's gone back in time. I've not had to use hypnosis; she's gone back herself – the coins have triggered something in her. I'll try to guide her but I don't know where we're going with this. Don't interrupt whatever you hear. Leave it to me, OK?"

Back in the room, Vivien said, "So you've buried her. Who have you buried?"

In the strange lilting voice, Sela responded. "My sister, she was wounded and then she died. We have buried her. The bard said the words; we burned her body and the urn has been placed in the hollow."

"Wounded, dead, by whom? Who wounded your sister?"

"They did it, in the great battle."

"They? What great battle?"

"The legions destroyed us. We should have defeated them. We were so many but they won, defeated us, wounded her and now she has gone."

"Yes gone, buried."

"No, gone, far away. They wounded her but they will not get her."

Vivien looked over at Steven with a puzzled expression on her face and then asked, "Who do you mean? Who are you talking about?"

"My mother of course – they will not get her. She is too clever, too strong. She defeated them many times. Destroyed their armies, and destroyed the temple to their false God. She was so victorious – so victorious. And now she has gone away and I miss her – miss them." Her face crumpled again but then she recovered herself. "My mother, my sister – both gone."

Steven felt a rising excitement within him. He knew his history; there had only been one woman leader with two daughters.

Vivien asked the question. "Who is your mother?"

"Boudica – she is Boudica, named for her victories. They will not get her, she has crossed the sea. Now I must complete my duty." Sela stood up suddenly, crying, "For the Gods," and threw the coins across the room. They clattered into the corner. "There, into the water! Guard her Andraste! Guard her Bel! There, my offering for the Gods; for my mother; for our people; for what we were." Her voice was breaking. "For my sister, now dead; for the memory of the death of thousands; for our lost freedom – our lost lands. May the Gods protect me now." She fell back onto the sofa still sobbing.

Vivien looked taken aback and quickly intervened. "Shhh, shhh, you must be calm – you must move on. Go forward to a happier time, now."

There was a silence again as Sela's sobs subsided and then she was calm and a smile lit up her face. Vivien looked over at Steven with a look of evident relief. She turned back to Sela and said, "You are happy now. Why are you so happy?"

"Aah, happy, yes." Still the strange lilting voice. "My daughter, so like her, the same copper hair – strong, like her grandmother, like my sister, like me."

"You are married then?"

"Yes, to the bard."

Vivien moved in front of Sela. "Who is this bard. Is he special?"

"Yes, he is the Druid who carried the Mysteries of Mona."

"The Mysteries of Mona? What are they?"

"I cannot, must not, say." The voice was beginning to sound agitated.

"So, he is from Mona. Therefore is *this* a sacred site?"

There was a silence; only the soft hiss of the tape could be heard. Vivien tried again. "So he knows of the Mysteries. What are they?"

"I cannot speak of them." Sela was shaking her head from side to side.

"Is this grove a sacred site?"

"I cannot speak of them, of this. I cannot, must not..." She was sounding distressed. Vivien changed tack. "Where is your mother now?"

"She has gone, far away. To escape." She had become calm.

"Why didn't you go with her?"

"She has left me to guard the burial site and protect the Mysteries of Mona."

"Where are they?"

"I cannot say, must not say... never tell – never..." Her voice began to rise in distress again and Vivien intervened. "It's all right. There now – rest, rest."

Sela became calm and in a while Vivien said, "Marian, Marian, it's me, Vivien. Can you hear me Marian? Sleep now, rest – you will wake up soon, refreshed."

"Yes, I'll sleep, Vivien." It was Sela's voice again, "I can hear you, I'll sleep... sleeeeep –." She was asleep.

Vivien and Steven left the room. Vivien lit a cigarette and sat on one of the kitchen chairs as Steven made coffee for both of them. They sat sipping it, thoughtfully, then Steven said, "That was weird. I've never seen anything like that. She sounded odd. So different."

"Yes, very strange but not unusual. What *is* strange though is that she managed to access the past all by herself; no help from me. I said that those coins were special to her."

"But, how reliable is all of this. She's taken a drug, after all. How do we know she's not hallucinating?"

"We don't. Only time will tell but it didn't sound as though she was imagining it, did it? Look at how she sounded – what she said."

"These 'Mysteries of Mona' – artefacts do you think?"

Vivien nodded. "Could well be – treasure, eh? God, how exciting – Jamaica here I come."

There was a snort and a gasp from the next room and Sela was sitting up blinking at them. "Wow! You two look so bright and gay."

"What do you mean 'gay'? I didn't know Stevie boy was like that." Vivien was back to her old, bantering self.

Sela laughed. "It's wearing off but still, its all colourful. I remember it all though. I couldn't see the girl; why do you think that was?"

"That's because she was you," said Vivien, "or should I say, your ancestor. That's what I could see when *I* tried – I saw you but not you – if you get my drift. My God, you're a descendant of Queen Boudica – I thought she was Boadicea – never mind." Vivien went down on her knees bowing before Sela. "Your Majesty, we are not worthy, not worthy."

Steven interrupted this pantomime. "Oh now, wait a minute – we don't know that. You could have been having a trip. It might not be real at all; how do you know it's not just your imagination enhanced by the drug?"

Sela said, "I could see the grove but it wasn't the same. Yes, that's it. It was *before* the landslide and there were different, older trees. There was a sort of passage and a hollow entrance to a sort of cave and I think that the landslide must have been deliberate, you know, to hide the burial site and the artefacts."

"What burial? What artefacts? We don't know that any of this is real," he said, trying to inject a note of reality into the conversation.

Sela shook her head. "No, they *are* there; she's there, I know that. It was all so clear. I was not only seeing the place, I seemed to know what had happened before and I was there, there just as I am sitting here with you now. I could *remember* the fear and the dreadful rush of the battle against the Romans – terrible, horrible and the sense of horror and fear at what happened in the towns that were destroyed. I could remember my sister, so ill with her wounds, and the sorrow of her death. I saw, or rather remembered, my mother, Boudica herself." She began to cry. "Such a sense of despair, sorrow, shame at defeat."

Vivien went over to her and took her hand. "There now, come on, sometimes it's the effect of the trip. These feelings though, do you *really* think they're true?"

Sela wiped her eyes, "Yes, oh yes. I didn't see Boudica in the grove, it was more like a memory of her – an impression I suppose but it was strong as though there was a memory imprinted there. I suppose if I was really channelling my ancestor's memory and standing at the burial site of my sister then the memory of our mother would be strong wouldn't it?"

She ended the sentence with a query and Vivien nodded, "Could be."

Sela got up and went over to the dictaphone. "Can I hear the tape? I want to know what I said. It's different being in a trance – full of impressions, like pictures flashing through the mind."

"Yes, sure," said Steven. "I'll play it."

They listened and Sela began crying when she came to the bit about the votive offerings. When it was finished, Steven said to Sela, "But is it possible, credible, that you should be still here, a descendant – what, nearly two thousand years later?"

Vivien said, "Hell yes. Why not? People didn't move around much before the last century. Did you know that they did tests on people in the area around Cheddar and found that a headmaster, at a local school, was related to the nine thousand year-old Cheddar Man? I've got two friends who had their DNA profile done by Oxford University and they've got the same DNA as the Iceman, you know, the mummy found in the Alps. In that case it showed that people certainly hadn't moved around much for one of my friend's family originates from the valleys of Northern Italy. So it's entirely possible that Marian is a direct descendant of Boudica. What *is* weird is this. What was Boudica doing here? The Iceni come from East Anglia if I remember rightly."

"Well, she did say there was a great battle and Boudica escaped. Did she escape? I thought she poisoned herself," Steven observed.

Vivien nodded. "True, but if I remember my history right it's all a bit of a mystery. You have this great battle and a great Roman victory but no captive queen. If she *had* been killed they would have moved heaven and earth to find the body. Can't have a *woman* beating all those men. Someone else says she died but where's the burial? Boy, can you imagine finding Boudica's grave?"[*]

"Perhaps it's here," he said.

Sela shook her head. "No, that was my sister."

Steven said, "Hey, not *your* sister remember; this is in the past."

Sela shrugged. "I feel it's now. But, OK then, it was her daughter, one of the two daughters of Boudica who were raped by the Romans so I, she, the other one, got married and had a daughter and now, after centuries, *I'm* here – weird."

"But what were they doing in a battle?" Steven asked.

"Celtic women fought alongside the men," Vivien said, "sometimes more ferociously according to the Roman sources. We're not all as meek as we look you know." She got up and looked out of the window towards the grove. "Strange isn't it. All this time buried there."

"We don't know that," said Steven. "Come on, we've found some coins. We don't know there's anyone buried there – do we?"

"There is," said Sela quietly. "*I* know. Yes, I really do believe she's there with whatever 'the Mysteries of Mona' are or were." She turned to Vivien, "What do you think it all means, taking into account your vision 'Wheels of Fire – Horns of the Moon', that sort of thing. Artefacts?"

Vivien nodded. "Almost certainly but what kind, God only knows. Could be a silver hoard from Mona, something like the Gundestrup Cauldron, or a coin hoard. If they knew the Romans were coming then they might have buried them to be collected later."

"Where is, or what is, Mona?" asked Steven.

---

[*] Tacitus – The Annals of Imperial Rome.

She lit another cigarette. "Mona is Anglesey, you know, the island off North Wales, though why *anyone* would *want* to live there I don't know. It was attacked by the Romans around the time of the Boudican Revolt. Very lurid descriptions of Druids and black clad women screaming curses. Mind you, *I'd* scream curses if I saw a whole lot of men in skirts coming towards me. All those men, bare legs, thighs, metal, ooooh! Anyway, the Romans were supposed to have found blood-soaked groves, decapitated heads, that sort of thing."

Sela had left the room and now returned carrying one of the encyclopaedias. She leafed through the pages and found what she wanted. She showed it to Steven. "That's the Gundestrup Cauldron."

He took the book and looked at the photograph of the great silver gilt cauldron found in Denmark. "Wow," he said, "just think if we found that. God, what's it worth?"

Sela looked at him. "Priceless I would say. You'd get money as treasure trove and then it would go to a museum. I tell you now, I'll not be part of anything that puts whatever we find in a museum." She looked upset and he hastened to re-assure her. "Hey, no, I didn't mean anything by that. I was just curious but, assuming something is there, what would we do with it?"

"Leave it there; respect it and respect the people who put it there. It's religious."

He was puzzled. "But I thought you didn't believe in religion."

She nodded. "Conventional, dogmatic religions, yes. I would probably be against anything like that but this is different. It's sacred to the memory of the past. It was important to them. It would be like grave robbing and I sensed the grief and despair that lay behind the burial."

Steven looked at her. Clearly this meant a great deal to her. He said to her, "But we don't know if anything is really there. We've only found a few coins. No burial, no treasure." He turned to Vivien who was sitting quietly observing the exchange.

She shrugged her shoulders. "There's *definitely* a burial there. Marian experienced it and I have felt the power of the place. Also, there is the Guardian, remember?"

"How could I forget," he said. "OK but what do we do now?" His attempts at being rational melted before the certainty of the two women and, in any case, he knew they were right. The memory of the Guardian was still with him and then there was Sela's behaviour under the trance.

Vivien said, "Look, let's go back to the grove, have a good look at it, eh?" She turned to Sela. "Do you feel OK?"

Sela nodded. "Tired now but yes, OK." She got up and Steven lent her his arm as they walked across to the grove.

As the three of them entered the trees, Steven studied the rocks. "Yes, I can see what you mean about the landslide and, yes, I can see the original course of the stream. If the burial is anywhere it has to be under all of that. I wouldn't know where to start. We need some expert help; what about the archaeologist you know?" he asked Sela.

She said, "But if you involve an archaeologist he would be bound to notify his department and if there is a burial there then the police will need to be informed." She gazed at the rocks. "Yes, there is a burial, I know there is – I can still feel what I felt earlier. It's in there."

Steven looked thoughtful. "Let's take a step back. What about Jane Trethowan? Is this what she wants? If she does, how the hell does she know about this?"

The others were silent as he continued, "I don't understand, how does she know about this? How *could* she know?"

Sela said, "She doesn't, at least she doesn't know where the artefacts are, hence the excavations. But how she got wind of the things, if that is why she wants the land, well that *is* a mystery unless she too is sensitive and can sense the energies."

The three of them walked back to the house and into the kitchen. "Do you think she sensed the energies?" Steven asked.

Vivien shook her head. "No, they don't emanate for miles. You have to be quite close. Perhaps she has some historical record." She paused, pondering her statement and then said, "No, not possible. Celts didn't write anything down and this would certainly have been a secret in case the Romans found out. The fact that it's still here means the Romans didn't know. *The plot thickens.* Got a black coffee?"

Steven handed the coffee to Vivien and Sela. "This Tim, you said he was into Earth Mysteries. Couldn't we use that in some way?"

"Good point," said Vivien. "What do you think Marian?"

Sela pondered for a while then said, "Suppose we say we've found some coins. We could point to another part of the garden then see what he says. We could sound him out, you know, 'what if, etcetera', give him some lunch, wine, get him relaxed…"

"Some pot," interjected Vivien.

"…perhaps, yes, why not? Then, when he's relaxed, give him the opportunity to say how he feels about these sort of things." She looked at the other two with an eager look on her face.

Vivien finished her drink, "Ah, that's better. Yes, that sounds like a good idea."

Steven nodded, "Yes, it does but what I *don't* understand is why would Druids come from Mona to Somerset. It's a bit of a trip isn't it? Wouldn't Wales, or even Cornwall have been better? What about the Romans?"

Sela said, "They didn't bother with this region much. Romans were very practical. They used client kings to rule. They generally settled or influenced only in areas that were productive, you know, grain, cattle, sheep, mining for iron, lead, tin, silver, that sort of thing. They were in the Mendips and the Brendons but didn't bother much with this region. They had a signal station up at County Gate, Old Barrow, but that was to watch the Channel in case the Siluries came across. Exmoor would have seemed inhospitable; too difficult to control and, in any case, the local people didn't put up much resistance. So it's entirely possible that Druids or a Druid, Boudica and her daughters, could have come here."

"And gone where?" he asked. "In your trance you said she'd gone away."

Sela considered this and then said, "Perhaps to Cornwall or no, more likely by boat across the Channel to Wales; to the Siluries, she'd be safe there. It's only about ten miles."

Vivien nodded, "Makes sense to me. So what about this Tim? What's he like, nice?"

Sela smiled. "I don't really know him well; only met him in college when he was giving a talk. We had coffee, seemed quite nice, a bit academic, you know, beard, glasses very into his subject."

"Well if he moves, he's mine," said Vivien and Steven laughed.

Sela wasted no time and telephoned Tim's number. He was in and after a short conversation she put the phone down. "OK, he'll come in a few days."

"He will indeed," interjected Vivien.

"God, don't you ever stop," said Sela in exasperation; she went on, "he said he would be interested in looking at the coins and anything else." She stopped, overcome by fatigue so Steven told her to have a rest.

Whilst Sela took a short nap to clear her head, Vivien watched some T.V. and Steven browsed through the encyclopaedias taking the opportunity to read up on the Boudican Revolt. There was not a lot in the Roman records but archaeology had revealed significant destruction of Colchester, London and St. Albans. The site of the battle was uncertain but most opinion favoured the Midlands. The fate of Boudica and her daughters was unclear, lending some credence to the possibility of Boudica's escape. He was studying the map of Britain when Sela, much refreshed, rejoined them. Anglesey lay off the north-west coast of Wales and his immediate thoughts were that it would have been far easier for any artefacts to be taken across the Straits into Wales or by boat, down the coast, to somewhere away from Roman attack.

"I'm puzzled," he said. "Why would artefacts come here? Why would Boudica come here, I mean, it's a long way from anywhere? Why would anyone come here when they could escape into Wales?"

Vivien nodded. "Yes, it does seem strange but it *did* happen so there you are. Who knows *what* they were thinking?"

They were silent for a while then Sela said, "Yes it happened so let's think it through. Boudica has this great battle and loses. She isn't killed and doesn't kill herself, OK? So, what does she do next? Where does she go? She can't go back to her tribal lands; she can't go west towards Wales 'cos the Romans have been there and the area's not safe. She can't go south 'cos there are tribes sympathetic to Rome there. So, she heads south west and then, eventually, across the Channel into Wales, avoiding patrols and capture."

"Yes, that makes sense," said Steven, "but why here? Is this a sacred area like Mona?"

"Could have been. There's a stone circle up on Porlock Common; stone settings on the moor; and there are barrows. Could have been a special area although there are more impressive circles elsewhere. Don't forget the Culbone bit about Jesus, you know, the legend that he came here; so there could be a sacred tradition in the area. But, it could be more simple than that. Perhaps whoever carried the 'Mysteries of Mona' to here did so 'cos he originated from this area and came home; it would be safer."

"And Boudica comes here by coincidence?" he asked.

"Yes, perhaps, or," she paused, "or, it was known to be a special area. If she was a Druid or priestess, as well as a queen, and there's good reason to think she may have been, then she would know of this area. Also, its proximity to south Wales would make it an ideal spot to hole up for a while."

"How do you mean, 'she may have been a Druid'?" asked Steven.

"Well, one of the histories states that, before the battle, she took a hare from beneath her cloak and set it to run across the field, watching which way it turned – a form of divination."[*]

Vivien nodded, "Yes I've heard of that. Yes, it makes sense to me darlings. But I've been visiting you for ages sweetheart," she said to Sela, "and I've never seen this stone circle."

Sela smiled. "Never occurred to me to show it to you; there's not much to see. In fact, if you didn't look at a map, you'd go right by it. Oh no, *you* wouldn't; you'd probably collapse in its near vicinity."

Steven said, "I don't know of it either. Could we go and have a look at it now?"

In a short while they had driven up the steep winding road of Porlock Hill and out onto the high moor. Sela directed him down a side road and after a mile or so she asked him to stop. They got out and Steven looked around. They were in an open area close to a stream. A farm gate lay to their right and Sela took them through it.

"How far is it?" he asked, seeing nothing.

"Oooh! Energy, oooh." Vivien had gone pale and had stopped walking.

"There you are," said Sela triumphantly, "definite proof of her sensitivity. We're in the circle now."

"Where?" he looked around and saw nothing.

"No, look!" She took him back a few paces and pointed to a stone set low into the ground.

"And here, and here, and there." She was taking him around the circumference.

---

[*] Dio Cassius – Historia Romano LXII.

"It used to be higher but some bloody vandal destroyed it. However, there are records. OK, not impressive like other circles but, nevertheless it's here – and look at Vivien."

Vivien had sat down, her face white and sweaty. Steven was impressed at this demonstration of Vivien's sensitivity. They helped her up and walked back to the car.

"There's a burial over there and a stone setting," said Sela, pointing across the road.

"What's a stone setting?" he asked, helping Vivien into the car.

"No one really knows," said Sela as she got in as well, "but you get lines of stones, in rows, across Exmoor, only low ones though, nothing impressive. It's to do with the type of stone up here but, as to their meaning and use, who knows?"

Vivien had recovered and lit a cigarette. "Well, ducky, you should have warned me. Bloody powerful that was. A place of sacrifice, no doubt of that. I wasn't expecting anything; didn't even know we were there, then, Shazam! Woo! Powerful, I must say."

Steven headed the car back. Sela continued to explain about the area. "There are the Whit Stones – no one knows their origin and, over there," she pointed out of the window, "is Culbone. That area is really weird. It's got the smallest church in Britain; stone rows; an inscribed stone with what looks like a lopsided Celtic cross and they found a Beaker burial there as well. And, of course, let's not forget Jesus."

"God forbid we do," said Vivien. "*He* seems to be everywhere. He follows me around, not only here but the Holy Grail as well, at Glastonbury. Do you think *He's* trying to tell me something? Should I be 'born again'?"

"Once is enough for the world," said Sela laughing. "They wouldn't have you anyway – too dark and mysterious for them. You'd be exorcised straight away."

Vivien took a drag of her cigarette, exhaled and sent a cloud of blue smoke into the car causing Steven to cough. "Oops! Sorry darling," she said and then continued: "Actually, my aunt did try to have me exorcised once. It was strange. I kept saying that I wasn't interested, that I had my own spiritual ideas but *they* kept saying that it wasn't me speaking; it was the *demon within*. They prayed, put their hands on me, yelling out the name of Jesus. In the end they gave up, said I was beyond saving and that I would burn in Hell when the battle of Armageddon comes." She threw the finished cigarette out of the window.

"You shouldn't do that," said Steven, "you could start a fire."

"And will I start a fire in your heart, baby?" asked Vivien, batting her eyelashes at him but ignoring his reproof. Steven didn't answer, concentrating instead on the difficult drop of Porlock Hill.

Back at the house Steven said to them, "So, a place of sacrifice. Were they really so bloodthirsty?"

Sela replied, "You have to try to put yourself back in ancient times. People lived on the edge, you know, close to life and death. They were much more conscious of their frailty than we are today. Average lifespan was probably around thirty years. And they saw death first hand, not like us today. How many dead people have your seen?" she asked him.

"Well, actually, I'm not typical. My first job was at an undertakers so I saw many but I take your point."

"Oooh!" said Vivien. "Spooky. Did you see *lots and lots* of dead people? I bet you had a good look at the girls, eh?"

He nodded. "Actually, when I first started I admit I was curious – who wouldn't be at sixteen years of age? But you soon get used to it and, in the end, you feel very little – it's just a job. I never really got used to the relatives though – all that sadness. At first, you look at a body and find it hard to think it was once alive, it's so still. Your brain tells you that it's breathing but, of course, it isn't – and no body warmth."

"Meet any necrophiliacs?" said Vivien.

"Oh stop it Viv," said Sela. "I was talking about life and death and sacrifice. Look, when you live close to Nature, on the edge, and you're aware of your frailty, your vulnerability, then you become aware of the Gods. You see the seasons changing; the weather coming; the storms frighten you and hail can flatten your crops. No rain means that the harvest could be late or non-existent; no game even. So, you feel the need to placate the Gods. You give some of your crop or you sacrifice an animal or what could be better than a human sacrifice, eh? What better than the tribal chief or an enemy prisoner of high status?"

"I see what you mean," he said.

Sela continued, "You remember we talked about the sacrifice of Jesus – in a way, that was a re-run of the sacrifice of the Corn King – an annual event in ancient times. Anyway, you offer what you can to the Gods and, if you've done it right, you're rewarded. I don't think they were any more bloody than we are today with our bombs, etcetera. Look what a nuclear bomb can do. There's a whole industry built up around the arms trade."

"Wow, that's a bit of a jump around – from human sacrifice in ancient Britain to corporate America and the arms trade." He laughed and she laughed as well. "I get a bit confused sometimes," she said as though to herself.

"I've noticed," said Vivien.

The evening was drawing in and Sela said that she ought to go back to the cottage to check on Tanith. It was agreed that Vivien would go with her, stay fora few days so they could do some shopping together and catch up on things. They would return to Steven in two days at lunch-time when Tim Hutchins would visit.

Steven waved them off, saw to Perry's needs and settled down for a quiet evening. He reflected on the events of the past days in a state of mixed

The Moon Temple

feelings ranging from bewilderment, scepticism, elation, excitement to real emotion when he thought about Sela. So much had happened to him and he pondered the implications of his new relationship.

He knew he would miss her company over the next few days. Could it be so that he and Sela would form a strong and permanent relationship? One side of his mind longed for this, the other urging caution. After all, he had felt 'love' for Jane Trethowan hadn't he? A memory of Jane came back to him but then he remembered what Sela had said about him being hexed. Sela, surely, had been right. Yet, what did he really know of this strange woman? There was the difference in their ages, though not extreme; there was her life style – she was very strange and, though he was open to new ways, new ideas, he knew it would take time before he could be so totally convinced of the power of witchcraft. Having thought that, he immediately recalled, with real fear and horror, the events of the past days. If it was not witchcraft than what *had* been going on? Was he going mad? He rejected that and considered that the grief and strain of the past years may have weakened his mental strength.

But no, what about Perry? The dog had also experienced the terror on the pathway; had experienced the 'attack' in the orangery, hence the frenzied barking; had an awareness of the energies within the grove. No, everything had been real.

And what about Vivien? She clearly, was sensitive. If he needed convincing of this then her reaction within the stone circle had been the clincher. She had never been there yet collapsed when entering its precincts even though it was not immediately visible to the casual eye.

But above all, he remembered Sela standing in the orangery and the memory of her bewitching actions there and up on the moor in the moonlight. Yes, witchcraft was a real power, terrible yet, at the same time, beautiful.

He got up and went into the orangery. He stood silently contemplating the now dark area and went over to the windows looking out into the garden. This time there was no horror, no void, no melancholy only the memory of Sela's eyes, so different to Jane's. Jane's eyes… following him and watching. He came to with a start. Why had he thought of Jane? Was it starting all over again?

He held his ground and cleared his mind, staring out into the darkness. No, it was all right. He turned back and stood in the centre of the room. A fleeting memory of Jane nagged at the back of his mind and, again, he dispelled it. He stood straight, pointed his finger forward and inscribed the sign of the pentagram in the air, saying the words Sela had taught him.

> *"Powers of Light be with me;*
> *Guard and protect me,*
> *Be merciful unto me*
> *Through Time and throughout Eternity."*

As he said this he visualised a sphere of light around his body. Immediately the nagging insistent memory of Jane and her watching eyes, vanished. He felt a sense of release and this feeling sustained him throughout the evening and through a peaceful night.

CHAPTER 20

Sela and Vivien arrived just after midday and were having a drink when the sound of car tyres on gravel announced the arrival of Tim Hutchins. He was a tall man, in his forties, with a greying beard, longish brown hair and spectacles. He looked every inch a stereotypical academic in his crumpled jacket and cord trousers. He re-acquainted himself with Sela, shook hands with Steven and seemed almost mesmerised by Vivien who, in turn, gave every moment of attention to him. Steven had to admit that Vivien could look quite striking when she chose to do so and, in this case, she had certainly done that. Her black hair was held across the crown of her head by a braided band and her blue eyes were set off to advantage by the dark gothic eye makeup so that they seemed to glow in her pale face.

After some preliminary small talk, Steven opened the box into which he had put the coins. Tim took out an eyeglass and examined them closely.

"Hmm! Extraordinary. No doubt about it, these are coins of the Iceni or Ecen. Prasutagus was the king – husband of Boudica – you may know her as Boadicea." At the mention of Boudica's name the others exchanged glances. So Sela's vision had been correct. Steven felt a sense of amazement at such a confirmation. Tim continued, "Hmm. Where did you find these?"

They went into the garden. Steven led them away from the grove and over to a flower bed which he had deliberately disturbed the previous day. "I was half-heartedly beginning to do a bit of gardening when I just turned them up. I've got a metal detector so I went over the area to see if there was anything else but no, nothing."

Tim examined the site then said, "Probably just isolated coins. You do get them every now and again. Roman coins have been found up near Selworthy and at various sites and odd locations all around Exmoor but these... well, it's a bit strange."

"How do you mean?" asked Sela.

"Well, Romano-British coins are not unusual nor would it be unusual to find a scatter of different types but to find three silver coins, from one particular tribe with no links to this area, is strange indeed. Have you got the detector handy?"

In a short while Tim was running the detector around the locality. There was a 'beep' and everyone watched as he probed the area but it was only an old rusty screw. "Hmm. No – no you're right, nothing else here and this is a good detector as well. No, must have been a simple coin drop. Iceni? Well, perhaps an auxiliary soldier – there was a signal station up on the moor you know. Perhaps a bit of loot after the rebellion." He stood looking at the site, stroking his beard in a gesture of puzzlement. He seemed about to say something but then shrugged and handed the detector to Steven.

They walked back to the house and Steven prepared a light lunch as they all sat in the kitchen talking. Tim told them about his work. It turned out that he was actually a historian not a professional archaeologist but he was very involved with a local group and had managed several site digs under the direction of a professional archaeologist. However, it was clear that he knew his subject and he enthused about a Saxon site found near Watchet. Steven was a bit puzzled, as the lunch progressed, for Sela did not raise the matter of a possible grave site and cut across Vivien when she seemed to be moving in that direction. Instead, she asked him about energy lines, stone settings and circles and, as the afternoon progressed and the wine flowed copiously, aided by Vivien's drug laden cigarettes, Tim relaxed.

"Yes, I do think the ancients had an insight into things now lost to us. We do not know why they erected lines of stones, or single stones, and we certainly know only a little about the great circles and henges. Oh yes, I know about the sun and the moon, astronomical alignments, that sort of thing but what were their *true meanings* – their *real* use?" He took a deep drag of the cigarette and smiled down at Vivien who was now nestled comfortably against him. She said nothing only looking up at him with admiring eyes.

Steven beckoned to Sela and she discreetly followed him out into the sitting room. "I thought you were going to raise the matter of the burial – you know, what would he do etcetera, etcetera."

"Yes but, to be honest, I don't trust him. I don't know what but, look, when you showed him where you found the coins he didn't ask the questions I would have expected an archaeologist to ask." She was speaking just above a whisper in case they could be overheard.

He did likewise. "But he's not professional."

"No, but that doesn't mean that he isn't an expert. It means he doesn't do it for his main income. He's noted for his excavation techniques. Also, he's saying little about Earth Mysteries – all superficial."

"Could be he's intoxicated by wine, drugs and Vivien."

"Ah yes, I hadn't thought of that. You could be right. Boy, he's really gone on her isn't he?" She looked towards the kitchen where a shuffling sound could be heard.

"Like I am on you,?" He pulled her to him and they kissed.

"God, I'd like to be alone with you now," she said. "Oh, listen."

There was a gasping and snorting coming from the kitchen. They peered in to see Vivien lying back on the kitchen table with Tim leaning over her in an awkward embrace. Sela coughed and they looked up.

"Oh – oops – sorry darlings but I couldn't resist him," said Vivien, clambering down and hanging on to Tim who seemed reluctant to let her go.

"Look," said Steven, "why don't you two make yourselves comfortable in the lounge; put some music on and have a drink. We'll tidy up in here." He winked at Sela who started collecting plates.

Vivien and Tim wandered out and Steven grabbed Sela. "Come on," he said and soon they were lying together in his room. Again he felt vital and potent with her and their love-making, though urgent and quick, was, nevertheless, extremely satisfying for both of them. Lying together he said, "I love you, you know."

"I know," she replied, kissing him, "and I love you too." They lay, holding tightly to each other and then pulled away as they got out of bed and re-arranged clothing. She stood in front of the mirror straightening her skirt.

Steven came up behind her and tucked a label back inside of her top. "So, why don't you trust him?" he asked her.

"I don't know. I thought he would ask more questions. Perhaps he wants to look at the whole site before saying more. I don't know but he seemed dismissive. It's possible he might want to investigate the site himself – he was clearly taken by the fact that the coins were from the Iceni. It would be a major coup for him to uncover a grave which might contain an archaeological sensation. Can you imagine what it would mean to discover anything relating to Boudica? He would be world famous – a sensation overnight – a book, serial rights in journals. He'd make a fortune." She sat down on the bed and started combing her hair into place.

"But he can't dig here unless I give permission," said Steven. He watched as she re-arranged her hair and he marvelled at the way she managed to get it all into place without the use of a mirror.

She shrugged and said, "No, but he could generate local interest. You'd get more unwelcome visitors."

"Like Dan?"

"Well, not like them but nuisance detectors – that sort of thing." She changed direction. "Look, he seems to be getting along with Viv so let's wait a bit until we know him better then tell him about our ideas."

"But don't you think Viv will have said something by now?"

She laughed. "Are you serious? Did you see the two of them? I bet they're at it like rabbits downstairs. No, she won't have said anything yet but she might later. I'll have a word." She stood up, came over to him and put her arms around his waist.

"Anyway," he said, "his identification of the coins with Boudica confirms your trance vision doesn't it?"

"I never doubted it for a minute," she said. "If you could have experienced it as I did, you'd have had no doubts either."

They went downstairs and peeped into the lounge. Tim and Viv were both dead to the world on the carpet, he with no trousers and she with no skirt – it was not a good sight. They closed the door and went into the kitchen. As they cleared up the plates and put things away she said, "I've got to go away

The Moon Temple

tomorrow to Exeter – just one night – a lecture but I'll be back by the following evening."

"Can I come?" he asked not bearing the thought of being parted for even a short time.

"No, not really. It's a talk to students so not open to the public and then I've got to attend a seminar. Why, will you miss me?"

"Of course I will but I'll survive I suppose." He sounded forlorn, like a lost child.

She stroked his cheek. "I'll be back quick as I can, OK?"

He nodded and kissed her. "It'll seem ages but you've gotta do what you've gotta do." Then, "They're still asleep so what do you want to do now?"

They decided to take Perry around the garden and spent the next half hour throwing a stick for him and discussing certain gardening points. When they got back, Vivien and Tim were in the kitchen drinking coffee.

"Have a nice walk?" asked Vivien.

"Yes. Have a nice… er… sleep?" asked Steven.

Vivien looked coyly at Tim, giving him one of her sidelong glances. "Oh yes, a lovely deep, deep sleep…" She patted Tim's arm.

He blushed, "Er, yes, sorry – I don't know what came over me. Too much of the old puff I guess." They all laughed and Tim relaxed again. "Look," he said, "I've got to get away. Thanks for the lunch. The coins, err, could I take them to the local group?"

"I'd rather you didn't, at least, not at this stage. I'll decide what I want to do; give you a call, maybe tomorrow, yes?"

"Sure," said Tim. He got up and looked at Vivien. "Er, would you like a lift anywhere?"

"Oh, you could drop me in the village," said Vivien, too quickly. She turned to Sela. "I'll be back later darling, OK? At your place," she winked.

Sela said, "Oh Viv, I've got something of yours," and she beckoned to her. Vivien followed her out of the kitchen leaving the two men alone.

Tim looked at Steven. "She's great – Vivien I mean – Marian is as well," he added hastily.

"Yes, both, I understand – don't worry. Yes, Vivien is certainly different."

Tim looked enthusiastic. "Yes, I'll say. I've never gone for those sort of goth looking girls – lots of them when I was at university but, somehow, it suits Viv don't you think? I mean it's quite a turn-on really."

Steven nodded in agreement, "Yes, I can see that it could be." For a moment he felt sorry for Tim. Clearly, he didn't know what he was getting into.

Sela and Vivien returned. Vivien was smiling. "OK then *darlings*. I'll be back soon." She went up to Steven, "mwah, mwah," and then to Sela, "mwah, mwah." She waved at them and was out of the door.

When Steven had shut the door Sela said, "Well, I won't see her for a while at least so that means I have you all to myself."

"How do you mean? She'll be back here soon."

"You're kidding. They'd obviously arranged that. No she's got Tim in her clutches and he, poor man, is in for an interesting ride."

"Yes, I was just watching them. I doubt he'll be able to handle her. I wonder that he can drive at all – in his state. Does that mean that I, too, am in for an interesting ride?" He raised his eyebrows in query.

She placed her hand on her hips, lowered her voice and, in a reasonable imitation of Marilyn Monroe she said, "Now what do you think – lover boy?"

The Wheel of Fire – The Horns of the Moon

CHAPTER 21

Tim opened the passenger door and Vivien climbed in to his 4-by-4.

"Oh, this is *too* much," she said as he got in. "I bet this can *really* take you to some interesting places."

He started the engine then turned to her. "Oh yes, some really good places. Look, I've just got to drop something off to a friend then, if you like, I could show you exactly what it can do."

"And what *you* can do, I hope," she batted her eyelashes and he laughed.

"Oh certainly – yes indeed." He drew her to him and kissed her, hard. He let her go and she smiled at him.

"Patience, patience..." she ran her hand along his thigh. He drove the car out onto the lane as Vivien began rolling a cigarette. She was engrossed in this when the car turned into another drive and pulled up.

"Come on," said Tim, "this won't take long."

She put the roll-up in her pocket and got out of the car. Tim was embracing a tall woman and, as he pulled away, the woman said, "Hallo Vivien, its been ages since I heard from you."

Vivien looked at her with shock and pain, her heart pounding. "Hallo Jane," she said, the lightness gone from her voice.

"Don't I get a kiss then?" Jane Trethowan came over to her, placed her hands on Vivien's shoulders and kissed her full on the lips as Vivien's body tensed. "Oh come on now. It was a long time ago."

"It was two years ago; to be exact, two years, two months and three weeks," said Vivien; she looked even more pale.

Jane turned to Tim, who was leaning against the car watching them. "Vivien and I have got a lot to catch up on. I'll call you later."

"Sure – no problem," said Tim. He smiled at Vivien in a casual manner. "I'll see you soon," he said, got into his roadster and was soon gone, leaving the two women together. Vivien stared after the car. What was happening to her? Tim had been all over her and then...

"Oh come on Viv – you are pleased to see me, aren't you?"

Vivien turned to see Jane looking at her with a smile on her face. "You bitch – you bloody cow bitch," said Vivien.

How could this be? What was Tim doing, going off like that? What was Jane doing here? She felt her mind spinning as Jane replied, "Oh, now that's hardly fair and doesn't make sense. A cow, a bitch certainly but a *cow bitch*?" She gave a little laugh as she said this.

Vivien turned to walk away but Jane caught her by the arm. "Don't go Viv – please. Look, I'm sorry. Come in... at least for a drink. Oh come on, don't cry... come in." She put her arms around Vivien's shoulders and guided her into the house. Vivien sat sobbing in the deep armchair as Jane prepared a vodka and tonic. "No ice, see – I remembered." She handed the glass to Vivien who took it, as though by instinct.

"You bloody bitch," sobbed Vivien. "You left me just like that – you made me ill, you know." She took a gulp of the vodka, fished in her pocket and pulled out the roll-up. She took a puff and stopped sobbing. Jane said nothing but handed her some tissues. Vivien got up and went over to a mirror. "God, what a bloody sight." The tears had formed black rivulets down her cheeks. "Where's the bathroom?"

Jane pointed to a doorway and Vivien got up, her mind calming under the effects of the vodka and marijuana. After ten minutes she returned, looking fresh and composed. "I'm going now," she said but there was no force behind her statement of intent. She was toying with the pendant around her neck, indecisive, uncertain.

Jane got up. "Oh Viv, look, I'm sorry really and truly sorry. I didn't leave you in the way you think, I had to go."

Vivien sat down. "You did. You did leave me. You just went leaving me alone – no word, no phone calls, nothing. God, I hate you. You ruined my life. Do you know I had a breakdown?"

Jane came over to her. "Oh no, really? I am so sorry. I didn't mean to hurt you – you know what I'm like; I don't always think."

Vivien took another gulp and finished the drink. Jane took the glass and refilled it.

"But you just went," said Vivien forlornly.

"It was you – your fault," said Jane.

"*My fault! My fault!* How? Why? What did *I* do? *You* were always in charge – in control. *You always are.*"

"What I mean is that I was getting too fond of you," said Jane softly. "You know me, I don't get attached to anyone. But you, you were different – I had to get away."

Vivien looked at Jane who did seem to be sincere. "I didn't mean to be so clingy," she said.

"I know you didn't but there you are – so I went and I'm sorry, so sorry you were ill. Viv, Viv, you and I had something special and now fate has brought us together again. You know all about fate, destiny – come on – you and I were special." She paused and then said, "Do you know, I missed you; me, can you imagine *me* missing anyone? But I missed you and now you're here again. Can't you forgive me?"

Vivien looked at her, gulped down her vodka and then held out the glass. "Well, I suppose I'd forgive you anything but even more so if you give me a refill."

Jane laughed and filled the glass. "So, where were you off to with Tim?

"You know *me*," said Vivien, "I met him today, got laid and we were off for another ride. He's not bad is he... for a man?"

"Where did you meet him?"

Vivien paused before answering but realised that Tim would know anyway. There could be no harm in telling the truth – after a fashion. "I'm visiting my friend Marian Hall and we were at a friend of hers, Steven Downs, he's just across the fields from you."

"Oh yes, I know them both," said Jane, "but now you're here and I want you to stay with me. We'll have dinner, yes? Oh come on, say yes."

To Vivien's ears Jane sounded as though she was being genuine – wanted her to stay. "Yes," said Vivien. The drinks and the cigarette had done their work. She was feeling relaxed, at ease and there was Jane, her Jane, back again – like old times. Jane came over to her and cupped her face. She gave her a lingering kiss, her tongue flickering between Vivien's lips. Vivien gasped, all the memories flooding back; all the happiness, all the heartache. "I need to freshen up," she said, "a shower."

Jane took her by the hand and led her upstairs and into a large bedroom. "There's the bathroom," she said. "I'll see you in a while."

Vivien undressed and stood under the warmth of the shower. She could not believe this. Jane was back in her life. She had not told Marian about Jane, only that she had experienced a distressing break-up after a love affair. When Marian and Steven had referred to Jane Trethowan she had decided not to say anything, not wanting to awaken memories which, inevitably, would have been dredged up under Marian's questioning. She did not want to compromise the matters relating to Steven's house and land, seeing herself as being long gone and back in Glastonbury when they, eventually, brought their investigation to a conclusion. But now Jane was back in her life. Should she say anything to either Marian or to Steven? Jane wanted whatever was on Steven's land – should she tell Jane of the past life regression? She decided not to out of loyalty to Marian and to Steven whom she liked. No, concentrate instead on rebuilding her relationship with Jane. God, she had loved Jane – she was so powerful, commanding and dominating, a perfect foil to Vivien's sexual compliance and insatiable appetite. She turned off the shower, towelled herself dry and stepped out of the bathroom and into the bedroom. Jane was there reclining naked on the bed. "Come here Viv. I need to do something."

Vivien felt her stomach quiver, dropped the towel and went over to Jane who pulled her down onto the bed and, for the next hour, Vivien felt herself floating on a sea of ecstasy as Jane explored her, exploited her and finally pushed her aside, the different desires of both women fully satisfied.

"Life is strange," mused Jane after a while. "I never thought I'd see you again. What have you been doing recently?"

Vivien chatted happily about her art, her psychic work, her varied relationships.

"But there has never been anyone to match you," she said.

"What about Marian? You said that you visit her a lot – is she with you?"

Vivien hesitated. This was an opportunity to make Jane jealous and it might throw Jane off the scent in case she became too curious about Marian's relationship with Steven Downs.

"Oh yes, now and again but not serious you know, not like with you; and we do psychic stuff."

"Yes, I know she's in the Craft," said Jane. "I asked her to join me once but she declined, something about being a loner; no good in groups, that sort of thing – her loss though."

"She is good at it, you know," said Vivien, defending her friend but then, sensing a sudden tension, she added, "but not like you – no one is like you. I've known many occultists. No, you, you're something *really* special." She felt Jane relax and looked at her, seeing a smile on her lips. She said it again, "You are extremely powerful in magic Jane; I've never seen anyone to match you."

Jane was positively enjoying the praise. It was disconcerting for Vivien. Jane could change moods so rapidly and took offence at the tiniest thing. Yet, a bit of praise and she positively glowed. Vivien remembered that Jane could also be vicious, verbally and physically, if she felt that someone wasn't giving due regard to her powers. She stroked Jane's face.

"I'm so happy to be with you again, Jane darling. But you won't leave me again will you? No, sorry, I don't mean to pressure you – sorry – it's just that you're everything I've ever wanted to be. I was devastated when you went."

Jane propped herself on her elbow and looked down at Vivien. She studied the pale face and the eyes looking up at her with evident adoration. "No, don't worry Vivien. I need you as much as you need me – no, I'll not leave you. In fact, I want you to join me – join my group. I need someone with your deep intuitive powers and your sensitivity. Just think, you and I, what we could do, eh? It will be perfect." She bent her head and kissed Vivien whose heart seemed ready to burst with joy.

"Oh Jane, you mean we could be together – a couple – you and me?"

"Of course darling – I told you. I missed you. Do you think I would let you go now?" She got up and stood at the foot of the bed looking at Vivien. "Come down in a while. I'll arrange for some dinner and we can talk –," she looked at her watch, "say, around 6 o'clock. OK?"

Vivien felt sleepy and exhausted and was soon asleep. When she awoke it was dark. She checked her watch – 8 p.m. She leapt up, showered and dressed, then went downstairs.

"I let you sleep – you must have been tired." Jane was standing in the doorway of the dining room. "Come, I've got some nice food for us – we can talk."

Vivien sat at a small table tastefully arranged and accepted the glass of wine Jane poured for her. "So, Jane, what have you been up to?" she asked.

"Oh this and that. I have a large business to look after remember? But, that's not what you're asking me is it? You mean, what do I want with Steven Downs? Oh come on – I know you and I know that you must have talked about me with Marian and him – that's why you came down here."

Vivien took a gulp of wine. It was very good and the warmth of it coursed down her throat. She toyed with her soup but didn't answer. The conversation was turning – disturbing her.

Jane smiled, but the smile did not reach her eyes, which remained cold. "Viv, Viv, you're with *me* now. Jane and Viv together – against the world."

It sounded comforting and Vivien attempted to bring the subject back to a more normal level. "I told you, I visit Marian regularly."

"But not Steven Downs – you can't know him, he's not been here long. So come on, tell all – tell me what's going on – what you were all doing."

Vivien took another drink, she felt a bit light headed. "No, nothing." She began to feel anxious. Something was wrong. Jane was becoming insistent, unpleasant almost.

"Vivien, I *know* why you're down here. You're looking for the hoard aren't you? That's why you're here isn't it?" She reached over and placed her hand over Vivien's free hand, digging her nails into the flesh.

"Hoard? What?" She felt uneasy now and put down her spoon. "Jane, don't... I don't know – oh... you're hurting – don't."

"Vivien, I know about it – all of it."

Jane took her hand away and Vivien looked at the indentations left in her skin by Jane's nails. "How could you? No one knows..." She tailed off, realising she was falling into Jane's trap. She rubbed her sore hand. There were tears in her eyes.

Jane got up, a look of triumph on her face. "How could I know? Well that's easy – you told me." She walked around to Vivien and stood beside her looking down at her.

Vivien's head was spinning. "*I* told you. I... How could I? I only found out myself..." Again she stopped, dismayed, bewildered.

Jane took her arm and helped her up guiding her into the lounge. Tim was sitting there. "Hello Vivien." He smiled. He was relaxed, arms draped along the back of the sofa; at ease, composed, at home.

"What? Tim! Jane! What?" Vivien sat down. Was she having another breakdown? She rubbed her hand again to ease the soreness.

"You told me, well, at least you pinpointed the area, roughly, where the things are buried but now we need to know exactly where and you can tell me, I know you can." Jane's tone was hard.

Tim said, "I wasn't taken in by that story about the coins. Three silver coins of the Iceni, just lying there." He was looking at her with an expression of contempt. Vivien could not believe the change in his demeanour.

Jane had gone to a cupboard and she returned carrying a tape player. "Now, I wonder who this is." She pressed the switch.

There was a soft hissing noise, as the tape began to turn, and then it came to life. "Take hold of the script." It was Tim's voice. "There, have you got it? Now, quest back in time to when this was written… back, go back."

"Back… yes, I can see, yes," softly Vivien's voice floated in the air. She stared at the recorder in disbelief. She must be going mad. This could not be. "Yes, back. I can feel it – see it – see him." Vivien listened in mounting horror. The voice, and the words, spoken softly were still recognisable. It was, without doubt, her voice.

Tim spoke again, "See who? Who can you see?"

"A scribe – he is reading it – reading this."

"Where is he?"

"On a fort – up on Hadrian's Wall."

Tim's voice sounded tense. "Where did the script come from originally?" Silence for a while until Tim said, again, "Come on Vivien, where did the script come from?"

There was a long silence, then Vivien's voice whispered softly, "Far to the south – in the land of the Dumnoni."

Jane's voice cut in, demanding answers. "Where? Where is that? Ask her – ask her."

"Shhh – you're disturbing the moment – be patient. The Dumnoni were a tribe in this area. She's been right so far. She couldn't have known that I got this from near the Wall." His voice continued. "Vivien, you've said 'the land of the Dumnoni,' can you sense where? Can you show us?"

Silence – then Vivien's voice, again. "Yes… yes, I know where it is."

Jane's voice cut in. "Get the map."

There was a rustling sound and then Tim said, "Take your pendulum and dowse for the location." A long pause, only the hiss of tape audible in the still room. "There, I have sensed it, there." Vivien's voice was faint and dreamlike.

Jane's voice said, "Where is it stopping, focusing? Ah, on Exmoor but where, where?" Her voice was urgent, impatient. "Read the script again." There was a silence and then Tim's voice. "Vivien, it says 'the Mysteries rest near the high hills where the trident of Neptune pierces stony arms to become part of the whole'. What does that mean? Can you sense what it means?"

Again silence and the hiss of tape.

Vivien was feeling sick as she listened. How could this be? When was this? She asked the question but Jane gestured for her to be quiet and the voice from the tape continued. "There on the moor; Porlock, there, here."

"She's pointing to my land," said Jane excitedly. "No – Rita Palmer's land – yes, look, the stream and up here look, two tributaries into one and then it flows into the Channel through the shingle ridge. OK, bring her out of it."

Tim's voice was heard saying, "Vivien, you will sleep now, sleep, you will not remember this; you will sleep; you will not remember me; you will not remember our meeting today nor that you have seen Jane. You will sleep and when you awake, you will be refreshed... No memory of our meeting, do you understand?"

Vivien's voice, faint, drowsy. "Yes, sleep. I will not remember, sleep, sleeping oh mmmmmm..."

Jane switched off the tape and looked at the bewildered and horrified Vivien. "There, you see. So it's no use feeling loyalty to Marian. You've already done it. Betrayed her if you like. But its not betrayal Viv." Her voice had become gentle coaxing. She sat down next to Vivien who was beginning to cry. "There, there, you're with me. Viv and Jane and Tim, all friends, close friends, more than friends. You and me," her voice was soft, insistent, repetitive and Vivien was beginning to slump against her. "Friends, you and me, lovers, companions. You, me and Tim, friends – lovers. You are nothing to Marian – she's just a friend. You are nothing at all to Steven Downs. You don't know him; he doesn't like me. He's been horrible to me. You won't like him, Viv. You and me, we're special, aren't we, aren't we, special, yes?" She was stroking Vivien's hair. "Special friends, we are, aren't we, lovers, you, me, Tim, all special, aren't we?"

"Yes... Yes..." Dreamily, Vivien answered, her mind completely absorbed by Jane's voice and the warmth of her body. She felt another hand on her and Tim's voice. "Yes, Vivien, we are all together, you, me, Jane. Friends, lovers, companions. You will be with us, work with us. You are nothing to Marian. She has gone away, left you. You don't care about Steven Downs do you?"

"No, Marian has gone away... Yes, I want to be with you, Jane, Tim... yes, with you both – friends – friends, companions..." She dozed off.

Jane stood up and she and Tim laid Vivien full length on the sofa. They went out into the dining room. "Soup?" asked Jane.

"Why not," said Tim. He took the bowl and sat down.

"Don't drink that wine – here, I'll open this one." She took the bottle already on the table and went into the kitchen where she poured it into the sink. She returned and opened a new bottle. "I don't want you sleeping on me tonight," she said.

"Don't worry, no fear of that. OK, so now what do we do?"

"She'll tell us what she knows when she wakes up. Then we'll fix Mr. Downs."

"What about Marian?" he asked.

"She's away. When she comes back she'll have no idea what's going on. I'll arrange for it to look as though he's gone away with Vivien. No problem. We'll think about Marian later. Maybe get her on our side. She might be useful. Viv's mine now."

"And mine as well," said Tim laughing. "You certainly are a kinky lady, aren't you?"

She shrugged her shoulders and took a drink of the wine. "Well, a bit of variety never did anyone any harm."

"I agree." He finished the drink, stood up and put his arms around her, pulling her to him.

They went back into the lounge where Vivien lay sleeping. Jane leaned over her. "Vivien, wake up when I count to three. You will be with me and Tim, friends, companions, lovers, friends. Part of my group, you and me. Viv, Viv, one – two – three."

Vivien opened her eyes and looked at Jane. "Oh, sorry. Slept did I? So tired, tired. Hallo Tim, sorry, tired, sleepy – got a ciggy?"

"Yes, I know," said Jane. "Come, time for bed, eh?"

She helped Vivien up and, supported by Jane and Tim, Vivien made her way slowly and unsteadily up the stairs. Jane smiled across Vivien's head at Tim as they escorted the sleepy, bewildered, helpless Vivien into the bedroom.

CHAPTER 22

As Steven breakfasted, Sela chatted, happily, about the trip to Exeter. "At least I'll get a chance to do a bit of shopping."

"Where will you stay?" he asked.

"Oh, in the Halls of Residence – not bad really, you get a good breakfast. Seminar is in the afternoon so I should be back in the evening."

"Do you want me to look in on Tanith?"

"No, I'll pop home now, put some food down, give her a stroke – if she's in that is. The problem is that she's got all the woods to hunt in. Cat food ain't so good after a fresh little birdy." He had a mind-picture of Tanith tearing a bird to pieces and he remembered the cat sharpening its claws in front of the fire.

He said, "Perhaps it was Tanith stalking me in the woods – you know, a sort of werecat changing its shape."

He looked up at her; she was regarding him seriously. "You don't really think that do you?"

"Of course not; mind you, nothing would surprise me after what I've been through." Seeing her serious face he hastened to re-assure her. "Hey, come on, just joking. No, of course I don't think that." He got up and came over to her, putting his arms around her and kissing her on the crown of her head. "So when will you leave?" He was trying to be nonchalant about the temporary separation but he hated the idea of their parting.

She looked at her watch and said she would go at ten o'clock. "Take me a couple of hours or more to get there."

He walked her back to her cottage, Perry in attendance, kissed her goodbye and then headed back along the terraced path. Hawkwood was so empty without her he thought as he tidied up the kitchen. He wondered what had happened to Vivien. His query about her to Sela had resulted in a shrug and a smile. "Knowing Vivien," she had said, "I would think that she has completely exhausted poor Tim Hutchins. She knows I'm away today and back tomorrow so she'll probably turn up here. Can you look after her?"

"Yep, don't worry. I'll be well on my guard from her predatory advances, although, come to think of it, bedding a vampire would be an experience."

She had kicked him under the table. "Hands off! The vooman is mine." She had said this in a deep gutteral tone.

"Oh, very Bram Stoker," he had replied. As he walked down the stairs and into the lounge, he smiled at the memory. He spent the next hour reading and then the doorbell rang.

"Hallo Steven darling," said Vivien. "The wanton returns." She looked pale, far more so than her usual goth appearance and the shadows beneath her eyes were not due to makeup. Obviously, she had spent a heavy night of passion, drink and drugs, with poor Tim, Steven found himself thinking.

"Hi yourself," he said. "Have a good time?"

"My *dear*, don't ask me. The man was absolutely insatiable – ooooh! I can hardly walk."

"Spare me the details," said Steven as he led her into the kitchen. "Coffee?"

"Oh *you sweetheart*, yes I could *murder* a cup." She perched on one of the stools and started to roll a cigarette.

"Marian's gone away but you know that, she said I'm to look after you. Back tomorrow evening." He switched the kettle off and spooned some coffee into a mug.

"Look after me, eh?" She batted her eyes at him and gave him the sidelong glance.

He ignored her. "What are you doing today – any good at gardening?"

"Gardening – are you *mad*? *Me*? Darling, the nearest I get to gardening is a trip to a flower stall. I am absolute death to plants I can assure you. No you potter about I'll go and have a nap. I'm absolutely done, darling. The man is…"

"Yes, I know, insatiable; here," he passed her a coffee and she sat, sipping it.

"I'll have this then I must have a shower and change."

Steven eyed her and said, "Did you say anything to Tim about the site?"

"No, no of *course* not. Marian asked me not to, although I don't know why. I had the *absolutely perfect* opportunity last night. God, he would have done absolutely *anything* I asked – anything." She looked at Steven with that coy sidelong glance but he did not respond to her. In fact he found Vivien tiresome; very attractive, yes, in a sort of 'S and M' way but tiresome, with her constant obsessive harping on about sex. She finished her coffee and went upstairs.

"I'll be in the garden," he shouted to her and went outside. He surveyed the untidy beds and vowed, again, to get a gardener in. It did not appeal to him to start weeding or forking the beds and he did not know much about pruning large established trees and shrubs. He picked up a loose branch or two and the scattered flowerpots, then went back inside. Vivien had changed and looked much fresher. She had made another coffee and pushed a mug over to him. He took it and drank some of the warm liquid.

Vivien sat nursing her cup as though gaining comfort from the warmth. "So, what have you been up to, you and Marian? I bet you were pleased when I didn't come back last night, eh?"

"Not at all, but, yes, it was nice to have time with her, I won't deny that. That doesn't mean you're not welcome. After all…" He stopped as a wave of dizziness engulfed him. Everything went black and he fell heavily off the chair and onto the floor. Vivien put down her cup and went over to him. She straightened him out and then went to the phone. Ten minutes later the bell rang and she opened the door to let in Dan and Ray.

"Where's that bloody great dog?" asked Dan nervously.

"He's in the lounge. I've shut the door. He won't do anything; he'll think Steven's got guests."

"OK, where is he then?"

She took them into the kitchen. Dan raised his eyebrows. "Wow, out for the count. What did you do to him – hit him with something?"

"Of course not. Now be careful with him." She was eyeing Steven's prone body with some concern and the way she was clenching and unclenching her fingers betrayed her agitation.

"Is he likely to wake up?" asked Ray. "Should I give him a whack?

"No need for that," said Vivien firmly, "he'll be out for a few hours after what I've given him." She watched as Ray bent over Steven and hoisted him up with ease onto his shoulder. "Don't hurt him, will you," she said nervously. "Put him in the car. I've got something to do."

They carried Steven out whilst Vivien wrote something on a piece of paper. She put it on the table and then, after collecting her bag from her room, she hastened down the stairs. She shut the door and got into the 4-by-4. Steven was slumped in the back snoring. Ray drove the short distance to Jane Trethowan's house where she was waiting accompanied by Tim.

"OK? Everything is OK?" Jane sounded agitated as she walked to the car and looked in at the unconscious form lying on the back seat.

"Yes," said Ray. "She did a good knock-out job all right."

"Well done, Viv," said Jane and put her arms around Vivien who looked up into her eyes adoringly. "Will it be OK, Jane?" asked Vivien, her tone still betraying some anxiety.

"You left a note?"

"Yes, like you said. He's gone off with me for a dirty weekend."

"And will she believe that?" queried Tim. "Is it credible?" He sounded scornful.

Vivien eyed him with contempt. "Credible? Of course it's credible. Marian knows what I'm like. If I get my hooks into someone well…" She left the sentence floating in the air. "Anyway, you didn't seem to mind when we…"

"Oh, just leave it," said Tim, eyeing Jane nervously but Jane was addressing the two men. "OK," she said to Ray and Dan. "Get him over to the Folly. Secure him, not so tight that you stop the circulation, but make sure he's made secure."

"Don't worry, we don't want him doing his Kung Fu bit on us again, do we Ray?"

Ray rubbed his bruised face, then grunted and got into the driver's seat. Dan climbed in and the vehicle disappeared around the back of the house.

Jane, Tim and Vivien went inside. Vivien was looking dejected. Something was bothering her but she could not place what it was. There was an insistent something or other at the back of her mind, trying to get through.

"What's the matter?" asked Tim, seeing Vivien's expression.

"Oh, look I know that you say this is for a higher purpose but you won't hurt him will you? After all Marian was my friend." *Was* my friend? Why did she say that?

Jane looked at her. "Viv, you trust me don't you? Would I do anything to upset you again now that we're back together? Look, when Marian comes back we can all meet and straighten things out."

"But she'll hate me. I mean, I've drugged him and you've kidnapped him..." She paused and looked at the others. "No, no, you've tricked me... You can't let him go – he'll go to the police."

"He won't," said Tim. "Viv, I'm an archaeologist. I only have to say he knew about the hoard and was intending to keep it and sell it. That's against the law. We can come to a compromise – he'll listen."

"Anyway," said Jane, "I'll let him have it all back when I've used the artefacts, OK? Now, come on, look at me, look."

She held Vivien's upper arms firmly and looked down at her. Vivien lifted her eyes and looked at Jane. "There," said Jane, "there now, come on, you and me Viv, you and me, together, together."

A dreamy look came into Vivien's eyes. She calmed down and smiled at Jane. "Yes, together, yes, yes, yes."

She sat down and rolled herself a joint, all thoughts of Marian and Steven gone from her mind.

Tim called Jane over to him. "We'd better get on with it then; I don't know how long it will take to get the artefacts. She said they were under rocks, a landslide, that could be difficult."

"OK, when Dan and Ray are back we'll start." She turned to Tim, smiling and said, "Oh who would have thought it, eh? I – we – we're so close, so close. It's all coming right – perfect, perfect. I'll just make that call, OK?"

"Sure. Will he be able to be here at such short notice? He's usually very busy, won't he find it difficult to get away?"

"Of course he'll be here. What do you think?"

"I don't know. You know how I feel about him. I don't mind you and girls, but I can't help it – I get jealous." He knew that Jane had several lovers, as he had himself – but he could never really accept her promiscuous nature.

She laughed softly and touched his face. "Don't be jealous darling. You know he means nothing to me – none of them do – just a means to an end and I need him to be there at the end – if you see what I mean."

Tim laughed. "Yes, indeed I do."

There was the sound of footsteps and Dan and Ray came in. "OK, nice and safe," said Dan. "Still asleep as well. He'll get a shock when he wakes up."

"Did you make him comfortable as well as secure?" asked Tim. "We don't want him dying on us, at least not yet."

"Don't worry, he's OK," said Ray.

Tim looked at Dan, who was no longer wearing a sling. "How's your wrist? Can you do any heavy work?"

Dan flexed his fingers and moved his wrist back and forth. "Sore, but usable, providing I don't lift anything too heavy."

Jane went out and returned wearing jeans and boots. "OK, let's go."

The five of them left by the back door, collected various tools and were soon crossing the fields that adjoined the rear of Steven's land. They walked up the course of the stream, through into the garden of Hawkwood and, led by Vivien they entered the trees and so into the grove.

"Where the hell are we going?" grumbled Dan. "And where's that bloody great hound?"

"I told you, he's in the lounge," said Vivien. "He won't be aware of us this far over. It's in here, here in this wild area. What about the Guardian?"

"Guardian?" said Ray. "What, have we got to sort someone out?"

"No one of this world," said Jane. "Viv, tell me again about the entity." She listened as Vivien told of the encounter with the apparition.

"Bugger me," said Ray, "what'll it do?" Dan was saying nothing but his eyes darted around nervously.

Jane reassured them. "Nothing, it's just like a projection, an image, but I can stop it. Now Viv, come with me. You three stay here."

Jane and Vivien entered the grove and approached the rocks. Jane stopped. "Yes, I can feel something, something strong."

Vivien was standing with her eyes closed. A chill seemed to fill the area and then, as though stepping through an invisible door, the black beastlike shape of the Guardian appeared and rushed at them and through them. Jane flung up her arms and uttered some words; the chill vanished instantly. Vivien opened her eyes. "Did it come?"

"Yes, I've banished it. We can proceed." She called to the others who entered the grove. Dan and Ray were clearly uncertain and nervous.

Tim went up to Vivien and asked, "Where?"

Vivien pointed to the rocks. "This is where the coins were found." She indicated the spot.

Tim bent down and then stood back examining the rock formation. "Ah, yes, look! You see where the water channel used to be? Well, just below are different rocks. Look, there's a long gap. We can lever that lot out. No problem – get the crowbars." He climbed onto the long rocky shelf above the gap. Dan and Ray returned and, under Tim's direction and with his support, the three men probed and levered, using the rock shelf as a platform, until, with a rumble, the rocks slid to the side exposing a man-made passage. Water gushed out and then became a trickle. "Brilliant," said Tim. "If it's there then that's been an anoxic environment until now."

Jane said, "What's that then?"

"It means there's been no oxygen to corrode whatever is in the ground there. The same as the script. You remember, I found the script along with others, in a boggy site. The same as the Vindolanda scripts; no oxygen to corrode or rot the items. Preserved as though just buried. Brilliant!" He crawled into the passage and brought out an urn.

"Typical early Romano-British pottery – hey." He looked inside the urn. "A burial – a cremation; that's not written in the script." Tim crawled in again and then returned. "It's like a small burial chamber." He scrambled back in and Jane followed him; she watched as he scraped at the soil around an object.

"Hmm, a sword but it's in bad condition." He leaned over it, examining it closely.

"Don't get carried away," said Jane, impatiently. "We didn't come for a full-scale archaeological dig. Where are the artefacts?"

Tim crawled out. "Pity – very interesting. Iceni, no doubt, but why here?" He paused then said, "It could take a while to find what we're looking for. We'll use Vivien's sensing abilities. Vivien, come here."

Vivien walked forward, slowly. She could feel the enormous energy pulse hitting her making her dizzy.

"Are you OK, Viv?" asked Jane, irritated.

"Give me a moment," Vivien said and composed herself. Something was nagging at her mind, the memory of Marian but it was distant like a dream. "OK." She walked forward then crawled into the hollow stretching out her hand. She moved it in a circular movement. Beads of sweat began to appear on her forehead. "Oh! Strong power, strong, pulling me – oh!" She stopped suddenly – tensed and collapsed.

Tim pulled her out. "What happened?" he asked Jane.

"I don't know – may be too powerful for her – ah!"

Vivien opened her eyes. "Anyone got a ciggy?" she asked.

"Oh for God's sake, will you get on with it," said Jane, tersely. "What did you feel? Where is it?" Jane was becoming even more impatient.

Vivien got up and edged her way back into the chamber, followed by Jane and Tim. "Here, beneath me, it lies here – the Mysteries of Mona."

Tim looked at Jane. They exchanged triumphant and excited glances. "That's it. Just like the script said – she couldn't have known that. The Druids took the sacred artefacts away and buried them here on sacred land. They're here. I only gave her one bit of the broken script. I read it on the tape – remember? I mentioned 'Mysteries' but she didn't see the other bit I had – that was more complete. It said, 'Mysteries of Mona'. She couldn't have known the legend was about druidic sacred instruments from Mona. Bloody hell, it's all true – she couldn't have known."

"I never doubted it for one instance," said Jane calmly. "Now let's get on with it. You two, come in here. Dig – there." She pointed her hand at the spot indicated by Vivien.

Using trowels, Dan and Ray began removing the damp earth. Seeing that Dan was having difficulty using his injured arm, Tim pulled him away and took his place. "Just remove the soil. Get it away from here." He was carefully trowelling at the wet soil and, in a relatively short time he stopped. "I've hit something. OK, Ray, you move out. I'll do this." He carefully removed the earth from an area which began to take the shape of a small chest.

"It's lead and sealed tightly," he said. In an hour, he had cleared the wet, clinging soil and exposed the lead chest. He pushed at it gently and it moved in the ground. "OK Ray, come here. Help me move it." Together they loosened the soil around the base and gingerly manoeuvred the box, which was extremely heavy, out of the chamber and into the open.

Outside, Jane leaned forward. "Open it, open it!" Her face was pale with excitement and her eyes were fierce, eager.

"Not now, not here," said Tim, "back at the house. We must get out of here now."

"It's too heavy to move," said Ray. "We'd never get it back."

Jane picked up a trowel and, kneeling beside the box, she began digging at the soft metal lid.

"For God's sake," said Tim, "what are you doing?" The latent conscience of an archaeologist surfaced briefly.

"I want it open now." Her voice was firm and frightening in its intensity. "Get the bags." Dan obeyed her and put the holdalls near the box. She levered at the lid and there was a crack – it opened. She pulled back the lid and immediately beneath was a leather hide, rotten and in pieces. She pushed it aside and gasped.

There, gleaming as though just laid in the box, was a golden wheel with spokes. "The Wheel of Taranis," she said softly. She lifted it out and it seemed to glow in the sunlight. Tim knelt down, reached into the box and pulled out a bronze, curved, sickle-like knife. Jane smiled. "Yes, you see, for cutting the mistletoe they say but I know what it was for."

"The Wheel of Fire... The Horns of the Moon," said Vivien softly – memory flooding back. The others ignored her.

"And this, look, what's this – this torc?" Jane pulled out a large golden torc with horse designs at the ends.

Tim took it from her and studied it. "I don't understand this," he said. "This is Icenian in design – why is it here? It's not written about in the script. Iceni coins, now a torc. It doesn't make sense."

"Boudica," said Vivien softly. They turned to her. "It belonged to Boudica," she repeated.

"What are you talking about?" asked Jane. She took the torc and held it, her eyes gleaming with sudden excitement. She looked at it and then at Vivien. "What do you mean? How do you know?"

"In the spirit vision. Marian sensed it. Boudica came here, with her daughters, after the great battle. One of her daughter's died of wounds and is buried there," she pointed to the urn. "Boudica crossed the Channel to the Silures; the other daughter remained here to guard the site."

Tim said, "It must be the case. There's no explanation, otherwise, for Iceni artefacts, and this torc is of great weight and would have belonged to an important leader." He studied it closely. "But Boudica was supposed to have killed herself..." He paused, as though pondering. "Although – yes – the accounts *are* very unsatisfactory. None of it's very definite. I suppose she could have – must have – survived, else this wouldn't be here now... God! This is amazing – a sensation!"

Jane looked at Vivien and then at the torc. "If this is all true, then this is even better. It'll lend even greater power to the rite. So, Boudica was here. She must have been of the Druids too and this torc must be druidic otherwise it wouldn't have been buried with her daughter. God, I can't believe my luck – perfect."

Tim said, "Our luck, you mean."

"Yes, our luck, I meant that." Then her voice changed, hardened. "Oh this is an omen. It was meant to be. It's a divine message to me – yes..." She turned to Tim and said in a deliberate tone, "This is a message *for me*."

Tim was full of mixed emotions. As a lover and supporter of Jane and of all that she stood for, he was certain that the artefacts would gain for her the power she craved. As an archaeologist though, he felt a great sense of sadness. The discovery of such a site, the artefacts and the links with Boudica and the Druids, would have made his name. He would have gone into the annals of archaeological history alongside Schliemann or Carter. He looked at the urn and its sad remains and then at the artefacts. He picked up the wheel. Such wonderful workmanship. He knew that she was right. This veritable gift from the Gods was a definite sign. Jane's destiny was being written by the Spirits themselves.

Jane broke into his reverie. "Come on then, let's get back."

He looked at her. Yes, he had to acknowledge the facts and, what was more, he loved her. "You're right. This *is* for you – not for me." He put the golden wheel down. The artefacts were placed in the bags.

She smiled at him and touched his arm. As though picking up his thoughts, she said, "It's fate, destiny – I have no control over this."

Tim sighed. "I know," he said to her, "it's all right."

"What about the site?" interrupted Dan, insensitive to the charged atmosphere.

"No time. Later – come on, we must get back." Tim picked up the bag and turned from the site, followed by the others.

They made their way across the garden, into the fields and so to Jane's house. Ray and Dan took themselves off under instruction to return at midnight. When they had gone, Jane opened the bags and took out the wheel and the curved blade.

She ran her finger along the edge of the knife. "Still sharp enough," she said, smiling at Tim. He was examining the wheel again. She said, "So, we have them. The sun and the moon. We begin the rite at around five o'clock, before sunrise. Will we see the sun, do you think? It would make it perfect."

Tim looked at the weather forecast in the newspaper. "Should be clear but you can never tell with the mist. Still, wonderful, eh? Tomorrow, you will achieve your goal, you will be the true supreme Druidic leader of the Islands; reclaiming your ancestral heritage."

She smiled at him. "Yes, yes, I will be and I will make those stupid politicians aware of it as well. I will make them see that once we were great and will be again. I will generate such power, such force, that nothing will withstand me. We will be able to throw off the choking Christian code that has held us down. This will give me political and religious credibility."

Vivien was watching the two of them in utter amazement and growing disbelief. What were they talking about? Could they be serious? Political and religious credibility? Jane was going to proclaim herself Supreme Druid of Britain? She would be a laughing stock. Couldn't she see that? Couldn't Tim? Clearly they could not and Vivien felt a shiver of fear. Were they both insane? Softly, she asked, "What about Steven and Marian? You said you'd return the artefacts so what are you going to do?"

Jane and Tim looked at her, a mixture of contempt and irritation on their faces.

"Do you really think I'd give them up?" said Jane. "No Viv, don't be so stupid. I know that you live in a hazy, candy-coated world. Why don't you go and have a smoke or a drink if you like, but don't be so bloody stupid. Marian? We'll deal with her later but Steven Downs, well, he's special."

She picked up the blade and the wheel. "Tomorrow, as the sun rises, Steven Downs will be tied to the Wheel of Taranis – a much larger one of course – and then, well," she raised the curved blade, "well then there will be a great reaping and I will be anointed in my rank with the blood of my *living, suffering, sacrifice.*"

Vivien looked at her in horror. "And Marian – she's my friend. Jane, you can't."

Jane ignored her and turned away, examining the blade. Vivien tried to get her thoughts together. Memories were coming back. Whatever Jane and Tim had done to her, their power was wearing off. Like a bad dream she recalled the tape recording and then, with disgust, the way she had been used by Jane and Tim through the night. There were blanks but, overall, she was beginning to remember. Now she knew that she, too, was in danger; she had to play along. Something nagged at her mind and then she remembered. "Jane, I can see how important this is, all of it. I just didn't realise. You know how I feel about you – you know you can count on me. It's true, I don't know Steven Downs and you said it was all for a greater purpose. I can see that now."

Jane put down the knife and smiled at her. "Yes, well how could you have known? Yes, you can see that this is destined can't you? You can see it... you're a sensitive and now you know, good."

"But Marian is my friend – let her alone, can't you?"

"Of course I can't," said Jane becoming irritated again.

"But, she's a descendant of Boudica."

She flung the words out and Jane looked up quickly and said, "What?"

"Yes, she saw it – in spirit vision. She saw Boudica's daughter and the Druid who brought the artefacts. She's a descendant of the daughter who stayed on."

"How do you know that it's true? She was deluding herself."

"No, no Jane, it couldn't have been so. I got a glimpse before she regressed. I saw a young woman – it was Marian or, should I say, her ancestor – same hair, everything. And Marian, well, well she knew of the artefacts and the burial. How could she have 'seen' this. You've only just dug them up and the torc was not supposed to be with them. Marian spoke of the Mysteries of Mona – how could she have known that they were there?"

Tim had been listening intently. He nodded. "I believe her. How could she have known? I suppose that's how you knew the name when you collapsed at the burial site. But, that doesn't matter now. It's all true. We've got the artefacts – it must be right because the torc is, without doubt, Iceni in origin and obviously belonged to someone of high status. Boudica's – it would be priceless. Just think."

"Priceless, yes and mine now – ours. Just think of the power. This is perfect, perfect." Turning to Tim, Jane said, "The artefacts, the torc of Boudica and now a descendant. What power. She must, and will, join us. I will use her."

Tim said, "But, why would she co-operate? Oh, yes, she would – she's an occultist, like you."

"Like me? Like me? Are you mad? No one is like me. No, she's just a silly little hedgewitch; spells, potions, no real power. She couldn't stand against me, not now. No, she'll join us. I'll make her join us – she will want to and you, Vivien, you will get her for me. Go and get her when she returns. Bring her to me. Use the thing about Steven Downs as bait but get her here." Jane smiled at Vivien, walked over to her and put her arms around her. She looked down into Vivien's eyes and said, "Remember Viv, you and me, together – you and me, you and me."

Vivien felt herself sinking again. She tried to hold on to the memories of Marian, conscious of the terrible dangers awaiting her two friends but soon, all she could see was Jane and her eyes which seemed to pull her down and down, eating into her soul, crushing her power to resist.

CHAPTER 23

Sela had finished her lecture and stepped outside to phone Steven. The phone rang for a while but there was no reply, so she went and had some tea. She tried again – still no reply. It was now 4.30 p.m. She tried again, a feeling of unease beginning to grip her. Where could he be? In a state of mounting anxiety, she phoned once more and, on getting no reply, she decided there and then to miss the seminar and to leave the University. At 9 p.m. she drove into Hawkwood's driveway to find the house in darkness. At the sound of the bell Perry barked from deep inside the house. Gripped by a sense of foreboding Sela went to the back of the house and found the kitchen door unlocked. Switching on the lights she saw the two cups and then Vivien's note.

*"Sorry sweetheart, but I've taken him off for a few days of debauchery. I'll bring him back **WHEN I'VE HAD ENOUGH.***
Luv Viv."

Sela read the note again. No, this made no sense, she knew how Steven felt about Vivien. Perry barked and she found him in the lounge in darkness. He fawned around her tail wagging and made his way to the front door. She opened it for him and he rushed out, in evident relief. Sela looked at the note again. No, Steven would not have gone off with Vivien and, even if he had, he would certainly have taken his dog. She went up to his room. The bed was still unmade, the room as she and Steven had left it. Again, that sense of foreboding. Something was very, very wrong. Her heart gave a lurch. It had to be Jane, but where was Vivien? As though obeying some deep, unspoken command, she found a torch and, with growing concern and trepidation, she made her way across the garden and into the grove.

Immediately, she knew what had happened for, amidst piles of excavated earth the lead container lay open before her. She peered into the hollow and saw the excavation. Jane – it had to be, and then she saw the urn. Sela pulled it forward and shone the torch in. Amongst the mess of burnt ashes were some fragments of bone – a cremation. It hit her – a cremation – a burial – Boudica's daughter, and her mind pictured the ancient grove. The long-ago link with her distant past made her feel deeply emotional. She held the urn for a while and then gently replaced it. As she did this, she remembered placing it there so many centuries ago. She shook her head. No, no, just her imagination or a flashback to the spirit trance. A trick of the mind but then why did she know *exactly* where to place it? There was hardly enough light to see but she felt the urn settle back into a recess in the ground, caused by its

The Moon Temple

weight. She crawled out again. Where was Steven? Where was Vivien? If it was Jane, and she was sure it was, then both of them must be in deadly danger. She had to find out more.

Sela drove her car to the cottage. Tanith was sitting patiently waiting for her. She stroked the cat, nuzzling its soft fur and then picked her up and carried her into the Moon Temple. Sela shut the doors, lit a candle and some incense and then invoked Hecate to give her aid.

She finished her invocation and, picking up Tanith, she sat down on a chair and began stroking the cat. Tanith purred and purred and then settled down as Sela continued to stroke her. Tanith seemed mesmerised as Sela began to speak softly into the cat's ears. "Yes… Yes… You will go, go, through the dark – through the woods – through the trees… To the hills yes… the hills… There – to the house – yes… yes…"

Tanith was now motionless, her eyes fixed, staring at the candle flame. Sela chanted softly.

"Through your eyes I will see;
Through your eyes I will be;
Through the trees, through the trees,
Now I'm you, you are me,
Through our eyes, we will see."

She was silent and began rocking gently to and fro. Then she began to speak again in a whisper. "Yes… in through the window… the hall… yes… I can hear them – they are there… I can see them… Jane, Tim, Vivien – talking… talking… Listen, listen."

She was silent and all that could be heard was her breathing. Then, suddenly, "Yes… I can hear, yes." Her voice suddenly became raised. "Oh – no, Steven… Where?" She was breathing heavily now and then she began in a whisper, "Yes… the Folly – the Folly… Vivien, Vivien, hear me Vivien… Vivien."

Her voice had become almost inaudible, as though she was concentrating and then suddenly it rose, almost hysterical. "No – Jane – she knows… She is looking, turning… searching. She knows… but she can't see – no, no. Now rising… s*hape-shifting*… Ah, Jane, no, no!" Sela was now breathing hard, her chest heaving up and down as if in a state of very great anxiety. "Go – now – go … quickly, through the trees – through the dark – ahh! The beast… the beast – following, seeking – out into the dark, it cannot follow – it cannot follow us, it is gone. Come now, back, back – here – now!" She ended with a shout and Tanith, roused from her trance, jumped off her lap. Sela was breathing quickly as though she had been running and slowly she brought herself under control.

So Jane *did* have Steven. But Tim and Vivien, why were they there? What was the Folly? All she knew was that Steven was in danger. Should she call the police? She went to the phone then put it down. What could she say? That her boyfriend had been taken by Jane Trethowan, a highly regarded landowner and politician? By witches? No, no good. She had to find Steven but now she was conscious that Jane was aware of her scrying. Jane had not seen Sela, only the ephemeral shape of a cat, but Jane would put two and two together – she would know it was Sela and, even now, might be coming for her.

The phone rang; she answered it.

Vivien's voice floated into her ear. "Oh good, you're back. I'll come over." The click came before Sela had time to open her mouth.

Twenty minutes later, from a vantage point on the hill, Sela spied Vivien alone, walking up the track towards her cottage. She got back to her house as Vivien opened the front gate. "Hi, darling – how was the talk?" Vivien's voice was lighthearted but her pale, drawn face belied her outward cheerfulness.

"Where's Steven?" asked Sela, tersely. "I know he's with Jane and Tim – why Tim? What's going on?"

Vivien was clearly thrown off guard now that she could see that Sela knew about the others. "He's all right, *really* – Jane wanted him to come and talk to her. He's with her now – why don't you come over as well?"

Sela looked at her friend. Clearly there was something very wrong if the light-hearted, generally affected, Vivien could maintain this pathetic deception so diligently. "Come on in, we'll talk about it." She decided to go along with the deception. "So you seduced Steven, you rotten little tart," she laughed. "I hope it was worth it."

"*My dear*, the man is an absolute machine but you can have him back now."

Vivien lit up a cigarette. "He's talking with Jane and Tim about the artefacts," she went on.

"Why? How did they find them?" Sela's voice was sharp.

This threw Vivien; she did not know what to say. "Err, oh, I don't know – oh, come on Marian, *you* know I never listen to anything."

Sela decided not to press Vivien. Instead she went to her cabinet and took down Jane's crystal pendulum. She sat across the room from Vivien and dangled the crystal from her hand in a casual manner, allowing it to twist and spin, sending sparkles of light across the room. The ceremony of 'Evocatio' had altered its vibrational energies enabling Sela to counteract Jane's influence over Vivien. "So, Viv, where did you go with Steven, you know, where did you do it?"

"At his place, of course, darling." Vivien tried to maintain an open, direct stare but her eyes were being drawn to the glittering pendant.

"So, why leave me a note?" Sela was speaking in a soft, yet firm, tone.

"Oh, I don't know – I just did." Vivien was now looking at the crystal.

Sela was silent for a while watching Vivien's eyes, then she said, "Where is Steven now, Vivien?"

"In the Folly." The voice was subdued, drowsy.

"Where is the Folly?"

"I don't know."

"Vivien, I want you to project yourself onto the astral. Gently now, rest and relax, relax – now you can see Jane's house."

"Yes."

"Go to it – go there now."

"Yes – go there, yes."

"Don't go in. Look across her land. Search for it – the Folly – an old building."

There was a long silence then Vivien said dreamily, "Ah yes, on the hill – on the promontory – like an old chapel. Yes, I can see it; through the gardens above the sea."

"Can you sense, see, Steven – go in?"

Silence – then, softly – "Steven, yes. He's there. With three men."

"Is he talking to them? Is he safe?"

"Not talking; can't speak... mouth is gagged... He's not safe. He is bound."

Sela felt her stomach lurch. She was dreadfully afraid for him for she knew that Steven was in mortal danger. There could only be one way out of this for Jane; she had kidnapped him and she could not let him go – alive. But what was her purpose?"

"Vivien, why has Jane kept Steven?"

"Sacrifice – blood sacrifice. She has the artefacts – they're special to her. She wants you, too – I must bring you to her..."

"Why, why does she want me – to kill me?"

"No. You're special – Boudica's descendant."

"How does she know that?"

"I told her – to save you – she needs you, you're special."

This held out a sudden hope and Sela thought for a moment and then said, "Vivien, Jane has been controlling you. Now you'll be free of her. You're *my* friend. We're good friends. That's true, isn't it?"

"Yes Marian. You are my best, my only friend."

"Then you will now be free of Jane. She can't control you now, nor in the future. You're with me now."

"Yes, with you."

"And what is Tim's role?"

"He's Jane's lover – her priest."

Sela felt a wave of anger run through her at the way she had been duped. "But how did he find the artefacts?"

"I told him."

"When? How could you have known?"

"Last year – Jane and Tim used me to scry on the astral. I didn't know. Didn't remember."

The audacious nature of the plan and the deception behind it was breathtaking.

"How, what, did they know?"

"Tim had a fragment of a Roman script. He stole it from a site near Hadrian's Wall. It spoke of a legend about the Mysteries of Mona hidden in the land of the Dumnoni – where the Trident of Neptune rises from stony arms."

Sela was puzzled. "What does it mean?"

"It refers to two streams, flowing into one stream which flows into the sea. The stony arms – that's the great shingle ridge of Porlock Bay. Jane researched maps and identified such a site on Exmoor and I dowsed for it on a map."

Hence the metal detecting; the searching; the attempts to get the land from Rita Palmer and then from Steven. Not realising that Rita had an heir, Jane had counted on buying the land and then, when that failed, gaining the land on Rita's death through sale by auction. It was now clear to her but why Jane wanted the artefacts, well, that was still a mystery. Greed? And Tim, why was he not just going about things through an archaeological dig? She questioned Vivien further and the reply astonished her. So that was why Jane wanted the Wheel of Taranis. It was a Solar implement and, therefore, a confirmation of what she saw was her ancient druidic lineage.

"But, Supreme Druid? It's ridiculous." Sela paused, pondering, then said, "How do you know Jane?"

"Jane was my lover, the one who left me, who ruined my life. I loved her so much but she just left me." Vivien's tone became sad.

This startled Sela. So *Jane* had been the long-term partner. "But why didn't you tell me that you knew her?" She felt compassion for her friend, who had been so ill following the break-up, but she also felt peeved that Vivien had not confided in her.

"I just wanted to forget. Didn't think it would matter. I love her and she has promised me we'll be together." This last phrase gave Sela cause for real concern. Jane would have power over Vivien no matter what. So that was it and now the woman was bent on a harebrained plan to assume some sort of religious-political role. Ridiculous, yes, but, clearly, highly deadly to anyone who attempted to thwart her plans. There had been enough historical precedents to demonstrate the dangerous link between political ambition and a sense of divine destiny.

"No, Vivien. We must stop her and save Steven. You will help me now. Do what I say. You will obey only me, only me but you will pretend to co-operate with Jane and Tim."

Sela had thrown away all scruples and had no sense of guilt about using the fragile nature of her friend's mental state to save Steven. Vivien had been an occultist all of her life and used her powers in the full knowledge of possible danger. Now there was an overwhelming need to save an innocent person caught in an occult web of deceit, ambition, greed and murder woven by a practitioner who obeyed no rules. Whatever Sela was doing in using her friend had to be balanced against the dreadful alternatives. She recalled her discussions with Steven. She had told him that she was for the Light against the Dark but it was never quite as simple as that, was it? When she had told him that she had once misused her powers to gain revenge for a friend, she had not told him that the friend had been Vivien. She had hoped that through her actions in aiding him against Jane, she would gain some form of redemption from her karmic debt. Now, though, her use of Vivien's fragile nature as a tool to thwart Jane's malevolence, was adding a new karmic burden. Sela knew only that she loved Steven and that she must save him; if that meant using her friend, well, so be it.

Vivien was compromised in any case, Sela told herself, in an attempt to justify her actions. Vivien's relationship with Jane Trethowan was too strong and Sela knew that such a relationship would always pose a threat; it would come between them now, whatever happened. The time for Sela to answer for her actions would come, eventually, when she stood before the dread Lords of Karma.

CHAPTER 24

Sela brought Vivien out of the hypnotic state. Vivien opened her eyes and looked at her. "Oh God, Marian, they've taken Steven – I don't know what happened – they're going to kill him."

Sela stood up, went over to her and put her arms around her friend, calming her. "I know, I know – you've just told me everything. Now, what must we do?"

"We must save Steven. I'll help you and I'll pretend to be with Jane and Tim." Vivien was clearly distressed. She fumbled in her pocket and pulled out the remains of a roll-up. She got up and found some matches.

As Vivien drew the smoke into her lungs, Sela could see her friend beginning to calm down. Satisfied that she now had control, Sela said, "OK now, you've come to bring me to Jane; you've convinced me that she has a destiny and I'll go along with this 'cos I am a descendant of Boudica and my duty is to help her."

"She called you a little hedgewitch, you know."

"Silly of her wasn't it? Never underestimate anyone. Does she know that Steven and I have been together? I know she knows I know him, if you see what I mean…"

"Gosh – too complicated," interjected Vivien.

"… but does she know we've been sleeping together?"

Vivien thought about this. "I'm not sure. *She* had him. She's so vain she might think you're not his type, you being younger and all that. I honestly don't know."

"Then we'll have to take a chance. I'll be the little hedgewitch. I'll be over-awed by her and grateful to be allowed into her circle; she wanted me to join her once, you know. I think she knows I was scrying her but I can explain that, if she bothers to ask. Now listen, I won't mention Steven, OK? We'll have to try to get to him, or you must. When is all this going to happen?"

"Tomorrow morning, at sunrise," responded Vivien.

"OK, look, you make yourself a drink, have a nap or something; I've got something to do." She put her arms around Vivien and gave her a hug. Vivien was so frail and sensitive and Sela felt her heart go out to this strange, psychic woman.

She left Vivien and went into her temple. She sat silently, lost in thought and allowed her mind to relax, placing herself into a state of receptivity, questing on the astral plane. After about an hour she came to, sighed deeply, her eyes moist, and then she went to the table where she sat and wrote for a while. She put the papers into an envelope, addressed it and put a stamp on it. Then she picked up Jane's pendant, put it in her pocket, and went out to Vivien. "Right, ready, let's go."

Soon the two women were making their way towards Jane's house. On the way, she posted her letter and then looked in on Perry. As she entered Hawkwood a great sense of emptiness, loneliness and anxiety hit her. How was Steven coping with all of this? Was he still alive? In her heart she knew he was because of Jane's dreadful intentions but, aware of Steven's warrior capabilities, she wondered if he had come into conflict with his kidnappers, and she missed him dreadfully. The memories of him were everywhere in the house and the dog was looking at her in a manner that seemed to ask questions about the whereabouts of his master. Sela bent down and fondled the dog's head then she saw to it that he had food and water and left him to guard the property.

Before starting up the driveway to Jane's house, Sela turned to Vivien and said, "I'm going to try something with Jane. I'm going to *make* her accept my presence without too many questions. I shall use 'the glamour', a witch trick. She used it to seduce Steven – I'll use it to gain her approval." She turned from Vivien and stood silently for a moment. "OK, ready, go ahead." To Vivien's eyes Sela looked the same but did seem to exude more confidence. Sela, on the other hand felt a sense of trepidation as Vivien rang the bell of Jane's house but she made a silent invocation for protection to Hecate and composed herself as the door was opened by the butler. Jane rose to meet them, a smile on her face but caution in her eyes. Her tone, though, seemed welcoming. "Marian, so glad you could come."

"Jane, Jane, I can't believe it – I'm so honoured that you want me," gushed Sela, wondering if she had overdone it but Jane looked pleased. She continued, "I can't believe what Vivien has told me. Can I see them? God, what a thing, eh – priceless, and so important – a link with our past; and this bit about me and Boudica – incredible, isn't it? I saw it, you know, on the astral."

Jane continued to smile relaxing a little. "Perhaps the honour is mine – you, a direct descendant of the great Celtic leader and now the artefacts as well. It's all perfect."

Tim came into the room, looked at Sela and said, "Well, well, I'm sorry I couldn't let you know but there was a greater purpose."

"Yes, of course, I completely understand. This is too important, too special – I can't believe it; to be here at such a time." Sela stopped and gulped as though overcome with great emotion.

Jane turned to Tim, still smiling, and said, "Fetch them. I want her to see them – then she will know that I am the one destined to lead."

Sela shivered. Jane's demeanour, her manner of speech with its grandiose tones, all pointed to a mind that was unbalanced, teetering on the brink. She knew that she must be cautious and must convince Jane that she had accepted her claims. Tim returned and placed the bag on the table. Jane reached in and pulled out the gold Wheel of Taranis. Sela felt energy vibrating from the wheel and a wave of emotion caused tears to start in her eyes as Jane held it up allowing it to glint in the light.

"The Wheel of Taranis, the Thunderer – symbol of the Sky God, the sun and of the ancient Order of Druids," she cried.

Then reaching into the bag she pulled out the curved bronzed blade. Again, Sela felt the vibrational energies emanating from the ancient artefacts as Jane cried out, "The Great Sickle, the Reaper – symbol of the moon."

"The Wheel of Fire and the Horns of the Moon," said Vivien softly and Sela, hearing her, remembered Vivien's vision.

Then Jane lifted from the box the great gold torc. Sela gasped as a wave of incredible power hit her. Jane looked up and Sela composed herself, heart pounding. "Oh this is all wonderful, wonderful," she said.

"Even more than you know, Marian," said Jane. "Come here and let me put this on you."

Sela stepped forward and Jane placed the torc around her neck. She felt something akin to an electric current run through her – enormous energy. She again composed herself as best she could.

"But this is beautiful, beautiful, and so heavy." She reached up, fingering its curved and scrolled shape.

"There, look Tim – the past and the present linked." Jane looked at Sela and said, "Do you know what this is? It was Boudica's, her great gold necklet as described in the Roman histories and you, Marian, you are her descendant – Vivien told me – you saw it all in the spirit. Yes, I can see it too. You have the red hair – ah, this is so, so perfect. You will assist me; you will help me; you will be my totem. How can anyone stand against me now? I have the instruments of power and a direct, unbroken link with our sacred past through you."

Sela felt the energy pounding through her veins and a great sense of atavistic resurgence brought, flashing into her mind, a sense of the past; of open grasslands; horses; warriors; the joy, yes, joy, of battle. She lifted the torc from around her neck and studied its intricate metalwork. She felt truly emotional at the realisation that this object was directly linked to her. Her heart was still beating rapidly and she strove to regain control of her breathing.

"No," said Jane, "put it on, keep it on. I will dress you as you should be dressed and you will be with me, with us," she looked over at Tim who was beginning to feel isolated. "We will all be together as the sun rises as we make our offering to Bel and, now, to Andraste, your ancestor's tribal deity."

"Offering?" queried Sela, trying to sound puzzled. She put the torc back around her neck prepared, this time, for the energy pulse.

"A sacrifice. But don't think of this now. No, now you will go and rest, meditate as I will; prepare yourself."

"But what is all this for?" asked Sela, determined to get to the bottom of Jane's obvious insanity and driving murderous ambition.

"Power, of course; political and religious power. You know of my work – now a pan-Celtic union – total independence – becomes necessary and unavoidable. A true Nationalist movement – not the pale, Anglo-Saxon version but a more ancient unification of all *true* Britons. Nothing can stop me now. Nothing and no one." Her voice had risen and she stared at Sela fixedly. "Are you with me?" she said suddenly, her tone and demeanour changing.

"With you? Yes, yes of course. How could I *not* be? How could I reject such a historical inevitability? I didn't think this could be possible and to be with you at this time – I can't say enough."

Jane stared fixedly at her and, with a cold voice, said, "You were scrying me earlier today. Why? What did you seek to find?" She lowered her tone and almost whispered, "What do you know?"

Sela was startled at the sudden change in manner but she had prepared an answer for this. "How did I think I could hide from someone like you? I knew as soon as I entered that you had sensed then seen me. Oh Jane, what am I to you? I know only a fraction of what you know. You asked me once to join you. I turned you down – stupid pride of course. I always worked alone – you know, spells, potions, that sort of thing. The truth is – I'm envious of you. You're so skilled. Sometimes I try to learn from you in secret – so I scry."

"Yes, go on, there is also the matter of Steven Downs. You haven't asked about him. You helped him when I was hexing him. Why? What is he to you? Is he your lover?"

Sela looked her straight in the eyes and giggled like a schoolgirl. "Lover? Me? First, he's too old and, in any case, I like women – ," she looked over at Vivien who was now quite anxious, " – don't I, Viv? Our secret must come out, sweetheart."

Jane looked at Vivien and then back at Sela. "Aha. Well then, that's interesting. But what about Downs? Why help him? Tell me what you know – tell me." Her voice had risen.

"He asked me," Sela said, simply, realising she must convince Jane if she was to save Steven. "He'd heard about me in the village, I think, and came to me. Said he was under psychic attack – so I helped him. I charged him £150."

Jane relaxed. "£150? You come cheap. But how did he *know* it was witchcraft?"

Sela hesitated. What could she say? Steven hadn't known until she had told him. Then, inspired, she said, "Oh, he's into New Age things – does Tai Chi, meditation, that sort of thing. He'd read about psychic self-defence so, instead of going to a doctor, he came to a witch doctor." She laughed at the pun. Jane also laughed and turned away putting the wheel and sickle back in the bag. She looked up at Tim and said, "OK? Satisfied?"

"Yes," he replied, "all makes sense. Anyway, if she *was* with Downs, she'd hardly have come here." He picked up the bag and left the room.

Jane stood looking at Sela as though measuring her up. "Yes, you would look good in a robe I have. I want you just right for the ceremony. I'm going to rest now and then prepare myself. You do the same. Vivien, take her up to your room – don't play around too much, you two, I want you fresh. It's eleven o'clock now, I'll call you at four and prepare you myself, personally." She left the room and Sela relaxed instantly. Now that Jane had gone the tension in the room had gone as well.

Vivien said, "Come on." They went upstairs and along the corridor. "Here's my room; Jane's at the other end." Tim came out of a bathroom and went to the far door. He entered it and it clicked shut.

"He's in with her now," said Vivien. "They're lovers." The memory of their hands on her made her feel sick. "They're bastards – the two of them – bloody bastards."

Sela wondered at this comment but there were things more pressing for her to worry about. She went over to the window and looked down. It was too high to climb out and drop down. She would have to find Steven before Jane came for her but she could see no way to do this from her room. She went out to the top of the stairs and drew back at the sound of men's voices in the hall below.

Disturbed and anxious she returned to the room. "We're stuck, at least for a while. I'll try later but I've got to get to him. Where *is* the Folly?"

Vivien went to the window and pointed through the trees. "At the end of the pathway there's a gate and this leads out to the promontory. The Folly is there."

"OK, I'll try later." Sela took off the heavy torc and looked at it, marvelling at the complex metalwork. "To think that the last person to wear this was Boudica. I can't believe it but it's true. I know; I could see her time as though through her eyes."

Vivien held the torc, sensing its power and she began questing. "Yes, I see the past – death and blood." She paused and put the torc down quickly.

"And? What else, what else, Viv? Tell me."

"The future; death and blood, death and blood." Vivien's voice was dull and somnambulistic. "Death and blood and loss – the end of things – and a final victory."

Sela felt hope. "A final victory for Boudica? For me? Is that it, is that what you see? Tell me, Viv."

But Vivien was staring at the torc, dully, as though in a trance. Then she looked up and gave a little smile. "Yes, victory for Boudica – for you, for what is Time? Past and present become one and a great battle will be fought again."

The Moon Temple

"A great battle? But Boudica lost her last great battle."

"And lives on and is back here in you again – nothing ends – all is a cycle; death, rebirth," she stopped then changed the subject back to the immediate and went out onto the landing. She returned saying, "They're still there. We'd better try to rest a bit."

"Rest? How can I rest with Steven in such danger?"

Vivien touched her friend's hand, comforting her. "I know, I know. God, I feel responsible. It's all my fault – all of it." She began to cry and Sela put her arms around her. "There now, there. It's not your fault – none of it. If anyone's to blame, it's me – I got you into this."

After a while, Vivien wiped her eyes. "No," she said. "Karma – it's Karma." She gave Sela a long look, staring deeply into her friend's eyes. Sela felt a sudden attunement with Vivien. There was no longer the sense of a vapid, drug-laden, fey woman. Instead, there was an impression of great compassion and strength, as though Vivien's human body was merely the temporary vehicle for a being who was set upon a high, spiritual path. Sela held the image as she held Vivien's gaze and then the sudden impression was gone and Vivien lowered her eyes. But Sela knew that she had glimpsed something – someone special. In that spiritual moment she had seen that she and Vivien shared a common, karmic mission which had to be, and would be, accomplished.

Over the next two hours, the women kept watch, trying to find the right moment to move. At last, Vivien came back. "They've gone, the men. If you are going to make a move it must be soon. You've got three hours before they come for him."

"Come with me – let's go."

"No," said Vivien, "I'll stay here. No, don't worry – I stumbled once but now I'll be all right. I'll cover for you if they ask for you. Go! Now!"

CHAPTER 25

Steven woke, aware of a thumping headache and that his mouth was gagged, making breathing difficult. He tried to raise his hand to rub his head and was instantly aware that his wrists were tied together in front of him and that his ankles were also bound. He was lying on a cold damp and dirty stone floor. He lay, attempting to loosen the gag and to gather his wits; the dull ache in his head was beginning to abate. What had happened? He remembered Vivien's visit but nothing else. All was blank and now he was lying here – where? He shuffled around until he was able to sit upright, his back against a rough and equally cold stone wall. Looking around, he saw he was in a stone-built room which looked like the inside of a church or castle. Light was coming in from a small glass panel above the heavy wooden door and was obviously the product of an electrical source. He lifted his wrist, and peered at his watch. Two a.m. – God, how long had he been unconscious? All day it seems. Footsteps. He listened and then heard a key in the lock.

"So, you've woken up at last." It was Jane's butler. He put down a jug of water and a bowl of something, undid the gag and then stood up, closing the door before Steven could say anything. Steven wriggled over to the jug and, taking hold of it with both hands, he downed the water in a few quick gulps. He looked at his bound wrists and tried to loosen the knots with his teeth but they were too tight. He picked up the bowl which contained some porridge, quickly ate it to satisfy his hunger and immediately felt better. What was going on? Clearly Jane was at the bottom of all of this, the butler proved that, but why was Vivien involved? Did Sela know? Was she involved? He quickly dismissed this. She was away but then, a sudden thought. Was she away? Suppose it was some sort of elaborate plan – some witchery. Three witches – like in Macbeth. Three aspects of Hecate.

The thought chilled him far deeper than the cold of the room. It was a perfect deception if it was so. Jane, Sela, Vivien. He knew he was in terrible danger, his imprisonment demonstrated that. There was no way that the women could let him go now even if they got whatever was hidden on his land – artefacts, perhaps. What artefacts? How did he know all of this was true? After all, who had said there were artefacts? Jane hadn't but Vivien and Sela had done so or implied it. All that nonsense about past lives. Vivien's sensitivity; fainting at stone circles – she said she didn't know about. Was that true? How did he know? He remembered his conversations with Sela, her patient erudite explanations; all so plausible, meaningful and full of occult knowledge, at least to his untutored ears, and then, that talk of blood sacrifice. Was *he* going to be sacrificed? A few days ago he would have considered such a thing the product of a movie like the one in which they burnt the policeman in a wicker cage.

He went over things in his mind. When had he first met Sela? Yes, after the terror attack in the woods – she was there at the bottom of the pathway. And then the horror in the orangery; she had phoned him and rescued him – or had she? Perhaps she had been trying to ingratiate herself with him, getting him to trust her. No, surely not. Look at the way they had made love and felt about each other. Each other? How did he really know she truly cared for him? Yes, he loved her but hadn't he loved Jane Trethowan as well? He had slept with both women and had felt strangely attracted to Vivien. God, was it possible that they were in it, the three of them together?

Another thought flashed into his mind. What about the rite in the Moon Temple? All that talk of 'evocatio', what was it she had done? Yes, yes, that strange eerie chant; something about 'you're mine now'. She said it had been to control the spirit of the pendant but how did he know this was so? Perhaps it was an enchantment, 'glamour' she had called it. And then what about when she had 'called down the moon'? A memory of her naked form standing in the moonlight and the intensity of the love-making which had followed filled his mind and he felt a sense of panic as he recalled their love-making on the high moor, in the moonlight. That had been, without doubt, bewitchment. He knew now that he was in danger of losing his life – a triple danger and he had to get out, get away, call the police.

Steven examined his bound ankles and saw that they were tied in a more amateurish manner. He picked at the knots, felt them loosen and soon he was standing flexing his legs. Now he could move and with bunched fists at the front he would be formidable. "Hey you!" he called, "anyone there?"

There was the sound of scraping chairs and the clatter of feet. Feet? More than one person then. A voice sounded outside the door – Ray's voice, "Shut up Downs."

"I need a piss. Do you want me to do it here?" Steven tried to make his voice sound weak yet urgent.

"I couldn't care less," replied Ray but the butler's voice cut in. "No, I'll have to clean it up. We'll get him out. He can hop along." Ray shouted through the door, "OK, we'll let you out – no funny stuff – no bloody Kung Fu or I'll finish you."

The key turned in the lock and the two men entered the room. Steven launched a kick deep into the butler's groin. The man gave a squealing cry and collapsed, writhing to the ground. Steven side-stepped the fallen man, grabbed the shirt front of the startled Ray and head butted him, breaking Ray's nose and sending him dazed and bleeding to the floor. He bent down and hit him with his bunched fists, knocking him out. The butler was clearly incapacitated but Steven did the same to him and then stepped over the prone bodies and out into the passageway. Three steps led to a room. There was no sign of Dan. He saw a bread knife lying on the table and, picking this up, he left the building and darted around the back.

Where was he? The sound of surf could be heard behind him so he had to be on some sort of headland. He paused, then squatted down holding the knife between his shoes and sawed through his bonds. He tucked the knife in his belt. As his eyes became accustomed to the gloom he saw that he had been a prisoner in what looked like a church tower. He oriented himself and was aware of the dark bulk of Jane's house a few hundred yards away so he made his way over to it. The house was quiet and dark at the front. He edged around to the back and saw lights downstairs and in some of the upstairs rooms. Peering through the window he could see Dan watching the television. He was about to move away when he heard a scuffling noise. Someone was creeping around the back of the house and was coming stealthily towards him.

Steven shrank into the shadows, all his senses alive and ready for action. He drew the knife. The stealthy furtive steps stopped. Had he been seen or heard? He waited, then the sound started again – only one person heading in his direction. He put the knife back in his belt and as the figure loomed out of the darkness Steven stepped from the shadows and aimed a powerful punch at it. His reflexes were honed by years of competition and, as he launched his strike, two things happened simultaneously. He sensed the shape in front of him, something about it, and, with incredible control, he stayed the force of the punch so that it just grazed the nose of the person. The second thing was that there was a soft gasp, a female gasp, and then he was holding Sela, his hand clasped over her mouth.

"Shhh! Quiet, quiet," his voice hushed but commanding. He pulled her into the shadows.

"Oh Steven, Steven. Oh God. You're all right. Quick, get away. They're going to kill you." Her hushed voice was urgent and she reached up to stroke his cheek but he took hold of her wrist and tugged her into the shadows. He said nothing and pulled her further into the surrounding trees until they were away from the house. After a short while he stopped.

Before he could speak she was holding him. "Steven, Steven, are you OK? I was so worried – so scared." Her voice ended in a sob.

"Were you? How do I know that?" His voice was hard as he pulled himself away from her embrace.

"What, what do you mean?" She was bewildered.

"Vivien drugged me and you, you're supposed to be away overnight and I find you here." She was silent. She could see what he was thinking.

"Well, go on, tell me. When shall we three meet again – here to meet with Macbeth or should it be Steven Downs?" He mimicked the tremulous witchy voices of Shakespeare's chant.

"You can't believe that," she said. "You think I've set you up? Why am I here? Because I couldn't get in touch with you, that's why; 'cos I was so worried I came back this evening; *because* Jane sent Vivien to get me to bring me to her but I hypnotised Vivien and she told me that they had you. I pretended to be overawed by Jane – she's off her head – and I hoped to rescue you. That's why I'm out here now. What else would I be doing creeping around in the dark?"

He looked at her as the words tumbled out. So plausible, so upset, so glad, no, relieved to see him. "How the hell do I know *what* you're doing – what are any of you doing? All I know is that Vivien, your friend, fixed me good and proper and then I woke up, bound, a prisoner on Jane Trethowan's land; and now you, you're here as well. No, I don't believe you – would you?"

Before she could respond, there was a noise of a door crashing open coming from the direction of the Folly and voices shouting. Dan ran out of the house in the direction of the noise.

"Quick, we must get to my house," he said pulling her quickly behind him. "They've recovered." With no further explanation he dragged her across the field towards Hawkwood, stumbling together in the dark as they crossed the rough ground.

She did not try to break away at first but then said, suddenly, "But Vivien, she's still there." She resisted his pull as she said this and he halted.

He turned on her, fiercely. "She can bloody well stay there. She's with them – she drugged me – you bloody bitches." He took hold of her wrist, again, in a tight grip.

"No, no, you don't understand." He was pulling her through the dark and she struggled to keep up still talking, gasping. "She was under Jane and Tim's control."

He stopped, puzzled. "Tim?" What the hell was going on?

"Yes, he's one of them – not me, not Viv."

He was pulling her again and she almost fell. He dragged her on and through to his land and into Hawkwood. "We'll call the police." What would she say to that? Perry came over to him, stubby tail wagging. He patted the dog as he spoke.

She went to the phone, "Yes, OK." It rang and Steven got to it first.

"Don't do anything stupid," Jane Trethowan's voice was full of menace, "or I'll kill Vivien now. I don't care about the consequences. The police have to come a long way and, by then, I'll have finished with her. Nothing is going to stop me fulfilling my destiny."

Steven was puzzled. Sela picked up the extension phone listening. Now he would know. He said, "Look Jane, your quarrel is with me. Let Vivien alone. We can sort this out; talk about a land deal – yes? What destiny, anyway?"

"You won't understand. You're not important now – put Marian on." He held onto his phone, paused, and then motioned to Sela to speak into the extension.

"What is it Jane? Let Vivien go. I'll come back to you. You need me for the rite, you know you do."

Steven, puzzled, looked over at her as Jane ranted, "I need no one, no one." Then she quietened, "But you can come back – yes, yes to witness the event. I was wrong. I don't need Downs now I have Vivien. Come back, yes. I mean it. Don't call the police – I'll do it anyway but if *you* come back well then, that might be different. I won't go after Downs if you come back. Perhaps, perhaps I can make a bargain with him." Jane's voice changed again. "I knew I was right – you're with him. All that rubbish about you and Vivien – you're with him. Who do you think you are, you little bitch – trying it on with me – scrying me. I knew it, knew it." She was ranting, shouting down the phone and then that sudden change as her voice became softer, "But you can come back – yes, the Boudica link will be helpful to me… you can be with me – yes – come back."

Steven looked over at Sela eyebrows raised in query as Jane continued, "I knew you were lying, pretending to be with me. Well, you can come back but don't call the police – I *will* kill her, yes, I'll kill her; but nothing will stop me, nothing." She was beginning to rant again as Sela cut in looking directly at Steven who was now listening intently on the extension. "All right, I'll come back. I'll be alone. No, no Steven. He won't do anything. He'll do as I say – you know what I mean. Don't hurt Viv yet. Wait till I'm there. We'll talk." She put the extension down and he put the phone back.

"Quick," Sela said, "get out of here now in case they come for us. She's mad, completely insane. She *will* kill Vivien believe me, unless, somehow, we can distract her. I can distract her while you get to Vivien. Oh Steven, Steven, you do believe me now don't you? Look," she picked up Vivien's note and handed it to him.

He read it and saw what had happened. Sela was right; she had not betrayed him.

"Oh God," he said. "I'm so sorry. How could I doubt you?"

"No time for that, we must get out." She was urging him towards the door.

"They won't come here. They're frightened of me and Perry. Why does she want you?"

Sela tugged at him pulling him to the door; she called Perry who followed them. "There are such things as guns you know. Your karate can't stop a shotgun."

They ran into the shrubbery and into the dark away from the house. When she considered them to be a safe distance, she stopped and told him the whole story as she had got it from Vivien. He listened as she spoke of Tim's excavations in the grove; of the discovery of the artefacts and about Jane's plans.

"But this is insanity. Who will take her seriously? It's ridiculous."

"Is it? I'm not so sure. The artefacts are immensely powerful if used in conjunction with a rite, a rite of which I have no knowledge. She needs human sacrifice. Yes, Steven, she's adopting the rites of the old Solar cults – there's always a need for blood sacrifice. You were going to be it and now she has Vivien. Oh, it's not the artefacts, it's a combination of things; the consummation of everything coming together. She wants me because she thinks it will add credibility to her cause – me, a direct descendant of Boudica. Perhaps she *will* be able to mesmerise millions; Hitler did. He was into the occult as well – always seeking the Grail. Some say he had the spearhead that went into the side of Christ. The Spear of Destiny as it's known. Such leaders become charismatic, fanatical and they attract other fanatics. It only takes a few, most voters are apathetic. She's already got a small following and some big people – like Roger Martin.

Steven recalled the man's behaviour with Jane. Then he said, "Yes but she's mad and people will see through her. Decent people will, surely."

He saw her smile in the darkness, "I wish we had more time to talk about this but we don't. She will expect me soon. There are decent people, yes, but there is always a dark side; polarity, remember? It's what someone like Jane can do with anything that seems to be special, superior even. She can twist things, mesmerise people and she has based it all on death. Now I must go to her, delay her, we've got to get to Vivien. Oh God, if only we had allies."

She looked over at Perry and then bent over him. She stroked his great head and seemed to be whispering into his ears and then she made a sign on his head. From her pocket she drew out the crystal pendant Jane had given to Steven. She attached this to Perry's collar. The dog looked at her with devotion as she turned back to Steven. "Listen, sweetheart, you can't go to the police. She *will* kill Vivien in the belief that the Solar Gods will protect her. Mad, yes, beyond doubt and dangerously so. I must go to her now. No," she put her hand up to his mouth, "this I must do. She *will* kill Viv but I don't think she'll kill me, at least not until the rite is done; it seems I'm special. I'll go to her. Of course, she'll ask about you, what you'll do. I'll tell her I've bewitched you and you won't, can't, do anything. She'll believe that – I'll make her believe me but she'll kill Viv regardless; she needs the blood. And she'll send the others to get you so you can't give her away. Me, well she'll assume I'll be so overcome by her power that I'll do nothing."

Steven went to interrupt but she stopped him again. "This is what you must do now. As soon as I leave here, you leave as well but go across the fields with Perry – I need Perry for my plan to work. You must isolate Dan, Ray and that other one – can you do that? I know you can, my warrior," she smiled at him and caressed his cheek.

He looked down at her. "Of course I can. It's what I *can* do. If I come at them from the dark I should be able to take them out." He put his arms around her pulling her close. "I doubted you. I'm so sorry. I was so bewildered."

"I know." She kissed him and smiled, sadly it seemed.

He looked into her eyes, "Oh, I love you. Don't go – I'm scared you'll get hurt."

"Yes, yes, I know," she said softly, "but I must. This will be a necessary battle. Gandulf against the Dark Lord, remember? You on the physical plane and me on the psychic levels. We must win. She can't, mustn't, use those artefacts…" she paused, then went on, "and they must *not* go to the police or to a museum, no matter *what* happens. Promise me, promise me that you'll put them back in the grove – promise me."

She was insistent and so earnest that he could almost feel the physical intensity of her demand. "Yes, I promise, but nothing will happen to us this *I* promise, OK? We'll bury them together, you and I."

She gave him one of those strange, deep looks, staring intently into his eyes "Yes, together. Now I must go to her."

She came into his arms and he held her closely, smelling her hair, kissing her eyes, her lips, not wanting to let her go into danger, a danger about which he had no understanding. But he knew her power, and felt a sense of confidence in her.

"There now," she whispered, "I love you, love you." She held onto him and he could feel her heart beating against his chest.

"I love you too, my sweetheart," he replied, puzzled by her apparent sadness and he felt a sudden sense of foreboding which effected his former confidence. "You will take care – don't trust her." What was it he was feeling, sensing?

She smiled, "Of course; you do your bit and we'll be OK – so no more worrying and premonitions of doom." She said this in such a matter of fact manner that he realised that she had, once again, demonstrated her strange ability to read his thoughts and his doubts were dispelled.

He kissed her again and then she was gone, like a wraith, into the shadows. He looked down at Perry, who was standing looking after the retreating woman, then he and the dog set off towards the fields. In a short time he had crossed over the border of Jane's land and he and Perry began silently reconnoitring. Then he moved towards the promontory from where a glow could be seen, the glow of a fire.

CHAPTER 26

As he got closer he could hear the crackling flames and then some sparks shot up above the bushes; he made for the glow and peering through the undergrowth he perceived something that sent a shudder through him. The blazing bonfire revealed the rough stone walls of the Folly and, fixed upright to this was a large wooden wheel. Bound to the wheel spread-eagled, gagged, was the naked form of Vivien, clearly still alive for the firelight glinted off her staring, terrified eyes. Dark marks, snaking down across her body and from her wrists were, he realised, blood. Standing alongside the wheel was a masked figure dressed in a white robe.

In front of this scene was a stone altar and behind this stood Jane Trethowan dressed in a flowing red robe. Beside her, also in red, was Tim Hutchins. Behind them stood Dan, Ray and the butler; Ray looked terrible with a bruised and swollen face. With a shock Steven realised that they were dressed in what was supposed to be the clothing of Celtic warriors. Their arms were bare, revealing tattoos; their faces were painted and each had a Celtic sword and dagger hanging from his belt. There was a sudden movement and Sela stepped into the firelight.

"Aha!" said Jane, a look of satisfaction on her face, "so you've come back. I knew you would. See, Tim, she knows what is right. Where's Steven Downs?"

Sela walked up to Jane. "At his house. I fixed him. Told him to forget everything. He was asleep when I left him."

"How do I know he won't go to the police? How do I know you've 'fixed' him as you put it?" Her voice was contemptuous and dismissive. The others had formed a semi-circle around Sela cutting off any hope of escape.

"I don't have your skills but I do know how to hex someone so that they'll forget." Sela turned and looked at Vivien and at the trickles of blood glinting in the firelight. "As for the police – well, you've got Vivien." She faced Jane again. "You said you'd not hurt her yet," said Sela keeping her voice steady despite the horror and nagging fear. "I haven't called the police because you've got her. You said you'd wait."

Jane smiled at her. "I lied. Anyway you asked me not to hurt her but I didn't agree, did I? Did you hear me agree? No, you heard only what you wanted to hear. Anyway, we were getting impatient weren't we?" She looked over at the others who laughed callously all, that is, except the masked man who stood, unmoving. Sela looked at this figure and a shiver went through her. The mask was grotesque, resembling a Green Man but the intricate carvings on the face gave the impression of a leering lop-sided grin.

She could see the firelight shining on eyes which peered through two dark holes. That same firelight sparkled, also, on the blade of a curved knife which was stained with Vivien's blood. So this was the priest and executioner, she thought to herself, wondering who he might be.

Sela recovered herself, turned to Jane and said, "Yes, I'm sorry. Steven grabbed me in the dark and dragged me back to his house. I was just coming to you when you phoned. You know I want to be with you, be part of this – this great venture."

Tim turned to Jane. "But this is rubbish. Why was she outside? She's with him – she's..." He stopped as Jane put up her hand.

"No, no, you're wrong. Of course she has to be here. She cannot help it. It's in her blood. She, too, craves it; wants to see it again – yes, I know what she wants, what she did. Impaled women, slaughtered thousands – yes it's all there – I read it."

Steven, listening intently, realised what was happening. Sela had somehow bewitched Jane who was becoming confused. She was seeing Sela as Boudica and was referring to the Roman histories. Tim again tried to speak but Jane turned on him. "Quiet, you stand before a great leader. Come, Queen Boudica, let me give you this." She picked up the torc. "But first we must robe you." She gestured to the butler who jumped forward carrying a red robe. He handed it to Sela who slipped it over her head.

"Yes, perfect," said Jane. "Now this," and she placed the torc around Sela's neck.

"Perfect, perfect – it's all coming right, yes, yes." Jane turned to the men, "Come forward – kiss our hands and swear loyalty to her." Her phrasing and tone was grandiose and theatrical.

Tim was beginning to look angry and puzzled. "Loyalty to her? To us, you mean. Why her as well?"

Jane flashed a pitying look at him. "Isn't it obvious? She is a direct link; she is Boudica... was Boudica." She looked confused, paused and then went on, "I will use her psychic link to enhance the rite."

Exasperated but conscious of the looks of Dan and Ray, who did not like Jane being questioned, Tim said, "Yes, I understand but she tried to sabotage our plans."

Before Jane could answer Sela cut in. "No, Tim you're wrong. I'm with you – *both*," she emphasised this last word and saw that Tim seemed pleased at her acknowledgement of his status. She went on, "I didn't understand but seeing Jane and you – and you," she gestured to the others – "I can see *exactly* what has to be done."

Jane stepped forward and kissed Sela. "Aah, my sister of the dark. Yes, I can tell you are with us. Yes, you see Tim she knows it *intuitively*. So now, swear," she paused and added almost plaintively, "for me."

Tim took Jane's hand, knelt and kissed it. He did the same to Sela and the others did likewise although the masked man remained by Vivien's side. Jane whispered something to Dan and then said to Sela, "You see, they are yours – ours. Everything is going to plan... perfect." She stopped and a look of puzzlement came over her face. She shook her head and looked around her as though waking up. "Yes, what was it? Ah yes," she turned to Sela, her voice cold, different. "So, you came back. You..." she paused as if just aware that Sela was dressed ready for the rite. A fleeting look of puzzlement came over her face and again she paused as though trying to remember something. Steven realised that Sela's spell was weakening. Jane looked at the others who were all watching her, unsure of what to do. Jane quickly got hold of herself and turned to Sela.

"Come, Marian, let's see if you *are* with us." Taking Sela by the arm she guided her so that they stood in front of Vivien who was pleading to Sela with her eyes.

Sela tried to remain calm. Her friend looked in a dreadful state. Utterly terrified and moaning through the gag, Vivien tried to break the bonds on her wrists. She had several cuts to her upper arms, across her belly and one down her side. None were so serious as to cause too much loss of blood.

Jane said, "Power and the Life Force emanate from the glorious fiery heart of the living sun and permeate all living things. But the sun must feed as we all feed, and blood – hot and red – is its food, as it has always been. Now we will feed it until it rises, renewed, across the hills and then..." She made a thumbs down gesture at Vivien.

So, slow torture and death for her friend – Sela was getting desperate. This was not working out as she had thought. What would Steven do? Was he out there waiting? And now poor Vivien was to die, bound on the wheel.

As though picking up her thoughts, Jane said, "Bound to the Wheel of Taranis, she will die and I will be anointed with her blood." She ran her finger into a trickle of blood and drew a line across her forehead. "Cut her again," she said to the priest.

Vivien struggled, making muffled noises as the masked man took hold of her head, held it firmly and sliced across her ear with a sickle-shaped knife. Vivien gave a stifled moan as blood spurted and trickled down her neck and across her shoulder. Caught amongst the group, who were crowding around the nightmare scene, Sela stepped back turning away from the gaze of her tormented friend. She realised that there was nothing that she could do at this stage and she averted her eyes as the masked man made several more wounds on the woman's body. Tim reached across and touched the blood, tracing a pattern with his fingers on Vivien's body. He drew a knife, cut across her ribs then held the knife up letting the blood run down the handle, some of it soaking into the sleeve of his robe.

Jane moved closer to Vivien whose terrified eyes watched her as though mesmerised. "There, Vivien, we have played our special games so many times you and I but now – no more games, no more games... ever." She leaned forward and whispered softly into the wounded and torn ear of the helpless woman, "I said we would be together didn't I? How much more together can we get than this?" She pressed her lips against Vivien's blood drenched neck then stepped back, smiling, her lips red and moist. "Good, good," said Jane to the others and then she turned and Sela did not see her nod to Dan. But Steven did.

He had been a horrified observer and, like Sela, was uncertain of what to do next. When the masked figure started his series of cuts, Steven rose. He could not allow this to go on and Sela too, was in dreadful danger. As he prepared to rush upon the group he saw Jane turn to Dan and saw Dan take the other two men aside. In a moment they were heading directly for him although he knew they could not see him in the dark. Clearly they were heading for Hawkwood thinking he was still there helpless and alone. He saw, with alarm, that Ray carried a shotgun.

As the men got closer to the shrubbery Steven made a quick assessment. The immediate danger lay with Ray and the gun and there would be no time now, for mistakes. These men were ruthless killers and torturers. His martial arts training and the ethical use of force to overcome an opponent had to be balanced against the need to save himself and the two women, one of whom was in imminent danger of losing her life. The prickling feeling, which he always felt as a portent of danger, ran across his scalp. A fighting elation came to him, an elation he had kept under control for years but which he could now unleash.

As Ray made for the opening in the bushes, Steven kicked the gun from his hand, caught him in a head-lock and broke his neck killing him instantly. The other two, unable to see clearly in the dark and startled by the shadowy violent shape, stopped, allowing Steven to attack the butler with a high kick to the face, followed up by a short powerful jab into the man's midriff. Dan, recovering swiftly, drew the sword and slashed out at Steven. Steven sensed, rather than saw, the blade and swayed back but his foot slipped on the damp ground and the flat of the blade caught him across the forehead, momentarily stunning him. Blood welled from a shallow gash. He fell to one knee. The butler, gasping and winded by the punch recovered himself and also drew his sword, both men closing in to finish Steven. Dan paused, stood over Steven and said, "Got you at last, you bastard." He raised the sword and Perry came out of the dark, intercepting the downward slash with a bone crunching bite of his powerful jaws which splintered Dan's arm. There was a terrible shriek from Dan as Steven, recovering, stood up to face the butler who, clearly, had no further desire to be involved. He flung down the sword and turned, running up the steep shale-covered slope of the high coomb-side.

"Leave!" ordered Steven and Perry immediately released the damaged and almost fainting Dan. Seeing that Dan was now out of action, Steven turned to follow the fleeing butler but something strange was happening. The man seemed to be moving in slow motion, his feet sinking into the shale; then Steven understood.

The shale was moving, sliding slowly down and building up higher and higher around the man's legs and thighs.

"Help me, someone," he cried but the shale was moving swifter now and rising higher. It had reached his waist, trapping him completely. There was nothing anyone could do to help the unfortunate man as a mass of stone, made unstable by the sliding shale and heavy rains, loosened from above and slid towards him, catching him in the chest, bending his spine backwards and then, in a moment, covering and burying him. Steven, perceiving his own danger, called Perry and retreated before the landslide which slid on and rolled over the now whimpering Dan who could not recover from the pain of Perry's attack. The two men vanished under the tons of shale.

All of this had happened so fast and the first thing that the group were aware of had been Dan's agonised scream. They had stood, stunned, as the beginning of the dawn light revealed the moving landslide which buried the men and now slid to a stop only yards from the scene of the rite. The four of them stared at the awful event and took a moment to recognise the two figures emerging from the shadows. But Sela knew them instantly and ran to them.

"Oh God, Steven, you, you're safe. Oh darling."

He held her in his arms and looked over her head at Jane, Tim and the masked man. "It's over Jane, give it up. You're finished and you know it."

With a mixture of hatred and contempt, Jane looked at them. The malevolence in her eyes was so terrible that Steven could hardly bear to look at her. "So, Downs and the little hedgewitch think they've won. Come here Marian, come to me, Boudica's heir. This is where you should stand. Here is where true destiny and greatness lies."

"No, Jane, it's over. You must see that. All of this," Sela gestured at the tortured Vivien and the altar. "This is wrong... wrong. You can't base a future on this. Look, your men are all dead. There, the Gods you believe in have spoken. Give it up. Let Vivien go... please."

But Jane was not looking at her. She was looking over Sela's head to where the beginnings of a new dawn could be seen in the eastern sky. "Too late for that! You fool, you could have been with me but now... let Vivien go? Yes, I'll let her go." She walked over to the wheel, "I'll let her go... go to a great glory." Jane took hold of Vivien's hair, cruelly bent her head back and slit Vivien's throat with her ritual dagger. Vivien died in a choking fountain of blood which spattered Jane, Tim and the masked man, who still stood facing towards Steven but who had now begun to move to stand alongside Jane.

Sela screamed and Steven shocked by the brutality stood paralysed as Jane began to rub blood stained hands into her hair. "See, see... I am anointed in the blood of sacrifice and I have the Wheel of Taranis and the great sickle blade of the moon."

Steven recovered from his horror and ran forward only to find his way blocked by the knife wielding Green Man. He parried the lunge and dropped the priest with a bunched fisted hammer strike to the side of the masked head. The man fell, unconscious, to the ground. Jane and Tim moved backwards, putting the altar between Steven and them.

"I have the implements of power. You will not stop me," cried Jane in a triumphant voice, although it was also clear that she perceived the threat to her plans posed by Steven. She held them up and the growing light of the sun made them glow as she began a high pitched, wailing chant. Tim joined her, their voices keening and wailing, uttering words which were incomprehensible to Steven. He looked over at Sela and saw her face, frowning with concentration. He tried to move towards the two at the altar but found he could not.

As Jane and Tim continued their eerie chant, something began to happen around them. A mist was rising and it swirled into a vortex spiralling in the air. Sela saw it too, and realised, with alarm, that Jane's rite was beginning to come to its climax – though what that would be she had no idea. The horrifying image of her dead friend was filling her mind but she knew she would need all of her skills to combat whatever was about to happen. Sela invoked Hecate and her mind cleared enabling her to concentrate as she faced Jane and Tim.

As they continued their eerie chant, the spiral became horizontal and seemed to expand and open up and it was as though it was opening upon a long, deep, corridor.

"Like a hologram," said Steven aloud, his eyes watching the events in utter disbelief.

There was a loud humming noise and Steven discerned the babble of many voices growing louder and closer and he saw a sight which had not been seen for almost two thousand years. Moving forward towards the edge of the corridor, was a vast army of Celtic warriors. He could see them, hear them, smell the dust and horse sweat and he felt terrified. How was Jane doing this? What was this energy, this power that she seemed able to invoke? Steven felt his thoughts swirling in chaos as he tried to make sense of what was happening before his eyes. What *was* Jane? Could it be that she would succeed, would accomplish her plans, even in the face of Sela's attempts to stop her? *Was Jane the more powerful of the two?*

He turned to Sela, who, as though aware of his chaotic thoughts, called to him, "Steven! The Moon Temple! Visualise it around us – for protection – help me. Use your mind, your magical mind." He looked at her and then at the approaching horde and he did as she directed him to do, trying his best to visualise her room and the two of them in it.

"Yes," he said, "yes – the Power of Light," and then he shouted. *"Let there be a circle of fire and shining light around us, as about us flame the pentagrams."* His mind remembered moments of the ceremony and the memory of his encounter with Hecate came to him. *"Oh Hecate, Hecate, help us, help me now."* His mind was in chaos as he did his best to focus and then his old training took over and he summoned up Chi. The kaleidoscope images, rushing through his terrified mind, began to calm, to coalesce. His breathing became more steady and he was able to concentrate on the imagery of Sela's Moon Temple. He remembered her words when she had spoken of the power within.

"You have to summon up the flame that lies within yourself. It's no good looking for the answer elsewhere. The power comes from within and is then focused."

He remembered what he had said in reply, about the ability to break a brick with the hand through a switch of the mind. Suddenly, there at that moment of terrible danger, everything became clear. He knew, and could use, the power of magic.

Sela saw the horde and she knew that whatever happened now, it must not come out of the vortex and onto the physical plane. She raised her voice in a language which, again, to Steven's ears sounded Welsh. Jane and Tim heard her and they faltered but Jane cried out, in theatrical tones, "Bow down, heir of Boudica, to me, yes, to me – nothing can stop me, not even you – nothing," and she resumed her chant.

Looking over at Steven, Sela saw his concentration and she sensed the energies of the Moon Temple protecting him; she knew that the protective circle around them was inhibiting a different power, one of which she was becoming more and more aware. She could feel a growing energy emanating from the torc around her neck. Knowing, now, that Steven was protected by his visualisation of the Moon Temple, Sela stepped out of the protecting circle and into the open, turning towards the horde. The energy and mind-sapping strength of the vortex was terrible but the vibrating power within the torc was growing stronger and she knew what she had to do.

Sela could feel an enormous force beginning to emanate from the torc and she evoked that power, calling upon her long dead ancestor to rise, to aid her. She felt something like a sustained shiver run through her body. Her skin was hot, then cold and she broke out in a fine sweat. Something, something alien seemed to overwhelm her spirit and she felt her brain reeling as the alien force entered her body. Memories of another time, long ago, flooded her consciousness. She saw the fenlands, open grassland; the legions of Rome; the dead, the dying, the destroyed towns and she felt the triumph of victory and once again the joy of battle.

Steven could not move. It was as though he was held by a gigantic vice. He looked at Sela as she stood there almost unrecognisable to him. She seemed taller, with her red copper hair flowing to her waist and she seemed to be shimmering with light. Above her, the pale shape of the waning crescent moon hung in the early dawn sky. The light of the rising sun blazed off the heavy gold torc around her neck. She seemed to personify everything he now knew about the physical and spiritual nature of womankind, with her feet planted firmly and strongly upon the earth, holding in balance the life–giving, but also destructive, power of the sun and the deep, mysterious, healing and intuitive aspects of Lunar knowledge. Sela raised her arms and called out to the vast horde in a strange tongue and with a powerful strident voice which Steven did not recognise.

The vortex host, which had been getting closer and closer, paused. There was the sound of many voices, rising to a great continuous shout and Steven, striving to understand, heard that multiplicity of voices, merge into a repetitive chant.

"Boudica! Boudica! Boudica!"

Jane faltered, as did Tim, who could no longer speak. Jane tried to raise her voice again but Sela now stood in the full light of the sun. The vortex host and the mist vanished in an instant. Jane fell to the ground. Sela held her position, arms raised and then she, too, collapsed, overcome by the enormous power that had possessed her but which had now vanished, leaving her feeling drained of all energy.

Tim ran to Jane and helped her to her feet. Steven, now able to move, went to Sela who seemed exhausted. He helped her up and then went over to the lifeless body of Vivien, stepping over the unconscious body of the priest as he did so. He was about to release the body from the wheel when he heard Jane's angry voice.

"You stupid bitch. Do you think it's over? I still have the Wheel, the Sickle and the Blood... hah, hah, hah! The blood... yes," and she uttered a stream of words.

Tim, as though impelled by a command, drew his knife and began moving towards Sela. With difficulty, the exhausted woman climbed away from him up the hillside as he pursued her. Steven, alerted by this new attack went after him. Tim was about thirty feet up when Steven closed with him. The archaeologist slashed at him with the knife; Steven easily evaded the thrust, caught him by the arm and, using the man's momentum, he swung him round so that Tim tumbled head over heels down the stony hillside to crash with force against a rock. When Steven got to him he saw that Tim was dead.

Jane screamed in rage and she too, began to climb away from the scene in an attempt to escape. She dropped the sickle blade but clutched the Wheel of Taranis in one hand as she used the other to steady herself.

Sela recovered her strength and, standing on the other side of the slope, looked over at the fleeing woman. "Jane," she cried, "you can't run. You can't hide from the Silver Shining One and her hound. Look!"

She lifted her right hand, finger pointing at the pale horns of the crescent moon, still visible in the dawn light and now, seemingly poised above her head. Jane stopped, raised her eyes towards the moon which, to her maddened gaze, seemed to be a sickle blade ready to strike. She gave a cry and turning, continued her frantic climb.

"Now," called Sela and she gestured with her left hand at Perry who rose and loped after the fleeing woman.

Jane looked back and saw the Hell-hound of Hecate, a great black beast, coming towards her, a glowing pentagram shining on its forehead and the crystal pendant gleaming at the dog's collar. She recognised the pendant which she had given to Steven. In a moment of terrible clarity she realised how thoroughly Sela had outwitted her. Jane gave another cry, a mixture of rage and frustration, and then she was overwhelmed by sensations of terror and panic.

She turned and scrambled up the stony hillside, the hound following her, inexorable but with no hurry. She felt breathless, gasping for air; her hands were bleeding from the sharp stones; her gold sandals were torn from her feet and the brambles and gorse bushes scratched at the skin of her feet and legs. In utter terror she reached the top of the hill as the great beast crept towards her, its eyes red and glowing as the sunlight glinted in them.

Jane knew, then, that this was death approaching and she cried out as a pain shot up her arm and exploded into her chest.

When Steven reached her he found her lying there, her red robe ripped; her hands, feet and legs torn and bloody and her dead eyes staring, sightlessly, at the great, yellow orb of the sun whose light was mirrored, like fire, in the golden Wheel of Taranis.

CHAPTER 27

Steven looked up and across at Sela. "She's dead," he called. "I don't know how but she is." The body of Jane looked, strangely, pathetic and, for a moment, he wondered how the woman could have engendered such fear in him.

"Yes – yes, I know. It had to be." Sela began descending the slope with some difficulty and Steven scrambled over to assist her. She was white and exhausted from the psychic battle and he felt a growing concern at her obvious frailty.

"Are you all right?" He held her to him and, embracing her, he kissed the crown of her head.

"Yes, yes, just tired, so tired." Her voice was soft, almost breathless.

"God," he said, "what was all of that? I wouldn't have believed it if I hadn't seen it with my own eyes. I was looking into the past – terrifying. That army – who were they? Ancient Britons?"

She stumbled and he held her elbow, guiding her down. "No, not really. It was more like a projection of dark energy. Jane was producing it – Jane and Tim and that murderous masked man. Oh, poor, poor Vivien," Sela sobbed.

He comforted her. "Yes – horrible, the whole thing. I couldn't get to her. My God, I still can't believe it – everything – and you – you changed into something, someone else. What was it? You – you didn't look like you. It was weird, as though you were another person..."

She stumbled again; he saw that she was looking utterly drained. "I'll get you back." He was becoming anxious. She was, clearly, extremely weak and exhausted and he had difficulty guiding her over the rough ground.

"I had to draw upon Solar energies." Her voice was faint and breathless. "It drained me – Boudica came into me... I felt her power... Oh, I'm so tired."

They reached the scene of the rite. "What about Vivien and all of this?" She gestured with her arm at the dreadful scene.

"We have to leave it, leave here, now." Suddenly, he was aware that something was wrong. Where was the Green Man? "I pole-axed him, he should still be unconscious. Perhaps the headgear deadened the force of my blow. I wanted him for the police but now..." He stopped as he saw the masked figure emerging from the bushes carrying Ray's shotgun. "Get behind me," he said to Sela.

The figure stopped a few yards away. The leering face was towards them, the gun held nonchalantly over one arm. Steven was about to speak when the

The Moon Temple

man reached up and, with a free hand, lifted the mask from his head, letting it drop to the ground. "Well, this is a terrible mess, isn't it?" said Dr. Paul Hammond.

"You!" gasped Sela.

Steven was stunned; he had expected to see Roger Martin.

"Surprised are you? Well, that makes two of us. I thought you were only good for brews and potions. How wrong can one be?" His tone was conversational, casual even, but as Steven made a tiny movement, the gun came up covering him.

"No. No don't move. I've got nothing to lose by killing you two now. In fact, I'll do it anyway and walk away. With everyone else dead who will be able to tell anyone, eh?"

Sela said, "Paul, Paul, you're a doctor, you don't want to do this. It was Jane wasn't it? She fixed you – you were under her control."

He laughed but there was no mirth in the sound. "Oh, you'd like that wouldn't you? Is it so hard to believe that a doctor would murder people? We do it all the time you know. But no, I wasn't under her spell if that's what you mean."

Sela looked at him, shocked. "But why you?"

"Oh, come on. If you're going to kill someone – sorry – *sacrifice* someone, slowly, then what better person could there be than a doctor who's also a surgeon, eh?" He turned to Steven. "It was going to be you, you know. You'd have lasted a longer time than the woman but she was more fun. I could have sliced at her for hours you know. It's amazing how long you can keep someone alive." The conversational tone continued adding a certain horror to the unfolding, highly dangerous, situation. "Actually, I wanted to go further. Did you know that the Aztec priests would flay the skin from a chosen woman victim and then wear it? They'd dance to the sun. 'Give me a skin for dancing in'." He sang in a bizarre falsetto voice then said, "Jane didn't want that – too messy – but all that blood and all that power. Why me? It's simple. I believed in her – in her plans. I loved her, admired her strength and vision and you, you killed her." His voice became hard and angry. "All of those plans, all that power, could have been ours."

Perry was watching the doctor. The dog knew that something was wrong; he could feel the tension in the air and he moved forward, alert and growling. Paul Hammond pointed the gun at the dog. "I'll blast him if he moves," he said, quietly.

Sela stepped out from behind Steven creating a space between them. "There are only two shots in that gun," she said. "You can only get two of us and whichever of us survives will do for you." There was no weakness in her tone and Steven noted that she seemed to have recovered her strength. He was about to say something – to urge her to be cautious but was interrupted.

"Oh, well said, well said – like a true Queen Boudica," said the doctor. "Yes, a good plan, I must say. If I kill the dog and you, he'll get me – I've seen him in action," he gestured at Steven, "and felt him. That was some blow you gave me – you'll pay for that." He eyed Steven and Sela then said, "If I kill you two, I'll get eaten up by that great brute. If I kill him and the dog, no doubt you'll tear into me like a true Celtic bitch. Oh dear, decisions, decisions." He paused as though thinking and then said, softly, "Eeenie, meenie, minie, mo – ." There was a flash and a bang.

Steven felt the wind of the shot pass him and heard it thud into Sela, lifting her with its force. She gasped as she hit the ground. He turned to her and was down beside her assessing the wound. He could see that it was mortal – the amount of blood, welling from her abdomen, said it all. She was pale, looking up at him, trying to speak.

He felt sick with shock, "Shh, darling – no, don't try – don't try." His mind was racing as he attempted to staunch the wound.

"Listen," she gasped. "Rhiannon will help you. Rhiannon – look for her." She grimaced with pain and coughed. Blood trickled from her mouth. He wiped it away but she was whispering again. He leaned down to hear her, desperate to keep her with him. "Put them back – in the grove – promise me." Her voice was growing faint – almost a whisper.

"Yes, yes I know – don't talk – shh, shh, shh."

He held her, his mind in turmoil and she gasped a few times then gave a long exhalation of breath. She was gone, her body heavy against him.

Steven felt a sense of sheer disbelief. He knelt, holding her, rocking back and forth in a silent agony of grief. This could not be. Not now – after everything that had happened.

"Now you know how it feels – I said you'd pay." The doctor's voice was quiet, almost musing.

Steven laid Sela back on the ground and got to his feet. Perry, startled by the shot and confused by the sudden events, looked up at him waiting for a command. The doctor was holding the gun loosely in his hands. He continued talking. "I loved Jane – loved her – yes and she," he pointed at Sela's still form, "she killed her. So there you are." He brought the gun up and pointed it at Steven.

Steven tried to judge the distance. Could he get to Paul before the doctor pulled the trigger? Did it matter? Sela was dead so he might as well die trying to get the man who had killed her so callously. He tensed, preparing to make his move. Paul smiled at him, a terrible cold smile and then his face became a mask of despair. "Oh, don't bother," and with a sudden movement the doctor spun the sawn-off shotgun, placed the muzzle into his own mouth and pulled the trigger.

It was a while before Steven was able to move. He felt as though he had died inside. The shock of the previous terrible events threatened to overwhelm him utterly, and he knelt beside the dead body of Sela as though in a trance.

The intrusive noise of squabbling crows brought him to his senses and he stood up to see a number of the big birds crowding onto the blood-stained body of Vivien. He ran towards the gruesome scene, shouting and waving his arms; the birds flew off. He realised that he would have to get off the site before the activities of the birds drew attention. This was a dangerous situation for him should anyone come to investigate. He was alone on the site surrounded by six dead bodies, and his own clothing was covered in blood.

Steven went back to Sela's still, crumpled form. Apart from the dreadful wound in her abdomen, she seemed to be lying, peacefully asleep. His mind could not grasp the enormity of the tragedy before him. The trauma of the horrible events were imposing a numbing sedation to his emotions and he was like an automaton as he bent over her and lifted her up in his arms.

With some difficulty, he carried her to the cars standing near the Folly. He commandeered one of them, placed her limp body across the back seat and then went back to collect the artefacts. He drove the short distance to Hawkwood. Unseen, he carried her body into the house and laid her down on his leather sofa. He found some kitchen gloves and went back out to the car where he sponged the blood from the back seat, wiped the door handles and driving wheel and then, still wearing the gloves, he drove the car back depositing it at the Folly. He made his way across the fields to Hawkwood. He was sure that there was no likelihood of anyone seeing him at that early time of the morning. He felt nothing – no real emotion – just a deadness of the soul as though someone had switched off a light and he was stumbling through the motions in utter darkness.

He returned to the lounge and sat with Sela, resting her head in his lap. The numbness was still with him – a sense of total unreality as though he was an observer of the scene. Steven stroked her brow and ran his fingers through the thick tresses of her copper hair as he tried to think of what to do next. Then it was clear. He went out into the garden and across the lawn towards the wild grove.

The sunlight was shining through the branches of the trees, glittering and sparkling off the rippling stream. Looking at the rock slide, created by Tim, which had exposed the hollow entrance to the burial site, he studied the layout of the scene. He climbed across the rocks and peered into the hollow entrance. He could see the excavation from which the lead container, lying outside, had, apparently, been prized, and he could see the urn which Sela had placed back in its original spot. He lifted it out and looked at the cremated remains, realising their significance. Placing the urn back inside again he studied the opening and then made his way back to the house.

Bringing his own car round to the back of the house, Steven carried Sela and placed her on the back seat. He picked up the bag containing the artefacts and put them beside her. Then he went upstairs and came back holding his Goddess statue and the crystal wand he had bought in Glastonbury.

He parked the car as close to the grove as he could get. Lifting Sela's body he carried her to the grove and laid her by the stream. His eyes moved from her lifeless form to the bubbling stream, and then to the new leaves appearing on the trees all around. The eternal rote of life, death and renewal became clear to him – almost as a revelation.

It was then that he recalled his early flirtations with mysticism. He remembered some Buddhist writings in which the concept of Impermanence and the continuity of Mind had been discussed. Everything was impermanent in life; all things die and, therefore, the acquisition of material wealth is, in the end, futile. All things, the great, the small, the weak, the strong; animals, plants, humans, will all end and sink back into the great, flowing, eternal vastness of creation. But the Mind, the Spirit go on and are reborn. Steven remembered how Sela had spoken of the continuity of the Life Force; of the great sea of energy permeating everything. A spark of positive hope came to him – just a glimmer for a moment, and then the feeling faded and he was held, once more, in the grip of total desolation. He stood for a while then sighed and began his sad task.

With some considerable difficulty he got her body up to the entrance of the hollow and managed to manoeuvre it into the dark opening. The body rested in an almost foetal position, her copper hair falling across her face. The urn, containing the cremated remains was close to her head. He climbed down and returned with the artefacts. These he placed in the lead chest and then, again, with some considerable effort, he was able to push it into the hole from which it had been removed, with such indifference, only the day before. He placed the little Goddess figure and wand within the curve of Sela's lap then leaned over her and kissed her. As he pressed his lips against her he whispered, "Goodbye, sweetheart, my dear, dear, love. Rest here with your ancestor and with the sacred things that were so special to you. You see, I've kept my promise and I vow to you now that I will never leave Hawkwood. I'll always be here to guard and protect you and the site." He stroked her hair and her cold cheek. The gold torc was still around her neck but he left it there.

He knew it should be so for the golden torc was a link with her ancestral past and she had seen, and experienced, those ancient days. If the torc had that power then perhaps, just perhaps, it would be a means of bringing her back to him and they would walk the moors by moonlight and be together, lying in each other's arms, once more. God, if he could only cry. There was a leaden lump in his throat and he ached – ached for her.

Steven crawled out of the hole and clambered up onto the rock ledge – the same ledge that Sela had stood upon, only a few days ago. He remembered her as she had asked for a coin. He sighed and then took from his pocket a piece of paper. Sela had written down the poem she had recited in the orangery when she had 'called down the moon'. She had named the poem,

'The Moon Priestess' and he read it through to himself until he came to the last verse. This, he said aloud.

> *"For I can feel the cosmic power in me,*
> *A force and brightness, fiercer than the sun,*
> *Immortal now, I face my destiny,*
> *Thus Goddess of the Earth and Moon are one."*

As he finished, he felt the numbness lift and tears began to run down his face. He was wracked with deep, gasping sobs as the tension, fear, anger, sorrow and overwhelming sense of loss, came to the surface. He found himself crouching, like an animal in pain, as the storm rushed through him and out of him. And then it passed.

He rose and, with a spade, he dug and prized at the earth and stone above the hollow's opening. With a sudden rush, the rocks loosened and he leapt to the side as part of the hillside slid down to cover the burial site. The little stream stopped. He waited and then, from here, from there, water began seeping from the landslide below the site and soon the stream was back again but this time following its ancient original course.

There was a heavy oppressive atmosphere around him, pregnant with a deep silence. Then the sky darkened and the grove was lit by a bright yellow flash of lightning. The crack of thunder was directly over him and he waited for the rain. But it never came – just flash after flash and the deafening thunder. Then, that too passed and the grove grew light. He knew then, that Sela's powerful spirit had torn apart the veil and she had gone through into that eternal world to meet whatever fate the Gods ordained.

He prayed – half remembered prayers of his childhood but it was no use and then, remembering her beliefs, he called upon those ancient Gods – that the Karmic Lords would be merciful to her. In doing this he felt close to her for she had fired his spirit just as she had seemed to glow and shimmer in the light of the rising sun. He knew her to have been an intrinsic part of the earth and her words had risen on the wind and had been carried to the High Gods. He had learned, too, of her hidden depths, mysterious like a deep pool, and he had wanted to plunge into those depths and drown in her – to become a part of her. But she was gone – forever gone.

Steven sat on the rock shelf, lost in thought, his mind full of the memories of Sela, hearing her voice, her laughter, her warmth, their times together at her little cottage. The memories and comfort of her home, with her cat curled in front of the fire, came to him – Tanith... Tanith! He would have to get the cat.

Back at Hawkwood, he cleaned the sofa and room of the smell of blood and death. He removed his soiled clothing, dumping them in a plastic bag for burning later. He showered and changed and then, taking his car, he drove up to Sela's cottage. There was no one around but Tanith was sitting outside, looking forlorn. Taking a chance, he left the car and collected the cat; she was compliant. He continued to drive up the rough track as though out for a morning drive and then he turned back to Hawkwood, passing no one. Tanith walked into the house with no show of trepidation. She went over to Perry and rubbed herself against the slightly puzzled animal, and then wandered into the lounge making straight for the leather sofa. The cat jumped up, sniffed at the spot where Sela's head had rested and, curling up, Tanith fell asleep.

Steven, watching all of this, was overcome by a dreadful, sadness. He picked up Sela's coat, buried his face in its soft familiar surface and smelt the lingering scent of her perfume. He sat there as daylight faded and only roused when Perry came to him, pushing at him with his big questioning head. Steven rose, looked down at Tanith, who was still asleep, and then went out into the hallway. He climbed the stairs to the landing and entered his, now lonely, room and looked at the bed where, just a short while ago, he had held the woman he loved and with whom he had been so happy. He lay on the bed until he slipped into a welcoming, all embracing darkness.

CHAPTER 28

The next day was dank and dismal, with a hanging mist blanketing the fields and hills as though Nature was seeking to hide from human view the obscenities that had taken place. Steven lay on his bed trying to sleep but his dreams were punctuated with visions of Vivien's mutilated body, the leering, masked face of Paul Hammond and the recurring vision of Jane Trethowan – Jane holding the Wheel of Taranis as it glowed in the light of the sun. He had not dreamt of Sela although he had wanted to. He hoped that, in that dream-world, kingdom of the night, he would see her again, smiling, loving, vibrant – but there had been only the images of terrifying horror. Again and again he relived those last terrible moments of her life – those last precious moments. He could hear her fading voice and the last, desperate breaths. Rhiannon would help him, she had said. He knew that Rhiannon was the name of a Goddess but that was all and, in any case, he could not concentrate, not now – not after all that had happened; not after all that tragedy, that desperate grief and that overwhelming trauma. He stayed within the house, not wanting to venture into the gloomy, wet environment which seemed to add to his sense of utter sadness and loss.

It was two days before the news broke. Steven turned on the T.V. to watch the morning news and the picture was of Jane Trethowan's Folly. The news announcer was talking of "… brutal murders. Police are saying that wealthy landowner and politician, Jane Trethowan, local archaeologist and historian, Timothy Hutchins, artist and psychic, Vivien Thompson and Raymond Birch, an employee of the Trethowans, had been found murdered in bizarre circumstances."
The news bulletin moved on to other matters and Steven switched off.

He felt some anxiety and went over in his mind whether or not he had left anything that could link him to the scene. He felt he was in the clear but he did wonder why there had been no mention of Paul Hammond. He put the radio on, keeping it tuned to a news channel. Throughout the day the story began to get bigger and more detailed. He turned on the T.V. news channels switching back and forth. Then there was an announcement by a senior police officer. After a preliminary statement about the four bodies, the police officer went on, "The body of Doctor Paul Hammond was also discovered at the site. He had died as a result of a self-inflicted gunshot wound. There was a lot of blood around the site which investigators are attempting to link to the bodies. Other evidence at the scene has shown that Doctor Hammond was, most likely, responsible for the brutal slaughter of Vivien Thompson. A post mortem is being carried out on the four bodies. We are seeking the

The Moon Temple

whereabouts of Daniel Wade and Robert Walton, both employees of Miss Trethowan. They may be able to assist us with our enquiries." There was a further puzzle, for it was clear that the shotgun had been fired twice, yet there was no sign of another victim.

The National Press got onto the scene and they had a truly lurid story to tell. 'Satanic Murders', 'Voodoo Cult Murders on Exmoor', screamed the headlines. Steven was studying the front page of one of the papers as he walked up the drive to Hawkwood. "Mr Downs?" queried a man's voice. He looked up and saw a burly, middle-aged man accompanied by a younger man.

"Yes – who are you?" He knew who they were. It had only been a matter of time before *they* called. He felt his heart pounding.

"Detective Inspector Willis and this is Detective Sergeant Black. Could we come inside?"

"Of course," said Steven opening the door. "Just let me put the dog in the kitchen." He shut the door and then said, "OK, come in – what can I do for you?"

They walked into the lounge and the two men sat on the leather sofa. "Did you know Jane Trethowan?" asked the Inspector.

"Only slightly," replied Steven.

"But you're neighbours," interjected the Detective Sergeant, "you must have known her quite well."

"Yes, but I've only just come down here. I only arrived in Porlock four weeks ago." He listened to his own voice. Was it steady? Surely they would see the stress, hear it in his words.

The police officers exchanged glances and the Inspector consulted his notes. "Ah – yes, I see. You've inherited the house from your late aunt – is that right?"

"Yes, she died whilst I was in Scotland."

"Found dead on the moor?"

"Yes. Very tragic and somewhat mysterious so I believe. But, you must know this; the police investigated her death." A memory of the ghostly Rita on the stairs came to him. The panic he had felt in the orangery – the panic she must have experienced.

The Inspector was watching him. "Yes, but it wasn't us. So you must forgive us if we seem to be going over old ground. Did you hear anything strange, say, three nights ago?" The other policeman was also watching Steven closely.

"Strange? What do you mean?" Steven hoped he wasn't overdoing it. Surely they could see the tension in him – hear his beating heart? What did they know?

"Mr. Downs, there has been a brutal massacre on Jane Trethowan's land – you must know of it," said the Detective Sergeant, his tone hard, probing.

"Yes, of course, but I don't know much about it – only what I've read in the press..." He gestured to the newspapers lying on the table, "...heard on the news."

"So, no noises, no screaming – nothing?" Clearly, the Sergeant was suspicious.

Steven frowned as though concentrating. "Nope – nothing, nothing at all. But, then, the news said the bodies were found at the Folly. That's more than a mile from this house. I wouldn't, couldn't, hear anything." He went over to the doorway and beckoned them to follow. They went upstairs and he took them into his bedroom and over to the window; he pointed, "Look – you can just see the beginning of the Trethowan property. The Folly is around that stand of trees. I wouldn't hear or see anything." The police studied the scene. They exchanged glances and the Inspector nodded to himself.

Back downstairs, the Inspector asked about his contacts with Jane Trethowan. Steven told him about the small 'get together'. "Paul Hammond was there – he was my aunt's doctor but I hardly knew him. There was a Colonel Simmonds, a friend of my aunt, and, oh yes, Sir Roger Martin, a local VIP. A couple of others – I didn't really know any of them. Jane was welcoming me to the village, neighbourly, you know."

"You got into a fight with Raymond Birch and Daniel Wade, didn't you? What was that about? They worked for Miss Trethowan."

"Do you know, I still have no idea. Something about me being an incomer – ask the landlord."

"We have." The Inspector nodded to himself again, as though confirming something. It was clear that the police had already investigated his background and his contacts in the village. It was also clear that he was seen as a very new arrival with no community links. They chatted for a while and then, satisfied, the police left. He watched them drive off and became aware that he must have been perspiring with the anxiety of their visit. His shirt was stuck to his back.

Over the next few days, further reports came out following the post-mortems. The media had a field day. They took the story, shook it and turned it into one of the great and lurid murder mysteries of all-time. A local doctor and surgeon, Paul Hammond, had savagely mutilated then murdered Vivien Thompson. He appeared to have murdered Raymond Birch and Timothy Hutchins and had chased Jane Trethowan to her death. There was blood on Jane Trethowan linking her to the murdered woman, but her role in the victim's death was unclear. Then the doctor had shot himself with a shotgun which was registered to Raymond Birch, proving he had killed the man to get it. This in itself was bad enough but, the fact was that all of the victims, apart from the naked Vivien Thompson – the papers made a great deal of *that* fact – all of the victims and Dr. Hammond were dressed in some sort of ritual costume. A grotesque mask was found next to Dr. Hammond's body. There was an altar and occult paraphernalia in front of a gigantic wheel to which

Vivien Thompson had been bound. There, she had been tortured, mutilated and finally, murdered. Clearly, this was some sort of satanic cult. An examination of Jane Trethowan's properties revealed a penchant for occult literature and she had a ritual temple in her Porlock mansion. All of this indicated that she was deeply involved in black magic.

Steven continued to scour the papers and listen to the news. He wondered if anything would come out about Sela. The fact that she was missing did not seem to arouse any suspicion and he put this down to the reclusive nature of her life yet, surely, the Visitor's Centre would miss her or she would be missed by the college where she lectured. He wondered if he should go to the Centre and ask for her but realised this could cause more problems. No, better to leave it and to let things take their course.

Because of his close scrutiny of the press, Steven began to notice certain events which, in isolation, seemed unconnected. Sir Roger Martin resigned from his executive position to spend more time with his family. Colonel Simmonds was found to have committed suicide by shotgun – an eerie echo of Paul Hammond's death; several Council officials resigned or left the County. During one of his trips to the shops, Steven saw that the office of Sean Thurlow was 'To Let' and he realised that Sean and Fiona, too, had moved out. All of these, seemingly, unconnected events were of interest to Steven for, possibly, they indicated the break-up of Jane's political following. However, he was still puzzled about the lack of any mention of Sela but then, one day, the local news reported that the police were looking into the mysterious disappearance of another person, Marian Hall. She had failed to report in at the Visitor's Centre for duty and for classes at the local college.

Again, he studied the press avidly and listened to the news bulletins. Finally, a police spokesman came onto the television to announce that they had examined blood deposits near the Folly and, using forensic techniques, had linked the blood to DNA taken from Marian Hall's cottage. Clearly, she had been another murder victim, perhaps killed by shotgun. Blood residue, in one of the cars, indicated that her body had been removed from the site. It was assumed that her body, which had not been found, must have been buried or thrown into the sea. It was also clear that she, too, must have been a part of the satanic group. Examination of her cottage revealed occult paraphernalia. There were interviews with a few of the villagers and the consensus was that Marian Hall had been a reclusive, strange woman, known for her herbal cures and that she had often been in conflict with Dr. Hammond. As Steven had only been out with Marian a few times, the relationship between them was unknown and he was not involved in the police enquiry.

He felt lonely and lost, still traumatised by the horrific events and mentally exhausted by the tensions caused by the police investigation and press coverage. But now it was over; no more loose ends. Sela's reputation had been sullied but he knew the truth and time would take care of the rest.

He visited the grove daily but the sight of the rocks and the knowledge of what lay behind them filled him with terrible grief. He took solace in walking. Up on the hills he looked down at Hawkwood House; he could make out the garden area where Sela's body lay. It was as though he was outside of himself observing the scene. There was no sense of reality as his eyes took in the panorama below nor even when his wandering eyes settled on the, just visible, chimneys of Jane Trethowan's properties. He felt a sense of desolation – a terrible deadness, like a small, still point within his inner core. Could he go on? What was the point of it all? Everything that had happened to him over the past weeks – was it only weeks? – everything that had happened had been for nothing. He had lost the woman he loved so what did he care about anything now – even his life?

He was standing on the edge of a particularly high, steep drop. A step, a tumble and that would be it. For a moment he stood until, lost in that momentary, final despair, he found himself floating, then soaring high, higher up and over the moors. He could see everything from his great height and he felt a joyful freedom as he mounted higher and higher to the sun. The wind rushed past him, lifting him, holding him. He had a sensation of lightness as though he was a part of the air itself and then he was diving and swooping just above the ground. Everything had a clarity beyond his usual human vision and he could see the minute details of plants, grass, stone, all rushing past at speed. There was a figure, standing on the summit of the hill, and he swooped towards it and into it, merging his spirit self with his mortal self.

"You are the hawk. It will protect you."

He came to with a start, remembering her voice, hearing her near him and he looked around. Steven knew that what he had felt had been a so-called 'out of body experience' but it had not been what he had expected. He had always thought that such experiences would have a floating, dreamlike quality about them. In this case, the sensations had been exhilarating, almost violent, with that soaring, diving, rushing speed of flight. Yet, at the same time, there had been a lightness of being. He wondered if this was what Sela had meant by shape-shifting and then he knew, instinctively, that what he had experienced was what shamans had discovered long ago. The totem creature within all humans, that link with the primeval past, can empower a person and give them a hidden strength. Somehow, at that moment of suicidal despair, his totem, the hawk, had risen and evoked an unknown psychic strength from within the depths of his being. It had unlocked the portal to his soul and had lifted him from out of the cold depths of darkness and death, up to the redemptive warmth and light of the life-giving sun.

He stepped back from the edge. She had been near to him – surely, but there was only the soft rustle of the wind, the warming sun and the empty moor, but he knew she was everywhere around him and he felt his sorrows lifting and, for a while, he was happy. He could look at things in a more positive way. Sela had told him that life went on – that she would return and he held on to this thought and it sustained him, for a while.

But it was not always like that. There were the long, long, sad nights when he wanted to sleep but could not; when he wanted to dream of her but could not. Each night, since her murder, he had longed for a tangible memory of her, for the feel of her upon him, her breath beside him. He wanted her to come to him, perhaps as a succubus, so that he could pour the power of his love into her and bring her back to life. Sometimes, he yearned for her so badly that he prayed she would rise from her stone-covered grave and come to him in the deep of the night as a vampiric lover, to drain his life's blood and carry his soul with her into the vast, eternal emptiness of the moor; but always there was nothing.

The indoctrination he had gone through as a Roman Catholic child rose once more and, in his grieving state, he re-examined aspects of his early faith. His prayers, though, faded away and he could find no solace in a religion which held no answers for him. He could not believe – it had been too long and Sela had shown him a gateway to the spiritual world that made any conventional religious practices insubstantial and insignificant. If he was to find any answers then, to his mind, there was only one pathway now. He would immerse himself in the development of those practices which she had begun to show him. He would awaken his own inner flame and seek his own pathway to the transcendent. How he would do this without her guidance, he had no idea but perhaps the Gods, if they were there, would help.

Sitting in his chair, lost in a sad reverie, he had a sudden image of Sela standing on the rock ledge. He went to the grove and cried to the Gods to bring her back. He asked for a sign, for something, anything, to show that his voice was being heeded. His eyes were caught by the gleam of something bright in the stream. Reaching in he pulled out a coin. It was the coin she had thrown from the ledge. He held it for a while, remembering, and then he placed it back, carefully. This had to be a sign, but of what? He did not know why but he felt a sudden hope. Here was a portent, perhaps, and he walked with a lighter step back to the house.

New Moon Rising

CHAPTER 29

The morning was bright and sunny so Steven decided on a walk to the beach. He fed Tanith, who had settled in very well indeed, looked at Perry, who had curled up by the fire, and then set off down to the beach. Halfway there his bootlace snapped. He attempted a repair but then decided to return home to change his shoes. Instead of going immediately into the house he felt a strong pull to visit the grove, and so he walked out into the garden and across to the burial site. The sunlight was warm on his face and then there was the sudden drop in temperature as he moved between the shadows of the grove.

His whole being seemed suddenly more alive and he sensed, before he saw, the figure sitting by the stream contemplating the jumble of rocks. His heart seemed to stop and then pound in his chest as the sunlight, striking through the gaps in the trees, glinted and danced along the length of her copper-coloured hair. He felt a shiver of fear run through him as he looked at the figure, its back to him, and at the hooded coat, dappled by the dancing sunlight – the same type of coat that she always wore. Was this her spirit come to visit the site of her burial? Had the Gods heard his call? The figure moved, rose, and he heard the physical sound of her clothing rustling. It was her, Sela, but how? Their eyes met and he felt giddy, his head spinning.

"Oh, my goodness, Steven…" She saw his pale face – the questions – the disappointment. "Oh Steven, I'm so sorry. I saw you go out. I didn't expect you back so soon. Oh, I am so sorry to have shocked you like this. I'm Rhiannon, Marian's cousin."

Back at the house he sat across from her looking at her with a sense of wonder and deep sadness. So like Sela but slightly taller. The same hair, though cut differently; the same grey eyes. Only the voice, with a soft Welsh lilt, deeper and different.

"I'm so, so sorry I shocked you like that. I thought you were out. I saw you go; I've watched you for a few days – giving you some time to adjust. I knew that when you saw me you'd be taken aback – we are so alike. Our mothers were identical twin sisters. I wanted to give you time and then I was going to phone you and explain before we met."

"Where are you staying?" He was still shaken by her appearance; the likeness to Sela was disturbing yet he felt at ease with her. For a moment he could pretend – pretend she was back, sitting with him.

"At the cottage; I have keys." She reached into her coat pocket and pulled out some keys, dangling them and then placing them back.

"She told me to look for you," he said quietly almost to himself. He heard Sela's faint, whispering voice, fading as the life drained from her. "I thought she meant the Goddess Rhiannon. I forgot she had a cousin – I should have remembered but she never gave me your name."

"Yes, I know. She wrote to me on that last day; she knew what was going to happen – it came to her in a vision – you know all about that now don't you? She knew that her battle with Jane would be titanic and that, in order to win, she'd have to use the very deepest limits of her power and that she would pay the price."

Steven listened to Rhiannon's words. How had Sela known that she would have to pay a price? He remembered the way she had given him that strange, deep look just before she had gone to face Jane. Why had she not told him? He looked at her, so like Sela, but no, different, different – or was she? "So she wrote to you – can I see it?"

Rhiannon got up and took a letter from her bag. She handed it to him, his hand shaking as he took it.

'My dear Rhiannon. This would be strange to anyone but you but by the time you read this I will be dead.'

– Steven gasped: how *could* she have known?

'You and I have walked strange paths in our present lives and, no doubt, will do so again. But now I must engage with someone so dark and dangerous that I cannot avoid it. She seeks to strike out at someone I love and she will succeed, one way or another if I don't stop her.'

Steven read on as Sela explained about Jane Trethowan and about the sacred site. He read about Vivien's visions; about the excavations; about the direct link with Boudica; the whole story set out and her own vision of the final outcome.

'So there you have it. Steven will follow my wishes of that I am sure. Of this I am also sure. He will bury my remains with the artefacts and with our ancestor.'

– How could she have known that?

'Now, my Rhiannon, we have always been so close, more sisters than cousins and certainly Sisters of the Moon. Look after my Steven, he is a wonderful warm man. He is lonely and will need you as you will need him.'

– What did she mean by that? He looked at Rhiannon who was sitting stroking Tanith. God – it was uncanny, the resemblance – was she real?

'He will not understand my death but it has to be. I cannot let that dark soul of Jane Trethowan walk the earth and corrupt our ancestral heritage. Look after him and perhaps, in time, you and he will be together and I will be with you in spirit. Look after Tanith but I am sure my Steven will have rescued her.

I love you and will see you again in spirit,

Your Moon Sister, Marian.'

He put the letter away, his eyes moist. He saw another small folded paper with his name on it and with trembling hands he opened it.

'My Sweet, Sweet Steven. I write this at a time when you are in great peril, but I know you will be all right for it's destined that we will fight our battle against Jane and we'll win. I know this will happen but there's no time for me to explain – it's too complicated. However, I'm sustained by the knowledge that you'll be all right.
Steven, I love you so much and you have made me happy but there are deep and hidden forces at work and you will not, at this stage, understand. From our day on the pathway I was destined to meet you, to help you, to love you and to die in your arms.'
How did she know all of this? – it made no sense.
'I pray that I will have paid back some of my karmic debt but it will be in the hands of fate now. Time will tell but I know that somehow, in some way, I will be with you again.'
So that was it – that karma thing again. She had believed in it, *knew* it was so – and it had killed her.
'My cousin, Rhiannon, will give this letter to you. Look after her. You two need each other although neither of you realise this as yet – that, too, is destiny.

Goodbye, my darling. My love to you through eternity.

Your Moon Sister and your love, Sela.'

He began to sob uncontrollably and Rhiannon rose and put her arms around him. He leaned against her until the sobbing subsided and then she placed her hand on his head and he felt a comforting wave of warmth and slid into a dreamless sleep.

When he awoke he smelled cooking and went into the kitchen. Rhiannon was just removing a roast from the oven. "You will be hungry and must eat. The body must be fed as must the spirit."

"Yes, yes indeed, thanks. You didn't have to you know." He felt ravenous and realised he hadn't eaten properly since Sela's death.

"I know – I wanted to," Rhiannon said simply.

As they ate he told her the whole story, confirming Sela's account. She listened to him mainly in silence, only asking questions to clarify something. At the point where he spoke of Paul Hammond, Rhiannon bowed her head, "Such violence – such terrible wasteful violence – my poor Marian." She lifted her head and he saw tears in her eyes. When he told her about the final burial of Sela in the grove she nodded. "Yes, yes, strange but I felt a strong pull to go there. I watched you leave and then I went into your garden. I felt drawn to the grove... I sensed it as a place of power but that there was something more special there I was certain. When you found me I was attempting to quest for it and then you arrived. Perhaps my questing brought you to me. You have done the right thing Steven; it was what she would have wanted."

He gave a sad little smile. "It's so strange. It was only a short time ago that she stood in the grove on a rock ledge and threw a votive offering into the stream. Now she lies in that grove. I can't get my head around it." He told her of his finding the coin Sela had thrown into the water. "It was as though she led me to it – to give me hope."

She nodded thoughtfully and in sympathy. "Yes, but is it so strange? She *is* there, linked with her ancient past and guarding the ancient artefacts. It was destined to be so. She is here with you, still, on your land and you too are now a guardian of the site – your destiny, you see." She said this in a matter of fact voice, as if such things were everyday occurrences to her. Perhaps they were, he found himself thinking.

Afterwards, in the lounge, with Perry at their feet and Tanith on her lap, he asked Rhiannon what she intended to do.

"I will clear her cottage in due course. She told me to do this. It will stay in the family but will be empty for a while. You are to have her magical tools and books. But I will stay there for a few weeks. She would want me to; I used to visit often."

Steven nodded feeling strangely comforted at the thought. "So you are a witch as well?"

"I don't like the term but yes, I am, just as you are, now."

"Me? No, I don't think so." Steven looked at her puzzled. Why had she said this?

"Well, more a moon priest really. She has told me – that you have done some work with her – and now you and I will work together in her cottage, this she has wanted." It was said simply, like a statement of truth and he accepted it without question. Perhaps this was his karma at work and Rhiannon had been sent to guide him along his new, chosen spiritual path.

Later, he walked with her to the cottage and went in with her, his heart thumping with the memory of Sela. It seemed that she was everywhere but the place had been tidied up by Rhiannon. He sat across from her, the juxtaposition of images flashing in his mind. But Rhiannon was different, not the same as Sela, this was now obvious. She looked quite like her as relatives often do but was taller and dressed differently. The eyes, though, were the same. The same grey deep eyes of wisdom as though they had viewed the ages of the past and he felt the same atavistic shiver as he looked at her.

They spoke easily together about this and that and when he left to go home he felt lighter in his mind. He saw her every day for the next two weeks and he tried to maintain a lightness of spirit – to forget the horror and loss but there were moments when he lapsed into deep sadness and depression and she was there to support him and help him.

He spoke again and again about the events at the Folly, as though in speaking he could cleanse the horrific events from his psyche. He remembered the electrical storm following the death and burial of Sela and he recounted this to Rhiannon. She cried as he told her and then she said, "Yes, yes, your feelings were right. When great spirits pass over there is often just such a manifestation of great power."

Despite his own abilities to utilise meditation as a means of release from his depression, the legacy of his loss and the constant flashbacks to the horrific events of that dreadful morning persisted.

"It's not surprising that you can't lift yourself out of the darkness," Rhiannon said to him, one evening. "You were psychically injured by Jane Trethowan and you would have been all right following Marian's intervention. However, the trauma of the events at the Folly and the death of Marian have fractured your defensive aura."

One evening, when in a particularly low state, she took him into Sela's temple and there she created the Moon Temple and he saw Sela again in Rhiannon's movements and in the way she spoke the words. Rhiannon held him and comforted him and blessed him with the clear light of the moon, cleansing his soul of sorrow and trauma, helping to erase the memories of that dreadful day, the death of Vivien and the death of his beloved Sela.

She knelt with him upon the floor of the temple and then spoke to him words of comfort. "In life we are faced with many trials and we don't know why. It is as though we are being tested or, perhaps, we are having to pay back for things we have done in another time. All of us who set out on the spiritual quest have to go through this. They say it makes us stronger but we don't see it at the time. Only later does it become clear that we have been tempered, like steel, in the fires of adversity. There is always the Dweller at the Threshold of Enlightenment." Then she began to speak softly in verse.

"The silent, secret, Master of Despair
Awaits all those unwary ones who dare;
Who strive, in solitude, to reach the Light,
Then dashes hopes into the pit of night.
Where lost, the aspirations of the heart
Are spread like shattered fragments, blown apart,
To scatter dreams in dust-like clouds around,
To lie, unheeded, broken on the ground.
Yet, in this deep affliction of the soul,
The one who seeks can know the Dweller's role,
And rises humble but with courage, bright,
To tread, once more with strength towards the Light."

At the end, she lifted him from his knees, held him in her arms and kissed him, comforting him, and he felt the sorrow gradually lifting.

"In a way" she said, "you have died a spiritual death but now, given time and with my help, you will be re-born and be strong. All great mystics have to go through this."

"I'm no mystic," he replied but she said no more and remained silent.

CHAPTER 30

Over the following days he began to feel more invigorated and he started to do his martial arts exercises again; but the sadness inside him was always there, if only as a persistent shadow, hovering in the background. Rhiannon knew this and gave him space and she would leave him, sometimes for a few days, remaining at the cottage. Steven found that he wanted to see her more and more; she was so like Sela and he felt reassured and comforted when Rhiannon came over to spend time at Hawkwood.

He had many questions for her and learned that her family had, originally, been in the West Country but that they had moved to Wales when she was ten years old. She had studied complimentary therapies and had been running a successful private practice for a number of years. Like her cousin, Rhiannon had grown up in a household tradition steeped in ancient occult practices; the two cousins had often worked together. Inevitably he asked if she knew Vivien.

"Yes, Vivien has been around for ages. She was very talented you know, in her psychic field."

"What I don't understand is this," said Steven. "If Vivien was so psychic – could see the future and all that, why couldn't she see what would happen just as Marian did?"

Rhiannon looked at him and her eyes had that strange, deep gaze he had first felt when he had met Sela. It was as though Rhiannon was reading his soul and contemplating her reply before answering him. Then, as if reaching a decision, she said, "Perhaps she did know. Vivien was deeply spiritual but she had drifted into a way of life that was hurting her. Bad company, too many 'trips', unhappy relationships; she was a deeply wounded soul. Perhaps she *did* know what would happen. Perhaps she knew she would die – wanted to die, to save you – I don't know." He shivered as she said this and she paused before continuing. "But I know Vivien, knew Vivien. She was complex. Perhaps she had a karmic debt to pay." The strange look had gone and she touched his hand in a gesture of reassurance.

"I wouldn't have wanted someone to die for me," Steven blurted out, almost angry at the thought and remembering the light-hearted Vivien, perched on his kitchen stool, smoking her marijuana. Then his mind flashed to the mutilated body and he felt sick.

"The decision wasn't yours to make. There are forces beyond our understanding so you will have to accept that you can't affect all outcomes." She looked at him intently and then said, "Don't dwell on the memories. She's gone on now – she's OK." She touched his hand again.

"OK? That seems a strange thing to say after such a terrible end." There was a note of irritation in his voice. Rhiannon seemed so detached, at times, but she had not seen what he had seen; experienced those horrific events. However, he knew that she was trying to help him, to console him. "This whole karma thing bothers me," he said. "It seems so cruel – so lacking in any sense of mercy or compassion."

She nodded. "Yes, I know. I don't understand it all but Marian and Vivien were sure that there is something beyond this existence; that we come back, and I'm sure as well – you'll see." Rhiannon gave him a sad smile and he remembered that she, too, was grieving for her cousin.

He went over to her and took hold of her hand. "Yes – well I hope you're right but thanks, anyway, for your help in all of this. I'm sorry if I sound so low at times but the whole thing bothers me. Look, my aunt died – terrified, alone. That death was mirrored by Jane's; she died in absolute madness and terror. Those others with her had violent deaths; Hammond killed himself in a state of anger and despair; Vivien died in pain and terror and my poor Marian died violently trying to stop a mad woman. Where's the justice in it all?" He remembered his Catholicism – prayers to the Madonna for comfort in 'this Vale of Tears'.

"Yes, it does seem to be all one way doesn't it? But, if it *is* down to karmic law – and I'm sure it is – well, you don't know what each of them had done to warrant such an ending."

"But Marian and Vivien were fighting for good."

Rhiannon agreed. "Yes, but you still don't know what they owed. Anyway, Marian didn't die alone, did she? She had you to hold her, comfort her."

He remembered her last whispered words – the final breath on his cheek. "Yes, yes – at least I was able to give her some comfort wasn't I?"

He clung to the thought but still pondered the vagaries of karmic law. His parents had died in a crash. Ginny had been taken by cancer. But, an uncle had spent his last day playing snooker in the morning, doing a bit of gardening and then he had enjoyed a pleasant lunch. He had gone upstairs for a nap and had died. Another elderly relative had been able to see all of her family during an extended holiday abroad; she had returned to England and had died in her sleep, contented. None of it made sense to him.

He related all of this to Rhiannon and she said, "There, you see, there are other events which balance things out. Believe me, the more you consider these matters, the more you will begin to accept."

"I know," he said, "but it's so frustrating and puzzling. Don't we have any control over our lives or is everything pre-ordained?"

"I wish I could answer that," she said. "If I could I'd really be a great teacher wouldn't I? Look, it's to do with choice, I think." She was silent for a while then said, "You know how Hecate is represented as a triple Goddess, yes?"

He nodded. "Sure, facing in three directions, right?"

"Yes. Well, in ancient times, Hecate, or Diana Trivia – Diana of the Three Ways – stood at the meeting point of three roads and travellers would place offerings to Her before setting out on their journeys – for safety, guidance and so forth. Or, some people would visit the place, at night, and ask the Goddess for favours or to curse an enemy, that sort of thing. To act for good or ill."

Steven nodded again. "Yes, Marian told me about that. Light and Dark."

"OK," Rhiannon continued. "Well, you see, at that point they had a choice. They could take either of the paths or return the way they had come. Perhaps they would ask the Goddess to grant a supplication – or not, as the case might be – or retract their request. So, it's true that Marian and Vivien knew what would happen if they continued to help you but – and this is the point – they *didn't have to help you.* It was their decision."

"So, what you're saying is that if they hadn't helped me, they'd still be alive? That's horrible." He felt deeply upset at the thought.

"Oh no! I don't know." She hastened to reassure him aware that he was very distressed. "I'm just saying that it might be so. As I said, if I *really* knew I'd be a fantastic teacher wouldn't I?" She took hold of his hand to reassure him.

"Yes, sure. I see what you mean." He squeezed her hand.

She smiled at him and the dark mood lifted but, as he pondered Vivien's terrible fate, he wondered, then, if the electrical storm had marked not only the advent of Sela in the after-world, but had also marked the passing of Vivien. He hoped that it had and that, somehow, the spirits of the two great friends had met, once more, and that they had been guided by the Goddess Hecate to the presence of the Karmic Lords.

Steven and Rhiannon began to develop a close relationship. He found himself feeling more and more at ease with her. She needed to see to her business in Wales so would be away for most of the week but, as the weeks passed, she began to spend more weekends at Hawkwood, sleeping in Rita's room. Initially, this had happened following a ceremony, held now in Steven's orangery which he had decked out on the lines of a Moon Temple. The ceremony had been particularly powerful and he had managed to bring through the power-rush of Hecate. The feeling had been overwhelming and it had left him feeling dazed and slightly disorientated as though he had drunk too much alcohol or he had smoked too much pot. He had felt elated and excited by the experience and he wanted to talk about his success again and again. Rhiannon, too, had been delighted by his growing abilities and by his evident grasp of the methodology employed in deep ritual practice. She had felt the power coming through and had been about to accept it when she had sensed Steven's readiness and had 'seen' his aura glowing, as the spiritual fire within him had blazed like a bright and flaming star. So, she had stayed that night to help bring him down again, back from the heavenly heights into which his spirit had soared.

Her presence in the house lent it an air of homely comfort. She enjoyed cooking and was continually experimenting with new ideas and recipes. She loved watching cooking programmes on T.V. and also loved acquiring books by personality chefs. However, although she was seemingly happy as she pottered around, Steven was conscious of her grief at the loss of her cousin. Rhiannon seemed to do everything possible to avoid going to the cottage. Sometimes, he would find her standing in the orangery staring out towards the grove and he was loath to intrude upon her at these moments. At other times, she would talk about Sela, about how the two of them had worked closely together, honing and improving their magical skills and, because of Steven's own growing magical abilities, Rhiannon was able to share with him and show him many different occult techniques, from scrying on the astral to the use of focus tools such as tarot cards.

It was at the end of one of these sessions that Rhiannon mentioned the buried artefacts. She was talking about scrying. "Obsidian – a polished, flat piece of obsidian, is very helpful," she was saying.

"What about a crystal ball – you know, like you always see in those depictions of fortune tellers?"

"Well, yes, but they're expensive. A really good way to tap into the subconscious is to have a dark bowl filled with water. Then, you sit beneath the moon and watch the clouds and the moon's reflection cross the surface of the water. It creates a lovely, moody atmosphere." She got up and went over to the window staring out into the garden. "I wish I'd seen them," she said, suddenly.

"Seen what?" He was stacking the tarot pack and wrapping them in a silk cloth.

"The Wheel of Taramis, the blade and, most of all, the torc. I wish I'd seen them."

Steven put the cards away and went over to her. Rhiannon sat down on the rug, knees tucked up to her chin, her arms enfolding them. He sat down beside her. "Yes, I can understand that. They were wonderful... but deadly or so it seems."

She unclasped her knees, lent back on her elbows and stretched out her legs. "No, they weren't dangerous in themselves, they're just objects. It's what you do with them – that's the danger – or not, as the case may be. It's how you draw on the stored energies within them, how you use it. It all depends. Didn't Marian tell you about magical paraphernalia?"

Steven nodded. "Yes, of course. I understand that but these seemed to have such power in themselves. They were like veritable dynamos."

"Yes," she replied, "they contained the stored vibrational energies of, perhaps, thousands of years of sacred practices but you have to know how to sense those energies, harness them and direct them. If, say, an ordinary archaeologist found them – you know, someone not into the occult, then he would have seen just beautiful, ancient artefacts. It needs a person who is adept at channelling energies to be able to read them and feel their power. Look, a sword can be deadly in the hands of a killer but can be seen, also, as an object of beauty, of skilled craftsmanship if it is displayed in a museum."

Steven remembered Jane Trethowan, her lips red with the blood of Vivien, holding up the Wheel and invoking its stored energies.

Rhiannon nodded as he recounted this memory. "Yes, she was invoking Solar Magic... using that stored power for her rite but it was the stored energy, the vibrational energies within the object, *not* the object itself, if you see what I mean – not its outer physical form but the inner vibrational core and fabric of the object – that was what was being harnessed. I could do it too, but for a different purpose."

"What purpose?" He was eyeing her with unease. "You're not saying you want them?"

"No," she said and waved her hand in a dismissive gesture. "I was just giving you an example. I was just saying I wish I'd seen them. The torc in particular. It's part of my history, my ancestry as well, don't forget – as much as Marian's." She seemed a bit upset. "Part of *my* ancestral heritage. We shared the same genetic link – don't forget."

Forget? How could he, with this living, breathing doppelgänger of Sela resting on the floor before him? He sat, pondering her words. So Jane had used Solar Magic. Steven knew there were different magical techniques, for Sela had begun to tell him about them during some of their discussions. She had told him of the great adepts of the past, adepts like Mathers who, with the Order of the Golden Dawn, had explored Egyptian texts and had blended Freemasonry, Egyptian magic, Kabalah and a rich imagination, to create a vibrant system of magical practice. Steven knew also of Aleister Crowley, that brilliant, magical maverick, who had taken the ideas of Mathers and others and had developed his own system of Magick, with its Book of the Law. Crowley, in particular, had used Solar Magic to great effect. Steven felt it might be advantageous to read more about these practitioners and their systems but, when he voiced this desire to Rhiannon, there was a momentary silence before Rhiannon answered and, when she did, her tone of voice was hard.

"Don't go there, Steven," she said, staring earnestly into his eyes. "Don't. Solar Magic is powerful and active. If used wisely it can be beneficial but it almost always corrupts the practitioner. No matter how well intentioned the practitioner may be, there always comes a time, a need, for sacrifice – a need to shed blood – to incorporate the shedding of blood into the rites." Her voice took on a harder edge, almost contemptuous. "Just look at all the sun worshiping cults – they reek with blood, with pain, sacrifice and death. Look back at history – the Bible, Greeks, Romans, Persians, Celts – the Aztecs. Even Christianity uses blood as a motif for adoration – yes, I know it's symbolic but look at *their* history. Just look at the iconography." She paused, then continued, "And if you want to bring it to modern times, then look at Hitler's armies and Japan's cult of Bushido. Both use Solar symbolism as icons; the swastika and the rising sun. No, Steven, don't go there. The Gods of the Solar Path are always hungry – waiting to be fed – wanting blood – always."

The intensity of her feelings was obvious to him and he attempted to lift the tense mood.

"OK! I hear you." Steven raised a defensive hand and he saw her relax visibly. Yet he knew he would begin to read up about the Solar Path. In a way, Rhiannon's warning had awoken his interest even more. Then, in his mind's eye, he saw Sela resting in the grave of her ancestor and he also remembered the artefacts as he had placed them back in the lead container.

Why had Rhiannon mentioned them now? Surely she did not want him to dig up the artefacts? She could not want him to disturb the grave – remove the torc from around...? His mind refused to consider, further, what lay beneath the rocks.

Rhiannon stood up and looked down at him, her hands resting on her hips in an unnerving likeness to Sela's usual stance. "Don't worry," she said, "I'm not saying I *want* to see them. I just said I *wished* I'd seen them, that's all."

He looked up into her eyes and saw the sadness there.

"In a way," she said, "it would have brought me closer to her – to see what she had seen." She sighed and said, again, "Don't worry, I'll honour your pledge to her and your wishes. The artefacts won't be disturbed by me."

He continued to look up at her saying nothing. She removed her hands from her hips. "What's wrong?"

"You – you looked the exact image of Marian just now – it was nice but a bit spooky."

Rhiannon gave him a strange look. "Sorry," she said. "It'll pass in time. I can't help it you know – looking like her – but try to look beyond. Try; you must get over this."

"Sorry," he said, getting up from the floor. "It's just weird, sometimes."

"Do you want me to go?" There was a note of irritation in her voice.

He was alarmed. "No, no way – no. Oh, I'm sorry. It's just so numbingly awful at times. I never really said good-bye... do you see?"

"Yes, yes, of course." She put her arms around him in a companionable hug and he felt her comforting warmth but he held on to the image she had unconsciously presented to him. It couldn't harm her if he pretended she was Sela sometimes. She didn't have to know but, then, remembering Rhiannon's uncanny ability to sense, or read his mind, he realised he'd have to keep those thoughts, and this fantasy, to himself and guard his mind with care.

CHAPTER 31

Steven came to: a sudden alert wakefulness. He lay listening. Had he been dreaming of Rhiannon? The memory of her whispering voice, calling him, faded and vanished in that ephemeral way dreams often do. Then – a soft sound and the almost inaudible closing of a door below. He was out of bed in an instant and, peering into the hall, he saw the door of Rhiannon's room ajar. He slipped on his robe and went to her room, where he saw her empty bed. The door to the en-suite was fully open, the room empty also. Crossing to the window he glimpsed Rhiannon, a ghostly shape in her hooded coat, as she moved swiftly between the pools of moonlight and the deep shadows of the trees. She was heading for the grove – for the artefacts!

Swiftly, Steven left the house and was soon moving silently, within the deep shadows into which Rhiannon had disappeared. He kept his distance until, through a gap in the laurel bushes, he caught sight of her kneeling before the pile of rocks which covered the grave and the buried artefacts. There was a flare of light and then the soft glow of three candles added their feeble light to the pale, soft moonlight bathing the grove. The scent of incense was carried to him on the night air. Curious, now, he waited and then, to his distress, he saw her shoulders shaking and heard the muffled sound of her sobs. Not wanting to intrude upon her he began to move backward when he saw her rise.

She let her coat slip from her shoulders as she stood up, revealing a long sleeved, white gown. He could not see if it was a nightdress or some sort of robe but it covered her from neckline to ankle in flowing, diaphanous folds and it had a sheen to it, as though it was made of satin or silk. She was standing sideways on to him as she looked up at the night sky. He heard her say something, softly, and then she lifted her arms up towards the moon. The sleeves of the garment fell back slightly revealing the glint of bracelets and he then became aware of dangling earrings and a pendant. She was dressed for a rite.

Rhiannon held the pose and then raised her voice in an obvious invocation. She was speaking in, what he took to be, her Welsh tongue. He remembered that Sela had sometimes used a similar language and he recalled her challenging Jane Trethowan and how she had cried out strange words in a similar language, as the vortex horde had advanced upon them. The succession of images and memories were beginning to unlock something within his being. He moved silently forward, still concealed within the bushes, just as the moon went behind a high, fast moving cloud and the grove was in gloom except for the feeble glow of the three candles.

He tried to see what Rhiannon was doing as he perceived some movement from her shadowy shape and then the moonlight returned to reveal Rhiannon lying full length upon the rock shelf. She was resting on one arm with her other arm stretched out, the palm of her hand touching the rock fall which covered the grave's entrance. Puzzled, he watched her, and then she began to sing softly, as though to someone, or something – like a mother crooning to a resting child, he found himself thinking.

Her voice continued to croon softly as she removed her hand and raised herself into a kneeling position. The song finished and she remained there. A series of fast-moving clouds darted across the face of the moon like spectral figures flying in the night sky. The grove was alternating between darkness and light as Rhiannon stood and looked up at the sky again. The moon came out clear and bright as she turned her body to face his hiding place. Somewhere, high in the wood-covered hills, an owl hooted, its voice echoing in the silence.

The bright light lit her form casting her in high relief against the rock-strewn hillside. Rhiannon was holding her arms by her side as she stood there, perfectly still. The night air, too, was still, without a breeze to ruffle her hair or the folds of her garment. Once more, the owl gave its mournful cry. He could see Rhiannon clearly, her eyes closed in her pale face and the sweep of her neck blending into the pale garment so that, for a moment, she reminded him of a Greek statue – the statue of a Goddess – carved out of the stones upon which she stood. Once more, memories of Sela came to him; Sela, standing in the orangery like a pagan Goddess. The scene in the grove was breathtaking, redolent with memories of an ancient and mysterious past.

The moon went behind a cloud again, plunging the grove into a deep and depressing darkness and the mournful call of the owl echoed and died away in the stillness of the night. There was a pregnant silence and when the moon appeared once more, Steven was taken aback for Rhiannon had moved silently down from the rock shelf and was standing only a few metres away beside the stream which separated Steven from the burial site. For a moment he felt a sudden fear. Her movements had been so silent, so stealthy; almost sinister – almost vampiric.

She was standing on a flat table-like rock and this gave her height but her feet were shadowed so that she looked as though she was floating in the air like an ethereal spirit, and her form was reflected, dimly, in the bubbling waters beneath her. The stream sparkled, glinted and danced as though a thousand invisible entities were there, holding tiny moon lamps in homage to the mystic power of this unearthly being. Steven's heart was racing, for the imagery presented to him was startling yet disturbing in the extreme.

There, before him, stood Sela as though newly risen from the grave and the shroud-like whiteness of her gown lent credence to the image as she stood in the eerie light of the moon. Yet, his rational mind told him that this could not possibly be Sela. He knew her spirit had passed over – of this he was certain. His lost love lay dead, her mortal body buried beneath the rocks and near to where this moonlit figure stood. No, this was not, could not be her. This was Rhiannon before him – surely? But then, as he watched her, the spirit form opened its eyes and looked directly at his hiding place although he was certain she could not see him. He was stunned by what he saw.

This *was* Sela – it had to be: and then she lifted her arms outwards from her sides, in a slow, flowing, wing-like movement. She held the pose and stood, arms outstretched, open and, yes, vulnerable, like an offering upon an altar.

He rose to go to her, to hold her, hold his Sela once again. The emotions locked within him, the sense of loss, the memories aroused by Rhiannon's strange actions at the burial chamber, suddenly coalesced into one blinding flash of spiritual insight. Rhiannon *did* know he was there even though she could not see him hidden deep within the shadows of the bushes. Rhiannon, conscious of his grief and loss; conscious that her unsettling likeness to Sela, was tormenting him, had taken on the spiritual persona of her dead cousin. She was there before him, offering him solace – an escape, for a while – a pretence that he could see, or be with, Sela once more, if only to say that final goodbye, a goodbye denied to him by the shocking and callous manner of her death.

All of his being wanted to go to her; to be with her and to lose himself in this potent memory form – but he did not move. The awareness of the reasons behind Rhiannon's actions came to the fore. He was conscious of the risks she was taking in offering herself to him in this way; the possibility that he might be so lost in the imagery that he might seek a physical union with what was, for a time, no longer a dead memory but a living, breathing personification of the woman he had loved.

Steven was mesmerised by the image of Sela and then his growing spiritual insight enabled him to see beyond the ephemeral likeness. This was *not* Sela – this was Rhiannon and he could not, would not misuse her to gratify a longing for something precious, now gone forever. This was not Sela – this *was* Rhiannon.

He stepped silently back and, as these thoughts raced across his mind, he saw, and realised, that Rhiannon had been aware of his soulful struggle for she lowered her arms, closed her eyes and turned away to kneel, once more, upon the ground. He saw that she was lost in her own grief-stricken contemplation of the site.

He left the grove, his mind ablaze, and returned to his room. Sometime later he heard her enter her room and the door closed with a soft click. As he lay there in the darkness, his mind was filled with the images he had witnessed. He had felt her grief and had wanted to go to her but he had not done so and that had been the right thing to do. When she had turned to him, though, should he have gone to her? Should he have accepted her offering – her sacrifice – for that was surely what it was? She had opened her arms to him in a clear invitation to come to her. She had offered him the pagan concept of sexual union – a sacred act before the Gods – not out of a form of lustful intent but as a means of assuaging his grief.

His mind was in turmoil and confusion. Rhiannon knew of his yearning for Sela and had attempted to help him in this very physical way. Didn't she realise that this act had only added to his torment – or had it? Hadn't she given him a final last memory? Perhaps she really did care for him and he had misunderstood her actions. *Perhaps she was hexing him.* No – Rhiannon hadn't seen him at all – didn't know he was in the shadows. He had stumbled upon her private ritual, a sort of memorial service to her cousin. But, what if she *did* care for him? Should he do anything about it? Should he say something to her in the morning and, if so, what? No, better leave it to her. If she wanted him then she'd let him know – surely? If she hadn't seen him in the shadows what on earth could he say – that he'd spied on her privacy? No, better to leave events to take their course.

He turned onto his side, trying desperately to quieten his racing thoughts, but the imagery of Rhiannon, standing in the moonlight, blended into a memory of Sela standing on the rock shelf there in that same sacred, mysterious and magical grove.

CHAPTER 32

At breakfast Rhiannon said nothing about the night and chatted, instead, about going to Taunton and did he want to come? So the days passed. Every so often Rhiannon returned to Wales to see one of her patients but always she would return, either to the cottage or to spend time with him.

They talked, shopped, went for drives and walks and practised magic. His abilities grew and he became immersed in Sela's documents so that, in time, he felt that he, too, had been a part of a long and ancient sacred tradition. As Rhiannon and Steven worked together he found himself beginning to want her. Her proximity to him throughout the days was unsettling. The knowledge that she was just in the next room at night was tantalizing in the extreme and he found himself fantasising about being with her, even dreaming of her. The dreams, though, were confusing, the images of Rhiannon alternating with those of Sela reminding him of the events in the grove.

It was on one of their walks that something changed between them. As he helped Rhiannon along a particularly difficult pathway, she stumbled and Steven caught her in his arms. She was breathless against him and, as they laughed and looked at each other, Steven suddenly bent and kissed her. There was a look of consternation on her face and she pulled away from him saying, "Oh!"

Steven was, immediately, apologetic. "I'm sorry – so sorry." He felt embarrassed by his clumsiness and the presumption that she would want him. She gave a shrug and a smile and said, "Oh, don't worry – it's all right," and she continued walking down the trail. But it wasn't all right, at least not in Steven's mind. He thought about the episode again and felt stupid. It had been like a bad movie or, worse, like a mushy scene from one of his aunt's novels – novels he had dismissed as 'women's books' – but now *he* was acting like one of those characters. Had he ruined everything – crossed a boundary? He hoped not for he wanted Rhiannon to be with him – she was so like her cousin and he felt happy with that.

Back at the house she sat down on the sofa, leafing through a magazine. He came into the room and hovered awkwardly at the entrance. "I'm sorry Rhiannon. I had no right to presume anything. It just happened."

Rhiannon put down the magazine and looked over at him as he stood, like a naughty schoolboy, in the doorway. "Oh, come here and sit down." She patted the sofa and he sat alongside her.

"It's all right," she said. "I suppose it was inevitable – we've been together for some weeks now. It isn't that I minded, no, but when you look at me and when you kissed me, I didn't feel that you were seeing *me* – you were seeing *her*."

He began to protest but, then, stopped because there was a truth in what she was saying, at least in part. If he was truly honest with himself, she did remind him so much of Sela but he also knew that Rhiannon was *very* different, and it was that factor that had begun to overcome his memories of his former love.

Rhiannon touched him on the arm. "Listen, I'll tell you something. I've never been comfortable with men – it's just that my early life experiences have not been good. My father died when I was six and my mother had several men friends and one steady man. He tried it on with me when I was fourteen; he didn't get anywhere with me but it frightened me. He was a violent man to both of us and, in the end Mum hexed him. He left the area but it scarred me and I have never been able to commit myself to any man. And now, you come onto the scene." She stopped as he murmured something comforting, uncertain of what to say. She touched his arm again. "Look at me, Steven, what do you see in my eyes?" He looked into her eyes and there was the moistness of tears. "You see," she said, "I'm not upset because you kissed me; I'm upset because I didn't know how to respond – how to react. I want you to love me Steven, but I want you to love *me* not my poor cousin."

"It's not like that," he protested, pleased and anxious at her revelation. "I *do* want you but the memories keep coming back."

"I know," she said. She took his hand. "Listen. That night in the grove, when I looked at you, I knew you were there – no, don't, I want to say this." She squeezed his hand then let go. "I knew you were there in the darkness watching me. I *wanted* you to be there – I *brought* you there, to comfort you, at least that was what I was trying to do. I suppose I was a bit confused about us – and irritated."

"Irritated? Why?"

"Oh, you know – it sounds silly but I knew you kept seeing me as Marian and you confirmed it, remember? You said I was standing just like her and then you said that you'd never been able to say goodbye to her. So... I suppose I thought I would try to help you." She paused and looked at him shyly. "I knew I was taking a bit of a chance. It's a problem I have. I don't always think things through properly. You've heard the saying, 'be careful what you wish for else it might come true' – well, it's a bit like that with me. I don't always get it right." She paused then said, "That's one of the main pitfalls in magic; the Fates don't always interpret things the way they should." Rhiannon continued, "I suppose I'm a bit arrogant in magic, if I'm honest – a bit over-confident about my abilities but, there you are. Not only had I never done that sort of working before, I didn't know how you'd react; particularly in the light of how I feel, felt, about men. It could have happened between us, in the grove, and I would've let you pretend I was her – to comfort you – at least I thought that was what I was doing, or was I kidding myself? You see, I'm as messed up about us as you are."

Steven didn't know what to say nor where these revelations were taking them. So she *had* been hexing him. He remained silent as she continued. "I could sense your turmoil and that you were struggling with your emotions and, deep down, I felt you'd do the right thing. When you didn't come to me I realised that you had understood what I was trying to do even if it was a bit weird and that you weren't rejecting me because you didn't fancy me."

He smiled at her, trying to reassure her. "Well, it certainly was a bit weird – a bit creepy really – and astonishing too. You gave me quite a shock at one point, especially when you opened your eyes and looked at me."

"Sorry, that wasn't my intention…"

"I know," he said, "and I knew you couldn't possibly see me in the darkness but clearly you knew I was there. You *did* look like her. I thought she'd come back but then I knew that couldn't be and you *did* help me by doing what you did. OK, so it was weird but it was also beautiful and, I suppose, sad but I felt better for it. No, I didn't reject you as *you,* if you see what I mean. I rejected the image when I perceived that it wasn't *her.* It wouldn't have been right to have taken it further – that would have been self-indulgence on my part. But, there was a moment when I wanted you – wanted her – God! Now it's getting worse because you're here with me. This is a mess, isn't it?"

She nodded. "Yes – exactly – see what I mean? Both of us are confused by our situation and that's why I must go now. I must leave you because to stay would lead me into a situation which would be taking advantage of your confusion and grief. I want you to be sure about us, Steven. If I *am* to be with you then I must be sure that you want me and not a memory of Marian. I tell you this; if it's of any comfort to you I can hardly stop myself from jumping into bed with you right now. But I want you to want *me.*"

He felt a sudden surge of happiness as she uttered the last sentence. He smiled at her. "So, I haven't made a total mess of it then, have I? But you're right. I'm confused but I know that I want you to stay with me. Don't go, not like this."

She was adamant though, and he knew that she was right. He wanted her but he had to be certain, in his own mind, that it was not her uncanny and unsettling likeness to Sela that was driving him. Perhaps some distance between them would resolve the situation, one way or another. So he let her go back to Wales and began to miss her terribly, the images of Rhiannon beginning to supercede those of Sela. He felt guilty and empty, wandering the hills full, now, of the memories of both women.

Walking high along the windswept paths and looking across the Channel towards Wales, he had a memory of the time when he had seen a shaft of sunlight piercing the distant, mist shrouded hills. Then he had wondered if it had pointed to some unknown future, like a beacon. His mind was filled with the memories of Sela and Rhiannon but then it cleared as though the wind, which blew strongly around him, had cleared away some of those memories. Like a mist lifting suddenly, his mind focused and it was the memory of Rhiannon that remained.

The Jane Trethowan mystery vanished from the newspapers as the months passed and his grief also began to lessen. With this came a growing longing for Rhiannon, a realisation that he missed her and needed to be with her. He spoke to her daily by phone but did not voice his need in case it was not reciprocated; he did not want to lose what they had but he let her know that he missed her. Then one autumn evening the bell rang.

"I've come to visit you," Rhiannnon said smiling at him. "I think I have been away enough?"

He stared at her, in astonishment. His mind had been full of her and he had been about to phone her. He pulled her into the hallway and held her in his arms feeling a wave of pleasure as he looked at her. "Yes, too long but it was right to do so."

"Yes," she said. "It was right but now it's wrong and I need to be with you and you with me, yes?" It was not so much a question as a statement of fact.

"Yes, oh yes. I need *you* my Rhiannon of that you can be sure." He kissed her, held her close and knew it to be true.

They pulled apart and she looked over at Tanith and Perry curled up together in front of the fire. "A good omen that," said Rhiannon, nodding over at the two pets.

"Yes, it is." He kissed the crown of her head and, as he did this, a memory of Sela flooded his senses. But this was more than a memory. It was the sense of a tangible presence, within him and around him, so powerful that he could almost 'see' her. He knew, then, that Sela was bestowing a benediction on their union – then the presence was gone. He held on to the feeling and the memories of Sela that the powerful presence had conjured up; and then he let it go in a pent-up exhalation of his breath. There was no more regret, no more sadness – just Rhiannon in his arms and now and forever in his soul.

"What is it?" Rhiannon was anxious. "I felt a presence – I felt you go away from me, for a moment, as if you weren't with me."

"It's all right," he said. "It was a memory, if you like – a happy one. I'll never go away from you, I promise you. I love you – do you know that?"

"Yes, yes, I know – I feel it – and I love you. Now we will always be together." She reached up and kissed him then pulled back, smiling up at him.

Steven looked into Rhiannon's grey and ageless eyes and felt a profound abiding love for her. For the first time, since the death of Sela, the shadowy, clinging world of sadness and despair lifted finally and forever. He felt an aura of security and comfort enfold them, like a gift from the Gods and, with this, his wounded spirit was healed and soothed by a deep, blessed, enduring sense of peace.

The Eyes of the Goddess

CHAPTER 33

Steven lifted Sela in his arms and carried her upstairs to bed. He lay her down and she looked up at him with her grey eyes. There was a sudden shock of memory. His daughter turned on her side into her favourite sleeping position, her hair falling across her face and, for a moment, he remembered that other Sela as he had lain her in her final and eternal sleep.

"Oh, she's tired, poor little mite," said Rhiannon and she bent down, kissing the child on the crown of her head, the copper hair of mother and daughter mingling on the pillow.

"My two lovely girls," he said softly and Rhiannon looked up at him, smiling.

"And their lovely dada, eh?" She tucked the bedclothes around their child whose eyes were beginning to close.

They tiptoed out, turning off the light and closed the door, the sound of the music box muted as they did so. Downstairs, Rhiannon went to the window and looked out at the clear spring night. "Oh, look, a lovely full moon." She gazed up at the full bright sphere of light and Steven joined her. He slipped his arm around her waist as he let his eyes travel from the moon to the shadowy trees which marked the boundary of the wild garden and the sacred grove.

"Do you think she's at peace?" he asked.

Rhiannon turned and put both arms around his neck looking into his eyes. "Yes, of course and she's also all around us; I sense her often. She has blessed us, this I know. Do you still miss her?"

"Yes, yes I do but not in the way you might mean. I love you desperately but she will always be in my mind. Too much happened, so strange and terrible – wonderful too but, yes, I can't forget her – ever. It's so hard to believe that it all took place in just a month. It seemed as though I was trapped in Time."

She smiled at him, "In a sense you were – you were between the worlds." She went on, "I know that you love me and I *do* understand. I miss her too, dreadfully. She and I were like sisters; you have no idea how close we could be. It's right that you miss her but don't be so sad. She's back again, in Sela asleep upstairs. Yes, really, it goes on. I sensed it. The spirit is always there. Nothing ever fades away, it just changes, becomes something or someone else. She's out there," she gestured out at the garden, "up there," pointing at the moon and stars, "and in our daughter and in our memories – always."

He knew that what she was saying was true for he, too, had sensed something of Sela's spirit within their daughter. He had put this down to hope – hope that Sela had overcome whatever debts she had said needed to be paid. But now, it was no longer hope. That sudden glimpse, within those grey eyes and the memory of his former love had convinced him. He knew that Sela's spirit had been re-born in their daughter and it would be his karmic destiny to protect and guide her in this new, and perhaps final, incarnation. He nodded and kissed her, "Thank you."

"What for?" She looked a little puzzled.

"For being you. For saying the right thing in the right way. For loving me."

She laughed. "Oh come on. She knew that you and I needed each other. It was destined to be – so that's it. What we must do, though, is guide her."

He was startled, for Rhiannon had picked up his thoughts once again.

"Guide her, yes but not influence her. *She* must choose the Craft – yes?"

"Yes, of course, but she'll choose it – it's inevitable – it's her destiny, her karma, if you like. She's come back of that I'm sure and when she's older she'll inherit all of this... and the sacred site as well... and the artefacts."

This surprised him. Rhiannon had never mentioned the artefacts, not since their discussion five years previously.

"Yes, of course. Yes, she'll know of them – but they must be safe and untouched, yes?" There was a note of anxiety in his tone.

"That will be for her to decide," said Rhiannon. She looked at him and, reaching up she touched his cheek. "Darling, look, even though you're bound by your vow, as I am bound by mine to you, we can't bind the future. When Sela becomes owner and guardian of the site, the decision will be hers not ours. They're her ancestral heritage. Anyway, we'll be long gone. Look, trust the Fates. Sela will know what to do. Now, let's go into our Moon Temple and honour her at this special time, yes? Come on, let's prepare ourselves. A rite of blessing for us, for Sela upstairs and Sela out there."

He kissed her again and nodded, following her up to their room where they prepared themselves. Outside of the orangery they composed their minds; and then Steven pushed open the doors. They entered.

The darkness of the room was relieved by the pale glow of moonlight and by the soft glow of two candles. One, a tall white taper, was set in an ornate silver holder; the other, glowing softly red, was suspended, in an exquisitely moulded silver holder, from chains set into the ceiling. In the centre of the room was an altar – its black and white shape mirroring the chequered black and white tiled floor. Upon the altar a silver chalice, a sharp white handled dagger, a sword with ornate hilt and a silver and crystal wand glinted in the soft light. The candles flickered as though, for a moment, a passing spirit had disturbed the still air and that faint flicker was sufficient to throw other objects into sharp relief, revealing a statue in the centre of the altar.

The Moon Temple

The statue, sitting impassively, seemed to be staring out across the darkness towards them. Its eyes were large and slanting, almost feline; the breasts firm and jutting above the swell of a rounded belly. The hair swirled snake-like down its back and across the shoulders. Upon the statue's head was set a crown in the shape of the curving horns of the crescent moon.

Rhiannon lit some incense and clouds of scented smoke rose around the statue of the Goddess. Steven, dressed in a black robe held at the waist by a silver cord, picked up a taper and lit it from the flame of the candle. He felt peaceful and calm, as he looked across at Rhiannon who stood on the other side of the altar. She, too, was dressed in the same way, her copper red hair falling in thick waves down her back and across her shoulders. She picked up the wand, moved to one of the corners of the room and began the rite which would create their special sacred space, calling out the words and making the ritual gestures which were now an integral part of Steven's spiritual life. Soft music swelled into the room as the priestess and priest entered into that timeless place between the worlds of Matter and Spirit.

After the blessing, they knelt together on the floor of the Temple, each of them intent upon the rite – each, for a moment, lost in their own particular memories of Sela resting within the sacred grove.

As Rhiannon's mind created the imagery of her dead cousin, she found herself thinking also of her daughter asleep upstairs. Rhiannon was certain that her daughter now held the life force – the spirit – of her dead relative but there was always that sense of doubt wasn't there? Her mind drifted, trying to visualise the future and then she saw it in a true spirit vision, a sudden, startling glimpse of some unknown future time. For there, before her, in the Temple, stood her daughter now grown into womanhood, dressed in ceremonial robes and with her deep, copper hair, tumbling over her shoulders. The vision was intense and real and the likeness of her daughter to her dead namesake was uncanny, unsettling and unmistakable. Here, before her, was psychic proof of the continuation of the life force. Here, before her, stood her daughter and yet it was her lost cousin as well.

Rhiannon, her heart beating, studied the image before her, the beautiful but haunting image of her grown-up daughter. Suddenly, she felt uneasy for around the young Sela's neck blazed a great golden torc. Upon the altar lay a golden, spoked wheel and in Sela's hand was a sickle shaped blade. Rhiannon knew, instantly, that these were the buried artefacts, now recovered, even though she had never actually seen them herself. Yes, she had heard Steven's descriptions but *these* were tangible and real. She saw her daughter's lips moving as though reciting something. Rhiannon used all of her powers in an attempt to break through the veil of Time but she could not. She could not penetrate *that* mystery, no matter how hard she tried.

The vision began to fade away and Rhiannon tried to hold on to it but it continued to slowly disappear. She looked at the fading, beautiful image of her grown-up daughter in the sure and sudden knowledge that neither she nor

Steven would be present at their daughter's strange and potent ceremony. She felt a momentary sadness for she knew that Sela would never excavate the site whilst her mother and father were alive. She held the image, that powerful image of Sela, standing there bathed in an unearthly, supernatural light and she put her trust in her daughter and hoped that whatever rite Sela was engaged in, would be for the Light and not the Dark.

As the vision vanished she found that she was looking at the statue of the Moon Goddess which was placed within the centre of the altar. Rhiannon tried to remember the vision of Sela and where her daughter had been standing but her eyes were held by the eyes of the Moon Goddess statue. She looked into those impassive eyes and offered a prayer to Hecate, that her hopes for her daughter and for the future would be fulfilled and that all would be well. This surprised her somewhat for she and Marian had always avoided the impulse to be devotional. Her eyes settled upon the carved pendant around the neck of the Goddess. It was a depiction of the three phases of the moon; waxing, full and waning. The pendant stood out boldly and the symbolism was clear to her and obvious.

The lunar phases showed the birth, bright vitality and eventual waning and death of the moon, as though it was a living entity. Thus, those phases also represented the stages of life and of the human spirit. Yet, although the moon and, therefore, the spirit appear to die and are lost for a time, they always appear again, re-born, renewed, full of potent promise but always, always it is the same moon, the same spirit. The vision of the two Selas and her evaluation of the lunar symbolism lifted Rhiannon's own spirit and she felt a strengthening of her beliefs. She vowed to continue her quest for further knowledge and enlightenment and to strive, always, for perfection, that blessed state which would bring her, finally, out of the Sea of Souls, as Jung had termed it, into eventual union with the cosmic source of all things. The biggest problem for her was that, in order to achieve such balance and perfection, she would have to work on that one major flaw in her magical personality. She had mentioned it to Steven on several occasions and he was now able to help her to curtail and to control her over-confidence – the tendency she sometimes manifested to be too carefree and a bit challenging towards the powers that she was seeking to control.

Rhiannon looked over at Steven. Clearly, he had not seen the vision of their daughter for he knelt there lost in a peaceful state of meditation. She remained kneeling and continued to ponder the matter. Should she tell him what had been revealed to her? She decided that she would or, at least, some of it. She would tell him about the vision of their daughter, the reincarnated spirit of Marian, but she would not tell him about the artefacts, for that would distress Steven, this she knew. The knowledge that their daughter would, one day, excavate the burial site – desecrate it, was how he would see it – would be too much for him too bear. Yet, how could it be a desecration if the young

Sela was merely claiming what was hers by ancestral right? Nevertheless, Rhiannon knew that Steven would not accept such actions.

She had vowed to strive for perfection and to try to curb her somewhat maverick tendencies, yet here she was already engaged in deception. Rhiannon convinced herself that she was acting for the greater good, for Steven's peace of mind. Was it right, though, to withold such information from him? Wasn't she interfering in the karmic flow of things? If Steven knew what she had seen then, without doubt, he would try to stop Sela from excavating the site and the future would be altered. The vision, though, told otherwise. Their daughter *was* holding the artefacts, that had been clear. It was also clear to her that neither she nor Steven would be alive when *that* ceremony eventually took place, so what was the point in distressing him?

Rhiannon looked into the eyes of the Goddess as though asking for reassurance – but none came. She lowered her head, remembering that no reassurance could ever be given. Such reassurance, such certainty would mean that the future was already written and that the laws of Karma would have no meaning. Rhiannon knew that this could not be, for hadn't she herself intervened, many times, in the lives of others – made things happen, changed things? Wasn't she doing it now by withholding parts of the vision from Steven?

Rhiannon looked up, again, at the statue. Seeking reassurance from the Goddess – who was, after all, only symbolic – and, worse still, praying to the statue, was ridiculous. Why pray, when the power to alter events comes not from outside but from within the spirit of the practitioner? It was the application of the Magical Will that caused changes to occur. That was part of the thrill in using magical techniques. She'd told Steven to 'trust the Fates', but *tempting* the Fates – playing with them – was what gave witchcraft that special *frisson*.

She was standing at the crossroads, metaphorically speaking. This was exactly the type of situation she had talked about with Steven. She was facing Hecate – facing a choice and, whatever decision she made, would have certain consequences. She'd seen the future, but did not know the purpose of the rite, so, could it be altered? Should she try to mould it – control it?

Rhiannon flung a dismissive, almost challenging, look into the statue's impenetrable eyes.

"All will be well," she whispered into the darkness. "I'll make it so."

There, that over-confidence again, she found herself thinking, but in this case, she would make sure that things would go well. After all, she was a skilled magical practitioner. She also had Steven to support her and his magical abilities were growing year by year, so how could they fail? Their daughter *would* choose the right path – it was inevitable.

She stood up and Steven, startled by her sudden movement, rose to his feet, a question on his lips. He saw the look in her eyes and felt the power within her as she raised her arms and cried, "All will be well! Let it so be!"

He repeated the phrase, realising she must have been inspired in some way – touched by the spirit and soon both were lost in the flowing and intricate movements of the rite, as they brought the ceremony to its final conclusion.

When it was done, Steven put his arms around Rhiannon and kissed her.

"What was it you were asking for at the end? You looked so powerful and determined – almost possessed."

Rhiannon laughed. "Did I? Oh – for our happiness," she lied, then spoke a half-truth. "I felt a great rush of power – a need to ask for a blessing for the future."

As he held her she felt a bit guilty. She was keeping a secret from him but one little secret could do no harm – could it? A small deception, something kept hidden from him, veiled, occult. She looked at the statue again and, just for a moment, she felt a shiver of superstitious apprehension as she remembered her dismissal of the deity's power. Rhiannon shrugged off the feeling, putting it down to fatigue from the potency of the vision.

"All will be well," she whispered to him as he let her go.

Steven smiled at her and went over to the altar to quench the candle, leaving the Temple lit only by the votive candle and the moonlight. His eyes rested upon the dagger and he had a fleeting memory of Jane Trethowan, holding her blood-stained blade aloft as the sun rose above the moorland hills. Many, many times he had gone over the events which had led to that dreadful and tragic day. He remembered how he had wondered about Jane and the extraordinary magical abilities she had possessed and how she had been able to conjure up such demonic forces. He had discussed this with Rhiannon and had even voiced an interest in studying elements of the path Jane had followed.

Then he recalled Rhiannon's warning – her warning about Solar Magic. What was it she had said? That the Gods of the Solar Path were always hungry for blood? That Solar Magic always corrupted the practitioner? As he stared at the dagger, he remembered those words but, still, somewhere at the back of his mind he held onto the idea that he might look into that form of magic one day. If it was dangerous and active then that would suit his own martial character.

He was about to turn away when his body was assailed by a series of powerful tremors. He felt cold and then very hot as the feelings coalesced into one all consuming sensation of flight. It was the same out of body experience he had felt when he had been on the brink of self-destruction; the same soaring, rushing, speed of flight that had carried him to the light of the sun and which had saved him at that dreadful moment of despair. Then it was gone, as suddenly as it had come to him and he remembered that his totem was a hawk and that a hawk was always associated with the sun. There, he had been given a sign and he *would* begin a study of Solar Magic. He felt a momentary regret that he would never see the artefacts again, especially the

Wheel of Taranis, that wonderful, Solar implement that had enabled Jane to wield such power but had also driven her to murder and to her final destruction. Then he felt guilty – guilty that he should even think of them as he recalled the dreadful events that had led to their burial.

Steven became aware that Rhiannon was near to him and he turned to her.

"Are you OK?" she asked him anxiously. "I thought you were going to faint."

"No – don't worry, I'm fine, I'm OK – just a power rush. Give me a moment to catch my breath."

He looked about him, remembering when the room had been just an orangery. He had a fleeting memory of Marian, as Sela, the Moon Priestess, standing in the moonlight 'drawing down the moon'. Was this memory also a sign or was it a warning, a warning from beyond, warning him against the Solar Path just as Rhiannon had attempted to warn him?

Steven considered this possibility but the lure of the Solar Path was now strong within him. He had learned to control his violent nature through the disciplines of the martial arts; he could learn to control the inherent dangers of Solar Magic, just as he had learned to deal with the potential dangers that lay in the practice of Lunar Magic. Both forces could be evoked from, and channelled through, the psychic being of the practitioner. All that was different was the focus, the methodology and intent of the adept. Lunar, Solar – they were spiritual forces and, in a way, they were linked; for the moon was seen only with the reflected light of the sun and the sun could only shine, in the darkness of the night, by using the moon as a mirror for its own reflected glory. Like mortal beings, the two spiritual forces, masculine and feminine, needed each other.

After all, it had been Sela, a Priestess of the Moon, who had discovered and revealed to him his totem, the hawk, that potent symbol of the sun. And then he remembered her again but this time she was at the Folly, facing Jane Trethowan, her body shimmering with an unearthly light and the great gold torc around her throat glowing like fire in the light of the rising sun. Yes, Sela had used Solar Magic to thwart Jane's plans. In Sela, the powers of the moon and the sun, Lunar and Solar, had come together as an overwhelming force. True, they had failed to save Vivien but, then, Rhiannon had said that Vivien may have chosen to die to save him, and Rhiannon had also said that the Solar Gods always needed blood. By allowing herself to be sacrificed, Vivien had enabled Sela to accomplish a great task – the total destruction of Jane's murderous and insane political ambitions. Of course, Sela had died as well but this was another part of the sacrifice demanded by the Gods. Sela knew it was her karmic destiny to die… *or even her duty?*

He was startled at this last thought. What was the matter with him? How could he think of those horrible events and begin to explain them away? Then a new thought came to him. Perhaps the sudden memory of Sela was not a warning but was a sign of approval – a sign pointing the way to this new magical path. Of course! That was it!

Steven knew, then, that he *would* work with the Solar energies but he would also try to combine the two paths, Lunar and Solar, to bring some balance into the chaotic lives of mankind. *That* would be his intention. No doubt Sela would have approved – but would Rhiannon?

Somewhere, at the back of his mind, he heard his mother's voice. "The road to Hell is paved with good intentions." It had been one of her favourite sayings. Now where did that come from?

He looked at Rhiannon who was watching him with questioning eyes. Had she read his mind again? Was it her voice he had heard and not the voice of his dead mother? *Did she know what he intended?* But, no – Steven had long since learned how to guard and mask his thoughts. Rhiannon didn't know and he would not tell her – at least not yet. It would only upset her.

He looked into her eyes, smiled and said, "Well, you certainly brought the power through that time."

"Yes, I did, didn't I? But my closing ceremony must have been flawed for you to get such a surge now."

He shrugged. "Don't worry about it. I'm OK."

Rhiannon lowered her head. Something wasn't quite right. She could not identify the source of her unease. Steven's reactions were strange but no, he seemed all right now. Perhaps it *had* been the power rush which had unsettled them both for, clearly, Steven had felt something too. Rhiannon looked away from him and surveyed the Temple trying to recall the vision of her daughter. Then she remembered the artefacts in the young Sela's hands and she wondered, again, if Steven should be told about them. He seemed relaxed and happy now – contented, if that was the right word. Why spoil the moment with her anxieties about their daughter? After all, she was certain that events *could* be controlled now that the vision had been given to her – that vision with a glimpse of a *possible* future.

Rhiannon raised her eyes and studied Steven's face and she knew that she loved him deeply. Things were going well for them in their marriage and in their magical partnership. The knowledge that their daughter would be following their ways filled her with happiness. No – she would not tell him.

Rhiannon smiled to herself and vowed, once more that she would make things go her way and if that seemed like a challenge to the Fates, then so be it. She took Steven's hand, raised it to her lips, and kissed it and then the Priestess and Priest left the Moon Temple closing the door behind them

The smoke of the dying incense hung upon the still air, masking the structure of the Temple and making the statue of the Moon Goddess appear as a disembodied shape, floating in its own Time and Space. For a moment the Goddess seemed to fill the room as though she had fed upon the words and thoughts of the mortals and had become imbued with a tangible form of life. She seemed to be pondering and waiting – waiting to see what would, eventually, come to pass.

One final arrow of moonlight pierced the darkness and glanced across the lunar crown of the Goddess. Then, this light faded as the moon continued on its silent and secret way across the night sky to vanish, lost, behind the grey and wraith-like veil of the swirling, moorland mist now touched with the blood red glow of the newly rising sun.

Disclaimer

All characters in this novel are fictional. Any resemblance to persons living or dead is entirely co-incidental.

Porlock is a real village in Exmoor but some locations are imaginary. Hawkwood House, the Trethowan mansion and Sela's cottage do not exist – the reader will search for them in vain. The mysterious valley is there, close to Porlock, though you will have to search for it. I don't know what it was I sensed in that hidden valley but, then, they say that the Exmoor Beast is imaginary as well.